# THE GRADUAL PSALMS:

## A TREATISE

### ON

## THE FIFTEEN SONGS OF DEGREES,

### WITH COMMENTARY,

### BASED ON ANCIENT HEBREW, CHALDEE, AND CHRISTIAN AUTHORITIES.

BY

### REV. H. T. ARMFIELD, M.A., F.S.A.,

VICE-PRINCIPAL OF THE THEOLOGICAL COLLEGE, VICAR OF THE CLOSE, AND MINOR CANON OF SARUM.
AUTHOR OF "THE LEGEND OF CHRISTIAN ART," ETC.

LONDON:
J. T. HAYES, LYALL PLACE, EATON SQUARE; AND
4, HENRIETTA STREET, COVENT GARDEN.
1874.

LONDON:
SWIFT AND CO., REGENT PRESS, KING STREET,
REGENT STREET, W.

TO THE

RIGHT REVEREND

GEORGE MOBERLY, D.C.L.,

LORD BISHOP OF SARUM,

WITH HIS PERMISSION.

# PREFACE.

This book, the product of work in the vacations of the past four or five years, is an attempt to work a new mine for English readers, which has never been opened to them before. It has been my aim, not indeed to incorporate here all that ever has been said upon this section of the Psalter, but at least to familiarise the reader with every *kind* of treatment of which it has been felt to be susceptible: and, therefore, in addition to the usual sources of Christian information, I have here systematically embodied what has been said by some of the Hebrew and Chaldee authorities upon the subject. It is the systematic presentation of this latter class of writings, which constitutes the speciality of my book.

There is, it is well known, a vast body of literature in these languages upon the Scriptures, the work of writers who, whatever be their own date, sometimes earlier and sometimes later, have preserved to us interpretations, that have been current in their nation from time immemorial; writers, whose value consists not in any unparalleled capacity of their own, but in their ceaseless employment of the formula, "Our fathers said," thus accrediting a traditional interpretation as old, it may be, as the passage which it explains; writers, who have examined the Scriptures with a microscope, who have analysed them with a minuteness to which all comment upon a Latin or English translation of them is necessarily a stranger; writers, whose thought may be now of greater and now of less weight, but who will always have a place in any exhaustive treatment of the Scripture, because of the very care and labour they have bestowed upon it; and because they are the men, who, in the eloquent words of Dr. Liddon, "read the Old Testament with at least as much instinctive insight into the meaning

*Value of Hebrew Writers.*

of its archaic language, and of its older forms of thought and of feeling, as an Englishman in this generation can command when he applies himself to the study of Shakespeare or of Milton."\*

There is in fact a pre-Christian as well as a post-Christian exegesis: and by setting out expositions from Hebrew doctors alongside those which have secured acceptance in the Catholic Church, I hoped to exhibit the continuity of the older with the younger, and to leave the impression that the Christian method of handling the Scriptures was not a thing introduced at a comparatively late epoch, when those Scriptures had already run out several hundred years of their career without it; but rather that it is in kind identical with the method which has at all times been applied to the Scripture, and which, for all we can say to the contrary, might be suspected of being as old as the Scripture itself.

*[margin: Continuity of Christian with Hebrew Exposition.]*

Abundant evidence might be found in our Authorized Version of the Scriptures that the trans-

---

\* Liddon: Bampton Lectures; Lect. ii., p. 90: ed. 1869.

lators were acquainted with the commentaries of the leading Hebrew writers.* This, in fact, is their safeguard. Many is the time in years gone by when I fancied I had caught them tripping, and marginated accordingly a correction, which subsequent reading showed me to be itself a blunder. They had gone out of the way for a translation; but it turned out to be, though perhaps not always the most obvious and direct, yet commonly the traditional acceptation, treasured up, from a period when the Holy-Tongue was as yet unfossilized and on the lips of men, in the writings of the Hebrew sages. The work of the old English translators may not, of course, be pronounced immaculate: but I have learned to be somewhat timid in attempting to amend it. That mankind has a more accurate knowledge of Greek now than it had two hundred years ago seems to admit of no reasonable doubt; and we may therefore safely affirm that we could considerably improve our English Version of the

\* For some details on this subject see Chapter xxiii. of this work.

New Testament. But it does not seem equally clear that the study of Hebrew literature has advanced proportionably, or that we are much more conversant now than formerly with the usages and instincts of its phraseology; so much more, at all events, as to justify us in affirming that we have attained an equally superior vantage-ground for the inspection of the renderings in the Old Testament.

The Hebrew commentaries, it must be admitted, constitute a field of theological literature that in these last generations has not received the attention which it seems to deserve. The standard of attainment in the Holy Tongue is certainly not high. When a Jewish minister once assailed me with the taunt that "you Christians are laborious and profound in the languages of Pagan philosophers and dramatists and poets; but of the tongue in which God spake by the Prophets you are content scarcely to know the alphabet," I felt the justice of the rebuke. Persons are able to be popularly dignified as Hebraists, when their knowledge is really of the slenderest and most elementary kind. Many of the

*Ancient Commentaries.*

passages chartered with the names of Kimchi, Jarchi, and others, in some of our current books bear the stamp, unmistakable to experts in the matter, of having been taken at second-hand, often from the Latin versions of some of the older workers in this field, and but rarely from a first-hand study of those writers in their own tongue. The result of this handing on of stock passages from book to book is, that the original author remains only partially and imperfectly known, while in some cases the precise colour of his meaning has become not a little changed. It is indeed easy to understand why English writers, with the press of modern business upon them, have been shy of approaching the Hebrew writers at first-hand. The labour involved in doing so is enormous. The man who can read his Bible tolerably in Hebrew has almost a new language to learn before he can touch the authors of the Rabbinic Schools; and even when he has acquired a fair proficiency in handling them, he is liable to be continually embarrassed and delayed by the excessive technicalities with which they abound.

It is, therefore, not superfluous for me to say that everything of the kind in this book is taken from the Hebrew authors in their own language. I have preferred to cite them under the names by which they are known amongst their own people—Rashi, Radak, etc., instead of calling them Jarchi, Kimchi, etc., as they are mostly known to English writers who quote them in recent times. If any other justification for doing so were sought, it would be found in the fact that the forms which I have adopted were those under which they were cited by Buxtorf, Reland, and the most famous Christian Hebraists of old time; and, further, in the consideration that the name Jarchi involves a blunder, while the name Kimchi is by itself insufficient as a designation. The latter name was borne by more than one man of distinction; and the former is not a man's name at all, but simply a Hebrew epithet meaning "One born at Lunelle"—a circumstance which is not true of the author before us, who was born at Troyes. For the information of readers who are unversed in such matters, it may be well to state that

*How cited.*

the names I have employed are acrostic names, formed by taking the initial consonants of a man's name and title, and supplying them with vowels.

Acrostic Names.

Thus, Rabbi Solomon (in Hebrew it is Sholomon) Isaac gives us Rashi; Rabbi David Kimchi gives us Radak; Rabbi Moses Ben Maimon (Maimonides) gives us Rambam, and so on. This kind of name, I may add, is the form under which almost every authority is cited in Hebrew writings.

The reader of the Gradual Psalms, who knows the kind of thing that the traditional Hebrew authorities have said, as well as the kind of thing that Christian doctors have superadded, knows really all that is to be said upon the subject, outside the pale of mere speculation. It is this kind of exhaustive combination that I have endeavoured here to present in what is, not indeed the first treatise on the Gradual Psalms *alone* in any language—though amongst all the languages there are but three such works in the new Catalogue of the Library of the British Museum— but the first such treatise for the English reader.

I have translated the Targum on every verse of the Gradual Psalms from the Chaldee text, as it is given in Buxtorf's great Rabbinic Bible. It contains some curious paraphrases in certain verses, and has never before, I believe, been given to the English reader.* *(Targum.)*

One speciality of my work is the presentation to the English reader of all that seemed to have value of any kind with reference to the group of Psalms in the Midrash Tehillim—the Ancient Hebrew Commentary upon the Psalms, full of traditional exposition handed down from pre-Christian times, and, so far as regards its substance, though perhaps not as regards its actual compilation, the oldest Commentary upon the Psalms extant. There are, indeed, in some of the current English books, occasional allusions to this venerable work, and every now and then even an extract from some of its tales of marvel and fancy; but no one of those books, so *(Midrash Tehillim.)*

---

* For information on this and the other Hebrew writings here quoted, the reader cannot do better than consult the very able articles under the several names given in Dr. Kitto's "Cyclopædia of Biblical Literature."

far as I know them, shows a systematic acquaintance with it in its original language. I call it a Hebrew Commentary; but a knowledge of mere Hebrew would not suffice to read it. A good deal of it is written in Chaldee, or in that mixture of Hebrew and Chaldee forms, in which the Gemoro part of the Talmud is written. Then, farther, the Midrash Tehillim is exceedingly difficult of access. One may try half over Europe before securing a copy of it. There are, of course, copies in the Printed Book Department of the British Museum,—"it would not be the British Museum if there were not," the Belgian Librarian paid us the compliment of saying,—but there is no copy in the National Library of Brussels. At one time I thought Bishop Pearson had a copy, because he quotes it so frequently in his famous "Exposition of the Creed;" but more recently I have begun to doubt it, as the passages which he quotes might have been transcribed from the *Pugio Fidei*, where most, if not all, of them are given in the original, and accompanied with a Latin translation. However, when I wanted a copy, I tried the usual dealers, both

Christian and Hebrew, in learned books in London; but without success. I went to Brussels, and was assured that such a thing was not to be found there. Nor at Antwerp? None. At Amsterdam I was told I was likely to find a copy; though I wrote there without result: and at last I succeeded in procuring one at Frankfurt-on-the-Main. The book, I was made to see, was difficult to get: but when it was got, I found it was still more difficult to read.

I have spoken of the labour involved in these studies. Yet many, I know, have been deterred from entering upon the study of the Holy Tongue by an exaggerated idea of its difficulty. It wants of course, like everything else worthy of notice, a certain degree of earnest work; but it may help the student who is hesitating upon the frontier, to tell him what has been accomplished by ordinary men. My experience at this College has enabled me to tabulate some statistics of what is possible to a man who decides upon the attempt to read the Old Testament in its Original tongue. From

*The Study of the Bible in the Original.*

time to time, then, we have had here several men who, in the course of a couple of terms—half an academic year—have, amid other studies, thoroughly mastered the accidence of the language, and become perfectly acquainted with three chapters of the Pentateuch in it. I put on record a definite result, not as any extraordinary achievement—for it may be accomplished by any one who chooses to try—but as an encouragement to others, who need only some definite prospect to spur them to exertion. The Universities of Oxford and Cambridge are doing much to improve the knowledge of the Sacred Tongue in this country; and even at this early stage of their efforts, the standard, I am informed, has begun to rise: but unless the many are tempted to enter upon these studies, there will not be any great result from the movement. If the multitude of students can be induced to undertake them, then the few will attain to excellence in them, and our familiarity with the language and literature of the Scriptures will have a chance of becoming once again what it was in the great epoch of the Stuarts.

Of one thing the student who is hesitating whether he would learn Hebrew may rest assured—that when he has acquired it, he will feel it to be a weapon worth all the labour he may have bestowed upon it. At the moment of indecision, let him only remember that S. Augustine was virtually expressing his own regret at the want of it, when he said that the man who would be a master of Scripture had need not only of Greek and Latin but also of Hebrew knowledge; and that S. Jerome, penance though he said the study was to him, actually went to Palestine to perfect himself in it. *Value of such Knowledge.*

Upon one department, too, of the many practical activities of the Christian Church, these studies, for which I plead, have a deeper influence than is sometimes thought. No Christian, I should suppose, who reflects for even a single moment upon the enormous obligations that his Christianity has incurred towards Hebrew life and usage; owing to them, as she does, not only her greater treasures of Prophecy and Psalm, but even so many of her petty, *Its effect on Mission Work.*

b

yet in their way precious, details of ritual and phrase, details most of them which had their Hebrew precedents in days long anterior to Christianity itself—no Christian, I say, who has attempted to make any estimate of such a debt would feel it otherwise than a duty incumbent on the Church to make some, even exceptional, provision in her Mission Work for attracting to her fold those scattered survivors of the nation, to whose ancestral past she herself has owed so much. It is a common taunt against us that our Missions in that direction have latterly been a failure. How far, I am disposed to ask, is such failure due to our neglect of the necessary studies? to our diminished familiarity with the accredited interpreters of the Hebrew nation? It was the boast of one of old time, who "mightily convinced" the Jews, that he was "brought up at the feet of Gamaliel," learned, that is to say, in all the traditional lore of the Hebrew nation: and when I reflect upon the astounding knowledge of Scripture and its interpretation to be met with amongst the leaders of Hebrew opinion—a knowledge amounting in some cases of my acquaintance to a knowing by heart of the entire Scripture in the original Hebrew—then I feel satisfied that we are not likely to carry persuasion to the heart of the Hebrew, unless we have acquired at least some share in that same accomplishment, that was the boast and the triumph of S. Paul.

As to the need of a special study of the Psalter, I never can forget Bellarmine's saying that when he was in doubt what portion of Scripture he should labour at, there presented itself the Book of Psalms, "which all ecclesiastics daily read, but very few indeed understand." The growth of daily services amongst ourselves has made men feel more widely the need of a more complete study of a Book of Scripture which they have daily to recite. At this College, whatever may be the press of other subjects, we make no intermission in the study of the Psalter, entering so largely as it does into future clerical life. Several of the Bishops, too, have adopted the happy expedient of setting some section of the Psalter as one of their subjects of Examination for Orders; and thus securing some detailed and critical knowledge of at least a portion of the book. No section would serve such a purpose better than the Book of the Gradual Psalms. I believe a real service would be rendered to the younger Clergy if the appearance of my book should in any case lead to a somewhat exhaustive study of these Psalms being required of them.

I wish it to be understood at the outset that I have written with the animus of one who believes in the Psalms, and not with that of one who enters upon the study of them with the object of finding out whether they are really what they claim to be. If the higher criticism means that we must set to work ostensibly with the mind a *tabula rasa* as to the Psalms, but really with a sly prepossession in favour of cleverly disintegrating them—if this be criticism, then I for one can have nothing to do with criticism. In so far as my book may be read now, or hereafter, it will be read chiefly, I venture to say, by those who approach the Psalms, as I do, with a profound belief in the character that our historic faith has handed down to us about them, and who wish to catch some few rays of the light that the Holy Tongue itself can shed upon them.

THEOLOGICAL COLLEGE, SALISBURY,
*September*, 1874.

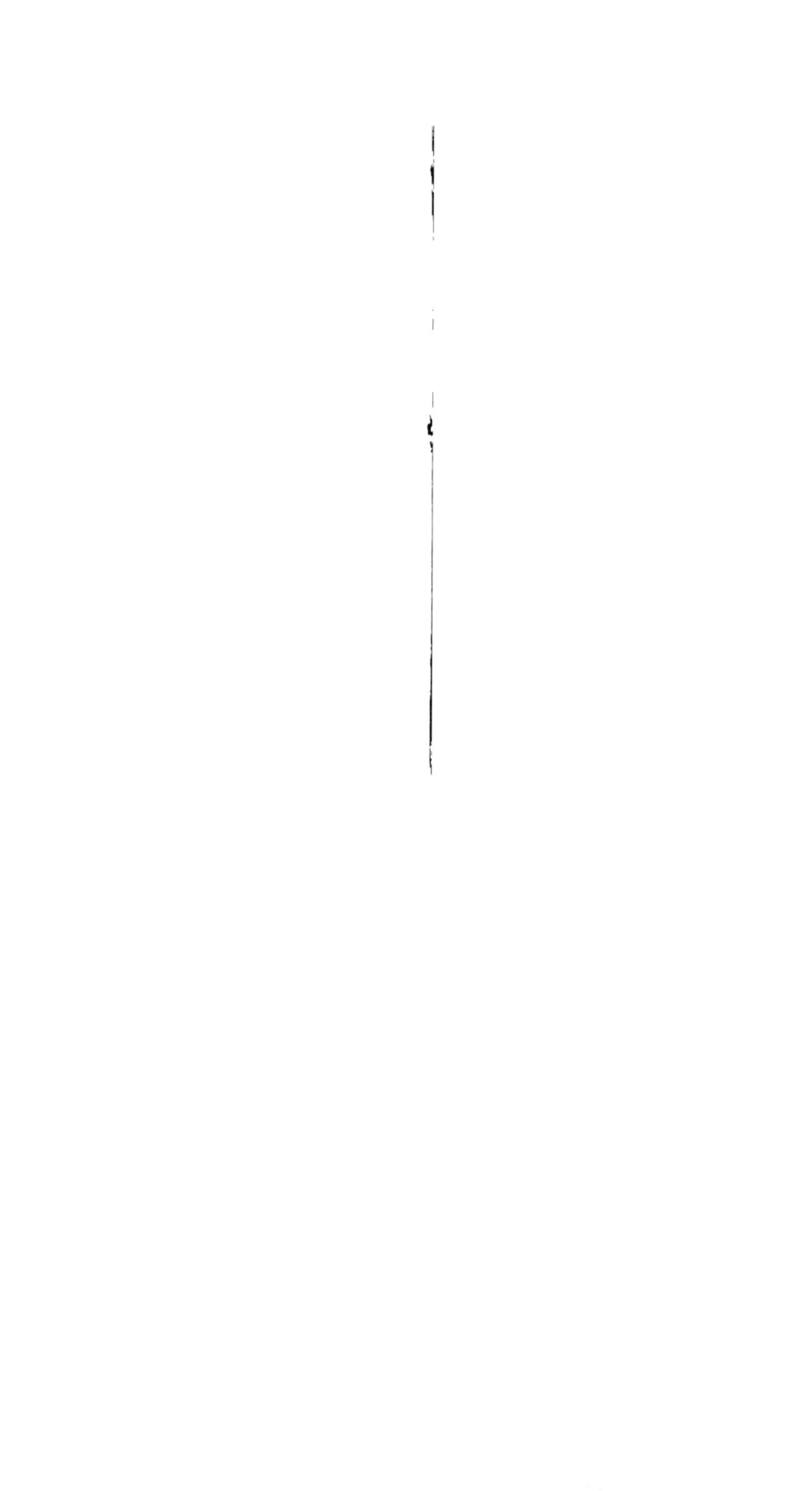

# CONTENTS.

| CHAP. | | PAGE |
|---|---|---|
| I. | The Gradual Psalms | 1 |
| II. | The Titles of the Psalms | 22 |
| III. | On Systematic Interpretation in the Church | 42 |
| IV. | Modes of Interpretation amongst the Hebrews | 66 |
| V. | The Use of the Gradual Psalms in Christian Worship | 91 |
| VI. | The Share of the Gradual Psalms in Israelitish Devotion | 120 |
| VII. | On Psalm CXX. | 130 |
| VIII. | On Psalm CXXI. | 148 |
| IX. | On Psalm CXXII. | 163 |
| X. | On Psalm CXXIII. | 182 |
| XI. | On Psalm CXXIV. | 191 |
| XII. | On Psalm CXXV. | 200 |
| XIII. | On Psalm CXXVI. | 212 |
| XIV. | On Psalm CXXVII. | 228 |
| XV. | On Psalm CXXVIII. | 246 |

| CHAP. | | PAGE |
|---|---|---|
| XVI. | On Psalm CXXIX. | 262 |
| XVII. | On Psalm CXXX. | 276 |
| XVIII. | On Psalm CXXXI. | 290 |
| XIX. | On Psalm CXXXII. | 299 |
| XX. | On Psalm CXXXIII. | 347 |
| XXI. | On Psalm CXXXIV. | 362 |
| XXII. | The Prevalence of the Odd Number | 370 |
| XXIII. | The Influence of Hebrew Writers upon the English Bible | 392 |
| | Supplement to Chapter I. | 407 |
| | Index | 409 |

# THE GRADUAL PSALMS.

## CHAPTER I.

### THE GRADUAL PSALMS.

The Gradual Psalms are those which form the group beginning with Psalm cxx. (When I was in trouble), and ending with Psalm cxxxiv. (Behold now, praise the Lord), according to the arrangement in the Hebrew and English Psalters. They are so called from the heading prefixed to each Psalm of the group,—in the Authorised English Version "A song of degrees" (more accurately, perhaps, "A song of the degrees"), and in the Latin Psalter, "Canticum graduum."

It is of course the Latin form of the heading that has given us the phrase "Gradual Psalms." Before proceeding to discuss the meaning of the phrase it may be well to say at once, by way of caution to the unwary, that the term *Gradual*, as applied to this group of Psalms, must be distinguished from the same term as applied also to a Psalm in the Eucharistic Office of the Christian Church. The Psalm (or portion of a Psalm) that was, and is still in the Western Church outside the English Communion, sung immediately before the recitation of the Gospel, is called the Gradual, because it is sung on the steps (*gradus*) to the pulpit or ambon,* from which the recitation of the Gospel takes place. The term *Gradual*, however, in this sense belongs not to any particular group of Psalms, but is applied promiscuously to any Psalm which the Office Book might have appointed for the service in question.

The Gradual of the Eucharist.

I say the term *Gradual Psalms*, as applied to the group of Psalms before us, must be carefully distinguished from the same term in this liturgical application. Yet there is some analogy between the two, if the name *Gradual Psalms*, as given to the group of Psalms on which I have undertaken to treat, has anything to do with their having been sung (like the Christian *Gradual*) upon certain steps of the Temple at Jerusalem.

---

* So Cardinal Bona (Rerum Liturg. Lib. II. c. 6, § 4) is careful to observe, and not from the steps of the Altar, as some of the more recent writers had affirmed.

The exact meaning that we are to affix to the term "Degrees," or its several equivalents, is a subject of debate, and has given occasion to much which one can hardly call otherwise than the wildest conjecture. Almost every conceivable shade of meaning that the etymology of the Hebrew word will bear seems to have been put forward by one or other of the later Christian inquirers.

The word in question is formed from a root which means to *go up, ascend*. About that there is no doubt whatever. But the precise meaning of the derived substantive is not so plain. *Sense of the Hebrew word.* In the Scripture itself it has more than one meaning. It has, first of all, the plain sense of *ascent*. This it has, for example, in Josh. x. 10: *1. Ascent.* "And the Lord discomfited them before Israel, and slew them with a great slaughter at Gibeon, and chased them along the way that goeth up (lit. the way of *the Ascent*) to Beth-horon." So again in 1 Sam. ix. 11: "And as they went up the hill to the city (Marg. In the Ascent of the city), they found young maidens going out to draw water."

It has also the sense of *exaltation, dignity;* as in 1 Chron. xvii. 17. ... "And hast regarded *2. Dignity.*

me according to the estate of a man of *high degree,* O Lord God."

Then, it means that by which Ascent is made—perhaps even *scaffold*, as the margin of the Authorised Version gives Neh. ix. 4. "Then stood up upon the scaffold, of the Levites. . . ." And in a multitude of passages, *steps* or *stairs*.

3. Stairs.

So it is in 1 Kings x. 19: "The throne had six *steps;*" in Neh. xii. 37: "And at the fountain gate, which was over against them, they went up by *the stairs* of the City of David at the going up (the *ascent*) of the wall." And in 2 Kings ix. 13: "Then they hasted, and took every man his garment, and put it under him on the top of *the stairs*, and blew with trumpets, saying, Jehu is King."

There remains the one sense of *degrees*, analogous to the preceding, which the word bears in all those passages about Hezekiah's recovery from sickness; as in 2 Kings xx. 11: "And Isaiah the prophet cried unto the Lord: and he brought the shadow ten *degrees* backward, by which it had gone down in the dial of Ahaz." I cannot help thinking that, by the choice of this particular rendering for the word, the English translators intended that the

4. Degrees.

"Songs of Degrees" should be associated in the reader's mind with the deliverance from sickness accorded to Hezekiah. I shall revert to this application, with Lightfoot's view upon it, further on. Meantime, I think it should be observed that it is only in one or other of these two latter senses, *stairs* or *degrees*, that the word occurs in the plural number, as it stands in the heading of these Psalms.

I. For the interpretation of the word as it occurs in the heading of the Gradual Psalms, some ideas have been suggested, not exactly agreeing *The name not structural.* with any of the senses tabulated above, though in some degree deducible from one or other of them. Gesenius, for example, appears to think the term has reference to the *structure* of the Gradual Psalms themselves. He observes that the ideas in the several Psalms mount by a kind of climax. A word or thought that has been used at the close of one verse being taken up at the beginning of the next. Thus in Psalms cxxi. 1, 2:—

"I will lift up mine eyes unto the hills, from whence cometh my help.

"My help cometh from the Lord, which made heaven and earth."

"Help" is here the idea which seems to him to link verse with verse. His words are "the language advances by steps (*gradatim*) in such a way that a part of a preceding sentence is commonly repeated at the beginning of the next, and everywhere is augmented with new resources of phrase, and, as it were, *ascends.*"[*] These Psalms would, in fact, according to his view be Gradational Psalms rather than Gradual Psalms. This observation of the laborious German lexicographer is, we are bound to admit, very ingenious.[†] It seems to me, in fact, only too ingenious. It is too fanciful, and too subtle, to be probable. The objections to it appear to be two.

[*] Thes. Ling.: Heb. p. 1032, s. v.

[†] His view is approved by Professor Delitzsch:—"Es ist Gesenius' Verdienst, den wahren Sinn der fraglichen Psalmüberschrift zuerst durchschaut zu haben, indem er seit 1812, und seitdem öfter gelehrt hat, dass die 15 Lieder von ihrem stufenweise fortschreitenden Gedanken-Rhythmus den Namen haben und dass also der Name, wie Triolett (Ringelgedicht) in der abendländischen Poetik, sich nicht auf den gottesdienstlichen Gebrauch, sondern auf den technischen Bau bezieht." (Biblischer Commentar über die Psalmen: Leipzig, 1867; p. 692). On the other hand, this view is rejected by Justus Olshausen (Die Psalmen. Leipzig, 1853; p. 28) "Ebensowenig Wahrscheinlichkeit hat die von Gesenius gegebene Erklärung, wornach die Benennung auf einen eigenthümlichen, stufenweise fortschreitenden Rhythmus deuten soll, der in jenen Liedern herrscht."

First, that this kind of chain-work in ideas is not *everywhere* observable through this group of Psalms. And second, that the same kind of structure is discernible elsewhere than in the particular group before us.

II. It may be convenient to class together two or three other meanings which are conjectural, as distinct from those which are in any degree traditional.

(*a.*) There is the view that the *Ascent* or *Goings up* spoken of in these Psalm titles were the goings up to the walls to repair them after the people's return to the Holy City from the Captivity in Babylon; the Psalms being called "Songs of the goings up," as being sung upon the walls by the guards and workmen.* It is possible; but it can hardly be said to be in any way proved.

<small>*a.* Ascent to walls.</small>

(*b.*) The *goings up* have been taken to refer to the going up of the male population to Jerusalem for the three great Feasts of the year. Some of the Gradual Psalms do, no doubt, contain language that might well be suggested by such journeys. Many of them, however, are of such a

<small>*b.* Ascent to Feasts.</small>

* Thrupp on the Psalms

character as to be very far from giving colour to this conjecture.

(c.) The *ascents* have been referred to the *elevation* of the voice with which these Psalms were sung. This view Gesenius thinks is indicated by Luther's translation of the Hebrew title,—" A song in the higher choir" (Lied im höheren Chor); though Delitzsch seems to be more correct in understanding Luther's translation to imply that the Psalms were executed by singers occupying an elevated position in the Church, and thus making Luther practically a supporter of the view, which I have discussed later, and which makes these Ascents have something to do with steps.

*c. Mode of performance.*

III. Another possible application of the Gradual Psalms is suggested in the words of Lightfoot, that great master of Hebrew studies: " The degrees of the sun's reversing, and the fifteen years of Hezekiah's life-prolonging, may call to our minds the fifteen Psalms of degrees; viz., from Psalm cxx. and forward. These were Hezekiah's songs that were sung to the stringed instruments in the house of the Lord: (Isa. xxxviii. 20); whether these were picked out by him for that purpose, be it left to censure. The Jews hold they were called

*Degrees on Sun-dial.*

'Psalms of Degrees,' because they were sung upon the fifteen stairs that rose into the Courts of the Temple. Whoso, in reading those Psalms, shall have his thoughts upon the danger of Jerusalem by Sennacherib, and her delivery,—and the sickness of Hezekiah, and his recovery,—shall find that they fit those occasions in many places very well. But I assert nothing, but leave it to examination." ("A Chronicle of the Times." Lightfoot, Works, ed. Pitman, vol. ii. p. 269. London: 1822.)

Amongst the interpretations that have been traditionally accepted in the Hebrew nation, we may take first of all—

IV. The view of the Chaldee Targum.* In that version, as will be seen in the pages of the following commentary, every single one of the Gradual Psalms is preceded by this singular enlargement and paraphrase of its Hebrew Title:—

---

* For the sake of the general reader, it may be convenient to say here that a Targum is a version of Scripture, of a more or less paraphrastic kind. It was a Targum that Ezra and his companions read when they "gave the sense"—the very word in Hebrew—of the Book of the Law of God. Neh. viii. 8. A Targum is commonly, but not necessarily, in Chaldee. The Septuagint version into Greek is, for example, a Targum, and not a strict translation.

"A song which was said upon the steps of the abyss."

What is "the abyss?" it will be at once asked.

*Steps of the Abyss.* The phrase refers to a strange legend that involves cosmical ideas long ago exploded, but which, if it has no critical value, is at least curious from its very strangeness. The story occurs in that one of the two parts of the Talmud, known as the Gemoro, which is in no form accessible to English readers. I therefore translate it as it stands there.*

"At the time that David was excavating the foundations of the temple, the deep (that is to say, the water under the earth) overflowed, and wished to destroy the world. David then said, Who is there that knoweth whether it is permitted to write the name of Jehovah upon a tile and cast it into the deep to quiet it. But there was no one who said a word. David then said, Whoever is capable of deciding it and does not do so, shall be hanged by his neck. Ahithophel accordingly weighed the matter in his mind, and applied the *a fortiori* argument. To make peace betwixt a man and his (suspected) wife, the

* The story is found in the Treatise Succah, fol. 53, 1. at the foot and over the leaf.

Law says, My Name, which must be written with sanctity, must be blotted out with the water.* To cause peace for the whole world, then, how much more so. He said therefore to him, It is permitted to write the Name of Jehovah and to do as proposed. He then wrote the Name of Jehovah upon a tile and cast it into the deep (abyss). The deep thereupon receded sixteen thousand cubits. When he saw that the water sank deep in the earth, he said, It is better for the earth that the water should rise higher, for it imparts moisture to the earth. He therefore said the fifteen Gradual Psalms, and made the water ascend fifteen thousand cubits, and caused it to remain at a thousand cubits from the earth."

The Gradual Psalms themselves are, it may be observed, supposed to contain some expressions referable to this wonderful story of the Talmud. When, for instance, David found the waters gushing out, he was in great distress. It is this distress that he reports in the very first words with which he opens the group of Gradual Psalms: "In my distress I cried unto the Lord."† He refers to it again in these Psalms under the image, "Then the waters

* See Numb. v. 23. † Ps. cxx. 1.

had overwhelmed us, the stream had gone over our soul."*

The fact upon which Ahithophel bases his reasoning is not immediately apparent in the passage from the Book of Numbers—the fact, I mean, that the Name of God was to be blotted out with the water. It must be observed that the sacred Name of Jehovah formed part of the curse (in verse 21) which was to be written in the book and blotted out with the water.

V. Another explanation, which in my judgment is not to be lost sight of even when we adopt another in combination with it, and which it will be seen in the following commentary has gained traditional acceptance among the Hebrew writers on the subject, is <small>Going up from Babylon.</small> that which finds in the *Degrees*, the *Ascents*, the *Goings-up*, an allusion to the going up of the restored Israel from its Captivity in Babylon, and the erection of the Second Temple.

There are unquestionably many, many phrases in this group of Psalms which exactly fit such an allusion. The verb ("go up"), which is at the root of the Hebrew noun in question, is certainly employed with reference to the motion betwixt Babylon and the Holy

* Psalm cxxiv. 4.

Land. Nehemiah, for example, says, "These are the children of the province that *went up* out of the Captivity."* Even the noun itself is applied by Ezra to the same event: "For upon the first day of the first month began he to go up (Marg. Was the foundation of the going up) from Babylon."† The only apparent difficulty in this acceptation lies in the fact that in the headings of these Psalms the noun occurs uniformly in the plural number. It is here "the goings up," and not "the going up." To this, however, it may be replied, that the captives went up to their country in detachments, not all at once; and that the heading of Psalms adapted (not necessarily composed) for them to sing upon their return naturally recognizes the fact.

VI. There is an extension of this kind of meaning given by that most ancient of all Hebrew commentaries on the Psalms, called the Midrash Tehillim. It is an interpretation which I have not seen noticed by any of the writers, Hebrew, Latin, English, or German, but which to my own thinking has more to commend it than any of the other many interpretations that have been offered. The Degrees,

*Deliverances.*

* Nehemiah vii. 6.   † Ezra vii. 9.

or goings up, are not the goings up from the Captivity of Babylon, as so many of the Hebrew and other writers have taken them to be, but the goings up out of any trouble or distress. The word is in the plural rather than the singular—" goings up" rather than "going up"—because Israel had experienced several such deliverances; to wit, that from the bondage of Egypt, and that of Shadrach, Meshach, and Abednego. The term "goings up," then, will not refer to the going up, in the sense of mere physical motion on the journey from Babylon to Israel, but rather to the deliverance itself. According to this interpretation, which has the advantage of being at once perhaps the most natural, the least objectionable, and certainly the most ancient interpretation extant, this group of Psalms would be properly thought of as the Songs of the (the article is found in the Hebrew) Deliverances, and would be applicable strictly not only to the return from the Captivity, but to any of those goings up from the depths of calamity and distress which the people of God may experience.

Before leaving this part of the subject, I would call attention to the word for "song" in the heading of these Psalms. There is, the ancient Hebrew Midrash seems to point out, a propriety in the use of the word in connection with the deliverances. It is the exact word used by Jeremiah in his distress, when he said, "*Sing* unto the Lord, praise ye the Lord; for he hath delivered the soul of the poor from the hand of evildoers."*

I confess that ever since I first became acquainted with this colouring of the Psalm-titles, from reading the old Hebrew Midrash, I have felt that it cannot be lost sight of, even though we may have to associate it with *steps*, or some other of the many senses that have been proposed for the word under discussion. It seems to justify, from the very oldest Hebrew tradition, that particular line of thought which the use of the Christian Church appears to have connected with the Gradual Psalms.†

VII. The last interpretation, which it will be necessary to notice, and from which the Gradual Psalms can hardly be divorced in the mind of a Hebrew reader, is that which connects them with a certain group of *steps* in the Temple. There

<small>Steps.</small>

* Jer. xx. 13.

† See, for example, the kind of thought that underlies the Office of the Gradual Psâlms, given in a subsequent chapter of this work.

was a flight of fifteen steps in the Temple, which led up from the Court of the Women to the Court of Israel; and, it is said, the fifteen Songs of the Steps were so called, because they were performed upon this group of fifteen steps. Radak, the Hebrew commentator, adds indeed the particular that upon each step one Psalm was said. But how? When? By whom? Why an arrangement apparently so eccentric was adopted, I never saw clearly stated in any of the current commentaries. I make no apology then for going to the fountain-head for information.

Describing the ceremonial practised on the first day of the Feast of Tabernacles, the Mischna* says that the Levites said in presence of the assembled multitude songs—literally, "Words of Songs," the same word as in the heading *Songs of Degrees*—and praises with harps and bow-instruments, and cymbals and trumpets, and instruments of music without number upon the fifteen steps that go down from the Court of Israel to the Court of the Women, which correspond to the fifteen Songs of the Degrees in the Book of Psalms, upon which steps the Levites were

* Talm. Bab. Succah., fol. 51, 2, at the top.

placed with the musical instruments and said the song.

It will be observed that this passage of the Mischna does not explicitly say that what they sang was the group of Gradual Psalms: the Gemoro, however,—that other division which with the Mischna makes up the Talmud,—explains that this was what they sang.

But let us push the matter a little further. What can be the significance of Psalms being said upon what we have called "a flight of steps" at all? The truth is that this flight of steps was something very much more than a mere staircase. The mental picture, alike of their form and of their functions, that is formed, I fear, by most English readers is very far from representing the strict reality. The so-called *steps* were, in fact, nothing less than what in modern English we should call the Orchestra of the Temple.

The shape of them is at once suggestive of such a purpose; for they were not straight, but semicircular in form. The Talmud explicitly describes them thus\*:—"And there were fifteen steps which went up from the midst of it (the

<small>Shape of Steps.</small>

* Talm. Bab. Middoth, fol. 35, 1 at the foot.

Court of the Women) to the Court of Israel, corresponding to the fifteen steps in the Psalms, upon which the Levites said the song. They were not straight, but curved like the half of a circular floor." Elsewhere we have the traditional estimate of their dimensions. Each step, says another treatise in the Talmud,[*] was half a cubit high and half a cubit broad. These steps, moreover, occupied a position at the east of the Altar, and very slightly removed from it. On them, in fact, it has been believed[†] the sacred orchestra was placed, as the Talmud indicates in the passage quoted above with reference to the service on the first day of the Feast of Tabernacles. And to crown the whole edifice, we have the fact that this position of the sacred orchestra exactly accords with that assigned to it in Scripture itself: "Also the Levites which were the singers, all of them of Asaph, of Heman, of Jeduthun, with their sons and their brethren, being arrayed in white linen, having cymbals and psalteries and harps, stood at the east end of the Altar."[‡]

[*] Talm. Bab. Joma, fol. 16, 1 past the middle of the page.
[†] See L'Empereur on Mid. 2, 5, ap. Surenh.
[‡] 2 Chron. v. 12.

This then, I venture to think, gives a somewhat different colour to the picture, which most English readers have sketched for themselves about the Gradual Psalms. Whatever view of the *Songs of Degrees* you may take besides, you cannot leave out some association of them with the steps, without ignoring the unanimous belief about them handed down from time immemorial amongst the people who gave them to us; without, in fact, implying that at some epoch or other this strange association of the steps with the Psalms was gratuitously invented and, being invented, secured general acceptance in the sacred literature of the Hebrew nation. It is quite impossible to believe such a thing, when we are dealing with a people so jealous of precedent and authority in religion as the Hebrews have always been. I see, in fact, no sufficient reason why we should not follow the leading of the Mischna and feel that Songs of Degrees, Songs of the Steps, is as much as to say Songs in the sacred Orchestra.

This fact, too, that they were performed with an exceptional majesty of ceremony and execution helps us further to understand the drift of them. We have seen that they were specially connected with the opening of the Feast of Tabernacles. But what was the Feast of Tabernacles? It was to the Hebrew nation the memorial of their dwelling in tabernacles in the wilderness—a memorial, that is to say, of their deliverance from Egypt. When, then, I am asked whether I adopt the steps-view or the deliverance-from-captivity-view,—(for the other views that I have noticed, are, in my judgment, though ingenious, yet too subtle, or too fanciful, or too conjectural for acceptance)—when I am asked which of these two views I adopt, I reply that I accept both. The one, when rightly and fully understood, seems to support the other. I see nothing to prevent our recognizing in the heading of these Psalms a kind of *double entendre*. I see no reason* why we should abandon the inherited

---

* Some writers have endeavoured to prove that these Gradual Psalms (amongst others) were not written till after the Babylonian Captivity, by observing certain peculiarities in their phraseology, especially the abbreviated form occasionally (*e. g.* Psalms cxxii. 3, 4; cxxiv. 1, 2, et al.) assumed by the Hebrew relative pronoun. In reality such forms do not prove what they are alleged to prove. See Dr. Pusey's masterly argument on the whole subject in his Introduction to the Book of Jonah. These arguments from language are enormously valuable as subsidiary arguments; but, when they stand alone, they seem to me to be generally too precarious to deserve confidence.

belief that they were originally David's Songs of the Deliverances—composed by him possibly in praise for deliverances accorded to himself and, naturally, with a memory of those earlier deliverances that God had effected for His people—and that they, so full as they were of this traditional meaning, were afterwards adapted by Ezra and his contemporaries to that special tide of devout feeling that was evoked by the deliverance from the Captivity in Babylon. Songs of the Steps, I believe them to be; Songs of the Sacred Orchestra, sung with all possible majesty of instrument and of voice; songs of a joy and trust that peep out even through the wail of the *De Profundis*;* songs not of this going up or that, but, as the ancient Midrash pointed out, Songs of the Deliverances—deliverances alike for all—for Moses, for David, for Hezekiah, for Ezra, for us; Songs of the Deliverances which God anciently accomplished for the Jew; and, not less, Songs of the Deliverances which God is now-a-days accomplishing for the Christian.

* Ps. cxxx.

## CHAPTER II.

### THE TITLES OF THE PSALMS.

ANY one who is at all conversant with the older writings on the Psalms upon the one hand, and with the modern commentators upon the other, will have observed that a remarkable change has taken place in the attitude adopted towards the Titles of the Psalms. Not to go back so far as the days of S. Augustine in the former class, a writer so comparatively recent as Dr. Hammond sees apparently no difference between the title and any other portion of a given Psalm, accepting the one for an integral portion of the Psalm just as much as the other. In the present day, on the contrary, it has become the fashion to discredit so many of the titles as to create a sense of insecurity in relying upon any of them.

I put the question, then, between the older critics and the new, in a pointed shape—Are the titles of the Psalms to be given up?

To begin with, let us have a clear idea of *what*

## THE TITLES OF THE PSALMS. 23

we shall give up, supposing we have to answer that question in the affirmative. It is not merely the erasure of what is in Hebrew a single word, "of David,"* that is involved. The Psalm-title extends often to a considerable length. In Psalm lxiii., for example, the title constitutes an entire verse:

A psalm of David, when he was in the wilderness of Judah.

In Psalm xviii., the title forms one entire verse, and begins a second; so that in Hebrew the first three verses stand thus:—

1. To the Chief Musician, a Psalm of David, the servant of the Lord, who spake unto the Lord the words of this song in the day that the Lord delivered him from the hand of all his enemies, and from the hand of Saul:

2. And he said, I will love Thee, O Lord, my strength.

3. The Lord is my strength, etc.

In Psalm li., the title in Hebrew occupies two entire verses. Thus:—

1. To the Chief Musician, a Psalm of David,

* As in Psalm xxv.

2. When Nathan the Prophet came unto him after he had gone in to Bathsheba.

The student of the Psalms in the holy tongue itself can hardly avoid having, in regard to these Psalm-titles, thoughts other than those suggested to the mere English reader. In the eyes of such a student they lose that 'deciduous' character with which the mode of printing in the Authorised Version can hardly fail to invest them. In that version, they look like something external to the Psalm itself; they are not unmistakeably included in the verse-numbering of the Psalm; they seem almost to challenge the verdict that they are the addition, the comment, the gloss of a subsequent editor to explain what he conceived to be the drift of the author's meaning. In the Hebrew Psalter, however, they look like nothing of the kind. There they read exactly like any other verse of the Scripture. The system of Hebrew accentuation, which indicates not only the connection of word with word and clause with clause, but also the traditional mode in which each is to be read aloud—this system is applied to the several words of the Psalm-titles precisely as it is to every other word of the Old Testament. If a Psalm is

*Their Character in the Original.*

recited in Hebrew, for example, in Israelitish worship, then, as a matter of course, its heading is recited too. In short, by their character in the Hebrew Psalter the titles claim to be integral parts of the several Psalms which they introduce, and vindicate their right to be treated by the same laws of criticism as those which are applied to other verses of the Psalter. If we are at liberty to amputate the title because it does not appear to square with the contents of its Psalm, then we are also at liberty to erase any other verse of the Psalm, because it does not comfortably adjust itself to the verses which may precede or follow it.

This fact that the titles are integral parts of the Psalms will be appreciated by the English reader, if he will notice one other fact, viz., that we have Psalm-titles in other parts of the Bible as well as in the Psalter itself. In the middle of a chapter in Isaiah we have for example this verse: "The writing of Hezekiah king of Judah, when he had been sick, and was recovered of his sickness"*—a formula which in structure and character is identical with the titles in the Psalter, and which is, in point of fact, nothing but a Psalm-title, precisely as the succeeding verses of

* Isa. xxxviii. 9.

Hezekiah's thanksgiving are nothing but a Psalm. Once more, the first verse of a chapter in the Second Book of Samuel,* is approximately what appears in the Psalter as the title of the eighteenth Psalm; the Psalm itself being substantially repeated in the chapter in Samuel.

Our acceptance then—to take the Hezekiah passage—of the title in Isaiah does not, surely, depend upon its obvious appropriateness to the verses that follow it? We should not, surely, be at liberty to cut this verse out of the heart of Isaiah's chapter, if we failed to discover such appropriateness? Yet if we are at liberty to reject the titles in the Psalter, because we fail to discover their suitableness to the contents of their several Psalms; then, we should also be at liberty to reject the verse containing such a title in the middle of Isaiah's chapter, if we failed to discover its suitableness; and then we should be at liberty to reject the verse next to it, or the next to that, upon the same grounds; then, in point of fact, we should be at liberty to reject *any* verse of the Scriptures if we failed to discover its fitness; and the right of this or that clause to a place in the Bible

* 2 Sam. xxii. 1.

would depend not upon external testimony, but upon our own faculties—a position which is obviously absurd.

The assumption, then, that the Psalm-titles are to be disregarded, involves consequences far too serious for us to acquiesce in it, unless we are driven to do so by evidence which is quite irresistible. A glance, however, at the books in which they are lightly treated, will show that the chief evidence against them is by no means of this kind, but that it commonly consists of nothing more than an apparent inappropriateness. The erasure of a Psalm-title is in fact nothing else but what is known to editors as a "conjectural emendation," and deserves no higher confidence than such emendations commonly receive. If a critic of a Psalm comes fairly forward, and says that the external evidence is against its title; that in fact such title is a late gloss; then we shall be bound to weigh his advocacy seriously. When, however, he says nothing more conclusive than that the title of a Psalm is inconsistent with the contents of the Psalm; that it involves, for instance, an anachronism; that it is a patent absurdity to attribute to David a Psalm containing expressions which

*The adverse evidence.*

can only be explained of the Babylonish Captivity; then we must invite him to look at the matter once again, and to consider whether a different hypothesis as to the intent and history of the Psalm might not dissipate the supposed anachronism. As an example, I take one of these Gradual Psalms. Ps. cxxii. is one that has been subjected to this kind of treatment. It is headed "A song of degrees of David." But it is said the Psalm contains phrases which can only refer to the Captivity. Therefore the title which ascribes it to David cannot be true, but is probably the addition of some later editor, who failed to see the true sense of the Psalm and the consequent impropriety of his title.

But supposing the external evidence in favour of the title to be insurmountable, it is surely possible to frame a hypothesis, which may at any rate help to mitigate the undoubted difficulty. If, for example, the Psalm were really a Psalm of David, and then by Ezra or some other were incorporated, possibly with some modifications, into the series of Pilgrim Songs for the return from Babylon, the internal difficulties against the title would, on such a supposition, almost entirely disappear.

And yet once again. I cannot refrain from observing that this rejection of a Psalm-title, not upon external evidence, but upon chronological phænomena presented by the Psalm itself, involves the assumption that Psalms are exclusively historic and not at all prophetic compositions. Those who do not feel it a difficulty that Isaiah should mention Cyrus by name will not suspect Psalmists because they use expressions which must be interpreted of an age much later than their own.

The pressure of an irresistible external evidence is then, as I believe, the only thing which can warrant us in surrendering the titles of the Psalms. But the amount of such evidence of which Europe is at present in possession is, so far as I know, almost infinitesimally small. It will, of course, at once occur even to the casual observer that they appear unchallenged in perhaps every printed Bible he ever saw. Yet too much must not be made of this fact. For these, it must be remembered, do not represent so many independent authorities, inasmuch as almost all the printed Hebrew Bibles come from a few early printed sources. These sources may be seen in Kennicott's "Second Dissertation," chap. iv.

p. 470, seq., ed. 1759. The Bibles that were early printed are themselves the product of late manuscripts.

With the view of conveying some idea *how* small the adverse external evidence is, I have been steadily through all the variations noted by Kennicott and De Rossi, so far as any occur in the titles of the Gradual Psalms. The following very slender crop of variants represents absolutely the whole result of my attempt to find such, of whatever kind they might be, in the titles of this section of the Psalter.

<small>External evidence in their favour.</small>

(a) In the title of Psalm cxxii. (a Song of Degrees of David), the phrase "of David" is wanting, according to De Rossi, in one MS. of the twelfth century, which Kennicott collated, and in one MS. of the thirteenth century.

($\beta$) In the title of Psalm cxxiv. (A Song of Degrees of David), the phrase "of David" is wanting in one MS. of the fourteenth Century, in one MS. of the twelfth century, and in one MS. of the twelfth or thirteenth century.

($\gamma$) In the title of Psalm cxxxiii. (A Song of Degrees of David), the phrase "of David" is wanting in one MS. of Kennicott's of the fourteenth century, and in one MS. of the thirteenth century.

As respects the titles of the Gradual Psalms—to take them as an example of the titles in the rest of the Psalms—this is all the external evidence against them which the Hebrew MSS. of De Rossi and Kennicott furnish; and this out of an array of 694 MSS. of Kennicott, and 958 of De Rossi! I submit that the external testimony to the authenticity of the Psalm-titles, which such a fact affords, is nothing short of overwhelming.

A concession is not unfrequently made with respect to the Psalm-titles which is at once most unjust and most damaging to the claim of those titles to cordial acceptance. By those who do not know the merits of the case, it is often supposed that the titles of the Psalms stand in much the same position as the subscriptions to S. Paul's Epistles, which subscriptions every body knows form no part of the genuine Epistles themselves. No comparison could be more unwarranted. They are alike indeed in one respect. The titles and the subscriptions alike came first under suspicion on account of internal difficulties. It was found to be hard to reconcile them with the apparent purport of the Psalm or Epistle which they accompanied. But *False analogy with S. Paul's Epistles.*

here the similarity ceases. When we begin to trace the history of the titles and the subscriptions respectively, the facts immediately strike off in two opposite directions. If the Psalm-titles be a subsequent interpolation in the Scriptures, then we shall expect to find some trace of the interpolation—that they occur in some copies of the Scriptures but not in others, for instance; some vestige of a protest or comment upon their introduction; and some indication that before a certain epoch they did not exist. Have we then any such trace? Absolutely none, I believe, of any weight. We can point to no era of sacred history and say, Then was the period when the Psalms had not their titles in the current copies of the Scriptures.

But with the subscriptions to the Epistles the case is entirely different. Not only do they contradict the apparent facts of the history, and so suggest their own spurious origin; but we know, so to speak, all about them. They crept into some copies of the New Testament; but from by far the most and the best of the copies that have survived to our day they are actually absent. We know then that they were not commonly accepted along with the Apostle's writings. We know, too, the period when they made their appearance in the world. We know even who made them. They were the work, says Dr. Mill,* of Euthalius, the Deacon of Alexandria, whose edition of the Epistles appeared† in A.D. 458. We know, I repeat, all about them. We have the very best evidence from without that they are an interpolation, in the fact that we can point to a period when the Apostolic Epistles did not carry them. And when we make some approximation to doing this in the case of the Titles of the Psalms, then (and not before) we shall be warranted in expunging them from our text and from our thought.‡

To sum up then. The evidence, whether favourable or adverse, that is attainable about the titles of

* Sed ad ὑπογραφὰς supra memoratas revertimur, in quibus ad calcem Epistolarum D. Pauli notatur locus unde, ut et persona fere per quam missæ sint. Has autem confecit Euthalius Diaconus; qui tum Paulinarum Epistolarum et aliarum quarundam Novi Testamenti partium editionem adornavit. Prolegomena in N. Test. ed. Dr. Mill, p. xc. 2 vols. folio. Oxford: 1707.

† So says Mr. Scrivener in his Plain Introduction to the Criticism of the New Test. p. 45, ed. Cambridge, 1861.

‡ Not to interrupt my argument, I have given at the close of this chapter a list of facts as to the non-appearance of the Epistle-subscriptions in the most famous MSS. There are no such facts that can be alleged about the Psalm-titles.

D

the Gradual Psalms is of two kinds, (1) external, and (2) internal; the external consisting in testimony, whether of ancient manuscripts, versions, or something else; and the internal consisting in a discoverable fitness or unfitness in the title when compared with the contents of the Psalm which each pretends to introduce.

*Two branches of evidence.*

Now it has never, so far as I know, been alleged that the external evidence is adverse to the authenticity of the Psalm-titles. On the contrary, that evidence is, we have seen, overwhelmingly in their favour. In the case of the Gradual Psalms, all the ancient manuscripts seem to contain them; all the ancient translations into the several languages seem to have accepted them; no hint is ever given that their origin is at all suspicious. No; it has been purely and solely upon internal evidence that their assailants have proposed to treat them with indifference. The argument has been, in brief, something like this:—A Psalm appears to a commentator to speak of events which belong to a given epoch, say the Captivity; the title assigns it to an author anterior to that event; ergo, the title is a blundering addition to the Psalm.

To this in the first place it might be replied, that it assumes the non-existence of the gift of prophecy, which would enable a Psalmist to speak of events posterior to himself; in other words, it assumes the falsehood of the Bible itself, which is really the very point at issue.

Secondly, the apparent anomaly between the earlier author in the title and the later substance in the Psalm, might be explained by the hypothesis that the Psalm was, *bonâ fide*, the work of him whose name it bears; but that in its actual form it is a recension of the original made by competent authority, Ezra or some other, who has given a colouring from later history to certain of the expressions of the original Psalm, and thus, as it were, has under the Divine guidance adapted the phrases of the earlier composition, so that they might the more readily reach the later sympathies and experiences of the Church. It is under some such hypothesis as this, I conceive, that the two ancient ways of interpreting "degrees"—that which refers it to *steps* of the Temple, and that which refers it to the (long posterior) *goings up* from the Captivity in Babylon—may be not rival interpretations, but simultaneously true.

And thirdly, it might be replied that, when the expressions of a Psalm appear to a commentator to have a meaning which sets the substance of a Psalm at issue with its title, such appearance is nothing but appearance. It is not reality. Rather, the fact of the title not suiting the apparent meaning is a proof that that is not the true meaning. The title and the substance of the Psalm come before the commentator on the same ground, on the same authority, with the same credentials. He has no more right to reject the title than he has to reject the substance. If he so interprets the Psalm as to set it in conflict with the title, then (if he *must* have this kind of argument) I should reply, in that fact is the proof that he has not got hold of the right interpretation.

But, in truth, this rejection of the Psalm-titles upon grounds of internal evidence is open to an objection which is still more fatal, as it lies nearer to the springs of thought. To follow the lead of supposed internal difficulties in the Psalm-titles, and quietly to ignore the enormous body of external testimony in their favour—what is this but to mistake the function of internal evidence altogether? When we are discussing whether a

<small>Internal evidence subsidiary, not paramount.</small>

given clause, that has come to us from antiquity, is genuine or no, the internal evidence presented by the clause is an instrument of enormous value in the hands of a sagacious critic; but when a certain amount of external testimony simultaneously exists, then it should be remembered—and this I venture to think has often been forgotten—that the internal evidence can only be *subsidiary*, and not paramount, in the investigation. When, for example, you find that a clause, say a Psalm-title, is present in one half of your ancient copies, while it is absent in the other half; then a difficulty in reconciling the clause with its neighbours forms a strong argument against it: but when you cannot show that there ever existed (I might almost say) even a single copy of your book without the clause in question, and yet affirm that the clause is suspicious, because, in fact, you cannot understand it—this, I make bold to say, has no right to be classified otherwise than as the merest conjecture. Your interpretation of the clause and of the whole book might suggest to you that the clause was spurious; but, supposing it to rest upon an external testimony which you have not cleared away, you would not be at liberty to reject the clause so long as there is any other conceivable hypothesis which might make its genuineness possible. In a word, we may apply to the Psalm-titles, and, indeed, to a play of Sophocles and every ancient book, the principle which a most eminent critic of the New Testament has laid down for his guidance in that department—that the just use of internal evidence "has no place unless where external evidence be evenly, or at any rate, not very unevenly balanced."*

I have made bold to put forward in English this line of argument upon the Psalm-titles, because they have been somewhat rudely swept aside in certain treatises of modern Germany, whose conclusions the publications of recent years have tended to make popular in England. In ancient days they were treated with respect. S. Chrysostom[†] compares them to the statues which kings erect to victorious generals. S. Jerome[‡] speaks of them as "keys" of the Psalms, by which alone the meaning can be

* A Plain Introduction to the Criticism of the New Testament. By Frederic Henry Scrivener, M.A. Cambridge: 1861. See p. 371.
 [†] In the homily on Psalm iii, at the beginning.
 [‡] Procemium to the Psalms.

unlocked. S. Augustine* dignifies them as "decorations upon the brow of Psalms."

Each Psalm-title must stand, of course, upon its own merits; but here I have to speak of what has happened to them as a class. It has become the fashion, then, to treat the Psalm-titles, as a class, with something like disdain, whenever they will not square with the demands of the current exegesis, and to assume (in the common phrase) that they stand in very much the same category as the subscriptions to S. Paul's Epistles. If what I have urged to the contrary has any influence in persuading my contemporaries that, until something very much more formidable is arrayed against them, there is no reason that we should withhold from the Psalm-titles the same frank confidence that we accord to the Psalms themselves, then my book will not have been written in vain.

* Enarratio in Ps. lviii, at the beginning.

# SUPPLEMENT

## TO CHAPTER II.

With a view of giving some idea of the extent to which the Subscriptions of the Epistles labour under the absence of external support, I have collected—chiefly from the stratum of textual criticism in Dean Alford's page—the facts about their non-appearance, so far as relates to names of persons and places, in the five most famous manuscripts of the Greek Testament, which scholars are wont to designate by the first four capitals of the alphabet, and by the first letter of the Hebrew alphabet.

In Romans the subscription does not
exist in . . . . A B¹ C D ℵ
,, 1 Corinthians . . . . A B¹ C D¹ ℵ
,, 2 Corinthians . . . . A B¹ D ℵ
,, Galatians . . . . . A B¹ C¹ D ℵ
,, Ephesians . . . . A B¹ D ℵ
,, Philippians . . . . A B D ℵ
,, Colossians . . . . B¹ C D ℵ

THE TITLES OF THE PSALMS.

In 1 Thessalonians . . . B¹ D ℵ
,, 2 Thessalonians . . . B¹ D ℵ
,, 1 Timothy . . . . A (?) D ℵ
,, 2 Timothy . . . . C D ℵ
,, Titus . . . . . C D ℵ
,, Philemon . . . . C D ℵ
,, Hebrews . . . . . C ℵ

## CHAPTER III.

### SYSTEMATIC INTERPRETATION IN THE CHURCH.

TECHNICAL theology has been so little studied in these latter generations in England, that I feel constrained to give some account of the methods of interpretation that have been recognised in Christian exegesis.

By the most famous expositors of Scripture, then, the meaning of it has been commonly set down under two distinct heads—(1) the literal, and (2) the spiritual. The latter again divides itself into three distinct branches, one of which treats of individual human action, and is called, in the Latin phrase, (*a*) Tropologia; the second branch is that which applies a passage of Scripture to the Church upon earth, and is known as (*b*) Allegoria; and the third, (*c*) Anagogia, is that which refers the phrases of Scripture to the life and conditions of future glory. In a word, according to the old Latin couplet, the literal sense informs

*[margin: The four heads.]*

you of fact; Allegoria, informs you of what you are to believe; Anagogia, of what you are to hope for; and Tropologia, of what you are to do.*

The exact bearing, however, of these terms will be best understood from some examples of their use. There are two passages in S. Jerome's works where he occupies himself with formally assigning a meaning to these terms, which he himself employs so frequently. The first occurs in his commentary on Ezekiel, chap. xvi. Starting from the Vulgate version of Prov. xxii. 25: "Lo, I have written it to thee threefold in counsels and knowledge"†—a version by the way which lies very close to one acceptation of the original Hebrew text—S. Jerome proceeds:—

It is enjoined upon us that we understand the oracles of truth, that is the Holy Scriptures in a threefold sense. First, according to the letter; secondly, in an intermediate sense, by

S. Jerome.

---

* Litera scripta docet; quid credas Allegoria;
Quid speres Anagoge; quid agas Tropologia.

† Ecce, descripsi eam tripliciter in cogitationibus et scientiâ. Have not I written to thee excellent things in counsels and knowledge? (A.V.). Luther's German version of the Hebrew substantially follows the Vulgate *tripliciter* with *mannigfältig*.

Tropologia; thirdly, in a loftier sense, that we may apprehend all mystic matters. According to the letter is the following:* 'Neither let us commit fornication, as some of them committed, and fell in one day three and twenty thousand.' And, 'Neither murmur ye, as some of them also murmured, and were destroyed of the destroyer.' But in an intermediate sense and by Tropologia, when we withdraw from the letter and mount a little towards loftier subjects, when the Apostle says,† 'It is written in the law of Moses, Thou shalt not muzzle the mouth of the ox that treadeth out the corn.' And at once there follows: 'Doth God take care for oxen? Or saith he it altogether for our sakes?' But the last, that is the third and sublime and sacred sense, according to that passage of the same Apostle:‡ 'For this cause shall a man leave his father and mother, and shall be joined unto his wife, and they two shall be one flesh. This is a great mystery; but I speak concerning Christ and the Church.'§

* 1 Cor. x. 8, 10.    † 1 Cor. ix. 9, 10.    ‡ Eph. v. 31, 32.

§ Et jubetur nobis, ut eloquia veritatis, id est, Scripturas Sanctas intelligamus tripliciter. Primum, juxta literam; secundo medie per Tropologiam; tertio, sublimius, ut mystica quæque noscamus.

It will be observed that here S. Jerome seems to amalgamate under one phrase, "mystic," the two branches, which others call Allegoria and Anagoge. Elsewhere he still groups the four branches under three terms, though in a somewhat different way. In his Commentary on Amos, he says :—

For we are bound to understand Holy Scripture first, according to the letter, doing, in the department of morals, whatever is enjoined. Secondly, according to Allegoria, that is, the spiritual sense; thirdly, according to the blessedness of the future state.*

Secundum literam illud est: Neque fornicemur, sicut quidam eorum fornicati sunt, et ceciderunt una die viginti tria millia. Et, Nolite murmurare, sicut quidam de eis murmuraverunt, et perierunt ab exterminatore. Medie autem et juxta Tropologiam quando recedimus a litera, et paululum ad altiora conscendimus, dicente Apostolo: Scriptum est, Non alligabis os bovi trituranti. Statimque sequitur, numquid de bobus cura est Deo? An propter nos utique locutus est? Extrema autem, id est, tertia et sublimis sacraque intelligentia juxta illud ejusdem Apostoli: Propterea relinquet homo patrem et matrem et adhærebit uxori suæ. Sacramentum hoc magnum est. Ego autem dico in Christo et in Ecclesia. S. Hieron. Comment: Lib: v. in Ezech.: cap. xvi: vol. v. p. 357, F. ed. Frankfurt-am-Mein.

* Debemus enim Scripturam Sanctam primum secundum literam intelligere, facientes in Ethica quæcunque præcepta sunt. Secundo juxta Allegoriam, id est, intelligentiam spiritualem. Tertio

Here, it will be observed, he connects with the letter that which in the former passage he classed separately as Tropologia. This is done, presumably, with a view to sustaining the threefold character of systematic interpretation; a character which some have supposed to be referred to in the saying, "a threefold cord is not quickly broken." (Eccles. iv. 12.)

A multitude of phrases and phænomena in the Scriptures have been adapted by subsequent writers to the fact of a threefold interpretation being required. Thus: the three senses of Holy Scripture have been compared[*] to the three loaves which the friend wished to borrow on account of his midnight visitor in Our Lord's parable. (S. Luke xi. 5.) They have been seen,[†] again, in the threefold end which he who speaks to the edification of the Church is to set before him: "He that prophesieth speaketh unto men to edification, and exhortation, and comfort." (1 Cor. xiv. 3.) And the same plurality has been seen, yet once again, in the threefold name given

secundum futurorum beatitudinem. S. Hieron: Comment. Lib. ii., in Amos. cap. iv., p. 69, H. ed. Frankfurt-am-Mein.

[*] Guerrici Abbatis. In Diebus Rogationum Sermo. ap. S. Bern. opp.

[†] Ibid.

to the Royal Apartment in the Canticles\*—*chamber* (iii. 4), *garden* (v. i.), and *cellarium* (i. 4. A.V. *chambers*). The contrast of these three terms is more apparent, it will be observed, in the Latin version of the Scriptures than in our own, which makes the variation (as the Hebrew does) by employing the same word "chamber" in the plural as well as in the singular number. In this imagery, the garden is the historic sense, the cellarium is the moral, and the chamber (cubiculum) is the mystic sense. We have seen above that S. Jerome sometimes classed the moral with the historic sense. Here, on the contrary, the same compression is effected by leaving the historic and the moral in separate classes, and grouping the Allegoric and Anagogic senses together under the epithet "mystic."

The four branches of Scriptural exegesis are most clearly defined by Dionysius the Carthusian in his work on the Psalms:—

Holy Scripture, then, is expounded in four ways that is to say, literally or historically; and spiritually or mystically. But the *Dionysius the Carthusian.*

---

\* S. Bernardi Abbatis, Sermo xcii. De Diversis. Tom. iii. p. 1220 : Ed. Paris, 1719.

mystic sense is threefold, to wit, the Allegoric, the Tropologic or moral, and the Anagogic sense. For the historic teaches us what was done, the Allegoric what is to be believed, the Tropologic, what is to be done, and the Anagogic what is to be hoped for.* History, however, is the narration of an event.

* Quatuor itaque modis exponitur Sacra Scriptura; videlicet literaliter seu historicè, et spiritualiter seu mysticè. Sed mysticus intellectus est triplex, scilicet allegoricus, tropologicus seu moralis et anagogicus. Historia enim docet quid sit factum, allegoria quid credendum, tropologia quid faciendum, anagogia quid sperandum. Historia autem est rei gestæ narratio. Sensus vero historicus, seu literalis, est fundamentum seu basis intellectuum aliorum, et ex eo solo valet argumentum ad fidei probationem: sicut in epistola contra Vincentium Donatistam asserit Augustinus. Denique sensus allegoricus est, quando ex dicto vel facto alicujus personæ, aliud aliquid intelligitur pertinens ad Christum et corpus ejus mysticum, quod est Ecclesia: sicut dum ea quæ in veteri testamento, ad literam sanctis patribus contigerunt, de Christo intelliguntur; vel ea quæ ad Synagogam spectabant, ad Ecclesiam referuntur. Omnia namque in figura contigebant illis, et scripta sunt ad nostram eruditionem. Sensus vero tropologicus est quando ea quæ de Christo vel de Sanctis scribuntur et recitantur, ad nostram moralem informationem aptantur et exponuntur. Sensus autem anagogicus est, quando ex his quæ temporaliter facta sunt, ad contemplationem æternorum perducuntur; et ea quæ ad militantem ecclesiam pertinent, ad statum triumphantis Ecclesiæ referuntur. Horum autem solet poni exemplum in hac dictione Hierusalem: quod quia commune est et pene omnibus notum omitto: ponam-

But the historic or literal sense is the foundation or basis of the other senses, and an argument drawn from it is the only one that avails for proof of the faith; as Augustine asserts in his letter against Vincentius the Donatist. Further, the Allegoric sense is when, from the saying or act of some person, something else is understood pertaining to Christ and His Mystical Body, which is the Church; as when those things, which in the Old Testament happened according to the letter to the Holy Fathers, are understood of Christ; or those things which regarded the Synagogue are referred to the Church. For all things happened to them in a figure, and are written for our instruction. (1 Cor. x. 11; Rom. xv. 20.) But

que exemplum in integra oratione. Id enim quod de manna scriptum est, secundum literalem sensum exponitur de cibo illo quem Deus pluit filiis Israel in deserto. Allegorice vero exponitur de superdignissimo corporis et sanguinis Christi sacramento: manna enim figura fuit Sacramenti altaris. Tropologice quoque exponitur de spirituali nutritione, qua Deus quotidie servos suos fideles in præsenti exilio interius alit, consolatur ac roborat, per charitatem et gratiam. Anagogice autem exponitur de felicissima illa refectione beatorum in patria ubi ipsa superessentialis divinitas est beatorum edulium per beatissimam fruitionem. Unde et scriptum est: Beatus qui manducabit panem in regno Dei. Et iterum, Inebriabuntur ab ubertate domus tuæ et torrente voluptatis tuæ potabis eos. Dion. Carthus. Procemium Psalmorum.

the Tropologic sense is when those things, which are written and recited of Christ, or of the Saints, are adapted to and expounded for our moral guidance. But the Anagogic sense is when some of those things which were done in time, are drawn out to the contemplation of eternal things; and those things which pertain to the Church Militant, are referred to the condition of the Church triumphant. But of these senses an example is ordinarily quoted in this word *Jerusalem;* but because this is common and known to almost all, I omit it; and will quote an example in an unattempted phrase.* For that which is written about Manna (Exod. xvi.), is expounded, in the literal sense, of that food which God rained upon the children of Israel in the desert. Allegorically, however, it is expounded of the most worthy Sacrament of the Body and Blood of Christ; for the manna was a figure of the Sacrament of the Altar. Tropologically also it is expounded of the Spiritual nutriment wherewith every day God inwardly feeds, consoles, and strengthens His faithful servants in their present

---

* This strikes me as the best of the renderings that offer themselves. This sense of *integer* occurs in classical Latin. For example, Juvat integros accedere fontes.—Lucret.

exile, by love and grace. But Anagogically it is expounded of that most joyous refreshment of the blessed in their home, where the super-essential Deity Itself is the food of the blessed, through their most blessed fruition. Whence also it is written, Blessed is he who shall eat bread in the kingdom of God. (S. Luke xiv. 15.) And again, They shall be satisfied with the plenteousness of Thy house; and Thou shalt give them drink of Thy pleasures, as out of the river." (Ps. xxxvi. 6.)

The example of *Jerusalem*, which Dionysius says he omits, is thus quoted by Dr. Neale from Durandus: "In like manner, Jerusalem is understood, historically, of that earthly city whither pilgrims journey; allegorically, of the Church Militant; tropologically, of every faithful soul; anagogically, of the celestial Jerusalem, which is our country." *Durandus. ap. Neale.*

Precisely the same classification is given by S. Thomas Aquinas, who, after explaining that the spiritual sense is based on the literal, shows how the several methods are connected together:— *Aquinas.*

This spiritual sense is divided into three parts. For, as the Apostle says in the seventh to the

Hebrews, The old law is a figure of the new law; and the new law itself, as Dionysius, in the "Ecclesiastical Hierarchy,"* says, is a figure of future glory. In the new law, also, those events which took place in the person of the Head, are signs of those things which we ought to do. In respect, then, of the fact that those things which belong to the old law signify the things of the new law, there is the Allegoric sense; but in respect of the fact that those things which were accomplished in Christ, or in what is significant of Christ, are signs of what we ought to do, there is the Moral sense; but in so far as they signify what belongs to eternal glory, there is the Anagogic sense."†

The same nomenclature may be observed amongst

* Dion. Areop. cap. v. Eccl. Hier. p. 1.

† Hic autem sensus spiritualis trifariam dividitur. Sicut enim dicit Apostolus ad Hebræos septimo, Lex vetus figura est novæ legis, et ipsa nova lex, ut dicit Dionysius in Ecclesi. Hierarch., est figura futuræ gloriæ. In nova etiam lege ea, quæ in Capite sunt gesta, sunt signa eorum, quæ nos agere debemus. Secundum ergo quod ea, quæ sunt veteris legis, significant ea, quæ sunt novæ legis, est sensus allegoricus: secundum vero quòd ea quæ in Christo sunt facta, vel in his, quæ Christum significant, sunt signa eorum, quæ nos agere debemus, est sensus moralis: prout vero significant ea, quæ sunt in æterna gloria, est sensus Anagogicus. S. Thom. Aq. Summa, Pars 1, Quæst. 1. Art. x.

the Greek writers in S. Chrysostom, whose adoption of the systematic spiritual interpretation gathers all the more significance from the fact that it is not uncommon for writers, who wish to depreciate it, to speak of him as the champion of the literal interpretation of the Scripture. Speaking of Psalm xlvii. (O clap your hands), he says : " It would be with propriety that any one should mount beyond the historic interpretation, and take the Psalm rather in the Anagogic sense. For though it derives both its beginning and its prooemium from the things of sense, yet it leads the hearer to things beyond sense."*

*S. Chrysostom.*

My object in this chapter is not so much to defend the plurality of senses in Holy Scripture—(for that has been amply done by able writers elsewhere)—my purpose, I say, is not so much to defend the plurality of meanings, as to draw together some facts upon it. Yet there is one feature enormously in its favour, which is observable in the original Hebrew of the Scriptures, but which I have never seen remarked

* Δικαίως δ' ἄν τις τὸν ψαλμὸν κατὰ ἀναγωγὴν μᾶλλον ἐκλάβοι, τῆς ἱστορίας ἀνώτερος γενόμενος. Εἰ γὰρ καὶ τὴν ἀρχὴν καὶ τὸ προοίμιον ἀπὸ τῶν αἰσθητῶν ἔχει, ἀλλ' ὅμως ἐπὶ τὰ νοητὰ χειραγωγεῖ τὸν ἀκροατήν. S. Joan. Chrys. in Ps. xlvi.

in any of the formal arguments upon either side of the question. It is this: there are certain phrases of the Hebrew which simply will not construe without it. From time to time the Hebrew reader encounters anomalies of grammar or of expression, which leave the mere literalist floundering in hopeless difficulties, but which acquire at once a sufficient explanation, if they are taken as the indications of some mysterious meaning hidden beneath the surface.

The first example I will take of this shall be from a Psalm—the clauses of the Compline Psalm, "For Thou, Lord, art my hope: Thou hast set Thine house of defence very high," or, as it stands in the Bible-version, "Because thou hast made the Lord, *which is* my refuge, *even* the most High, thy habitation."[*] The italics stand as I have put them, and the need of inserting such words suggests the difficulty surrounding these clauses. Who is the "thou?" The Lord? or the Psalmist? or some third person addressed in the previous verses? We should have expected something like this: "Because thou hast made the Lord thy refuge, the most High (thou hast made) thy habitation." The perplexity is admitted by most

[*] Ps. xci., 9.

## SYSTEMATIC INTERPRETATION IN THE CHURCH. 55

of the modern writers on the subject. Delitzsch gets over it by the dramatic artifice of making three different speakers in the Psalm. Justus Olshausen, who ignores everything but a primary or historic meaning in the Psalms, is driven conjecturally to reconstruct the clauses, and affirms that one would have expected for the first part of the verse, "For thou hast said, The Lord is my hope."*

All this will give some idea of the kind of difficulty that the Hebrew is supposed to present. But once grasp the fact that the phrases of the Psalm, whatever else they might mean, were so framed as to point to the mystery of the Christ, and the supposed difficulty immediately disappears. It is the Christ Who has been addressed in the former verses of the Psalm; and it is the Christ (as the Tempter saw upon the pinnacle of the Temple) Who is addressed afterwards; and it is equally the Christ Who is being addressed in these verses, but with a parenthetic glance at the Divine Nature in His Person. And now with this key in our hands we can construe the

* Der verschiedenartige Bau der beiden Parallelglieder hat Anstoss erregt, und allerdings würde man für das 1. Gl. eher eine Fassung erwartet haben, wie etwa diese, u. s. w. Die Psalmen. p. 374. Leipzig, 1853.

Hebrew, going plainly forward, without insertion and without change. "Thou"—the Christ—"Jehovah, art my trust: the most Highest"—so the Jews of the Septuagint took the word; sc. Jesus Christ—"Thou hast made Thy dwelling." What is this but a Hebrew anticipation of the doctrine which the Apostle, "an Hebrew of Hebrews," afterwards put into Greek—"In Him (sc. in the Person of Jesus Christ) dwelleth all the fulness of the Godhead bodily"?* But, as my desire is to show how even slender Hebrew learning may minister to the requirements of Christian theology, what I have to put into prominence is this—that it is, in fact, the mystery of the Christ, and nothing else, which enables you to construe the Hebrew of your Psalm without apology, without awkwardness, and without strain.

I shall now give an example of an anomaly in grammar in the Old Testament, which none of the ordinary expedients serves to explain, but which becomes, at least, intelligible, if it was purposely employed to suggest that there is something beyond the superficial meaning in the phrase where it occurs. If a writer has nothing to convey by his words

* Colos. ii. 9.

more than their ordinary, every-day meaning, then of course he adopts the ordinary, every-day usages of speech; but when he goes out of his way to do violence to the observed usages of his language—when, for instance, he uses a future tense in describing a past act—the question is, What are we to say then?

There is in Hebrew a particle which means "then;"* and which, of course, like its English counterpart, may be used with either past or future tense, and of either completed or uncompleted acts. But we meet with this anomaly in the use of it: it is used in some cases with the future tense—strictly, perhaps, the tense of incomplete action—when matters, apparently past, are to be described. The Gradual Psalms furnish an example of this:† "Then was our mouth filled with laughter, and our tongue with singing; then said they among the heathen, The Lord hath done great things for them." It is all plain enough in English as a description of the past restoration of the captives of Israel. "Then was our mouth filled;" "Then said they." But the verbs in Hebrew do not stand like this. There they are

\* אָז        † Ps. cxxvi. 2.

unmistakeably in the so-called future tense. "Then shall our mouth be filled." "Then shall they say."

So again in another famous passage:\* "Then sang Moses and the children of Israel this song unto the Lord." Very good; if the sacred writer meant only to describe the praises which in the past they offered for their deliverance from the bondage in Egypt. But the misfortune for such a limitation of the meaning is, that the Hébrew words do not say this. There it stands thus: "Then shall Moses sing."

The common way of resolving the difficulty is to say—as, for example, amongst the Hebrews, the grammatical commentator Aben Ezra says—that it is the usage of the holy tongue to put the future tense to designate the past with the particle in question. But I deny the fact. There are numerous passages where this particle occurs with the future tense, and where the meaning of the whole is unquestionably future too. "Then the eyes of the blind shall be opened, and the ears of the deaf shall be unstopped."† You could not possibly take these verbs as past

\* Exod. xv. 1.  † Isa. xxxv. 5.

in meaning, which this received explanation would require you to do.

An inspection of some of the other passages where the same juxtaposition of tense and particle occurs, would satisfy the reader that the facts of sacred phraseology do not bear out the alleged explanation of our difficulty. At the close of this chapter I have appended a list, drawn up for me by a friend, of passages where the same collocation of tense and particle occurs.

But to return to the facts under notice. We have before us two passages, which undeniably refer (whatever further scope they may have) to past actions—what had been done in the case of the rescued captives, and what had been sung by Moses. Yet each of these past actions is described by a tense which is vulgarly and roughly called future, but which even the most advanced modern philology agrees to call the tense of uncompleted action. The supposed explanation by the aid of the particle turns out to be a fiction, invented (it cannot be doubted) for these occasions. Where then are we to look for a solution of the anomaly? In the interpretation, I believe, of the words themselves. When the sacred writer thrusts in this amazing future tense with a fact that is obviously past, such a liberty with language seems to me intelligible on only one hypothesis. The language itself was designed to indicate that the transactions were not entirely past; that there was an element of future in them as well as an element of past. It was true of Israel's deliverance from captivity in the past that their "mouth was filled with laughter." But that deliverance itself was the foreshadowing of the rescue from a still sorer spiritual captivity which the Christ was to accomplish in the future. And if I may say that in this Psalm, apparently so Israelitish, so nicely squared with the ascertained facts of national history, so adequately explained in its every phrase and thought (a merely literary critic would admit) by the impression that would be made by these facts upon the nation's mind—if even in such a Psalm I may say that there was a kind of divine *double entendre;* that even in the most matter-of-fact narration of the past, God was hinting to the world about, and was educating the world for the future Christ; then I can understand that such a purpose should declare itself in a subtle turn of phrase as well as in a general

SYSTEMATIC INTERPRETATION IN THE CHURCH. 61

analogy of thought; then I can in a measure account for the intrusion of this future verb, which but for such a significance would have seemed irrelevant and out of place. With the Christian hypothesis, in fact, we can in a degree understand the grammar of the Hebrew Scriptures: without it we are hopelessly foiled. The interpreter can help us, where the grammarian, I believe, is powerless.

This key for reaching the solution of such difficulties in Scripture phraseology is, in reality, furnished us by the ancient traditional exposition of the Hebrew nation. The Gemoro part of the Talmud tells us why the Law says:* "Moses shall sing this song," and not "Moses sang this song." Hereby the Scripture was hinting at the future Resurrection. It was a song of Redemption—true of the Redemption in the past, but true also of the still greater Redemption in the future. In the Resurrection, the strange tense seems to say, when that Redemption shall have been consummated, Moses shall sing that song—every Moses, every one who participates in that final rescue effected by the Christ, shall sing

* Talm. Bab. Sanhedrin, fol. 91, 2, towards the foot of the page.

that song. A modern Jew would be astounded to learn how exactly such a piece of exposition, traditional in his nation from time out of all mind—how exactly it accords with the Christian doctrine of the New Testament, that the Saints in their triumph before the throne of God shall " sing the *Song of Moses*, the servant of God, and the Song of the Lamb." (Rev. xv. 3.)

Before leaving this part of the subject, I should like to call the attention of the English reader to the famous aphorism of the ancient Hebrew interpreters : " Scripture never evacuates its literal sense ;" that is to say, whatever may be the spiritual interpretations of which it is susceptible, it always has a primary, historic, literal, or (as the Hebrews call it) simple sense besides.

And finally, it will interest those who have followed me thus far to see the further elaboration of the subject in the table given by Waterland, which he has himself digested from the bulkier Latin treatise of Glassius, *Philologiæ Sacræ*. The table is appended to the General Preface to Waterland's work, *Scripture Vindicated*. It stands thus :—

## SYSTEMATIC INTERPRETATION IN THE CHURCH.

INTERPRETATION.
- Literal
  - Historical.
  - Doctrinal.
- Figurative.
  - Trope
    - Metaphor.
    - Metonymy.
    - Synechdoche.
    - Irony.
      - Catachresis.
      - Hyperbole.
      - Meiosis.
      - Allegory, *verbal*.
  - Scheme.
    - Proverb.
    - Riddle.
- Mystical.
  - Parabolical
    - Probable.
    - Improbable, Fable.
    - Impossible, Apologue.
  - Symbolical.
  - Typical.
    - Historical.
      - Rites, Ceremonies.
      - Actions.
        - Good.
        - Bad.
    - Prophetical.
  - Allegorical, *Real* Allegory.
    - Didactical, or Prophetic.
    - Tropological, or Moral.
    - Anagogical, or Sublime.

I here subjoin the list of passages for reference alluded to on page 59.

Gen. xxiv. 41.
Exod. xii. 44.
,, ,, 48.
Levit. xxvi. 34 (2).
,, ,, 41 (2).
Deut. xxix. 19, (20, A. V.)
Josh. i. 8 (bis).
,, xx. 6.
Judges v. 11.
1 Sam. xx. 12.
2 Sam. v. 24.
1 Chron. xxii. 13.
Job xi. 15.
,, xxxiii. 16.
Ps. li. (19 A. V.) (bis.)
,, lvi. 10 (9 A. V.).
,, xcvi. 12.
,, cxix. 6.
,, cxxvi. 2 (bis.)
Prov. ii. 5.
,, ,, 9.

Prov. xx. 14.
Isaiah xxxv. 5.
,, ,, 6.
,, xli. 1.
,, lviii. 8.
,, ,, 9.
,, ,, 14.
Jerem. xxii. 22.
,, xxxi. 18.
Ezek. xxxii. 14.
Micah iii. 4.
Zephan. iii. 9.
,, ,, 11.

From several of these passages it will be seen that when the future has to be translated as a past tense, some further reason must be given than the mere presence of the accompanying particle, or the colouring of the context, in which the solution has been sometimes imagined to lie.

## CHAPTER IV.

### ON HEBREW INTERPRETATION.

It would be a vast satisfaction to Christian readers if we could show, even with any degree of probability, that this fourfold method of interpretation demanded by the Scriptures is not the invention of Christian theologians—not a thing of comparatively recent growth, and traceable (it might be suspected) to the exigencies of Christian controversy; but rather that it is a thing which we have inherited along with the Scriptures themselves from the Hebrews who gave us them—a method which has been handed along from we know not when, as the traditional key for the devout understanding of the Scriptures, and which, so far as we can judge, those Scriptures have never been without.

By the nature of the case, it is not possible to give a mathematical proof of such a position; because the older Scriptures date from an age of which they are the sole surviving monuments. But in the earliest

Hebrew writings that we have, the method in question discovers itself, and the expositions so conveyed and ascribed to their national tradition\* are carried back to an antiquity of which no one knows the date. Many examples of such exposition will be found in the Targum and the Hebrew doctors quoted in the following commentary; examples which may make us feel that Christian exegesis is but a part of a chain very much longer than Christianity itself; and that when S. Jerome, one of the most systematic of the early writers on Scripture, was working at exposition with his Rabbi in Palestine, he was employing a method that was perfectly familiar to the Rabbi.

Indeed, it would not be too much to say that the multiplication of the senses of Scripture has been carried to a much greater extent in Hebrew exegesis than it has ever reached among ourselves. The Law has seventy faces, says the great grammatical commentator, Aben Ezra, at the close of his rhythmical Preface to the Pentateuch. And the methods by

\* Maimonides actually puts down, name by name, the literary descent of pupil from teacher, beginning with Rabbi Judah, the compiler of the Talmud, back to Ezra, and thence to Jeremiah. Maim. in Seder Zeraim Præfat.

which the scope of Scripture has been developed are very much more formal and more systematic than any which (so far as I know) Christian writers have ever tabulated. As to the exact number of these methods, there is no uniformity of opinion amongst the ancient authorities of Hebrew interpretation. Hillel, for example, who was President of the Sanhedrim at the time of our Lord's Nativity, expounded seven modes of handling the phrases of Scripture.*
Another authority laid down thirteen modes, which some have thought should be extended to sixteen; while, finally, we have no less than thirty-two modes recognised by some writers.

These, however, are rather rules for arriving at the senses of Scripture than senses themselves. They may be seen discussed at length in the Rabbinic treatise quoted above; but inasmuch as they have never, to my knowledge, been submitted to English readers before, it will be worth while to give some idea of them here. It is often very hard to understand them; but I have done my best to put them into intelligible English, and to exemplify them.

The first rule is the argument from the greater to

* See the Rabbinic treatise הליכות עולם Gate 4, Section 1.

the less (à *fortiori*). Thus, about Miriam, when she was leprous (Numb. xii. 14), "The Lord said unto Moses, If her father had but spit in her face, should she not be ashamed seven days? Let her be shut out from the camp seven days, and after that let her be received in again." By this argument, if she was to be shut out from the camp, all the more was she to be shut out from the Lord.

The second rule is the argument from parity of reasoning. By this rule, Samuel is proved to have been a Nazarite, though it is not explicitly stated that he was so. The vow of his mother was that "no razor should come upon his head." (1 Sam. i. 11). The same phrase is used of Samson, with the addition (Judges xvi. 17), that he was a Nazarite. By this rule, then, Samuel was a Nazarite too.

The third rule is the development of a principle;* as when Scripture unfolds and explains a thing in one passage, and from it a similar teaching is understood to belong to other similar passages. Thus, with respect to the feast of unleavened bread, it is laid down, "that which every man must eat, that only may be done of you."† Under this rule,

\* בנין אב   † Exod. xii. 16.

the same restriction is understood to the other feasts, even though about them the Scripture does not give the same detailed directions.

The fourth rule is called "the general followed by the particular." Thus, for burnt offerings the regulation is, "Ye shall bring your offering of the cattle, of the herd, and of the flock."* Here the general term "cattle," would include (say the Hebrew doctors) every kind of beast; but because it is followed by the particular "herd and flock," therefore it is restricted and interpreted by them. So, I may observe, the English translators show that they understood it, on the authority of this Hebrew principle, by inserting in italics the word *even*, which is not there in the original Hebrew.

The fifth rule is called "the particular followed by the general." Then every particular is understood to be intended. It may be said, perhaps, that this would have been attained by the mention of the general, without the notice of any particular. The formula in question, however, has its use in preventing the chance of some particular being excluded under some one of the other modes of Scriptural

* Lev. i. 2.

expression. This rule applies to the case of lost things; in which, first, particulars are specified: ox, ass, sheep, raiment; and then the general follows, "Any manner of lost thing."

The sixth rule is when a particular comes between two generals. Then the expression includes everything like the special, and excludes everything unlike. Thus, "Thou shalt bestow that money for whatsoever thy soul lusteth after, for oxen, or for sheep, or for wine, or for strong drink, or for whatsoever thy soul lusteth after."* Here the particulars, oxen, sheep, wine, include only moveables; by this rule, therefore, the general "whatsoever," does not reach to things immoveable.

The seventh rule is when a general requires a particular, or *vice versâ*. Thus "Number all the first-born of the males."† First-born would include females, who are therefore excluded by the subsequent particular.

The eighth rule is that when a particular is contained in a general, but yet has special regulations applied to it, those regulations apply not only to the particular, but to the general also. Thus, the wor-

\* Deut. xiv. 26. † Numb. iii. 40.

ship of Moloch was but one of many forms of idolatry. The man who gave his seed to Moloch was to be stoned to death.* And under this principle, the penalty was not meant to be greater in the case of Moloch than in any other of those abominations, but was meant to extend to them also.

The ninth, tenth, and eleventh rules deal with other relations between the general and the particular.

The twelfth rule determines the interpretation of what is unexplained by what is explained next after it.

The thirteenth rule is, when two passages of Scripture seem to contradict each other, they may be reconciled by a third. For example, it is said (Exod. xix. 20), "The Lord came down upon Mount Sinai on the top of the mount;" while in the following chapter Moses was to appeal to the people (Exod. xx. 22); "Ye have seen that I have talked with you from heaven." By *heaven* is to be understood the supernatural fire, as appears from a subsequent passage (Deut. iv. 36); "Out of heaven He made thee to hear His voice, that He might instruct thee; and upon earth He showed thee His great fire; and

* Lev. xx. 2.

thou heardest His words out of the midst of the fire."

Leaving now the rules and methods by which the senses of Scripture have been reached, we turn to those senses themselves.

The systematic exposition of Scripture ranges itself amongst the Hebrews under four heads. It will therefore be observed that they have the same number of heads of interpretation as is adopted by many of the Christian expositors. Yet the Christian division hardly corresponds, head for head, with that of the Hebrew. These heads are called: 1. *Peshet*,* The simple (rendering of words). 2. *Remez*,† Indication (of meaning). 3. *Derush*,‡ Illustrative exposition by way of allegory, etc. And 4. *Sod*,§ The mystical esoteric signification. With the initials of these four words they make one of those acrostics that are so common in Hebrew literature. The letters are the consonants—and a Hebrew word has no vowels —of the Hebrew word for Pa Ra Di Se, a term which aptly describes the Divine Word when understood in all the completeness of its several meanings.

One caution is necessary in this part of the sub-

\* פשט.     † רמז.     ‡ דרוש.     § סוד.

ject. It must be admitted that most of the books (I do not undertake to say all of them) of the Hebrew doctors are posterior in date to some of the books of Christian interpreters. Even the Talmud itself—Maimonides says* the Jerusalem Talmud was compiled about three hundred years after the destruction of the Temple, and the Babylonian Talmud about a hundred years later than that. At the date of the former, therefore, S. Ambrose was probably writing, while S. Jerome and S. Augustine had hardly begun; at the date of the latter the last of the "four doctors" in the West, S. Gregory the Great, had not yet appeared upon the scene.

Christian interpretation, then, it might be admitted, had at least opened its mouth, though it certainly had not said much before the compilation of most of the accepted works in Hebrew interpretation. The surmise, then, may possibly arise that the Christian method of looking beyond the letter of Scripture was, after all, a novel method—the invention of Christianity; and that if we find any points of similarity between the old method of the Hebrews and the new method of the Christian doctors, it is

* Rambam. יד החזקה Preface.

because the old method has, so far, been influenced, instructed, extended, and developed by the happy versatility of the new.

There is just one consideration which negatives such a surmise as that. The Hebrew books are, so to speak, very much older than themselves. Whatever may be the date of the actual compilation of the Talmud and the Midrash, there is no reasonable doubt that the bulk of their contents is very much older. Such works were but the formal collection into a book of material that had long been in circulation amongst the learned. And so amongst the later Hebrews whose works I have employed in this book—their chief value lies not in any exceptional ingenuity or insight of their own (though these, of course, are considerable); but it lies in the fact that their works are the repositories of expositions so long anterior to themselves—in the fact that they are so often able to introduce what they have to say with the formula incessantly recurring in Hebrew exegesis: "Our Doctors said."* Individual interpre-

* So frequent is the phrase that it is never written in full, but is indicated by the initials of the two Hebrew words which express it, thus:—א״ר

tations* in any one of these books may, of course, belong to the date of the book itself—may be due to the happy thought of this doctor or that, whether in ancient or more recent times; so all that it concerns me to contend for is that the expositions which I allege as forecasting, as generating, as in a sense warranting the Christian method—that these are of a *kind* whose beginning we cannot date, and which therefore, so far as we know, the Scripture has never been without.

There is, indeed, one term—Aggadah—in common use amongst Hebrew expositors which is roughly rendered into English "mystic exposition," and which might at first glance be thought to at once attest a branch of Hebrew interpretation analogous to the spiritual interpretation as received amongst Christian Divines. This ready analogy, however, exists only in name and in appearance. True; the word is explained by Buxtorf as, "Mystic nar-

---

* Though a certain restraint is apparent against license, even in this direction. Maimonides says that whosoever put forth, or enforced an interpretation bearing upon conduct (הלכה) without the authority of the Consistory, or the High Priest—he was reckoned amongst presumptuous sinners, and not amongst those who sinned in error. Rambam. מורה נבוכים 3, 41.

ration, allegorical exposition, historic illustration (discursus.)" Yet there is much in Hebrew Aggadah which has no counterpart among ourselves. I give one example of it out of a few taken at random from the pages of Rashi. When Jacob was going with his family into Egypt, it is said, "And he sent Judah before him unto Joseph, to direct his face unto Goshen."* Now the Aggadah adds a particular as to the purpose of this act. Jacob sent his son before him to prepare him a house of instruction (as the Hebrew literally has it), a theological school, from which sacred knowledge of the Law might issue. It would be easy to give a multitude of examples of this method; but I dare not burden my pages. This one example will be enough to suggest that there is here a something in spirit and in principle not altogether unlike methods familiar to ourselves, though in detail the Hebrew method often moves off in directions quite foreign to the lines of Christian thought.

It should be observed that the Hebrew theologian is quite as Messianic in his exposition of Scripture as ever the Christian can be. *Messianic interpretation.* From one end to the other of the Old Testament,

* Gen. xlvi. 28.

in the most unexpected places, in the most casual phrases, he sees the Messiah incessantly. The controversy, in truth, betwixt ourselves and him is not generally whether this passage or that refers to the Christ, but whether it refers to Jesus of Nazareth. Indeed, it would be quite safe to say that the Hebrew expositor often sees the Christ where the Christian has never thought of looking for Him; often in some analogy of a Hebrew word, which a translation, whether in Greek or Latin or English, almost necessarily loses; often in some piece of jugglery with a Hebrew word, of which its equivalent in any translation would, of course, not be susceptible; often in the particular phrase of the most casual, the most unavoidable kind, chosen to express a fact in question.

I take an example in the latter department from the Pentateuch. There are hundreds of them. Moses has to remind the people of Israel that in their passage to the promised land the command of the Lord was that they should not meddle with the Edomites, and he rehearses the command thus :*
"Meddle not with them : for I will not give you a foot of their land; no, not so much as a foot breadth;"

* Deut. ii. 5.

or, more literally, according to the Hebrew as the margin gives it, *even to the treading of the sole of the foot*. The literal meaning is plain. But this is not all. The word for *even to* is used quite as often for a certain limit of time as it is for a certain limit of space. Apply it so here. "I will not give you a foot of their land up to (*i. e.* before) the treading of the sole of the foot." Whose treading, then? Whose sole? Whose, but the Christ's? According to the prophecy of Zechariah, "His feet shall stand that day upon the Mount of Olives.* Not until the treading of the foot of the Christ should the people of God really take possession of those that knew not God. This is, in fact, the upshot of the little phrase, when Rashi points the way to the mystic interpretation of it—an interpretation, I may add, which, whether we take it of the Ascension from Olivet, or of the Second Advent, contains a truth quite as dear to the Christian as ever it could have been to the Hebrew.

Another good illustration for my purpose of exhibiting whatever affinity there is between the Hebrew mystic interpretation and the Christian, is

* Zech. xiv. 4.

furnished by the Hebrew exposition of the present made by Boaz to Ruth. The verse runs thus :—

"Also he (Boaz) said, Bring the vail that thou hast upon thee and hold it. And when she (Ruth) held it, he measured six measures of barley and laid it on her. And she went into the city." (Ruth iii. 15.)

But why "six" measures of barley? The present was a weighty one. Amongst the Hebrew writers, the difficulty has always been felt that women were not in the habit of carrying so large a burden. Some of them accordingly have disposed of it by the hypothesis that Ruth was divinely and supernaturally endowed with an exceptional strength to enable her to carry it. Let that be as it may, the particular number *six* that Boaz chose has a special propriety in the analogy of Holy Scripture. Rashi reminds us that from Ruth there was to spring that Son upon Whom were to rest those *six* famous gifts,—the spirit of wisdom and understanding, the spirit of counsel and might, the spirit of knowledge and of the fear of the Lord—that Son whom Rashi himself explains to be the Messiah. We thank him for the key to the "six measures of barley;" and we can even enlarge the parable. We remember how the Christ not only had a fulness of this Spirit Himself,* but how He has also shed forth this same gift upon His Church; and then calling to mind the teaching of S. Ambrose† that in the sacred idyll, Boaz—the "redeemer,"‡ the one who did what the kinsman failed to do—is the figure of the Christ, and Ruth, his bride, the stranger, the non-Israelite, is the figure of the Church—gathering all this together we see in the six measures that Boaz presented to Ruth a foreshadowment of that gift of the Spirit wherewith Christ has endowed His Church.

Again. It is the habit of Christian expositors to seek for a significance in (what in any other book would be called) the accidents of expression that present themselves in Scripture. If a phrase is any way strangely presented, then what is the import of such presentation? That is the question which Christian interpreters have, in most cases, made some attempt to answer. But the habit of doing so is one which they probably learned from

<small>Peculiarities of phrase.</small>

* S. John i. 16.
† S. Ambrose in Evang. Luc. cap. iii. p. 61. Tom. 3. Ed. 1586. Paris.
‡ Ruth iv. 14.

the received methods amongst the Hebrews. Thus, for example, in the Psalm (Ps. xiii.) *How long wilt Thou forget me, O Lord?* it may be remarked, that the question "How long?" is four times repeated. There have been "holy men," says the learned Dr. Neale, who have seen in that fourfold question an indication of the four tyrannising monarchies who oppressed the Hebrew nation—the Assyrian, the Babylonian, the Syrian, and the Roman. It is true that Christian writers, agreeably to their usual method, have given the interpretation; but (what is to my purpose to remark) it was given in the Hebrew Midrash before them.

In the department, too, of what is called the moral interpretation or *Tropologia*, as it is technically termed, the way has been pointed out by the ancient Hebrew expositors; though I doubt whether this branch of interpretation was ever so fully matured amongst them as it has been amongst Christian writers. When, for instance, Rashi comments on the verse in Genesis,[*] "And Joseph knew his brethren, but they knew not him," he quotes an interpretation older than himself. Joseph, it says, knew his

[*] Gen. xlii. 8.

brethren, in that he recognised the fact that they were his brethren, and took pity on them; while they knew him not, in that they did not act towards him in a brotherly way when he fell into their hands. Any one, who is at all acquainted with the method in which principles of moral action are drawn from the Scripture by the expositors of the Christian Church, will have no difficulty in recognising at least the same spirit here.

One of the most characteristic habits of the spiritual interpretation, as it exists amongst Christian theologians, is the practice of seeing a significance in the numbers that are mentioned in Holy Scripture. The most cursory reader has some inkling of this branch of the subject when he remarks the frequent recurrence, in leading situations, of the number seven. The principle, I would observe, seems to be a necessary corollary to a belief in the divine origin of the Scripture; and stated in its fullest development stands thus in the phrase of Origen, Nothing in the Scripture without its purpose —Nihil in Sanctâ Scripturâ otiosum. This habit, then, of seeing a significance, a design in numbers apparently the most random and undesigned, is by no

*Numerals.*

means the invention or speciality of Christian interpretation. It is a method which was always applied to the Scriptures, even as far as we know in the oldest Hebrew times. It is one which we have inherited from the Hebrews. It is one which they in fact have brought to a far greater development than ever it has attained amongst ourselves. You have been sometimes astonished at the minuteness with which Hermas, or S. Augustine, or S. Jerome, or S. Ambrose tracks one of the numerical statements of the Scripture to its possible source and significance; but their method, after all, is little more than a shadow of the same thing as it exists in the traditional Hebrew interpretation of the Scriptures. With the Hebrews, in their efforts to penetrate that which is veiled beneath the letter, the Scriptures have been literally examined with a microscope. Not the most abstruse coincidence, not the most casual enumeration, not the most ordinary detail seems to have escaped their notice. Sometimes, it must be admitted, the combinations which they succeed in making with the numbers of Scripture are such as to leave upon the English mind the impression that they are too ingenious to be intentional, and in place of conducing to any genuine edification seem to invite rather the kind of admiration that we might feel at the feats of a professor of legerdemain. But when every allowance has been made that could reasonably be claimed, there still remains a vast harvest of numerical coincidences that have been traditionally noticed in Hebrew exposition, and that have bequeathed at least their spirit to Christian exegesis — coincidences, of which we might not pretend to have discovered the precise import, but at whose existence we cannot fail to be amazed. It is at least a strange thing that the words and facts of the Holy Word should be *capable* of developing some hidden meaning: and if any one would feel the force of this, let him ask himself whether the last month's articles in the *Times* newspaper would, under any amount of ingenuity, be capable of doing the same.

To take an early example of this in the Book of Genesis. Every Christian theologian is familiar with the method in which the earliest Greek writers under Christianity dealt with the number assigned to Abraham's servants—three hundred and eighteen.*

* Gen. xiv. 14.

In the three Greek letters, with which that number is written, they saw the form of the Cross and the first two letters of the Sacred Name of Jesus. Whether the fact be accepted as significant or no, there can be no denying that the fact is as they represented. But the Hebrew interpreters have handed down another phænomenon, not less remarkable but not so generally noticed in connection with this part of the narrative. The name of Abraham's steward—the representative, as it were, of the band of servants—was, it will be remembered, Eliezer. "And Abram said, Lord God, what wilt Thou give me, seeing I go childless, and the steward of my house is this Eliezer of Damascus."* The name of the steward, it should be observed, seems to be thrust in here in a portion of the story where it would seem almost irrelevant, if there were not some under current of meaning in the mention of it. Now it must be borne in mind that in the Holy Tongue the only way of expressing numerals is by the letters of the alphabet, each of which has a numerical as well as a phonetic significance. And the ancient Hebrew expositors† have not suffered the remarkable

* Gen. xv. 2. † בראשית רבה

fact to escape them, that the letters of the word Eliezer in their language exactly make up the number three hundred and eighteen—the muster of which Eliezer was the representative and head.

Once again. The same precise regard to numbers is seen in the traditional exposition of the *two* " good kids of the goats," that Rebekah directed Jacob to fetch for his dying father.* Why *two?* says the expositor. Two were not necessary as food for the aged Isaac. No; but it was Passover time, says the ancient tradition of the Hebrew nation, and one of the two kids was for his Paschal Offering, the other for his "savoury meat." A Christian (I cannot help remarking) may well cling tenderly to this ancient belief that it was Passover when Isaac sent his son for "savoury meat;" for it makes Isaac, " with desire desiring to eat this Passover,"† before his death, and "sending" to have it prepared—it makes the story of Isaac quite a rehearsal of what was afterwards done by our Lord Jesus Christ immediately before *His* death. The Hebrew theologian, when he thus associated Passover with the "Last Supper" of Isaac, probably did not observe how un-

* Gen. xxvii. 9. † S. Luke xxii. 15.

mistakeably he was making the whole narrative point to Jesus of Nazareth.

It would be possible to carry this branch of the subject on to considerable length by exhibiting coincidences that ancient Hebrew expositors have remarked in the numerical equivalents of words in the Scripture; till the reader, who began by thinking the subject fanciful, would find himself yielding under the sheer force of the accumulation of instances. The Law of Moses, for example, is observed to contain a certain number of affirmative precepts and a certain number of prohibitive or negative precepts. All these may be said to be contained *implicitly* in the Covenant of Circumcision, which God gave to Abraham. "Be thou perfect,"* perfect in the keeping of this Covenant, said God to him at that moment. But at that moment also God changed his name from *Abram* to *Abraham*; that is to say, in the Hebrew name God inserted one letter, H. What is the meaning of this mysterious H? It is at least remarkable that the letters of this elongated name exactly make up the number of the affirmative precepts implicitly contained in the one precept "Ye shall circumcise."

* Gen. xvii. 1 *seq.*

I will not multiply examples; but Christians, as it seems to me, are not without an interest in a system which teaches us that *Amen*, the name of our Blessed Lord, is the equivalent of the words *Lord Jehovah* in the Holy Tongue; and which seems, moreover, to have the stamp of a divine sanction when in the Revelation a number is given as the equivalent of a name: "Here is wisdom. Let him that hath understanding count the number of the beast; for it is the number of a man; and his number is six hundred threescore and six."*

It only remains for me to invite the attention of the reader to the analogy that is observable between this system of the Hebrews and the kind of treatment that has been applied by Christian writers to the numerical phenomena of the Scriptures in general, and specifically to the number associated with the Gradual Psalms. They are fifteen in number, Christian expositors have been careful to remark; exactly one-tenth of the entire contents of the Psalter. Now the number fifteen is made up of eight and seven, which symbolize respectively the New and Old Covenants. Seven is the index of the Old Testament, on account of the pro-

* Rev. xiii. 18.

minence which is given therein to the observance of the Sabbath—an institution which in all its forms was associated with the number seven. The New Testament, on the other hand, has eight for its index, owing to the resurrection of the Lord upon the first, that is the eighth, day of the week. In this alliance of the two numbers some have found an interpretation of Solomon's text (Eccles. xi. 2.), "Give a portion to seven, and also to eight." But the combination of them gives us fifteen—the number of the Gradual Psalms, which have thus been said to contain in their grades, degrees, or steps, all the doctrine of both Old and New Testaments.

## CHAPTER V.

### THE USE OF THE GRADUAL PSALMS.

IT might not be incorrect to say that the Gradual Psalms have penetrated the devotions of the Christian Church to an extent which no other portion of the Psalter can rival. True, at first glance, Psalm cxix. might seem to have the best claim to this distinction, from its having been said through every day from beginning to end in the Offices of the West.[*] Or

---

[*] In the East it appears to have been appointed for recitation, not every day, but every Lord's Day. See the homily upon Psalm cxxi. appended in some editions to the works of S. Chrysostom. The author begins his homily thus: "As a great treasure, and spiritual wealth and most delightsome benefit of souls, and for the praise and glory of God, and for the security of our life and a pattern of good works, the noble chiefs and teachers, our Holy Fathers, have directed us to sing and play Psalm cxviii. (A. V. cxix.) upon the first day in the revolution of the week, which day is with us also called the Lord's Day, because of the Lord's resurrection upon that day." (S. Chrysost. Opp. vol. 5, p. 675, Migne). In the Sarum Portfory and in the Roman Breviary it is said daily at the lesser Offices:—At Prime, verses 1-32; at Terce, verses 33-80; at Sext, verses 81-128; at None,

again, the group of Penitential Psalms might set up a counter claim from their adaptation to so many circumstances of the Christian life. But when all such claims have been fairly heard, the Book of Gradual Psalms, in fragments or in its entirety, has entered into so many Offices of the Church, and has developed such an elasticity in adjusting itself to almost all possible shades of Christian feeling, that after all it might be doubted whether as a devotional instrument it had not fairly the right to the post of honour in the Psalter.

<small>Introductory Versicles.</small> I begin with facts which lie nearest home. The Gradual Psalms have fur-

verses 129-176. In every case the *Gloria Patri* is said at the end of every sixteen verses (and not at the end of every eight, as the Book of Common Prayer directs), presumably in order to preserve the ancient usage of making the number of Psalms odd. I specially note this, because there are modern books in circulation which appear to have lost sight of this ancient Catholic principle. It might with advantage be carried in mind by those who have the selecting of Psalms for Harvest Festivals and other exceptional occasions. So careful was the ancient English Church of this principle of the odd numbers, that she never allowed the number of Collects to be even, except during the octave of Christmas. Compare the words, "As often as occasion shall serve," in the Rubric to the occasional Collects at the end of our own Communion Service.

nished the Versicle and Response with which nearly every Office in ancient times commenced.\*

℣. Our help standeth in the Name of the Lord.

℞. Who hath made Heaven and earth.

This couplet is nothing but the last verse of Psalm cxxiv., and with this the ancient English Rite directs that all Benedictions of things and persons should begin. With this also began the ancient Sarum Office for Confirmation; it has sur-

---

\* To convey some idea of the frequency of this use I have compiled the following list from a Pontifical in Sarum Cathedral Library. The couplet occurs at the beginning of these Offices:

De Chrismandis in fronte.
De clerico faciendo.
De monacho faciendo ex electo seculari.
De patenæ et calicis consecratione.
De benedictione sacerdotalium indumentorum.
De benedictione mapparum seu linteaminum sacri altaris.
De benedictione corporalium.
De benedictione novæ crucis.
De benedictione sacrorum vasorum et aliorum ornamentorum.
De benedictione capsarum pro reliquiis et aliis sanctuariis includendis.
De benedictione et impositione crucis proficiscentibus in subsidium et defensionem fidei Christianæ seu recuperationem terræ sanctæ.
De benedictione armorum.
De benedictione ensis.
De benedictione et traditione vexilli bellici.

vived also in the Confirmation Office of our own Prayer-Book.

There are some facts which seem specially to connect the Gradual Psalms with the close of the day. The last of them, for instance, both in the ancient English Book and in the Roman Breviary, forms the last Psalm of the Compline Office, and thus has the honour of furnishing day by day the invariable cadence of that long sequence of Psalm and Canticle which formed the thread of every day's devotions in the ancient Church.

<small>Compline Office.</small>

Further than this, the other fourteen Gradual Psalms, though not distinguished by an invariable place in the last Service of the day, yet had among Psalms a prerogative not far removed from that. In both the English and the Roman Rite provision was made for the recitation of them at Vespers on four successive days of the week. At Monday's Vespers, together with three other Psalms (to make the odd number) Psalms cxx. and cxxi. were said. On Tuesday's Vespers Psalm cxxii., cxxiii., cxxiv., cxxv., and cxxvi. were the only Psalms. At Wednesday's Vespers Psalms cxxvii., cxxviii.,

<small>Gradual Psalms at Vespers.</small>

THE USE OF THE GRADUAL PSALMS. 95

cxxix., cxxx., and cxxxi. were said without addition; and at Thursday's Vespers the two remaining ones of the series, Psalms cxxxii. and cxxxiii. were said with three others; the last of the Gradual Psalms being never said at Vespers, for the obvious reason that it was said every day at Compline. Thus did the Church of the West never let a week go round without the recitation of the entire group of Gradual Psalms towards the close of the several days. With this feeling on the part of the Christian Church might be compared the use (noticed elsewhere) which still survives in the Hebrew nation, of reciting the Gradual Psalms in the afternoons of the winter months.

One of the most striking uses of the Gradual Psalms as a whole, consists in the beautifully constructed office of the Gradual Psalms, which is contained in the Roman Breviary. Whether the English Rite had any similar office I have not been able as yet to ascertain. This Office is said on all the Wednesdays in Lent (the Penitential Psalms being said on the Fridays), unless one of the greater Feasts happens to fall then. Bona, though he omits to notice this last exception, both mentions the usage and gives the reason for

*Office of the Gradual Psalms.*

it. "Inasmuch as," he says, "it is proper that we be holier than usual on those days, we add these (Gradual) Psalms to the task of our wonted Service, that by them we may be admonished that an ascent, as it were by steps (graduum), to perfection in spiritual life is prepared for us."* The Office consists of the fifteen Gradual Psalms, said in three groups of five each, the first group being said without any Gloria Patri, and without Antiphon, but with a Versicle Memorial of the departed at its close. Each group is followed by the Lord's Prayer, some Versicles, and a Collect. The first section seems specially to refer to the literally dead; the second to the spiritually dead; and the third to those who are dead to the world in the religious life. The whole forms one of the most beautiful of the Offices; and it would be a great gain if something of the kind could be adopted amongst ourselves as an acquisition to our devotional exercises for Lent. With a view of furthering this object I have trans-

* Quia enim hisce diebus decet nos solito sanctiores esse, Psalmos istos ad consuetæ servitutis pensum adjungimus, quibus etiam moneremur ad vitæ spiritualis perfectionem quibusdam velut gradibus ascensum parari. Bona. De Divinâ Psalmodiâ. cap. 15, sec, 1., p. 487, Ed. 1723. Antwerp.

lated the office entire, and placed it at the end of this chapter.

The question, of course, arises whether the Ancient Use of the English Church employed the Gradual Psalms in any similar way. I have looked through the "Pars Hiemalis," of the Sarum Portfory, printed by Henry Kyngston and Henry Sutton, in 1556, to see if in the Use of Sarum they had an Office of the Gradual Psalms or anything analogous to that Office in the Roman Breviary. I have not been able to find the Office entire; though a reminiscence of it with one Gradual Psalm (cxxx.) and the same Collect occurs before the second Vespers of the First Sunday in Advent. I have translated the office on a subsequent page* of this work.

A similar feeling too hangs about the rite of Sarum in its placing three Gradual Psalms (cxx., cxxi. and cxxx.) at the head of the first Office (Vespers) *In Vigiliis Mortuorum.*

Amongst all the uses of individual Gradual Psalms one of the most beautiful examples is the employment of Psalm cxxxii. as one of the Psalms in the Ancient English Office for the Burial of

<small>Burial of the Dead.</small>

* See page 114.

the Dead. Nothing could surpass the exquisite turn of meaning given to the Psalm by the Antiphon under which it was said:—

"This shall be my rest for ever: here will I dwell, for I have a delight therein."

Said, as the Psalm was, just when the sepulchre was closed upon its new tenant, this adaptation of its meaning forms one of the most touching examples of the marvellous flexibility of the Psalter that it would be possible to find.

An excellent meaning was given by the old English Use to Ps. cxxiii., *Unto Thee lift I up mine eyes*, by its being appointed to be said after Compline and after Matins—mark the clinging of the Gradual Psalm to the extremes of the day—almost every day in the year, as part of a little intercessory office for the peace of the Church. The Office in its original form is not accessible to everybody, so I have transcribed it from the Sarum Portfory for those who may care to see it.*

<small>Psalm cxxiii.</small>

Closely connected with this is the employment in the Sarum Rite of Ps. cxxi., *I will lift up mine eyes*, in a little Office for the recovery

<small>Psalm cxxi.</small>

* See page 116.

of the sick. The Office is directed to be said at Prime on all those days when the office for the peace of the Church is said after Matins. After some versicles which follow the Psalm, it contains the Collect at the end of our Modern Communion Office: *Assist us mercifully, O Lord.* And it concludes with this beautiful Collect :—

Almighty and everlasting God, the eternal health of them that believe, hear us in behalf of Thy servants, for whom we implore the help of Thy pity; that health being restored to them, they may render Thee thanks in Thy Church. Through Christ. Amen.

I have given this admirable Office entire on a subsequent page.*

In the devotions of the Roman Church, all the Gradual Psalms are interwoven in the Office of the Blessed Virgin, being mostly said under Antiphons, which give a new turn of meaning to the several Psalms. In this connection they occur as follows :—

At Vespers (out of Advent) Ps. cxxii., I was glad when they said unto me.

Antiphon. I am black but comely, O ye daughters

* See page 118.

of Jerusalem. Therefore hath the King loved me and brought me into his chamber.

Ps. cxxvii. Except the Lord build the house.

Antiphon. Lo, the winter is past, the rain is over and gone: rise up, my love, and come away.

At Compline. Ps. cxxix. Many a time have they fought against me.

Ps. cxxx. Out of the deep.

Ps. cxxxi. Lord, I am not high minded.

At Terce. Ps. cxx. When I was in trouble.

Ps. cxxi. I will lift up mine eyes.

Ps. cxxii. I was glad when they said unto me.

All under the Antiphon, Maria Virgo assumpta est ad æthereum thalamum in quo Rex regum stellato sedet solio.

At Sext. Ps. cxxiii. Unto Thee lift I up mine eyes.

Ps. cxxiv. If the Lord Himself.

Ps. cxxv. They that put their trust.

All under a common Antiphon, To the odour of Thy ointment do we run. The damsels loved Thee too much.

At None. Ps. cxxvi. When the Lord turned again the captivity of Sion.

Ps. cxxvii. Except the Lord build the house.

Ps. cxxviii. Blessed are all they that fear the Lord.

All under the Antiphon, Thou art beautiful and comely, O daughter of Jerusalem; terrible as an army with banners.

A similar Use is found in the famous arrangement of the Psalter by S. Benedict for his rule. Here also Psalms cxx.—cxxix. are said in groups of three at Terce, Sext, and None, on Tuesday and all succeeding days of the week, the rest of the Gradual Psalms occurring at Vespers or Compline.*

<small>Benedictine Psalter.</small>

The reader will not fail to notice in these Antiphons the fondness of the Ancient Church for that book which in modern times has been so much neglected among ourselves—the Song of Songs. It might almost be said that there is no book of Scripture which the early writers quoted with so much frequency and delight.

The same Psalms are some of them used in the Office of the Blessed Virgin, with different Antiphons at other periods of the year. But the examples I have given above are sufficient as specimens of the

* Bona. De Var. Rit. Div. Psalm. cap. iii. s. 2, p. 546. Antwerp: 1723.

use of the Gradual Psalms in this department of Christian devotion.

Another characteristic use—for I cannot pretend to notice every single individual use—of a Gradual Psalm lies in the employment of one of them (Ps. cxxviii., Blessed are all they) in the Weekly Office—said on most Thursdays of the year—of the venerable Sacrament of the Eucharist. It occurs likewise in a sacramental aspect at Vespers on the feast of Corpus Christi, with a paraphrase of one of its own verses as Antiphon :

As the olive branches may the Sons of the Church be round about the Table of the Lord.

A further employment of Ps. cxxviii. (Blessed are all they that fear the Lord), which has survived in our own Marriage Service in the Book of Common Prayer, is found in its presence in the Ancient Service for Holy Matrimony, where it was said without Antiphon and without musical accompaniment (*sine nota*). This employment of the Psalm does not seem to have had any precedent in the Hebrew Office for the same purpose.

<small>Marriage.</small>

Closely connected, too, with the same idea is the ancient use of the same Psalm in the Office for the Purification of Women after Childbirth. At the door of the Church, the rubric ran, "Let the Priest and his Minister say the following Psalms:" the Psalms in question being Ps. cxxi. (I will lift up mine eyes), and Ps. cxxviii. (Blessed are all they). They were said, I specially remark, under one *Gloria Patri*, as it seems, said at the end of the second of them only; with the view, presumably, of welding the two as it were into one, and so preserving the ancient practice of keeping the number of Psalms odd.

Churching of Women.

In our modern English Office upon a similar occasion these two Gradual Psalms have disappeared. Yet one of the alternating Psalms provided for the Office is still taken from the group of Gradual Psalms. As is well remarked by Mr. Blunt,* where the sorrows of the mother "have been added to by the death of her infant," the use of Ps. cxxvii. (Except the Lord build the house) "is very inopportune."

In the Sarum Office for the Confirmation of Children, the fifth and sixth verses of Ps. cxxviii. were used at the close of the Office with an obvious appropriateness to the occasion:—

Confirmation.

* Annotated Book of Common Prayer, p. 305.

"Lo, thus shall the man be blessed: that feareth the Lord.

The Lord from out of Sion shall so bless thee: that thou shalt see Jerusalem in prosperity all thy life long."

They had been used in the Confirmation Office at least from the time of Egbert, Archbishop of York, *circa* 950, and are now in Roman use.

With an obvious propriety Ps. cxxxiii., (Behold how good and joyful) was said in the Sarum Office at the Anointing of a Bishop in his Consecration, with two of its own verses for an Antiphon, which was to be repeated after every verse of the Psalm. The Antiphon was as follows:

<small>Consecration of Bishop.</small>

The ointment on the head, which ran down unto the beard, even Aaron's beard, which ran down to the border of his garment. The Lord commanded his blessing for evermore.

The character of the Psalm with its eulogy of brotherly unity, caused it to be used in old time at the profession of a monk and other analogous occasions.

And last of all, a Gradual Psalm had the distinction of furnishing the very first words of the Office used for the Coronation of

<small>Coronation.</small>

Queen Victoria, when verses 1, 5, 6, 7, of Psalm cxxii. (I was glad when they said) formed the anthem with which she was received on her entrance into the church.

Upon the use of the Gradual Psalms in the several Churches of the Eastern Communion it is not so easy to obtain information. I have inquired of one, who of all living men is one of the most accomplished upon such subjects, whether in any of the Syrian, Coptic, Russian, or other Eastern Service-books there is any Office of the Gradual Psalms at all analogous to the beautiful one which I have described before as occurring in the Roman Breviary. And the reply which my learned friend, the Rev. S. C. Malan, Prebendary of Sarum, makes to my inquiry, is as follows: "I can find no actual Services for the Gradual Psalms, nor Offices of them in the books I have. But in the Greek Church, by which they are called 'Proskyria' (from the first words of Ps. cxx.), they are said or sung at evensong from September to Christmas. They are also said or sung in the Russian Church during the special service for Thursday in the first week in Lent. They form of course," he adds, "one of the

*Eastern Uses.*

'kathismata' into which the Psalms are divided in consequence of Can. xvii. of the Council of Laodicæa, and of Can. lxxv. of the Sixth Œcumenical Council. Those kathismata obtain throughout the Greek Church, in the Russian, Georgian, etc., and also in the Armenian division of the Psalter."

The same division of the Psalter, I would observe, *Armenian Division of the Psalter.* does not appear to prevail through all the Churches of the Eastern Communion. While the Greeks divide the Psalms into twenty groups (kathismata), the Armenians divide it into only eight, which are called Canons. This arrangement has this result upon our present subject, that the Gradual Psalms go (as we find some trace of their going in the mind of Rome and Sarum) in one group with all the Psalms that follow, and with them constitute the eighth canon of the Psalter.*

From the above passage, and from the account of the Greek rite given by Bona, one can detect some traces in the Eastern usage of that tendency which I have already noticed as existing (though not without some grave exceptions) in the devotions of the

* Bona. De Var. Rit. Div. Psalm., cap. xv. s. 2, p. 554. Antwerp: 1723.

West—the seemingly instinctive clinging, I mean, of the Gradual Psalms to the later hours of the day. This seems even more clearly observable in the East than in the West; the East probably, according to its notoriously conservative disposition, reflecting with more faithful uniformity than the West the older practice of the Hebrew Church, which also used and still uses them at a similar period of the day. In the Greek rite, the use of the group of Gradual Psalms was different at different periods of the year. From Low Sunday up to Sunday after the octave of the Exaltation of the Holy Cross (which with the Greeks is kept on Sept. 14th,) the whole Psalter is traversed once in the week, the *kathisma* of the Gradual Psalms being said on Friday at Vespers, precisely as it is in the Synagogue to this day in the Sabbath afternoons of the winter months. From the Sunday after the octave of the Exaltation of the Holy Cross up to Quinquagesima, the Ordinary Psalms for Vespers on Monday, Tuesday, Wednesday, and Thursday, are displaced, and the *kathisma* of the Gradual Psalms is said in their place. From Quinquagesima up to Wednesday in Holy Week, the entire Psalter is traversed twice in the week, the group under notice being said at Vespers of Monday, Tuesday, Wednesday, Thursday, and Friday. I have compared this account of the arrangement of Psalms with the rubric of a Greek Psalter in modern use, and I do not find that the modern directions differ in much that is material from the directions I have quoted.

An analysis of the various Rites of several Churches of the Eastern Communion is given by Bona,* but beyond what is stated above, I have been unable to discover any employment of the Gradual Psalms amongst them which has any special character of its own, or which adds anything to the conceptions familiar to us in the West.

### THE OFFICE OF THE GRADUAL PSALMS.

The Gradual Psalms are said in Lent on the Wednesdays of every week, if not hindered by a Feast of Nine lessons, (*i.e.*, one of the greater feasts), in choir before the matins of the day; out of choir as opportunity shall occur.

The first five Psalms are said without *Glory be to*

* De Var. Rit. Div. Psalm. capp. 13-19.

## THE USE OF THE GRADUAL PSALMS.

*the Father.* But at the end of the last of them, *Grant them* is said.

It is incepted at once without Antiphon.

### Psalm CXX.
When I was in trouble, etc.

*No Gloria.*

### Psalm CXXI.
I will lift up mine eyes, etc.

*No Gloria.*

### Psalm CXXII.
I was glad when they said, etc.

*No Gloria.*

### Psalm CXXIII.
Unto thee lift I up mine eyes, etc.

*No Gloria.*

### Psalm CXXIV.
If the Lord Himself, etc.

*No Gloria.*

Grant them, O Lord : eternal rest.

And let light perpetual: shine upon them.

*Then is said kneeling:*

Our Father, etc., *secretly.*

℣. And lead us not into temptation.

℟. But deliver us from evil.

℣. From the gate of hell.
R︎. Deliver their souls, O Lord.
℣. May they rest in peace.
R︎. Amen.
℣. Lord, hear my prayer.
R︎. And let my crying come unto Thee.
℣. The Lord be with you.
R︎. And with thy spirit.

Let us pray.

### The Collect.

Absolve, we pray Thee, O Lord, the souls of Thy servants and handmaidens, and all the faithful departed, from every chain of their sins; that, being raised again amongst Thy Saints and Elect, they may be refreshed in the glory of the resurrection. Through Christ our Lord. R︎. Amen.

*After the Collect the other Gradual Psalms which follow are said immediately; and at the end of each Psalm* Glory be to the Father *is said.*

### Psalm CXXV.

They that put their trust, etc.
Glory be to the Father, etc.

### Psalm CXXVI.

When the Lord turned again, etc.
> Glory be to the Father, etc.

### Psalm CXXVII.

Except the Lord build the house, etc.
> Glory be to the Father, etc.

### Psalm CXXVIII.

Blessed are all they, etc.
> Glory be to the Father, etc.

### Psalm CXXIX.

Many a time have they fought, etc.
> Glory be to the Father, etc.

*Afterwards there is said kneeling*:
> Lord, have mercy.
> Christ, have mercy.
> Lord, have mercy.

Our Father, *secretly*.

℣. And lead us not into temptation.

℟. But deliver us from evil.

℣. O think upon Thy congregation.

℟. Whom thou hast purchased and redeemed of old.

℣. Lord, hear my prayer.

℟. And let my crying come unto Thee.

℣. The Lord be with you.
℟. And with thy spirit.

Let us pray.

### The Collect.

O God, Whose nature and property is ever to have mercy and to forgive, receive our humble petitions; and though we be tied and bound with the chain of our sins, yet let the pitifulness of Thy great mercy loose us, for the honour of Jesus Christ, our Mediator and Advocate. Amen.

*After the Collect the other Gradual Psalms which follow are said immediately; and at the end of each Psalm* Glory be to the Father *is said.*

### Psalm CXXX.

Out of the deep, etc.
    Glory be to the Father, etc.

### Psalm CXXXI.

Lord, I am not high-minded, etc.
    Glory be to the Father, etc.

### Psalm CXXXII.

Lord, remember David, etc.
    Glory be to the Father, etc.

### Psalm CXXXIII.

Behold, how good and joyful, etc.
>Glory be to the Father, etc.

### Psalm CXXXIV.

Behold now, praise the Lord.
>Glory be to the Father, etc.

>*Then is said kneeling*

>Lord, have mercy.
>Christ, have mercy.
>Lord, have mercy.
>Our Father, etc. *Secretly.*

℣. And lead us not into temptation,
℟. But deliver us from evil.
℣. Save thy servants,
℟. O my God, which hope in Thee.
℣. Lord, hear my prayer,
℟. And let my crying come unto Thee.
℣. The Lord be with you,
℟. And with thy spirit.

>Let us pray.

>The Collect.

Stretch forth, O Lord, to thy servants and handmaidens the right hand of Thy heavenly aid; that they may seek Thee with their whole heart, and that what they ask worthily they may be counted meet to attain. Through Christ our Lord. R̥. Amen.

This Office stands in the Breviary next the Office of the Dead. It seems from some of its clauses to form a part of that Office, though all the printed Breviaries that I have consulted refrain from continuing the page-heading, *Officium Defunctorum*, upon the pages occupied by the Office of the Gradual Psalms. Bona makes mention of a Monastic Office consisting of fifteen Psalms, which was said before the night Office. Of these, five were said for all the faithful living on earth; then five for all the departed; and then five for those who were recently departed. But whether this was the Office of the Gradual Psalms, Bona says, is not clear.*

#### THE ENGLISH OFFICE WITH A GRADUAL PSALM.

As a memorial of the departed.

*Every day in the year, except Good Friday, after Mass, at the last retreat before dinner, in the place of*

---

* Bona *De Divinâ Psalmodiâ.* Cap. xv. s. i., p. 487, ed. 1723. Antwerp.

the boys\* Ps. cxxx., Out of the deep *is said for all the faithful departed without note, and without* Glory be to the Father, *with*

    Lord, have mercy.
    Christ, have mercy.
    Lord, have mercy.
    Our Father, etc.

And lead us not into temptation,
℟. But deliver us from evil.
℣. Grant them eternal rest, O Lord,
℟. And let light perpetual shine upon them.
℣. From the gate of hell,
℟. Deliver their souls, O Lord,
℣. I believe to see the goodness of the Lord.
℟. In the land of the living.

*According to the Use of Sarum,* May they rest in peace, *is not said before the Collect for the departed, but after the Collect, in place of* Let us bless the Lord, *there is said,*

---

\* *I.e.*, on the floor of the Choir, and not in the *secunda forma* or *superior gradus*, where the Ecclesiastics usually sat. So, in my opinion, *in statione puerorum* ought to be translated; though I have obtained many different views upon it. My friend, Rev. Preb. Dayman, the learned editor of Ducange, thinks it means *in the boys' schoolroom.*

The Lord be with you.
And with thy spirit.
Let us pray.

Absolve, we pray thee, O Lord, the souls of thy servants the bishops, priests, our parents, benefactors, and all the faithful departed from every chain of their sins; that being raised again amongst thy saints and elect, they may be refreshed in the glory of the resurrection. Through Christ our Lord. Amen.

May they rest in peace. Amen.

### THE SARUM OFFICE ON A GRADUAL PSALM.

For the Peace of the Church.

*Omni die per annum post Compl. de die et post Mat. de die, præterquam in duplicibus festis et per Oct. Corporis Christi et Visitationis, Assumptionis et Nativitatis B. Marie, et Dedicationis Ecclesiæ, et Nominis Jesu, et in die Animarum, et in Vigilia Nativitatis Dñi, et abhinc usque ad inceptionem historiæ* Domine ne in ira, *et a IVta. feriâ ante Pascham usque ad inceptionem historiæ* Deus omnium *dicitur pro pace Ecclesiæ cum genuflexione sine notâ iste Ps..*

Ad te levavi oculos meos.
Gloria Patri.

*Finito Psalmo sequitur :*

Kyrie eleison.
Christe eleison.
Kyrie eleison.

Pater noster.

Et ne nos.
Sed libera.
Exurge Domine adjuva nos.
Et libera nos propter nomen tuum.
Domine Deus virtutum converte nos.
Et ostende faciem tuam et salvi erimus.
Domine exaudi.
Et clamor.
Dominus vobiscum.
Et cum spiritu tuo.

*Oratio.*

Ecclesiæ tuæ Domine preces placatus admitte; ut destructis adversitatibus et erroribus universis, securâ tibi serviat libertate; et pacem tuam nostris concede temporibus. Per Christum Dominum nostrum. Amen.

*His dictis surgat Sacerdos et omnes Clerici à prostratione osculantes formulas.*

## THE SARUM OFFICE WITH A GRADUAL PSALM.

### For the Recovery of the Sick.

*Et sciendum est quod quandocunque dicitur Ps. Ad te levavi oculos post matutinas, tunc ad Primam post tabulam lectam dicitur sine nota iste Psalmus* cxxi.

Levavi oculos meos in montes.

Gloria Patri.

Kyrie eleison.

Christe eleison.

Kyrie eleison.

Pater noster.

Et ne nos.

Sed libera.

Ostende nobis Domine misericordiam tuam.

Et salutare tuum da nobis.

Salvos fac servos tuos et ancillas tuas.

Deus meus sperantes in te.

Mitte eis Domine auxilium de Sancto.

Et de Sion tuere eos.

Esto nobis Domine turris fortitudinis.

A facie inimici.

Nihil proficiat inimicus in eis.

Et filius iniquitatis non apponat nocere eis.
Domine exaudi.
Et clamor.
Dominus vobiscum.
Et cum spiritu tuo.

Oremus.

Adesto Domine supplicationibus nostris, et viam famulorum tuorum in salutis tuæ prosperitate dispone; ut inter omnes viæ et vitæ hujus varietates, tuo semper protegantur auxilio.

*Oratio.*

Omnipotens sempiterne Deus, salus æterna credentium, exaudi nos pro famulis tuis pro quibus misericordiæ tuæ imploramus auxilium; ut redditâ sibi sanitate, gratiarum tibi in Ecclesia tua referant actiones. Per Christum.

R⁊. Amen.

## CHAPTER VI.

### HEBREW USE.

THE Hebrew ritual employs the group of Gradual Psalms upon two occasions, which show that in the national mind they were especially associated with protection from excessive rains. This connection is probably due to the phrase in Ps. cxxiv. 4: "The waters had overwhelmed us, the stream had gone over our soul."

The entire group of fifteen Psalms is said on the afternoons of Sabbath during the winter months. *Winter Use.* The reason of this usage is a tradition that the Flood took place in the winter. Here is an example of a tendency which I have elsewhere pointed out, as surviving even in the Christian uses of these Psalms—the tendency, I mean, of the Gradual Psalms to secure for themselves a place towards the extreme hours of the day.

This same group, too, formed a prominent feature in the Ceremonial practised on the first day of the Feast of Tabernacles—called the Festival of the Water-drawing, a festival of the very highest joy, of which the Talmud says that "he who has not seen the rejoicing at the feast of the Water-drawing has seen no rejoicing in his life."* On that occasion the Gradual Psalms were sung, the Levites standing upon the fifteen steps which led from the Women's Court to the Court of Israel, and accompanying the song with harps and bow-instruments and cymbals, and trumpets, and musical instruments without number. Here again the reason for the use of these Psalms seems to be much the same as before. The world, say the Hebrew sages, is judged by water. These Psalms are said as a protection against its excess. Observe here too, once again, the clinging of the Gradual Psalms to the close of the day. It was, I gather from the same passage of the Talmud, at the close of the first day of the Festival that all this ceremonial of illumination and music took place.

*Feast of Tabernacles.*

\* Talm. Bab. Succah 51, 1 at the foot of the page.

Yet once again. The entire group of these Psalms is said on the occasion of the Consecration of a house or Synagogue.

*Consecration.*

Individual Psalms of the group are used in Hebrew ritual upon various occasions, very much as they are with us. I give a few examples.

The first is one of great importance to us, as being a Hebrew precedent for the unanimous use of Ps. cxxxiv. as a Compline Psalm in the Christian Church. If the evening service of Weekdays is read at night, then the Hebrew direction is that it shall begin with this Psalm, with the verse, "The Lord of Host is with us, the God of Jacob is our refuge. Selah," repeated after it three times as a kind of Antiphon.

*Night Use.*

In the Benediction said on the appearance of the new moon, Psalm cxxi. (I will lift up mine eyes unto the hills) is one of three Psalms with which the Benediction closes. The reason of this selection is probably to be found in the verse, "The sun shall not strike thee by day, neither the moon by night."

*New Moon.*

The joyous, hopeful character, which has always been felt to attach to the Gradual Psalms, makes one of them well fitted for use at the Feast of Purim—the feast wherein the Hebrew nation commemorates its deliverance from the plot of Haman, narrated in the Book of Esther. Psalm cxxiv., which contains the verse, "Our soul is escaped even as a bird out of the snare of the fowler," is employed on that occasion.

*Purim.*

In domestic life among the Hebrews a Gradual Psalm occupies a foremost position. The Grace after meat is with them a somewhat lengthy service, and it always opens with a Psalm. On Sabbath and Holy-days, Ps. cxxvi. is the one appointed to be said (When the Lord turned the captivity of Sion). On other days this is replaced by Ps. cxxxvii., By the waters of Babylon.

*Blessing of Food.*

One passage in the Talmud[*] prescribes that three of the Gradual Psalms (cxx., cxxi., cxxx.) shall form part of the twenty-four Benedictions to be said on certain fast days. These three Psalms, in fact, form the last three out of six forms added to the celebrated "eighteen" Collects—the group of petitions, which is to the Hebrew what the Lord's Prayer is to the Christian. By the "eighteen" and the six "addi-

[*] Taanith cap. 2, s. 3. fol. 15, 1 near the middle.

tions," the prescribed number of twenty-four is made up. From another passage in the Talmud* it is inferred that these three Psalms would thus form part of the service for the first day of the year. I have, however, looked through the volume of Hebrew service for that day as used in England, without succeeding in finding the Psalms in question. Moreover, a Hebrew minister to whom I referred was not able from his experience to confirm my belief in the usage. Nevertheless, I give the facts as I find them in the Talmud.

In the Service to be said before retiring to rest at night, Ps. cxxviii. is one of the Psalms ap-

*Night Use of Ps. cxxviii.* pointed to be said. Just before it, as a kind of Antiphon, the verse of another Gradual Psalm (Ps. cxxi, 4), "Behold, he that keepeth Israel shall neither slumber nor sleep," is appointed to be three times recited.

Once more. The last four verses of a Gradual Psalm are embodied in the long meditative formula that is read in the "Additional Service" for Sabbath. I transcribe the piece as a specimen of such forms. "Rabbi Eliezer says that Rabbi Chanina thus taught:

* Rosh Hashshanah cap. 4, s. 5, fol. 32, 1 at the top.

'Wise men promote peace in the world; as it is said, All thy children shall be taught of God; and great shall be the peace of thy children. Read not 'thy children,' but 'thy builders' (the letters are the same in Hebrew). Abundant peace have they who love thy Law; none shall obstruct them. May there be peace within thy walls, and prosperity within thy palaces.* For the sake of my brethren and friends, I will say, Peace be within thee. For the sake of the house of the Lord our God, I will seek thy good. The Lord will give strength unto his people; the Lord will bless his people with peace."

There are indeed many occasions in the Hebrew ritual when fragments of Gradual Psalms are introduced. A curious example of this is found in the Service of Blessings said by the Priests—significantly called in Hebrew "The Order of lifting up of the hands." I say, significantly called; because it may perhaps guide us in the interpretation of the ambiguous phrase in another Gradual Psalm, "Lift up your hands in the Sanctuary," addressed to those who are occupied in the service of

*margin note: Blessings by the Priests.*

---
* Ps. cxxii. 6 to the end.

the Temple.* In that Service they pronounce the blessing with which Aaron was divinely commanded to bless the children of Israel:—(Numb. vi. 24-26.)

The Lord bless thee, and keep thee:

The Lord make His face to shine upon thee, and be gracious unto thee:

The Lord lift up His countenance upon thee, and give thee peace.

But the method in which this blessing is delivered is peculiar. The fifteen Hebrew words which compose it are separately recited, and at each separate word the congregation responds with a verse or phrase of Scripture appropriate to the word. The second verse of Ps. cxxiii.—"Behold, as the eyes of servants look unto the hand of their masters, and as the eyes of a maiden unto the hand of her mistress; so our eyes wait upon the Lord our God until He have mercy upon us,"—forms the response to the one Hebrew word which represents the phrase, "And be gracious unto thee." This kind of use may be thought of as bearing some analogy to the intercalary Antiphon put in between the verses of a Psalm—for example, the Invitatory Psalm (Ps. xcv.)

* Ps. cxxxiv. 2. See Comment. there.

in daily Matins of old time—in some rites of the Christian Church.

Another fragment of a Gradual Psalm forms part of the formula which is said on entering the Synagogue before the Daily Morning Service. I translate the whole prayer, which it will be seen is made up entirely of selections from the Psalms:—

"A song of the Degrees of David.* I was glad when they said unto me, We will go into the house of the Lord. I am as glad of thy word as one that findeth great spoils. Hearken to the voice of my crying, my King and my God; for unto Thee do I make my supplication. O Lord, in the morning Thou shalt hear my voice; in the morning I will direct my prayer unto Thee, and will look up. I called upon Thee, for Thou shalt answer me, O God. Incline Thine ear unto me; hear my prayer. My foot standeth right; I will praise the Lord in the congregations."

Two remarks occur to me upon this formula. First of all, the English reader should observe the tenacity with which the Hebrew clings to the heading of the Psalm. Only one verse of the Gradual Psalm is employed in this prayer.

*Tenacity of a Psalm-title.*

* Ps. cxxii. 1.

Yet the heading of the Psalm is traditionally recited, as forming an integral part of the verse. I have argued this point at length elsewhere in this volume in a separate chapter on the subject. For the moment I only wish to throw up the Hebrew usage into strong contrast with what would probably have been the English method under similar circumstances. With those loose ideas about Psalm-titles that have become prevalent amongst ourselves, it is perhaps not too much to say that, if the opening of a Psalm had to figure in a prayer for English Christians, the title of it would almost certainly be discarded.

And, next: I wish to allege this as an example of the extent to which Psalms enter into Hebrew devotion. In ancient times, the same was true of Christian devotion. But in recent days, there has been rather a disposition to abridge the quantity of Psalms said in Christian Offices. This, it should be noted, is a disposition in antagonism with the spirit not only of Christian, but of Hebrew precedent too. Psalms constituted by far the largest portion of the offices in the ancient Church. Its chain of Psalms was the back-bone of every service—the thread, upon which the pearls of Collect and Versicle were strung. So absolutely was this character supreme, that the title of the old Breviary of Sarum is simply this—*The Psalter of David according to the Use of Sarum.*

# CHAPTER VII.

## PSALM CXX.

1. A song of degrees. In my distress I cried unto the Lord and He heard me.

<small>Radak.</small>
<small>Rashi.</small>
These Gradual Psalms are fifteen in number; and it is said that the Levites used to say them on the fifteen steps which were on the Temple-mount between the Court of Israel and the Court of the Women, and by which the ascent from the latter to the former was made, one Psalm being said upon each step.

Further, it is possible to interpret thus: that "Degrees"—or "goings up," as the Hebrew word means—refers to the going up of the Children of Israel to their own land from the Captivity of Babylon; the Psalms being all spoken in the persons of the Captives, and containing allusions to the distress of their exile, their expectation of deliverance, and their trust.

Haggaon says the title indicates the tone to which the Psalm was sung, the performance demanding an elevated* voice. Aben Ezra.

If the word for "Degrees" be thus taken for the name of a Psalm-tone, it might stand in the same category with *Alamoth,*† *Aijeleth Shahar,*‡ *Jonath-Elem-Rechokim,*§ and *Mahalath.*‖ This is noted by Aben Ezra in his comment upon the title of the fourth Psalm.

The Psalmist speaks in the person of the children of the Captivity, using throughout the singular for the plural. While concurring in Radak.
this exposition of the general character of the Gradual Psalms, Aben Ezra remarks upon the absence of the name of the Psalmist. He Aben Ezra.
suggests that this Psalm is the utterance of the Holy Spirit with reference to the men of the Captivity, who were in "distress," and knew of no resource but calling upon God. The "distress" in the Captivity was manifold; but the present Psalm appears to be

---

\* It should be noted that the fundamental idea in the Hebrew word for "Degrees," is that of ascension, or elevation.

† In the title of Ps. xlvi.     ‡ In the title of Ps. xxii.

§ In the title of Ps. lvi.

‖ In the titles of Pss. liii. and lxxxviii.

directed against that particular form of "distress" which arose from what was *said* against the captives by their conquerors.

"Distress," an intensified form of the ordinary Hebrew word. Compare the intensified form of the word for "help" in Ps. iii. 3: "There is no help for him in God."

"He heard me." The past tense employed in place of the future, as often in Scripture.* So Radak.

In that interpretation of these Psalms, which sees in them the "degrees" of Christian virtues, this Psalm aptly describes the first of such steps—the renunciation of the evil and vanity of the world. It thus divides itself into two parts. I. The Psalmist, in the person of one beginning the grades of virtue, finds many opponents in the shape of slanderers and ill advisers. II. He laments the admixture of evil— "Woe is me."

Targum.
Excepting in the title, which has been noticed already,† the Targum introduces no new feature into the verse: "A song which was

* This usage is commonly called the prophetic past, and is designed to express a certitude in what is yet future.

† Chapter I.

said upon the steps of the abyss. Before the Lord, when distress was upon me, I prayed, and He received my prayer."

2. Deliver my soul, O Lord, from lying lips, and from a deceitful tongue.

"From the nations," says Radak, "amongst whom Israel is exiled, who are false, fraudulent, and calumnious." Such remarks, which are not infrequent in Hebrew Commentators on the Scriptures, doubtless are no inaccurate description of the oppression that Israel underwent in the Captivity of Babylon; but one cannot help further feeling from their tone of bitterness that they are meant to convey a contemptuous criticism of the character of those nations, Christian and other, amongst whom the Israelitish people is at this moment in exile and dispersion. I notice the remark here, as giving a specimen of a line of exposition that is, of course, superciliously condemnatory of ourselves; but it will readily be understood that I have not thought it worth while to notice such remarks in *every* place where they may occur.

*Radak.*

Into the category of lying lips Rashi at once puts all the descendants of Esau, the hereditary opponents of the sons of Israel.

<small>Rashi.</small>

From the lying lips and the deceitful tongue, the Christian writers seem agreed in putting it, of those who would deter a beginner from any earnest, costly, and unmistakeable following of Christ. The phrase gives one at least of its meanings to our Lord's saying: "Woe unto you when all men shall speak well of you."—(S. Luke vi. 26.)

The Targum is exactly as the Hebrew:—

"Deliver my soul, O Lord, from the lips of falsehood, and from the crafty tongue."

<small>Targum.</small>

8. What shall be given unto thee? or what shall be done unto thee, thou false tongue?

Spoken in respect of Babylon, who spoke false and insidious words against Israel in the Captivity.

<small>Radak.</small>

Two interpretations seem to be possible according to the letter. "What gain shall thy false tongue be unto thee? What shall it (mark the subject of the verb) give unto thee? or what shall it add unto thee?" So Radak, who makes the verse to be addressed to the calumniator of Israel.

On the other hand Rashi takes God for the subject of the verbs. What shall God give unto thee? What shall he add unto thee? sc. as a protection and a fence; probably, that is, as a restraint upon thy license. Who is competent to check the wilfulness of the false tongue? Anyhow the verbs in this verse are transitive, and not intransitive, as they appear in the Authorised Version. *Rashi.*

The ancient Hebrew Midrash gives a curious meaning to "false." The tongue of man is false to its own mission. Its characteristic function is speech. But the tongue does nothing with that function to deter a man from evil. When a man is about to break the command of God, the tongue does not interpose with its function of speech and say, "Do it not." Hence it is addressed as "thou *false* tongue." *Midrash Tehillim.*

The Targum follows the Hebrew: "What shall one give unto thee, O slanderer; and what shall one add to thee, thou calumniator with the crafty tongue." *Targum.*

Similarly Radak compares the words of the false tongue to coals of juniper, because such fuel is excessively hot and does not become extinct for a long time. Moreover, while outwardly it appears extinct and like ashes, yet inwardly it remains all on fire. Even so are the words of the deceitful tongue, which speaks evil against a man, while it carefully veils the malice of the heart in order that he may not be upon his guard.

*So also Rashi.*

Rashi likewise refers the "sharp arrows" of the mighty not to the retribution that should come upon the false tongue, as the English Version does, but to the words themselves which such a tongue utters. "For thou, O false tongue, slayest men afar off as such arrows do." He gives as an alternative interpretation that which the translators of the Authorized Version have adopted: "What will God Almighty in the end decree against thee? Arrows of the mighty with coals of juniper—arrows from above and Gehenna from beneath." This latter line of interpretation is as old as the Targum, which puts the verse thus:—
"Sharpened arrows of the mighty (or *the*

*So Aben Ezra.*

*Targum.*

*arrows of the mighty are sharpened,*\*) as lightnings from above with coals of juniper, which are kindled in Gehenna below."

## 4. Sharp arrows of the mighty, with coals of juniper.

The difficulty is this: Do these words form an answer to the question in the preceding verse? or are they a further description of the false tongue and its words?

In the latter way they are taken by the Midrash, Radak and others. According to them, the Psalmist compares the evil words spoken by the people of Babylon to arrows sharpened and discharged from the hand of the mighty. <small>Radak.</small>

When the tongue is compared to arrows, there is a reference (according to the Midrash) to the irrevocableness of the tongue's work. <small>Midrash Tehillim.</small> Even the lifted sword may be stayed, but the shot arrow may not.

The special point to be drawn out in the mention

---

\* So Walton translates it (Polyglott, ad loc.), and also Buxtorf, Lex. Chald. Talmud. et Rabb. s. v. נְרְדָא

of "coals of *juniper*," is the inextinguishableness of such fuel. There is a marvellous story in the Midrash which illustrates this very well. Two men in the desert sat down under a juniper tree, and gathered sticks of it wherewith they cooked their food. After a year they passed over the same spot where was the dust of what they had burned; and, remarking that it was now twelvemonths since they had the fire, they walked fearlessly upon the dust and their feet were burned by the "coals" beneath it, which were still unextinguished.

<small>Midrash Tehillim.</small>

The Latin writers, following their version, have given a turn to the phraseology of this verse which should be noticed. With them the preceding verse stood in rather a different shape to what it has with us. What defence shall be given to thee *against* the deceitful tongue—*against* all these dissuasives from virtue? And the answer in the present verse is Arrows and coals—the Word, Incarnate (may we not say?) as well as written, and the burning examples of the Saints.

5. Woe is me, that I sojourn in Mesech, *that* I dwell in the tents of Kedar!

It is not easy to identify the words *Mesech* and *Kedar*.

To begin with, the Hebrew word here translated *Mesech* is not necessarily a proper name at all. It may be intended to convey the idea of prolongation or extension. The ancient Hebrew Midrash obviously takes it in this latter way. Woe is me, because men have the rule over me from Babylon to Media, and from Media to Greece, and from Greece to Edom. Midrash Tehillim.

Or again, taking another meaning of the word rendered *Mesech* from its root, which means simply "to draw," Woe is me, that I sojourn with the people that is *drawn* to Gehenna. So the Midrash comments.

Or, as a third alternative, we might put the clause as Radak does: Woe is me, that my captivity is so greatly prolonged. Radak.

With respect to Kedar, there seems no reason to doubt that, as Radak goes on, it denotes the leading families amongst the Ishmaelites.*

---

\* Cf. Gen. xxv. 13. "And these are the names of the sons of Ishmael, by their names, according to their generations: the firstborn of Ishmael, Nebajoth; and Kedar, and Adbeel, and Mibsam."

Of those who take Mesech as a proper name there are some, says Radak, who interpret it to be the same as Kedar, which is so called because they *drew*\* the bow.

One Hebrew writer makes Mesech equivalent to Tuscany, interpreting the verse apparently of the woe of Israel in being scattered amongst Christian persecutors since the conquest of Jerusalem by the Roman army. I consider this worth mention only as one of a few specimens which I shall give of the turn which national disaster has given to the Scriptural exegesis of Israel. Rashi puts the verse into the mouth of the whole people of Israel—a Shemitic race—who lament their misfortune in having to dwell in exile amongst descendants of Japheth. It will be remembered that Mesech was one of the sons of Japheth. Gen. x. 2: "The Sons of Japheth; Gomer, and Magog, and Madai, and Javan, and Tubal, and Meshech, and Tiras."

<small>Joseph Ben Gorion.</small>

In the Targum, Mesech is taken as a proper

---

† מָשַׁךְ, the root of *Mesech*, = he drew. Cf. Is. xxi., 17, where "the mighty men of the children of Kedar" are presented as archers.

name, and apparently as identical with Kedar: "Woe is me, for I dwell with Asiatics, I abide with the tents of Arabs." See [Targum.] Kedar thus associated with *Arabia* in Isa. xxi. 13-17.

Modern writers mostly take Mesech for the name of a race living in the neighbourhood of Caucasus. This, however, seems to rest upon analogies more or less precarious. Upon the whole, I incline to take Mesech either as a word expressing duration, or as another name for the bow-drawing Kedar; Kedar being the name of an Ishmaelite race, and the whole verse being thus a lamentation on the part of the descendants of Isaac that they are forced to sojourn amongst the descendants of Ishmael. We have only to remember S. Paul's comment* upon the relations subsisting between Isaac and Ishmael—"But as then he that was born after the flesh persecuted him that was born after the Spirit, even so it is now"— and the Christian application of the verse under discussion is obvious at once. It is the regretful longing of the Church to be freed from the perpetual antagonism of the world.

* Gal. iv. 29.

In a similar direction, S. Augustine, in one of his sermons on penitence, takes these verses as the very wail of a contrite soul in its exile from the face of God. "Who then hastens and desires to return to his country, and face to face to contemplate that sight as it is, but he who repents of his exile? From which sorrow of the penitent there bursts forth this pitiable voice, which says: 'Ah me! since my exile is prolonged.' And lest you should think that these are the words of one who as yet has not faith, see what follows: 'I dwelt in the tents of Kedar: with those who hated peace, I was for peace: when I spake to them, they assailed me mightily.' These are the words not only of the man of faith, but also of the most unflinching Evangelist and the bravest martyr. For from the same feeling springs also that saying of the Apostles: 'For we know that even if our earthly house of this dwelling be dissolved, we have a building of God, a house not made with hands, eternal in the heavens. For in this we groan, earnestly desiring to be clothed upon with our house which is from heaven.'"*

*S. Augustine.*

---

\* Quis ergo festinat atque optat ad patriam remeare, et illam speciem quæ est facie ad faciem contemplari, nisi quem peregri-

6. My soul hath long dwelt with him that hateth peace.

"Long." The form of the word is unusual.* It is not in regimen, though in that form. The Psalmist refers to the long captivity that he has had with a nation that hateth peace. Radak.

Aben Ezra gives the same explanation of the strange form, explaining that it is a genuine adjective with the substantive—"period," מדת זמן "measure of time,"—understood. He quotes a similar form in Ezek. xlvi. 17. "After it shall return (וְשָׁבַת) to the prince." The identical word, it Aben Ezra.

nationis suæ pœnituerit? Ex quo dolore pœnitentis, etiam vox illa miserabilis erumpit et sonat: Heu me! quoniam peregrinatio mea longinqua facta est. Et ne putes nondum fidelem ista loqui, vide quid sequitur. Inhabitavi in tabernaculis Kedar; cum his qui oderunt pacem, eram pacificus; cum loquerer eis, impugnabant me valde. Non solum hominis fidelis, sed etiam evangelistæ firmissimi et martyris fortissimi hæc verba sunt. Nam inde est etiam illud Apostoli: Scimus enim, quia et si terrena nostra domus hujus habitationis dissolvatur, ædificationem habemus ex Deo, domum non manu factam, æternam in cœlis. Etenim in hoc ingemiscimus, habitaculum nostrum quod de cœlo est superindui cupientes. Serm. 351. De utilitate agendæ pœnitentiæ.

* רַבָּת in place of רַבָּה.

may be added, occurs again in the Gradual Psalms. Ps. cxxix. 1.

In the Targum he "that hateth peace" is particularized as Edom. It is difficult to see the meaning of the opening phrase into which the Targum has enlarged the word for "long:"—
"More than they, my soul dwelt with Edom that hateth peace."

<small>Targum.</small>

Strangely enough, the initial words of this old paraphrase seem to offer exactly the addition that the verse needed in order fully to describe the tribulation of the Church; who would say that "more than they"—more than the literal Israel in the literal Edom, she bewailed her sorrow in dwelling with a generation hating Him Who is our Peace. (Eph. ii. 14.)

7. I *am*‖ *for* peace : but when I speak they are ready for war.

<small>‖ Or, *a man of peace*.</small>

I am for peace, sc. with them : but when I speak of peace* to them, they come to fight with me.

<small>Rashi.</small>

\* It should perhaps be noted that "Peace" (שָׁלוֹם, the root of the modern "salaam") has been from ancient times the ordinary

## PSALM CXX.

The first clause in Hebrew would be literally, "I am peace," *i.e.*, a man of peace, as Aben Ezra explains it, and the English margin after him. The bareness of the phrase has a parallel in another Psalm: "But I give myself unto prayer," which in Hebrew is, "but I am prayer." Ps. cix. 4.

<small>Aben Ezra.</small>

The Targum imports a new turn of thought, though it leaves the phrases as bald as they are in Hebrew: "I (am) peace,* for I will pray: they are for war."

<small>Targum.</small>

I wish it specially to be noted as an argument for the Christian interpretation of the Psalms, that if

---

formula of salutation in the Hebrew nation. It was, for example, the address of Ahimaaz to David in 2 Sam. xviii. 28. Cf. Gen. xliii. 23; 1 Sam. xxv. 6. It appears, too, in the New Testament in our Blessed Lord's greeting of the Apostles, S. John xx. 19; and it has been even appropriated by ourselves in the Eucharistic Office, and the opening clause of the Order for the Visitation of the Sick. This may possibly give a different turn of thought both to the Psalm and to Rashi's interpretation of it. "I give a 'Peace:' but when I say Peace, they come to fight with me."

* Walton in his Polyglott translates this "Ego pacem proinde orabo, ipsi vero bellum." I speak with profound respect for his colossal work, but I have been unable to find any warrant for translating אֲרוּם (for) by "proinde." The order of the words, moreover, in the Chaldee, seems to me against taking it in his way.

you do not apply them to the Christ, you can get absolutely no meaning at all from these bald phrases of the Hebrew and its corresponding Targum without taking liberties with them. "I am peace," is perfect as applied to the Christ. You have only to translate the Hebrew literally, putting in nothing, and you get at once the Christian interpretation. That interpretation is not one which has to be apologized for; it is *the* one which entails no straining of the text. Reject it, and you are at once in difficulties with the Hebrew, and are reduced to guess-work as to the particular italics that have to be supplied. There are other passages in the Psalms where the Christian interpretation is the only one that admits of a simple unassisted translation of the Hebrew.

Believing as I do profoundly in the Christian interpretation of the Psalms, I consider this fact of great importance, and have made some further remarks about it elsewhere in this work.

The Midrash puts the verse into the mouth of God: "I am peace." In peace I begin to speak to the nations of the world. Their opposition should be overcome by the Messiah,

<small>Midrash Tehillim.</small>

who should "rule them with a rod of iron,"—a verse of the second Psalm, which, it should be observed, the Midrash here quotes and applies to the Christ. (Ps. ii. 9.)

It has been seen that the verse has been thought to demand the insertion of some word, which the Hebrew does not present, before "peace." But I wish to point out that the Christian interpretation of the verse requires no such liberty to be taken with it. —"I am peace," it stands. What is that but S. Paul's statement (Ephes. ii. 14) : "He is our Peace," put into the mouth of the Lord Jesus Himself, who may well be thought of as the speaker in the verse— the dialogue, as it were, shifting for the moment (as it so often seems to shift in the language of the Psalms) gently and imperceptibly like a form in some dissolving views—shifting from the Church to her Lord, the Leader and the Model of the Saints as they traverse the successive grades of virtue?

## CHAPTER VIII.

### PSALM CXXI.

### A Song of Degrees.

1. I ‖ will lift up mine eyes unto the hills, from whence cometh my help.

‖ Or, Shall I lift up mine eyes to the hills? whence should my help come? So Lyra.

This Psalm seems to be a prayer for the well-being of the chosen people rescued from captivity. Its theme is the completeness of the divine protection, and the reliance thereon of the servant of God. That reliance forms the second step in the fifteen grades of Christian virtue.

Amongst all the Gradual Psalms, the present one stands alone in having לַמַּעֲלוֹת in its title, in place of the usual הַמַּעֲלוֹת. The Hebrew commentators bestow some pains upon both the grammatical and the mystical significance of the change.

Radak.

Radak takes the ל as the equivalent of the definite article, just as it is in 2 Kings vii. 2, "Then a lord, on whose hand the king (לַמֶּלֶךְ) leaned, answered the man of God."

The Midrash Tehillim interprets the preposition (לְ) "with reference to." The Psalm looks forward to the final restoration of Israel at the Day of Judgment, when Israel should no more fall into the hands of its enemies. And it is *with reference to*—the Midrash here gives עַל as the equivalent word—that deliverance, that David, who according to the tradition of the Midrash is the author of the Psalm, says, "I will lift up mine eyes unto the hills."

*Midrash.*

I gather that here the Midrash understands the hills of Jerusalem. It is there that Hebrew tradition fixes the appearance of the Judge, in accordance with the prophecy of Zechariah (Zech. xiv. 4), "His feet shall stand in that day upon the Mount of Olives, which is before Jerusalem on the east:"—a passage, again, which Christian writers have associated with the angels' declaration at the time of our Lord's Ascension, "This same Jesus, Which is taken up from you into heaven, shall *so* come"—in the same place, amongst other resemblances—" in like manner as ye have seen Him go into heaven." (Acts i. 11.)

Rashi gives a mystical interpretation to the strange preposition, and, it would seem, applies the Psalm to the services which angels render to men: "Degrees" he takes in the sense of orders, ranks. The Psalm is a "song to (with reference to) the Orders,"—sc. of angels. "I find," he says, "that the peculiar heading in the second of the Gradual Psalms points to the Orders which go up in the presence of (lit. "for") the righteous in the world to come from beneath the tree of life to the throne of God." The strange preposition, which the Psalm-title here introduces, stands in Hebrew for the number thirty, and thus is made to serve another purpose in the mystical interpretation. Rashi goes on to quote a Hebrew poet, who records a belief of his nation that below the seven highest Orders of Angelic Being there were thirty other Orders, one above another, up to the throne of God, "who fly and ascend in grateful chanting of the Song of the Degrees." This, upon the whole, seems to me the best way of understanding the very troublesome note of Rashi.

*The hills*,—literally, no doubt, in allusion to the hill-country of Palestine,—that feature of his country which the Hebrew mind seems always to have dwelt upon with so much pleasure. Figuratively it may stand here (as so often in Scripture) for holy men, whose character is eminent above the world. The eyes of my heart I will lift towards the saints, emulating their attainments, and taking courage from their triumphs. The suggestion that by *hills* angels are meant (from strength and greatness) seems less apposite. S. Jerome even applies the figure to the Divine books of the Law and the Prophets, in which the Lord is seen as the helper of all.

<small>S. Jerome.</small>

*From whence cometh my help.* This clause is taken by Aben Ezra (and apparently by Radak also) as an interrogative phrase. "I will lift up mine eyes unto the hills. From whence cometh my help?" This is the question which the Psalmist answers in the following verse.

<small>Aben Ezra.</small>

It seems more agreeable to Hebrew usage thus to take the particle מֵאַיִן as introducing an interrogative rather than a relative clause, though the English translators seem to have taken it sometimes as one, sometimes as the other, and sometimes (as in the present case with the Margin) to have left the matter in doubt. Gen. xxix. 4 is a good example of the strictly interrogative force of the word: "And Jacob said unto them, My brethren, whence (מֵאַיִן אַתֶּם) be ye?" It is quite possible, it must be admitted, to quote an apparent justification of the use of the particle as a relative. Josh. ii. 4 is sometimes alleged as furnishing such justification: "And the woman took the two men and hid them, and said thus, There came men unto me, but I wist not whence (מֵאַיִן הֵמָּה) they were." I question, however, whether even here it might not be explained as an indirect interrogative.

This view of the particle "from whence," which takes it as an interrogative rather than a relative particle, has the further support of the Targum, which puts the verse as follows:

<small>Targum.</small>

"A song which was said upon the steps of the abyss. I will lift up mine eyes to the mountains. From whence shall my support come?"

The great Lexicon of Buxtorf gives no example of the Chaldee particle here being used otherwise than interrogatively. When the extreme antiquity of the Targum is considered—in substance it dates probably from the time when a Temple was standing—the paraphrase seems decisive that the traditional way of taking the clause amongst the Ancient Hebrews was interrogatively, and not as the English version puts it in the text.

2. My help *cometh* from the LORD, which made heaven and earth.

The language either of prediction or of expectation. I have no need of the help of men, but of the help of God alone. Even though I lift my eyes to the mountains, it will profit me nothing, for none can help me save God. To Him therefore will I lift my eyes, for He will help us, and gather us from among the nations; and all things—"heaven and earth"—are in His hands, to do what seemeth Him best. Aben Ezra. Radak.

The ancient Hebrew Midrash refers the Psalm to the Day of Judgment, when the final restoration of Israel shall take place. In the distress of that time righteousness alone will avail. No man shall deliver his brother, nor father the son. They shall then lift their eyes to their Father in heaven, and say in the words of Isaiah, Midrash Tehillim.

".Doubtless thou art our Father, though Abraham be ignorant of us." (Isa. lxiii. 16.) So here it is said, " Our help cometh from the Lord."

The spirit of this Hebrew interpretation, I would remark, exactly accords with our Lord's warning: " Think not to say within yourselves, We have Abraham for our father."

The Targum adds nothing to the Hebrew:

<small>Targum.</small> " My support (or " help") (is) from the presence of the Lord, who made heaven and earth."

3. He will not suffer thy foot to be moved: He that keepeth thee will not slumber.

<small>Radak.</small> Words of consolation addressed, in the exile, by every Israelite to his fellow. Thy confidence in the Lord is well placed; for though the Captivity seem to be prolonged, and thy God seemeth to slumber, yet He will not suffer thy foot to be moved.

There seems, however, no reason why the Hebrew should not be taken (with the Old Latin Gloss) as the address of the just man to himself. He soliloquizes that, owing to his reliance upon the help of the Lord, his moral position—"thy foot"—will not be ruined by pride, as was that of the fallen angels.

The use of אַל for the negatives in this verse is equivalent, according to Aben Ezra, to the more usual לֹא. It is matched by the negative in Prov. xii. 28: "And in the pathway thereof there is no (אַל) death." The other passage which he quotes as a parallel—Gen. xlix. 6, "O my soul, come not (אַל) thou into their secret,"—does not seem apposite as an illustration of the usage under discussion, for there it has, like the Latin "Ne," its ordinary force expressing a prohibition.

<small>Aben Ezra.</small>

The Midrash, interpreting of the Last Judgment, quotes the parallel expressions in Deut. xxxii. 35: "To me belongeth vengeance and recompence; their foot shall slide (the same word as here) in due time." It does not, however, notice the peculiarity of the negative. Indeed, it does not contribute much else to the understanding of the present Psalm; as all the rest of its long commentary hereupon is rather an enlargement of Psalm

<small>Midrash.</small>

cxxxvii., showing how its phrases about Babylon are to be realized. I do not feel that it has repaid me for the immense trouble of making it out.

The Targum is as the Hebrew:

*Targum.* "He will not suffer thy foot to be moved: thy keeper slumbereth not."

## 4. Behold, He that keepeth Israel shall neither slumber nor sleep.

The relation between the two Hebrew verbs is well expressed by "slumber," and "sleep;" the former being used, as Radak explains, of a state of somnolence less profound than the latter.

*Radak.*

*Israel,* with an allusion to Jacob, who slept at Bethel, and to whom the promise of God took this form, "And, behold, I am with thee, and will *keep* thee in all places whither thou goest." (Gen. xxviii. 15.)

*Aben Ezra.*

The Targum is word for word as the Hebrew, except that of the two verbs in Hebrew in the same tense, the first is represented by a participle in the Chaldee: "Behold, He slumbereth not, neither shall He that keepeth Israel sleep."

*Targum.*

PSALM CXXI.     157

5. The LORD is thy keeper: the LORD is thy shade upon thy right hand.

A curious Talmudic illustration of the phrase *upon thy right hand*, is furnished by taking it in connection with the last verse of the Psalm, "The Lord shall preserve thy going out and thy coming in." With regard to the words of the Law, it is said in Deut. vi. 9: "And thou shalt write them upon the posts of thy house." In an Israelitish house the direction is literally obeyed, and the sacred parchment (called, from the door-post itself, מְזוּזָה Mezuzah,) carrying certain verses* from the Law is affixed to every door, but always rigorously affixed to

* The passages actually so written upon a מְזוּזָה in my possession are: "Hear, O Israel: The Lord our God is One Lord: And thou shalt love the Lord thy God with all thine heart, and with all thy soul, and with all thy might. And these words which I command thee this day shall be in thine heart; And thou shalt teach them diligently unto thy children, and shalt talk of them when thou sittest in thine house and when thou walkest by the way, and when thou liest down, and when thou risest up. And thou shalt bind them for a sign upon thine hand, and they shall be as frontlets between thine eyes. And thou shalt write them upon the posts of thy house; and on thy gates." (Deut. vi. 4-9.) This is followed by the similar passage from Deut. xi. 13-21, which particularizes the blessings that should follow obedience.

the *right hand* post, as a continual reminder to every Israelite of his obligation to live according to the Law. We thus obtain a beautiful interpretation of the clause, *The Lord is thy shade upon thy right hand*, no less acceptable to the Christian than to the Israelite, that man will find his shelter and protection by living always with the law of God written in his memory.

Closely akin to this is the interpretation adopted by many of the Christian writers. *Upon thy right hand*, that is, so that the sinister powers of evil shall not impede thy course of righteous action. The right hand is a common index in Scripture of rightness, and the left hand of wrongness. The just, for example, shall be placed upon the right, and the wicked upon the left of the Lord in the Day of Account.

<small>S. Jerome and others.</small>

The Targum puts it:

"The Lord shall keep thee, the Lord shall shade thee upon the side of thy right hand."

<small>Targum.</small>

6. The sun shall not smite thee by day, nor the moon by night.

Keep thee, that is, from the extremes of heat and cold, and so from diseases as caused by those extremes. <sub>Radak. Aben Ezra.</sub>

S. Jerome, on the contrary, and many of the Latin writers, refer the verse to the security of the just man under the Divine protection—neither elated in prosperity, nor desperate in adversity.

With S. Augustine and the Gloss, a line of interpretation is adopted which could have suggested itself only to those who read the Scriptures exclusively in the Latin Version. With them the Sun is God; the Day is Wisdom; the Moon is the Church; and the Night is the Flesh of Christ, which (as I suppose is meant) in the Incarnation shrouded, veiled, hid the Godhead. The man who is under this Divine protection errs not in that wisdom which consists in the knowledge of God, nor in misapprehending that Incarnation of the Lord, which the Church has been the instrument of promulgating. It is quite possible to take the Latin for "by day" (per diem) in this way, as meaning "by the instrumentality of day;" but the corresponding Hebrew phrase is certainly not susceptible of such a turn.

The expressions are slightly enlarged by the Targum:

*Targum.*

"By day when the sun rules, morning spectres shall not smite thee;\* and by night when the moon rules, with (those of) night."

7. The LORD shall preserve thee from all evil: He shall preserve thy soul.

From all that may assail a man, from within as well as from without.

*Aben Ezra.*

The Targum makes a significant comment at the beginning of the verse:

*Targum.*

The word of the Lord shall preserve thee from all evil: he shall preserve thy soul.

This furnishes an example of that foreshadowing of the Christian doctrine of the Word which is frequent in the Targums. In numberless passages of Scripture where the sacred text says the Lord did so and so, the Targum paraphrases it that the Word of the Lord did so and so. Several easily accessible

---

\* Walton (in the Polyglott, ad loc.) appears to have inverted the grammar of the Chaldee when he translates it, "non feriet te spectris matutinis." But the verb is clearly plural.

instances will be found in a note of Bishop Pearson's work on the Creed. A whole collection of them too is given in a little work "On the Christology of the Targums," published by Young of Edinburgh. See a most striking indication that the authors of the Targum conceived of a *Personality* attaching to the Word of the Lord, below on Psalm cxxiv. 8.

8. The LORD shall preserve thy going out and thy coming in from this time forth, and even for evermore.

Thou shalt go out from thy Captivity in peace, and in peace thou shalt come in to the land of Israel. So Radak. Aben Ezra, however, interprets the *going out* of the going out to war, and of course the *coming in* of the return from war; basing the interpretation apparently upon the use of the same two words in the blessing upon Israel in Deut. xxviii. 6: "Blessed shalt thou be when thou comest in, and blessed shalt thou be when thou goest out;" where the words certainly seem to be applied to warfare, from the fact that the following verse proceeds to enlarge upon the enemies of Israel being smitten

M

before their face. While, however, we may adopt one or other of these as giving the primary significance of the verse, it is well not to forget that wider exegesis of them indicated by the pertinent observation of S. Chrysostom: "The whole of life con-sists in these—in goings in and comings out;" including the 'goings in' to temptation with a healthy faith, and the 'comings out' of them victorious, yet untainted by the breath of pride, as others have put it; and reaching even (in S. Jerome's thought,) to the final 'going out' from life, and the preservation of the just in the bosom of Abraham for evermore.

*S. Chrysostom.*
*S. Aug. Gloss.*
*S. Jerome.*

An entirely new colour is given to the verse by the Targum:

"The Lord shall preserve thy going out to business, and thy coming in for the study of the Law, from this time forth (lit. and from the year,) and for evermore."

*Targum.*

## CHAPTER IX.

#### PSALM CXXII.

### A Song of Degrees of David.

**1. I was glad when they said unto me, Let us go into the house of the Lord.**

AMONGST the Gradual Psalms, the name of David is prefixed only to Psalms cxxii., cxxiv., cxxxi., and cxxxiii. Of these, says Radak, David is to be taken as the composer. With regard to the rest, which do not bear the name of David, it is quite possible they were composed by some other of the singers,* whose names are not recorded.

<small>Radak.</small>

This Psalm, Radak continues, exhibits the language of the Israelites in their exile. So ardent was their longing to rebuild the Temple of the Lord, that

---

\* For "singers" here, Radak employs the technical word drawn from the Temple Service in 2 Chron. v. 12: "Also the Levites which were the singers (הַמְשֹׁרְרִים), all of them of Asaph, of Heman, of Jeduthun, with their sons and their brethren ...."

they mention the going up of Israel to Jerusalem to keep the holy feasts (*Let us go into the house of the Lord*). The language is not their own, for the house of the Lord existed no more; but they adopt the language of their fathers, who lived while the Temple stood. The expression is supposed to be taken up by each one of the captive children: hence the singular number of the verb, *I was glad*.

When Radak thus makes David the author of the Psalm, and yet refers it to the period of the Captivity, of course he was not ignorant that David lived and died long before that disaster. There seem therefore two ways open, in one or other of which Radak's interpretation must be taken. Either (1) David spoke in the spirit of prophecy; or (2) the Psalm was composed in the first instance by David, with some intention of his own, and was afterwards adopted into the collection of the Gradual Psalms, and applied to their own circumstances and aspirations by the Children of the Captivity.

Rashi not only makes David the author of the Psalm, but finds the explanation of its language in the life of David. When it was revealed that the Temple should not be erected in

*Rashi.*

the life of David, but in that of Solomon his son, there sprang up in the heart of Israel a longing for the departure of David, and the accession of Solomon. David himself was able to sympathize with this longing: and as he heard men in his old age sighing for the time when they might "go into the house of the Lord," he himself "was glad" at the thought of it.

The Midrash Tehillim gives the same remarkable exposition of it. *Midrash Tehillim.*

In the opinion of Maimonides, the Psalm was composed by David with a view to its use at the time of the building of Solomon's Temple. *Maimonides.* Others, however, of the Hebrew doctors quoted by Aben Ezra, refer it (1) to the abode which David prepared for the Ark upon Zion; or (2) even to the third Temple, which existed at the beginning of the Christian era.

Amid all this diversity of Hebrew opinion, it does not seem possible to say exactly what circumstance in the life of David—whether the preparation of the house of curtains for the Ark, or the prospective erection of his son's Temple—gave rise to the Psalm: but all the phænomena that it presents—

its being ascribed to David, and its position in the series, which, by unanimous consent, is admitted to have one of its interpretations in the going up from the Captivity—all, I submit, would be explained by the supposition that it was originally a Psalm of David—whether spoken prophetically, or historically, or both—and that it was subsequently adopted, and perhaps embodied in the series of Gradual Psalms, by Ezra and his companions in reference to their own prospects and condition.

The Psalm forms the third step in the 'ascents' of Christian virtue, which it represents as consisting in the hope of reaching the home —the "house of the Lord"—of the Christian's aspiration.

*They said.* The invitation reaches us, says S. Jerome, through the Law, the Prophets, and the Apostles.

<small>S. Jerome.</small>

The Targum follows the Hebrew, except in the inscription of the Psalm:—

"A song which was sung upon the steps of the abyss. I was glad when they said unto me, To the Temple of the Lord we will go."

<small>Targum.</small>

2. Our feet shall stand within thy gates, O Jerusalem.

The verb here is, strictly speaking, in a past tense—not "shall stand," but "did stand." So, moreover, it seems to be taken by the Hebrew writers, who interpret the verse as a memory of a happier past on the part of the Children of the Captivity—a recollection of the multitudes who used to gather within the gates of the Holy City at the three great feasts of the year. <small>Radak. Aben Ezra.</small>

Rashi, however, adopts a different exegesis. He thinks "stand" is used of success in warfare. Our feet stood—we were everywhere victorious; and the secret of our triumphs lay within —they were vouchsafed on account of—the gates of Jerusalem, where men were occupied with the Divine Law. The future verb—"*shall* stand"—of our own translation is thus not without its propriety, when viewed as a Tropological interpretation of the verse. Men's success and progress always *did* stand, and always *shall* stand, only in their faithfulness to the Law of God. <small>Rashi.</small>

The Midrash gives the same exposition as
Rashi.

*Midrash.*

The verb is expressly put into the past tense by
the Targum :—

*Targum.*

"Our feet were standing in thy gates, O Jerusalem."*

3. Jerusalem is builded as a city that is compact together.

Rather an exclamation, or reflection than a fresh proposition. Their feet stood within the walls of Jerusalem—Jerusalem, that was builded.

*Radak apparently.*

N.B. The definite article is found in the Hebrew, and must be translated like the article with participle in Greek.

The apparently superfluous mention of "builded" in connection with Jerusalem is due, as Rashi seems to take it, to that great addition in the way of "building" that was made to the city by Solomon in the

---

* It may be noted here, that our form of the word *Jerusalem* not improbably owes its origin to the Chaldee, where it is printed with exactly the same vowels. The ordinary Hebrew vocalization of the word is different.

erection of the Temple—an addition, which David, the original Author of the Psalm, contemplates by prophetic anticipation, and upon which the Children of the Captivity gratefully look back.

The latter clause of the verse, " as a city that is compact together," has given rise to much difference of opinion. First, as to mere translation. The several translations that have been proposed seem to divide themselves into two classes; (1) those in which the relative (שֶׁ) is taken as the nominative of the verb, as in our Authorised Version, and (2), those in which it is joined, by a common Hebrew usage, with the subsequent personal pronoun (לָהּ). The former class makes this personal pronoun redundant. Yet even this may be justified by the similar instance in another of these Gradual Psalms, cxx. 6. This, however, is avoided by the second class of translations; and the question then is, What is the subject of the verb? It would, no doubt, be quite possible to take (as Radak appears to do) "the congregation of Israel," (עדת ישראל) as the subject. The gender is suitable, and the sense of the context suggests some such subject. But might not the verb, I would suggest, be taken impersonally? It would then stand thus, "As a city, for (to) which there is a union (it is united) together." This would lead very well to the translation (which is, in the present case, really paraphrase) offered by Dr. Leeser*—"Wherein all associate together."

For Jerusalem, then, there is a union together. But a union of what? Both in ancient and in modern times many replies to the question have been conjectured. Gesenius, for example, amongst the moderns, refers it to the reconstruction of the demolished city, the re-union of its scattered elements —lapides diu disjecti, iterum conjuncti sunt.† This line of interpretation is indeed somewhat akin to that suggested by one of the Hebrew Commentators, who refers it to the buildings of the city, which (the Psalmist alleges under this interpretation) were pervaded by a unity, though the city had been built and

---

* I take this opportunity of saying that those who interest themselves in the accurate translation of the Old Testament, would do well to see the translation of the learned Dr. Leeser, (London: Trübner). A Christian scholar will not be likely to accept his rendering of all passages; but such as have not time to read the Hebrew writers for themselves, will find in his book the results of a very extensive acquaintance with the traditional interpretation of the Scriptures.

† Thesaurus Ling. Hebr. s. v.

restored at several different times. But if we pay regard to the statement of the following verse, the interpretation of Radak appears to be the most tenable of all—that the union or association referred to was the gathering of the tribes at the Holy City for the celebration of the three feasts of the year. At those times, says Aben Ezra, Jerusalem was like a city, whose children were gathered into her from all the country round about in a time of fear and siege. <sub>Radak.</sub> <sub>Aben Ezra.</sub>

There remains for notice yet another and an entirely different interpretation offered by Rashi. He, as it appears, would translate strictly every word of the Hebrew; *Jerusalem that is builded as a city which is joined with it together.* But *joined* where? and how? Joined in the promise of God and in the deliverance from Egypt. And what is the city to which Jerusalem is compared and which is thus joined with her? Shiloh, the place where the people rested and the tabernacle was set up on the arrival in Canaan.\* Further, the passage where Shiloh is joined with Jerusalem in the phrase of God is Deut. xii. 9: " For ye are not as yet come to the <sub>Rashi.</sub>

\* Joshua xviii. 1.

rest and to the inheritance, which the Lord your God giveth you." Shiloh is the "rest," and Jerusalem—that was builded, I suppose, *as* Shiloh in being an element in the promise of God—is the "inheritance." Under this interpretation I would remark—what really adds colour to it though Rashi does not notice it—that Holy Scripture once again explicitly compares Jerusalem with Shiloh, as 'builded' like it for ultimate destruction. Jeremiah's prophecy (Jer. xxvi. 6) against the Holy City took precisely this form: "Then will I make this house like Shiloh." There may have been a touch of sadness, then, as well as a record of hope in the captives' utterance of a verse which spoke of Jerusalem being *builded as a city which is joined with it together*.

Reverting, however, to the translation adopted by the preceding Hebrew authorities, who see here a reference to the union of the multitudes at Jerusalem for the Feasts—the Christian writers carry us forward to that which those assemblages prefigured, the gathering of the Saints in the heavenly Jerusalem, and not in the Jerusalem which slew the prophets. And here the "union" in the building is unmistakably the union existing between the living stones that "are built upon the foundation of the Apostles and Prophets, Jesus Christ Himself being the chief Corner-stone." (Eph. ii. 20.) The union of all with each, arising (as S. Augustine hints in his treatise on the Trinity*) out of the union of each with God.

The Targum introduces the notion of the "Jerusalem that is above." Targum.

"Jerusalem which is builded in the firmament as a city for which there is union together in the earth."

4. Whither the tribes go up, the tribes of the Lord, unto the testimony of Israel, to give thanks unto the name of the Lord.

The tribes are "the tribes of the Lord," as being the keepers of His commandments. Radak.

The 'going up' of the tribes of Israel to Jerusalem alludes to the festive gatherings there three times a year in obedience to the command of Deut. xvi. 16: "Three times in a year shall all thy males appear before the Aben Ezra.<br>Radak.

---

* De Trin. Lib. iii., cap. 2.

Lord thy God in the place which he shall choose; in the feast of unleavened bread, and in the feast of weeks, and in the feast of tabernacles."

Rashi gives an entirely different turn to the verse.

*Rashi.* The preceding verse, we have seen, involves (according to him) a mention of Shiloh in the phrase, "as a city." He continues this reference in the present verse—"Thither (to Shiloh) the tribes went up," (he preserves the past tense of the Hebrew verb,) when they came from Egypt, and there they set up the tabernacle of the congregation. (Josh. xviii. 1.)

"Unto the testimony of Israel." None of the Hebrew Commentators to whom I have access adopts the word "unto;" which, moreover, has no equivalent in the Hebrew text, and is not necessary for the explanation of the clause. It seems, upon the whole, best to treat the clause (with Radak). as a kind of parenthetic clause, explanatory of what has preceded: "Whither the tribes go up, a testimony to Israel." The command that they should go up three times a year to Jerusalem was, in fact, "a testimony to Israel," that God had made them his chosen people.

A different interpretation is given by Rashi, which is at least ingenious, and curious as a specimen of that microscopic kind of examination to which the Hebrew doctors have submitted the text of Scripture. He makes "a testimony to Israel," an explanation of the unusual form (יָהּ) in which the preceding word LORD stands. The tribes of Israel, it should be observed, are explained to be the tribes not of Jehovah (יהוה) but of Jah (יה)—the tribes, that is, distinguished by י and ה; and he applies the fact thus:—

*Rashi.*

When the tribes came up from Egypt to take possession of the promised land under their prerogative as the chosen people, amongst other taunts that they had to encounter from the nations of the world would be this: that if the Egyptians had exercised a lordship over the bodies of the men of Israel, *à fortiori* they had done the same over those of their wives, and hence the generation that issued from the bondage were nothing but bastards. Accordingly, God said, I testify of them, that they are the children of their reputed fathers; and He put His own name (יה) upon them, one letter (ה) before, and one (י) behind their name :* and this name יה thus becomes a testimony to Israel.

<small>Midrash.</small> The Midrash likewise puts a special emphasis on the clause, *the tribes of the Lord*—not a mixed race, that is, from intermarriage with their oppressors in Egypt.

<small>Targum.</small> The Targum fixes the meaning of the "testimony of Israel "—For thither the tribes went up, the tribes of the Lord, who testified to Israel that His Presence (Shechinah) dwelled amongst them as they went to praise the Name of the Lord.

5. For there‖ are set thrones of judgment,

‖ Heb. do sit. the thrones of the house of David.

---

* He refers to the introduction of the form הָרְאוּבֵנִי, with ה prefixed, and י affixed to the name of "Reuben" in Numb. xxvi. 7, (so too with "Simeon," ib. 14,) when Moses at God's command numbered Israel after the plague. The form in question was not used in the previous numbering of Israel in Numb. i. 17-46. The English reader will notice the recurrence of the formula, "the family of," throughout Numb. xxvi.—*e.g.*, in xxvi. 12, " of Nemuel, the family of the Nemuelites." It is this formula which is the equivalent of the two mystic letters in Hebrew.

"Thrones," in the plural—the throne of the Divine Presence in the Temple, and the throne for the sovereigns of the house of David. So Radak takes it. Aben Ezra sees in the expression an allusion to Solomon and his brethren; or, if the Psalm be referred to the future dispensation, the thrones are for the Christ and his children. *So the Midrash.* All these ideas are combined in Rashi's exposition— the residence of the Shechinah, the judgment of the nations of the world from Jerusalem (in the time, I presume, of the Christ), and the regal thrones for the line of David.

It is but a very easy step from this region of thought to the fully developed view of Christian writers, who see in the "thrones of judgment" either (1) an allusion to the association of the chosen ones with the Christ in the future Judgment ("When the Son of Man shall sit in the throne of his glory, ye also shall sit upon twelve thrones," (S. Matt. xix. 28); or, (2), a reference to those Apostles themselves, who are themselves "thrones," as having God in a special manner resident upon them; who are "there," in Jerusalem, the Church of God; and who are, too, "of *S. Jerome.*

the house of David,"—the flock which has the true and literal David for its shepherd (Ezek. xxxiv. 23),—as being the founders, the rulers, and the guides of that Church.

By the Targum the thrones are assigned to the temple:

*Targum.*

For there (sc. in that place,) are set thrones in Jerusalem, thrones in the temple for the kings of the house of David.

6. Pray for the peace of Jerusalem: they shall prosper that love thee.

The peace of Jerusalem, (which, a Christian may add, is the figure of the Church,) consists in the gathering into her of her children from their Captivity, when the nations of the world shall no more contend for the possession of her.

*Radak.*

*Rashi.*

Pray for her peace, and say unto her, They shall prosper, &c. So Rashi.

"They shall prosper that love thee." The captives themselves, says Radak, are the lovers of Jerusalem.

*Radak.*

In the Targum the form is similar:

Pray for the peace of Jerusalem: they that pity thee shall dwell in tranquillity. <sub>Targum.</sub>

**7. Peace be within thy walls, *and* prosperity within thy palaces.**

The word for "walls" (חֵיל) is explained by Radak to mean the moat around the walls (it is distinguished from "wall" in Lam. ii. 8); while "palaces" (אַרְמְנוֹת) refers to strongholds built within the city. Aben Ezra, it should be observed, pointedly gives the same exposition of the words.

With the Christian interpreters, "Peace" is the Lord Jesus Himself—the Centre of all strength, and the Spring of all virtue (so the Latin Version interprets "walls"), within that Church, of which Jerusalem is the figure.

The Targum follows the Hebrew:

Peace be within thy fortress (*or* thine army), and tranquillity within thy palaces. <sub>Targum.</sub>

**8. For my brethren and companions' sakes, I will now say, Peace *be* within thee.**

Each one of the captives prays that his brethren in captivity may be restored to dwell in Jerusalem. Aben Ezra, however, interprets "brethren and companions" of the Priests and Levites; and thus links the verse closely with the following verse, which mentions "the house of the Lord."

*Radak.*
*Aben Ezra.*

A beautiful turn is given to the verse by S. Jerome, who seems almost to place it in the mouth of our Lord Himself. He is our "Peace;" and, viewed in this light, the verse sounds like a forecast of our Lord's prayer for His "brethren," that "they may be with Me where I am" (S. John xvii. 24); within the earthly Jerusalem first, and then within that of heaven—with Him in the Church Militant now, and with Him, too, in the Church Triumphant hereafter.

*S. Jerome.*

The Targum gives no assistance:

For the sake of my brethren and companions, I will say now, Peace be within thee.

*Targum.*

9. Because of the house of the LORD our God, I will seek thy good.

That is, because of its devastation, if we take the Psalm as being uttered by the captives of Israel. *Radak.*

The Targum is exactly as the Hebrew, save that for "house" it makes the usual Chaldee substitution, "house of the Sanctuary":

Because of the Temple (house of the Sanctuary) of the Lord, I will seek to do good to thee. *Targum.*

## CHAPTER X.

### PSALM CXXIII.

A Song of Degrees.

1. Unto Thee lift I up mine eyes, O Thou that dwellest in the heavens.

"I LIFT up." There are two ways of explaining the use of the singular number, while we apply the Psalm to the Children of the Captivity. Either (1) it is a collective singular, as Radak observes *[Radak.]* that when the Psalm writer speaks the language of the Children of the Captivity, he uses sometimes the singular, and sometimes the plural; or (2) the general sentiment is put into the mouth of some principal person amongst the people who were in captivity or distress. This last is Aben *[Aben Ezra.]* Ezra's mode of explaining it.

"O Thou that dwellest in the heavens," from which all decrees come, says Aben Ezra. The clause expresses (according to Radak) the speaker's sense that he has no hope of help from any but God.

The form יֹשְׁבִי is explained by Radak to be equivalent to יֹשֵׁב. Rashi always remarks upon the redundant י, and elsewhere accumulates several examples of the same use. See Ps. cxiii. 5, 6, 7, 8, 9:
מוֹשִׁיבִי, לְהוֹשִׁיבִי, מְקִימִי, מַשְׁפִּילִי, מַגְבִּיהִי.

Notice the advance in the degrees of Christian perfection. He who began (in the first Psalm of the group) with "calling" unto the Lord; who next "lifted his eyes unto the hills," and then had been gladdened at the thought of entering the house of the Lord—he now ventures to lift his eyes unto the Lord Himself. S. Jerome and others.

The Targum is substantially as the Hebrew, except that it has the enlargement in the inscription, which runs throughout the Gradual Psalms:

A song which was said upon the steps of the abyss. Before Thee I have lifted mine eyes, Who dwellest upon the glorious throne in heaven. Targum.

The Midrash Tehillim gives nothing upon this Psalm.

2. Behold, as the eyes of servants *look* unto the hand of their masters, *and* as the eyes of a maiden unto the hand of her mistress; so our eyes *wait* upon the LORD our God, until He have mercy upon us.

<small>Radak.</small> Servants, masters. A comparison that draws out the completeness of our dependence upon God; servants being supposed to owe their food and maintenance to their masters.

Radak observes that his father, the famous Joseph Kimchi, interpreted the figures of this verse—the eyes of servants toward the hand of masters, and the eyes of a maiden towards the hand of her mistress—of the glance in appeal for pity while under chastisement. So Israel in its distress looked for pity to Him Who was the Author of the visitation.

The leader, who (in Aben Ezra's view) began the Psalm in the singular number, here speaks in the name of himself and the whole people.

It seems to have been reserved for the Christian expositors to assign a separate meaning to the "master" and the "mistress" mentioned here. There is no difficulty in seeing that when our eyes wait upon the Lord, we are "as" servants, and the Lord is "as" their master. But who are the "maiden" and the "mistress" in the next clause? We, they reply, are still the "maiden," that is, the Church; and the "mistress" is Christ, Who is declared by the Apostle (1 Cor. i. 24) to be "the power of God, and the wisdom of God;" power and wisdom being the two attributes which are presented in combination under the word "mistress." *So S. Aug., S. Jerome, and others.*

In the Targum "unto the hand" is represented by "from the hand:"

Behold, as the eyes of servants look from the hand of their masters, and, behold, as the eyes of a maiden look from the hand of her mistress, so our eyes look in the presence of the Lord our God, until He take pity upon us. *Targum.*

The servants who "look from the hand of their masters," are, I presume, servants that are on the alert for any indication or command which the master may give with his hand.

3. Have mercy upon us, O Lord, have

mercy upon us: for we are exceedingly filled with contempt.

The word (רַב) here translated "exceedingly" is explained by both Radak and Aben Ezra as having זְמָן (time) for its substantive understood—"A long time"—in reference to the duration of the Captivity.

The Targum is exactly as the Hebrew:

*Targum.* Take pity on us, O Lord, take pity on us, for we are exceedingly filled with contempt.

The answer which S. Augustine makes to the "contempt" of this verse deserves, from its striking form, to take rank with the story of S. Filippo Neri's famous question to the worldly youth, "What next?" "They are derided who call that happiness which they cannot see with their eyes, and it is said to them, What believest thou, madman? Dost thou see what thou believest? Hath any one returned from the world below, and reported to thee what is going on there? Behold, I see and enjoy what I love. Thou art scorned, because thou dost hope for what thou seest not; and he who seemeth to hold what he seeth, scorneth

*S. Augustine.*

thee. Consider well if he doth really hold it. . . . . What he holdeth slippeth from his hands, or he slippeth away from what he holdeth; either he must needs pass through his property, or it through him. Through whom do his possessions pass? Through him who is ruined while living. Who passeth through his property? He who dieth in his riches; for when he dieth, he carrieth them not away with him to the world below. I have my house, he hath boasted himself. Thou askest, what house of his own? That which my father left me. And whence did he derive this house? My grandfather left it him. Go back even to his great-grandfather, then to his great-grandfather's father, and he can no longer tell their names. Art thou not rather terrified by this thought, that thou seest many have passed through this house, and that none of them hath carried it away with him to his everlasting home? Thy father left it: he passed through it: thus thou also wilt pass by."*

4. Our soul is exceeding filled with the

* S. Aug. Enarr. ad loc. Oxf. Trans.

scorning of those that are at ease, *and* with the contempt of the proud.

As with רַב in the preceding verse, so here Aben Ezra explains the form רַבַּת as a feminine adjective, which has for its substantive מִדַּת זְמָן (measure of time) understood. The same form occurs in the first of the Psalms (cxx. 6).

"The scorning of those that are at ease;" that is, of the nations of the world, who were in peace and quiet, while Israel was in affliction and distress.

<small>Radak.</small>

A grammatical difficulty is discussed here in considerable detail by some of the commentators. It consists in the presence of the definite article with לַעֲג which on that account cannot be in regimen with the following word; although the sense apparently requires that it should be so. Radak says that the word really in regimen is omitted, and that another לַעֲג (without the definite article) must be understood. "Our soul is filled with the scorning—the scorning of those that are at ease." As a similar instance of the definite article attached to a noun apparently (though of course not really) in regimen with another he quotes הָאָרוֹן הַבְּרִית.* (Josh. iii. 14.) This way of explaining the anomaly has the additional weight of the name of Aben Ezra—eminently a grammatical commentator—in its favour.

"The proud." The word גְּאֲיוֹנִים is noticed as a peculiar word by the Hebrew writers. Radak, both in his "Book of Roots," and in his comment upon this passage, thinks that it is equivalent in meaning to the more ordinary גֵּאִים, and that in form it is similar to עֶלְיוֹנִים, being connected with the root גאה the third radical ה being changed into the kindred י and the נ being formative. That, no doubt, is a perfectly philosophical account of the form. But then comes in a strange traditional usage with respect to the word which very materially affects the exegesis of it. The Massorah here remarks in the margin that though written as one word it is read as two לִגְאֵי יָאנִים which Radak translates (for the literal sense) "the proud oppressors."

* This, I presume, must be the example—and it is certainly an apposite one—intended by Radak; though in my copy it is wrongly pointed, and caused me some trouble. Some editors seem to have erased it altogether, in despair.

(cf. Zeph. iii. 1, הַיּוֹנָה)—a sense which lends an additional bitterness to the lamentation of the verse.

<small>Rashi.</small> A mystic sense is found by Rashi in this traditional reading of two words in place of one as written. He renders the clause "the contempt wherewith they despise," (that is, I suppose, the contempt directed at) "the valley of the Doves," (גיא היונים), which last is a name for Jerusalem, connected with the expression about the remnant of Israel in Ezek. vii. 16. "But they that escape of them shall escape, and shall be on the mountains like doves of the valleys."

The Targum makes but a slight change in the Hebrew:

<small>Targum.</small> Our soul is excessively filled with the derision of the prosperous, the despisers and the proud.

The word that I have here translated "despisers," is rendered by Walton "despectorum." Buxtorf seems more correct when he puts it "Contemptores." See Lex. Chald. s. v., fol. 327, ed., 1639.

## CHAPTER XI.

### PSALM CXXIV.

### A Song of Degrees of David.

**1.** If *it had not been* the LORD who was on our side, now may Israel say;

The Psalm is spoken of the rising of their enemies against Israel in their Captivity to destroy them. Radak.

"On our side." So the preposition (לָנוּ) is explained by Radak. Aben Ezra, too, compares the usage in Josh. v. 13. הלנו אתה אם לצרינו.

"Now." On the particle נָא Aben Ezra observes that in the Scripture it is always equivalent to עַתָּה (now.)

The Targum likewise renders it as a particle of time:

A song which was said upon the steps of the abyss. If it had not been the Lord who was our support, Israel now may say. Targum.

The Psalm corresponds to the fifth step in the Christian "ascents." In the preceding Psalm there was an advance upon what had gone before. Here is the next "degree" of virtue—the recognition of God as the source of that advance.

The "Israel" spoken of in this Psalm may be <small>Midrash Tehillim.</small> Israel in the house of Laban, in whose person the Midrash Tehillim imagines the Psalm to be said. There are certainly some of its phrases which acquire an appropriate meaning from being interpreted in this connection.

2. If *it had not been* the LORD who was on our side, when men rose up against us;

"If it had not been the Lord." The repetition of <small>Aben Ezra.</small> the clause from the first verse points to the successive attempts against Israel that were made from day to day in their Captivity.

The Targum introduces here its characteristic substitution of "Word of the Lord" for "Lord:"

If it had not been the Word of the Lord Who <small>Targum.</small> was our Support when the child of man rose up against us.

Upon the change of "Lord" into "Word of the Lord," see the remarks above on Ps. cxxi. 7.

Think of the "Word of the Lord" as the Word which "was made Flesh and dwelt among us;" and then this ancient Targum seems almost to anticipate the Christian application of this Psalm to those who suffer for the Gospel, and to whom literally the "Word of the Lord" was a support when men rose up against them. <small>So S. Augustine.</small>

3. Then they had swallowed us up quick, when their wrath was kindled against us.

"Quick:" alive. Such was their haste to destroy us that they would have violated the common instinct of men, that rejects flesh, in its living state, as an article of food. <small>Radak.</small>

The same idea underlies S. Augustine's exclamation on the phrase, "O inhuman, O cruel men! The Church swalloweth not thus. To Peter it was said, '*Kill and eat,*' not '*Swallow quick.*'" The Church, he explains, fulfils the command to Peter, when she reckoneth no man amongst the true members of Christ except he be slain (in <small>S. Augustine.</small>

his carnal self, of course) first. This sense comes out strongly when the Psalm is put into the mouth of the martyrs. If the Lord had not supported them, they would have yielded to the persecutions of men, who thus would have swallowed them "quick;" swallowed, that is, their true, their spiritual life.

"Then." אֲזַי is said by Radak to be the same as the more usual form אָז.

The Targum is as the Hebrew:

Targum.
"Lo, then whilst alive they had swallowed us; when their wrath was augmented against us."

4. Then the waters had overwhelmed us, the stream had gone over our soul.

"Waters." The Psalmist describes troubles under this figure. The Christian writers concur with the Hebrew authorities in this.

Radak.

"Stream." The form נַחְלָה gives rise to remark in most of the Hebrew writers, because it might easily be mistaken for a feminine. The observations of Aben Ezra are the fullest. He says (with Radak) that here the accent

Aben Ezra.

is on the first syllable; and that there are three Hebrew words with these consonants, which are to be distinguished by the accent and the pointing of the ה; (1) where ח carries ־ַ and the final ה is the mark of the feminine, with the accent of the word of course upon it, meaning "inheritance;" (2), where, as in the present instance, ח carries ־ָ, but the accent is on the last syllable, and the word is therefore a Niphal participle from חָלָה, *Sick*. Rashi, by the way, gives "sickness" for the meaning of the present word; and (3) where ח still has ־ָ, but the accent is on the first syllable, the ה being paragogic (as in לילה *night*), the word being masculine (and therefore accompanied by the masculine form of the verb, עָבַר), which is the present case.

<small>Rashi.</small>

S. Augustine seems to have been the first to illustrate the verse in the waters through which Israel passed safely, while the Egyptians were overwhelmed.

<small>S. Augustine.</small>

The Targum differs slightly from the Hebrew:

"Lo, then the waters had overwhelmed us, sickness had passed over our soul."

<small>Targum.</small>

5. Then the proud waters had gone over our soul.

Two accounts may be given of the dual noun ("waters") being followed by the verb in the singular. It may be an anomalous use, which, nevertheless, has a counterpart in Numb. xix. 13: "Because the water (מֵי) was not sprinkled (זֹרַק) upon him." So Radak takes it; though he offers as an alternative the explanation adopted by Aben Ezra. The latter says that the real subject of the verb here is another נַחַל (stream) understood and carried on from the "stream" of the preceding verse: "The stream of the proud waters had gone over our soul."

<small>Radak.</small>

<small>Aben Ezra.</small>

"The proud waters," that is, says Radak, the waters which overwhelmed us with wickedness and pride.

<small>Radak.</small>

An excellent commentary on the figure is given by the Targum:

"Lo, then there had passed over our soul, a king who is like the proud waters of the sea."

<small>Targum.</small>

6. Blessed *be* the LORD, who hath not given us *as* a prey to their teeth.

A return to the idea of the third verse— "they had swallowed us." <small>Aben Ezra.</small>

For the spiritual sense, it is well to connect this with "the snare of the hunter" of Ps. xci., as applied to him who "goeth about seeking whom he may devour.".

The Targum is nearly as the Hebrew:

"Blessed be the Name of the Lord who hath not delivered us, as a thing to be broken, to their teeth." <small>Targum.</small>

What I have ventured to translate "as a thing to be broken," Walton renders "sicut prædam." The idea, however, in the Chaldee root is rather "break" than "plunder." Buxtorf turns this very passage "Sicut fractionem dentibus eorum."

7. Our soul is escaped as a bird out of the snare of the fowlers: the snare is broken, and we are escaped.

A description of their powerlessness. We had no

*Aben Ezra.* more power to escape from our troubles, than a bird has when it is snared.

The Targum varies the word for "fowlers" in a way that seems almost to anticipate the application of the Psalm to the advance along the "Degrees" of spiritual growth :

*Targum.* "Our soul (is) as the bird (which) has escaped from the snares of hindrances : the snare is broken, and we are escaped."

8. Our help *is* in the name of the LORD, who made heaven and earth.

Though we had no power, God has all power. Hence the clause "Who made Heaven and earth."

The Targum again enlarges "Lord" (see above on Psalm cxxi. 7) :

*Targum.* "Our support is in the Name of the Word of the Lord, who made Heaven and earth."

This is a most important instance of the introduction of the phrase "Word of the Lord;" because it tends to show that the authors of the Targum conceived of the "Word of the Lord" as a Person, and not merely as an attribute, an emanation, or an abstraction. If in their phrase "the Word of the Lord" meant no more than "the declaration of the Lord," "the saying of the Lord," they could hardly have spoken of its "Name."

It should be remembered that the two parts of this verse have secured themselves a place as Versicle and Response in a vast number of the varied services of the Christian Church. See them still surviving in this character in the Confirmation Order of the English Church. Some details upon the subject are given elsewhere in this book, in the dissertation upon the use of the Gradual Psalms in Christian devotion.*

* See Chapter V.

## CHAPTER XII.

**PSALM CXXV.**

A Song of Degrees.

1. They that trust in the LORD *shall be* as Mount Zion, *which* cannot be removed, *but* abideth for ever.

<small>Radak.</small>
<small>Rashi.</small>

THE italics of this translation rest upon the authority of Radak, who connects the somewhat disjointed expressions of the Hebrew precisely in this way. Rashi, too, proposes to supply the necessary links in a similar way: "They that trust in the Lord shall not be moved (he supplies ימוטו), as Mount Zion, which shall not be moved."

*Abideth for ever.* An allusion to the permanence of Zion under the reign of the Christ.

<small>Aben Ezra.</small>

Our translators have correctly represented the

force of the Hebrew word by "abideth." It is a pity they have not preserved the same idea in their rendering of Ps. xxii. 3. "But thou art holy, O thou that inhabitest the praises of Israel." This latter passage Radak quotes as an illustration of the present verse. He sees in it an assertion of the permanence of God. "But thou, O Holy One, continuest—abidest." And the same attribute is here assigned to Zion. יֹשֵׁב<br>Radak.<br>יָשַׁב

The Targum makes one or two additions:

"A Song which was said upon the steps of the abyss. The righteous who trust in the word of the Lord (are) as the Mount of Zion; it shall not be moved, it shall be inhabited for ever." Targum.

On the introduction of "Word of the Lord," see above on Ps. cxxi. 7.

In the degrees of Christian virtue, this Psalm represents the sixth step—the confidence which the Christian places in the Lord. It "teacheth us, while we ascend and raise our minds unto the Lord our God in loving charity and piety, not to fix our gaze upon men who are S. Aug.<br>Enarr. ad<br>loc.

prosperous in the world, with a happiness that is false and unstable, and altogether seductive; where they cherish nothing save pride, and their heart freezeth up against God, and is made hard against the shower of His grace, so that it beareth not fruit."

*Midrash.* The Midrash Tehillim may be said to treat this as a Psalm of individual security amid general disaster. At the time when the Temple was destroyed a decree went forth against the houses of the just, to destroy them, according to Isaiah's saying: "Of a truth many houses shall be desolate, even great and fair, without inhabitant." (Isa. v. 9) Yet here in the Psalm we have a prophecy that, in the case of the righteous who trust in the Lord, this judgment should be reversed, and that God would bring them back to their homes again.

2. *As* the mountains *are* round about Jerusalem, so the LORD *is* round about his people from henceforth, even for ever.

The protection afforded by the mountains had not,

Radak remembers, always been complete; for enemies had captured the city and ruled in it; but with the Lord in the midst of His people, they will be absolutely safe, so that no enemy shall approach them, "from henceforth even for ever." *Radak.*

Aben Ezra's remark is good as explaining the singular position of "Jerusalem," which stands by itself at the beginning of the verse. *Aben Ezra.* According to him, Jerusalem forms the subject of the entire verse. She has the mountains round about her, and the Lord round about His people, in the midst of her (the Divine Presence in the Sanctuary); therefore she is permanently secure. It would be quite possible to preserve the exact form of the Hebrew clauses, and yet make good English. The word "Jerusalem," it should be observed, is in the Hebrew marked off by a strong accent from its attendant clause. "Jerusalem—mountains are round about her; and the Lord is round about His people." The Targum indeed seems to contemplate some such form:

"Jerusalem, the mountains are around her: and the word of the Lord is round His people, from now and for ever." *Targum.*

The arrangement of the text in the Latin versions is different from ours, so that it is difficult exactly to adopt the interpretation which the Latin writers suggest. S. Augustine takes occasion here to enlarge upon the significance of the term "mountains" in Holy Scripture. It stands as a figure of the Saints, and specially of the preachers of truth, whether Angels, or Apostles, or Prophets. "They are the mountains who are enlightened by God; and they are enlightened in the first place, that light may descend from them into the valleys." Thus interpreted,—and, as Dionysius observes, it is scarcely true to restrict the expressions of these two verses to the literal Jerusalem or Zion, which has been several times moved, captured, and destroyed—the name "mountain" applied to the Saints furnishes one more little point of likeness to their Lord, Who is Himself described by Daniel as a "mountain." "And the stone that smote the image became a great mountain."*

It does not indeed seem altogether possible here to preserve that application, which in many passages of the Psalms is so apposite, of "Zion" to the Church

* Dan. ii. 35.

militant, and of "Jerusalem" to the Church triumphant; but if we think of Jerusalem in this latter special sense, it is at least true that just as perpetuity is one feature of the Lord's protecting His people on earth, so it is a feature of the rest of the Saints "standing about" the Church in Heaven, that it shall be a rest "even for ever."

3. For the rod of|| the wicked shall not rest upon the lot of the righteous; lest the righteous put forth their hands unto iniquity.

|| Heb. *wickedness.*

*The Righteous.* This will be best interpreted by a reference to the prophecy of Isaiah:* "And it shall come to pass, that he who is left in Zion, and he that remaineth in Jerusalem, shall be called holy." The righteous, the holy, then are the rescued from Captivity, whether literal or spiritual; and the lot of the righteous is the city of their abode. In that city there shall be no place for the rod—the sceptre, the symbol of the strength and might—of the wicked.

Radak.

\* Isa. iv. 3.

In applying the clause to the heavenly Jerusalem of the future, notice our Lord's declaration: "They shall gather out of His kingdom all things that offend." (S. Matt. xiii. 41.)

*The Rod.* The leading idea of the word seems to lie, according to Radak's view, in chastisement and punishment—that chastisement, namely, which the very presence of wickedness in their midst inflicts upon the people of God. It is susceptible, however, of another meaning. Aben Ezra appears to see in it the symbol of possession. To the whole verse indeed he gives a much wider scope. *The righteous* are, of course, the Israel of God. But the *lot of the righteous* includes nothing less than all the earth, the same lot that is spoken of in Ezekiel xlv. 1: "Moreover, when ye shall divide by lot the land (rather, the earth) for inheritance, . . .": and the drift of the whole clause is that the wicked shall have no permanent inheritance in the earth.

<small>Aben Ezra.</small>

Either of the two senses of "rod," whether sceptre or scourge, enables us to see in the verse an encouragement to that confidence in God, which is the specific theme of the Psalm—an encouragement to look forward to the "restitution," the rectification of all things—an answer to that most unsettling of all the anomalies of life, which a Psalm has phrased: "I do also see the ungodly in such prosperity." The answer is that it shall not be always so. Their rod shall not "rest." This consideration may check the righteous from being tempted to put forth *their* hands unto iniquity. And so S. Augustine takes it.

*Lest the righteous put forth their hands unto iniquity.* Iniquity is contagious. The wicked should have no contact with the people of God, lest these latter should learn their ways. Both Radak and Aben Ezra refer to the reason which God gave Israel for the utter eradication of the Canaanites. It was, "that they teach you not to do after all their abominations." (Deut. xx. 18). They did not utterly destroy these nations, says Radak, and so they stumble themselves: but in the future dispensation—including probably in the term both the time of the Christ, and the world to come—there will be no stumblingblock inviting to wickedness, for all the evil shall be destroyed.

By way of addition to the Hebrew, the Targum

only limits the meaning of "iniquity" at the close of the verse:

> "For the rod of wickedness shall not rest upon the lot of the righteous, that the righteous put not forth their hands unto falsehood."

<small>Targum.</small>

This limitation of "iniquity" to "falsehood," may possibly be due to the remembrance of calumny, which appears to have constituted a chief element in the sufferings of Israel under the Captivity.

4. Do good, O LORD, unto *those that be* good, and to *them that are* upright in their hearts.

*Good*, that is the good in act, as well as the upright in heart. *Do good* to them; give them, that is (says a mediæval commentator) temporal things for sustentation, spiritual things for justification, and celestial for remuneration.

<small>Radak.</small>

The Targum is exactly as the Hebrew:

> "Do good, O Lord, unto those that are good and upright in their heart."

<small>Targum.</small>

The ancient Hebrew Midrash gives a curious enlargement of the verse. It seems to imagine the Psalmist speaking in the person of one who lived before the time of Moses, and  *Midrash.* who contemplated the "good" that should accrue to Israel from the giving of the Law. It paraphrases thus:—"There shall come one who is good, and he shall receive good from the good for the good."

One who is good—that is, Moses; as it is written of him, "And when she saw him that he was a goodly child ... (Heb. that he was good)." (Exod. ii. 2).

Receive good—that is, the Law; as it is written of it, "I give you good doctrine, forsake ye not my Law." (Prov. iv. 2.)

From the good, that is, from God; as it is said, "The Lord is good to all." (Ps. cxlv. 9.)

For the good, that is, for Israel, according to the present verse.

5. As for such as turn aside unto their crooked ways, the LORD shall lead them forth with the workers of iniquity: *but* peace *shall be* upon Israel.

That is, even in Israel itself, if any are perverse in their ways they shall have no inheritance amongst their brethren, but shall share the fate of the wicked in the preceding verse. So Radak.

*Turn aside.* Aben Ezra implies that the participle is to be taken transitively, as the same word is taken in Mal. iii. 5, "That *turn aside* the stranger from his right, and fear not me, saith the Lord of hosts." Then he says there is an ellipsis of בְּ with עֲקַלְקַלּוֹתָם (crooked ways), just as there is in 2 Chron. xxxiv. 30: "And he read in their ears all the words of the book of the Covenant that was found *in* the house of the Lord" (הַנִּמְצָא בֵּית י'). The whole clause would thus stand, "As for such as turn people aside by (or, in) their crooked ways."

Aben Ezra.

*Peace shall be upon Israel.* When the wicked shall be thus rooted out from their midst, then shall there be peace to the residue of Israel, and they shall "lie down and none shall make them afraid."

Radak. So also Aben Ezra.

The Targum appears to refer the verse to the future severance of the just from the unjust:

"But those, who turn after their own perversities,

he shall lead into Gehenna; their portion (shall be) with the workers of falsehood. Peace upon Israel." <sub>Targum.</sub>

Notice again the specification of falsehood as the particular form of what the sacred text calls simply "iniquity." See the remark on the Targum of Psalm cxxv. 3.

## CHAPTER XIII.

### PSALM CXXVI.

A Song of Degrees.

**1. When the LORD turned again the Captivity of Zion, we were like them that dream.**

SPOKEN, says Aben Ezra, like the former Psalm in the person of the Captives, returned from Babylon. So likewise says Rashi.

*Like them that dream.* Two ways have been suggested for explaining this comparison. Either (1) the distress of our Captivity became as a dream that has passed away, in the excess of joy that we had upon restoration. This is the interpretation given by Radak, and adopted by him from his father, the celebrated Joseph Kimchi. Or (2) so great a marvel was our restoration, that the imagination of waking man

[margin: Radak.]
[margin: Joseph Kimchi.]

never conceived the like: it belongs only to the extravagance of the dreamer. Aben Ezra interprets it in this latter way. In either case, the gist of the verse is to express the exuberance of their joy in thinking of their restoration.

<small>Aben Ezra.</small>

This sentiment is well conveyed by the Targum, though it is expressed by an entirely different figure.

"A song which was sung upon the steps of the abyss. When the Lord turneth the Captivity of Zion, then should we be like sick people who are cured."

<small>Targum.</small>

This, I imagine, nearly expresses the tense-relation between the two verbs in the Chaldee, the verb ("turneth") in the protasis being in the imperfect tense, while "should be," in the apodosis is in the past.

In its Christian aspect the Psalm represents the seventh of the "degrees" in our ascent to the Jerusalem that is above. The Christian's exultation at his deliverance from the spiritual Captivity of Sin.

The Church on earth is well represented under the usual figure of "Zion," as distinguished from

"Jerusalem," the Church above. The Captivity in which men were held by the devil was "turned," first of all, when Christ took man's flesh. Such appears to be the channel of S. Augustine's thought. It was "turned" again in a sense which still more exactly fits certain expressions in the Psalm, in the Resurrection of our Lord. A beautiful light is thrown upon many of the verses, if we put the Psalm specially into the mouth of those who had been "sad" (S. Luke xxiv. 17) at His removal in the Crucifixion, and then "became consoled"—so the ancient Latin gives the word for "dream,"—had their mouth filled with joy, and their tongue with exultation when they found that His Resurrection was an accomplished fact. The latter verses of the Psalm are a true expression of thoughts which have been carried on from the Resurrection of the Lord to the resurrection and reward of the redeemed in Him.

2. Then was our mouth filled with laughter, and our tongue with singing: then said they among the heathen, The LORD hath done great things for them.

A difficulty, which has been much discussed, lies in the tenses of the verbs. In the former verse, the verb (הָיִינוּ) was in the past tense. Here they are in the other tense,* which commonly represents uncompleted action, either future or imperfect. The latter of them is actually taken as a future (of course with a mystical intention) in the Vulgate, Tunc dicent inter gentes. Any historic interpretation of the verse, however, plainly requires that the verbs be here, as in the preceding verse, substantially in the past tense. The question is whether the usage of the Scriptural language elsewhere will at all justify us in so taking them. Sometimes, indeed, it has been proposed to take them in a kind of aoristic sense, indicating an act that might be done now and again —a method of explanation which is strictly faithful to the instinct of a tense that speaks of *uncompleted*†

* יְמַלֵּא יֹאמְרוּ

† This is the character which Ewald gives of the second tense of the Semitic verb. I say "the Semitic verb" rather than "the Hebrew verb;" for the same pair of tenses exists in Arabic, Syriac, and Chaldee, as well as in Hebrew. Some grammarians call it *imperfect*, while others call it *future*. Ewald's words about its function are :—

Das imperfectum beschreibt das unvollendete sei es das nochnichtseiende oder das werdende, erst in erfüllung gehende;

action. It might then stand in English idiom, Then would our mouth be filled with laughter; that is, it has been habitually so filled—whenever we have thought of the deliverance in question, and will be so filled again: then would men say among the heathen; they have said it before and will say it again. Such a mode of accounting for the tenses here is by no means unphilosophical; but there seems to be really no reason for resorting to it. The strangeness of the tenses here has, I believe, a significance of its own, as I have pointed out further on. But the usage of the holy tongue will bear us out in boldly taking them as past in sense, though not in form. One very famous parallel there is. "Then sang Moses and the children of Israel this song unto the Lord." אָז יָשִׁיר־מֹשֶׁה. (Ex. xv. 1.) There can be no doubt that the verb here is past in sense, though not so in form.

The whole difficulty has been thought to be solved by the remark of Aben Ezra on this latter  Aben Ezra.

daher aber auch weiter das was erst werden solle d.i. das nach dem gedanken des redenden von etwas anderem erst abhängige. Ausführliches Lehrbuch der Hebräischen Sprache des alten Bundes. 7th ed. Göttingen, 1863, p. 352.

passage; "It is the usage of the holy tongue to put the future for the past with the particle אָז : *Then did Solomon build* (יִבְנֶה). 1 Kings xi. 7. *Then spake Joshua* (יְדַבֵּר). Josh. x. 12. *Then Moses severed* (יַבְדִּיל). Deut. iv. 41." I have shown, at pages 64, 65, by a list of all the passages, where this combination of tense and particle is found, that the alleged usage is by no means uniformly observed in Scripture. But Aben Ezra's brief series of examples is, I consider, of great importance to us, as showing that the tense-translations (apparently so anomalous) which the Christian Church has adopted, Latin as well as English, can be justified by the observable usages of Hebrew grammar.

The truth of the matter seems to be this. The combination of a *future* tense with the attendant features of *past* narration indicates a double meaning. It *was* true in the past that our mouth was filled with laughter, and it *will* be true in the future that our mouth is to be filled with laughter. Hence we find some of the Hebrew authorities (as Aben Ezra above) insisting upon the past sense of the verbs, while others insist upon the future sense of them. This latter is done by the doctors of the Midrash. There

Simon ben Jochai (who is older than S. Jerome, and probably even older than the first Latin Version of the Scriptures) is quoted as giving a mystical or future interpretation of the verse before us. "It is forbidden," he says, "to man to fill his mouth with laughter in this world; for it is said, Then shall our mouth be filled with laughter, and our tongue with singing." This kind of fact is, I consider, of great importance to us; because it shows that when the Christian Doctors began to write commentaries, giving mystical or Christian senses to the Old Scriptures, they were doing nothing new, but were only adopting a method that had been always traditionally employed by the Doctors of the Hebrew nation.

<small>Midrash Tehillim.</small>

Rashi, on the passage in Exodus, endeavours to explain the anomaly by an ellipsis (it entered into the mind of Moses that *he should sing*), and—what is perhaps of more value—enumerates other passages where the same phænomenon presents itself, a verb in the future (imperfect) tense in the midst of historic narrative having unmistakably a past meaning. Such instances will be found in Josh. x. 12: אָז יְדַבֵּר יְהוֹשֻׁעַ לַיהוָֹה. And in 1 Kings

<small>Rashi.</small>

vii. 8 : וּבַיִת יַעֲשֶׂה לְבַת פַּרְעֹה. Amongst the moderns, Delitzsch, following Aben Ezra, though without quoting him, appears to make all depend upon the presence of the particle אָז and observes that in past narrative the future after אָז has always a past sense.*

I should be unwilling to leave this subject without noticing the confirmation which this tense-anomaly appears to give to the mystical interpretation of the Scripture. In the passage of Exodus, for example, a tense which is confessedly future is used to describe a fact which is unmistakably past. Why is this? It seems to be in a measure explained when we learn that there is a meaning in the Law of Moses beyond itself; that the words do something more than describe a mere historic fact that Moses sang the song; and that they are written "for our sakes;" that they have an interpretation in Christ and Christians as well as in Moses and Israelites—a future meaning as

* His words are ". . . denn zwar hat das Fut. nach אָז in Zukunftgeschichtlichen Zusammenhängen wie (Ps.) 96, 12. Zef. 3, 9 Futurbedeutung, immer aber Imperfektbed. nachdem einmal vergangenheitsgeschichtlicher Ton angeschlagen. Ex. 15, 1. Josh. 8, 30, 10, 12. 1 K. 11, 7, 16, 21. 2 K. 15, 16. Iob. 38, 21."

well as a past one—a meaning, (as Rashi in substance puts it) in that song which those who have been redeemed from a Captivity sorer than that of Egypt shall sing in the day of resurrection and restitution of all things. It has been the fashion to deride this explanation of the tense in Exodus as one of the "Conceits of the Rabbins;" but I cannot refrain from reminding Christian readers that it seems at least to have found its way into the New Testament, which tells us (Rev. xv. 3)—in a phrase that is not easy to explain apart from this connection—that the redeemed, standing on the Sea of Glass, "sing the Song of Moses, the servant of God, and the Song of the Lamb."

The Targum puts the verbs in the same tense as the Hebrew—the imperfect:

Targum. "Then would our mouth be filled with laughter and our tongue with praise: then would they say, among the peoples, The Lord hath abounded in doing good with them."

3. The LORD hath done great things for us; *whereof* we are glad.

The nations saw their joy and exclaimed, What a miracle was that deliverance! Yes, replies Israel in this verse, the joy that you see in us is caused by this miracle that God has performed with us. Radak.

The Targum is exactly as the Hebrew:

"The Lord hath abounded in doing good with us; we were glad." Targum.

4. Turn again our captivity, O LORD, as the streams in the south.

*Turn again.* The language of Israel while they were in Captivity. So Radak.

*As streams in the south.* A south land is a Scriptural figure for a parched, waterless land. Thus (Judges i. 15) Achsah, the daughter of Caleb, "said unto him, Give me a blessing: Radak. So, too, Rashi and Aben Ezra.
for thou hast given me a south land: give me also springs of water." Just as the introduction of water into such a land would renew and fertilize it, so restoration from their bondage would refresh and gladden the captive Israel.

The difficulty which seems to lie in the verse is

this: that here they seem to pray for a deliverance from Captivity, whereas in the first verse they had used language which implies that such deliverance was already past. But the difficulty is not a real one. It may only indicate, as S. Augustine says it does, that the speakers looked forward to another deliverance—the spiritual and greater one—beyond that which they had already experienced in the literal Babylon. It might, indeed, be fairly said that the seeming difficulty actually *demands* the spiritual interpretation of the Psalm; because, without it the difficulty must be left, real and unexplained.

*S. Augustine.*

This exposition is exactly conveyed by the paraphrase of the Targum:

"Turn, O Lord, our Captivity, as the earth is turned when springs of water burst out in the drought."

*Targum.*

The Hebrew Midrash applies the verse to Jacob, who sowed the blessings (I suppose, the blessings he received from his father in Esau's stead, for in the blessings which he gave to his sons there is no mention of tears) in tears. He reaped in joy, according to the blessing, "Therefore

*Midrash Tehillim.*

God give thee of the dew of heaven and the fatness of the earth, and plenty of corn and wine." (Gen. xxvii. 28.)

5. They that sow in tears shall reap in joy.

A continuation of the comparison in the preceding verse. It describes, in fact, the action of people in a parched land which receives water. They sowed seed in anxiety and dejection, because there seemed but little chance that the seed would spring up. Yet such people would reap in joy, because of the yield which the unexpected waters had produced. So Rashi takes it literally. *Rashi.*

Radak adds to this a mystic interpretation of the figure. The sowing on the part of Israel is the keeping of the Commandments of God. *Radak.*
The harvest which should be reaped is blessing sent from God. They who had kept his Commandments in the tears and distress of the Captivity, should afterwards be rewarded with blessing in the joy of restoration. The same mystic interpretation of the sowing is given by Aben Ezra. *Aben Ezra.*

Closely akin to this is the mystic interpretation given by S. Augustine, who applies the figures of this and the following verse to the sorrows of the just in the present life, and the harvest of joy which such shall reap in the life to come. See S. Augustine's Sermon (Psalmus qui cantatur Domino) on this text—De Sanctis, 45. The verse seems almost an anticipation of the Apostle's phrase about those who "sow to the spirit" in tears, and "reap in joy" everlasting. (Gal. vi. 8.)

*S. Augustine.*

The Targum makes no material change:

"They who sow in tears shall reap in praise."

*Targum.*

6. He that goeth forth and weepeth, bearing precious seed, shall doubtless come again with rejoicing, bringing his sheaves *with him.*

The hope of the Captives still expressed under the figure of the seed. If Israel sowed the precious seed of righteousness with tears in their exile, then they should reap it with joy, when their future reward was paid them. So it is explained substantially by Rashi, Aben Ezra, and Radak.

*His sheaves.* Aben Ezra takes it differently. The pronoun, in his view, refers to the seed—*its sheaves*, the sheaves which it will bear—rather than to the reaper.

*Precious.* There is a difference of opinion amongst the Hebrew writers as to the meaning of this word מֶשֶׁךְ. Radak, in his Hebrew Lexicon (Book of Roots), observes, that (excepting where it is used as a proper name—Meshech) the word occurs only twice in the Scriptures, viz., here and in Job xxviii. 18, where the Authorised Translation has "price." In both instances, he says it means "precious,"—" Wisdom is more precious than rubies," he would translate the passage in Job—and he gives the more common adjective יקר as the synonym of it. On the other hand, Aben Ezra—with whom Radak respectfully disagrees—explains that the word in question means a vessel for holding seed. As the seed is, in his interpretation, the righteousness and obedience of Israel, so the "vessel" must apparently be the souls and bodies of the Israelites themselves, in which the

Radak.

Aben Ezra.

"seed" was, as it were, contained. This interpretation of the word has been adopted by some modern writers, under the apparently mistaken idea that it derives some countenance from the analogy of a similar word in Syriac. It seems, however, to labour under the fatal disadvantage of being inapplicable to the passage in Job, where, I observe, the learned Aben Ezra passes the word over entirely without remark.

There is yet a third sense of the word for "precious"—not wholly alien to that adopted by Aben Ezra—which is given by the Targum. This connects it with a root which means *to draw:*

"Going, he shall go with weeping, bearing a draught"—so the word literally is—" of seed. Coming, he shall come with praise, when he shall carry his sheaves." [Targum.]

Christian writers have seen in the verse a picture of the contrast between the trouble of the present life and the joy of the future. "We fast," says S. Cyril of Jerusalem,[*] "refraining from both wine and meat, not hating them as abominations, but waiting for our reward; that, looking higher than

[*] S. Cyr. Jerus.: Catech. iv. 27.

things of sense, we may enjoy a spiritual and rational table, and that now having sown in tears, we may reap in joy in the world to come."

And, finally, the Psalm which begins with "dream" and ends with "sheaves" invites us to think of Joseph; Joseph, "in whom" acccording to S. Ambrose's beautiful application,* "there was revealed the future Resurrection of the Lord Jesus, to Whom both His eleven disciples did obeisance when they saw Him gone into Galilee, and to whom all the Saints shall on their resurrection do obeisance, bringing forth the fruit of good works, as it is written, 'He shall doubtless come again with rejoicing, bringing his sheaves with him.'"

* De Joseph Patriarcha Liber. c. 2.

## CHAPTER XIV.

**PSALM CXXVII.**

A Song of Degrees for Solomon.

1. Except the LORD build the house, they labour in vain that build it: except the LORD keep the city, the watchman waketh *but* in vain.

*For Solomon.* It appears to be generally conceded that the preposition here (ל) is to be rendered "for" and not "by" or "of," as in the frequent heading, "A Psalm *of* David," where, however, the preposition is the same. Both Radak and Aben Ezra give as its equivalent a preposition (בַּעֲבוּר) which means "on account of," "for the sake of," "in reference to." There are other passages where this is unquestionably the sense of the preposition that occurs in the present heading. For example, Deut. xxxiii. 8: "And of (ל) Levi he said, Let thy Thummim and thy Urim be with thy Holy One." Or, better still, Gen. xx. 13: "I said unto her, This is thy kindness which thou shalt show unto me; at every place whither we shall come, say of (ל) me, He is my brother."

Rashi interprets the Psalm under the light of a Hebrew belief in the Talmud, that upon the same day Solomon laid the foundation of the Temple and made affinity (1 Kings iii. 1.) with Pharaoh, by taking his daughter to wife, which, he intimates, was a violation of the command in Deut. vii. 3. This association of wickedness with church-building is the explanation of God's saying in Jer. xxxii. 31: "This city hath been to me as a provocation of mine anger and of my fury, *from the day that they built it*, even unto this day:" and David, by the inspiration of the Holy Spirit, foreseeing this association, spoke the present Psalm with reference to it, that the labour of the builders would be vain, except the Lord built the house, except the builders themselves acted in accordance with the Law of God.

*Rashi.*

The immediate occasion of the Psalm was, according to Aben Ezra, Nathan's announcement to David that not he but his son should

*Aben Ezra.*

build the Temple. This criticism falls in exceedingly well with the language of the Psalm. The first verse sounds not unlike acquiescence in a message, that must have inflicted grievous disappointment upon the king; that the Lord, in fact, was not with him in building the house himself; while the promise that his son should build, in a measure explains the transition of the poet's thought to the blessing and strength of children in the last three verses of the Psalm.

Radak also concurs in this exposition of the Psalm. His treatment of it, however, is worth especial notice; because it presents a detailed example of three out of the four lines of scientific interpretation known to Christian commentators. He says explicitly that the Psalm admits of three several interpretations: it may be interpreted of Solomon, as above; or, it may be interpreted of the Christ; or again, it may be interpreted of the children of the world. In other words, he formulates here what are technically known to Christian theologians as the historic, the allegoric, and the tropological methods of interpretation. The historic bearing of the Psalm points to the building of the Temple. In the allegoric interpretation of it with reference to the reign of the Christ, the "house" is still the Temple, and the "city" is Jerusalem. The kingship of the Christ will make the city secure; but in the meantime, until the Christ appears, it passes from the hands of one enemy into those of another: one builds it; the next destroys it: and so it must be in continual sequence, because the building and the watching of such is not pleasing to God. Finally, and tropologically, the building of the house may be interpreted of the establishment of any of the kingdoms of the world, according to the figure in Nathan's message to David : "Furthermore I tell thee that the Lord will build thee an house;"* and the Psalmist thus declares that no king can make a kingdom secure to himself and his posterity, except in accordance with the pleasure of God.

The Targum appears to take Solomon for the author of the Psalm:

"A song which was said upon the steps of the abyss by the hand of Solomon. If the Word of the Lord do not build the city, labourers in vain are the architects of it: if the

*Targum.*

\* 1 Chron. xvii. 10.

Word of the Lord be not a guard of the city of Jerusalem, in vain a guard waketh."

Viewed as one of the "Degrees" in Christian virtue, the ninth, the Psalm is directed against self-reliance.

Nor, if we adopt that sense of the preposition in the heading—which we have seen the Hebrew will very well bear—"for," "to," "in reference to" Solomon, must we forget that in the Song of Songs the Christ is explicitly called "Solomon." I say explicitly called Solomon—just as in Ezekiel* He is explicitly called David, the literal David having been dead hundreds of years in Ezekiel's time—explicitly called Solomon in the Song of Songs, because there are phrases in that book which hardly admit of any but a grotesque explanation, if they are to be restricted to the literal Solomon. Well then, by the "house," the Temple of Solomon's building, we are instinctively reminded of what S. Augustine puts so prominently forward—that the Lord Jesus spake of His Human Body under this very figure: "Destroy this Temple, and in three days I will raise it up."† And thus by the opening phrase

*S. Augustine.*

* *E.g.*, Ezek. xxxiv. 23.    † S. John ii. 19.

of the Psalm a line of thought is opened, which is felt to be not out of place in a Psalm which goes on later to speak of the "Fruit of the Womb." It was on the resurrection morning at the holy tomb that the watchmen woke in vain, expecting to find this "Temple" which the Lord *had* built for Himself, which they had intended to destroy, and which He had designed to "raise up," still in their unholy keeping.

The moral interpretation is given by the Hebrew Midrash. The instruments in God's hand for "keeping the city" are the scribes and teachers of the Law of God.  <small>Midrash Tehillim.</small>

2. *It is* vain for you to rise up early, to sit up late, to eat the bread of sorrows; *for* so he giveth his beloved sleep.

In the former verse we were taught the futility, apart from the help of God, of the efforts of builders and watchers in the city: here the same truth is extended to the labours of the traders and the money-getters.  <small>Aben Ezra.</small>

The whole verse, however, seems to receive the

most harmonious interpretation possible by referring every one of its clauses to the possession of the kingdom. [Radak.] The Psalmist had begun with the thought of the building of the Temple by Solomon: in this verse his thoughts have passed to Solomon's occupancy of the throne of Israel, and the several efforts that were made to defeat his succession.

*Rise up early.* An allusion to the rebellion of Absalom, of whom it is said (2 Sam. xv. 2), [Radak.] "And Absalom rose up early—the same word—and stood beside the way of the gate." *Sit up late*, or rather, *ye who are late in sitting;* sitting, that is, upon the throne of Israel. A reference to Adonijah, who deferred making any claim to the throne of David, until the latter was prostrated by extreme age.\*

*To eat the bread of sorrows*, or more strictly, *eaters of the bread of sorrows.* We may interpret this by the light of the phrase in Gen. iii. 17: "*In sorrow shalt thou eat of it*," where the word for "sorrow" is substantially the same as the word here in the Psalm. The phrase thus points to the anxious effort

\* 1 Kings i. 5.

—analogous to that which man must make for his own sustenance—the anxious, yet futile, effort to secure the crown, that was made by these would-be supplanters of the line of Solomon.

*His beloved*—Solomon, that is. The word for "beloved" is that from which Solomon's name of Jedidiah is constructed: "And he called his name Jedidiah,‖ because of the Lord." (2 Sam. xii. 25.) ‖ That is, *Beloved of the Lord.*

*So*, that is to say, in accordance with His purpose indicated in the foregoing clauses—His purpose of defeating the efforts of those who would supplant Solomon. They made efforts to get the kingdom; and the efforts were vain. To His beloved on the contrary He gave *sleep*, repose, exemption from effort: and he entered upon the kingdom without labour of his own, because his was a house that the Lord had built.

There is a self-consistency here which, to my mind, very strongly recommends this as the historic interpretation of a verse that has puzzled some of the English and German commentators not a little. The Allegoric interpretation too, in this way of taking it, gives us a beautiful image of the certainty of the progress of the Gospel in the teeth of oppositions of every kind. Solomon, His beloved, is then of course the Christ, the "Beloved Son"* of the Gospels; and the present verse speaks of the establishment of the Messiah's kingdom, notwithstanding all the efforts of various enemies to prevent it. "He that dwelleth in Heaven shall laugh them to scorn" (Ps. ii. 4); and compare the second Psalm throughout.

It was upon the Cross that God gave "His Beloved" sleep.

The unusual form שֵׁנָא with א as its final is pronounced by both Radak and Aben Azra to be equivalent to the more ordinary form שֵׁנָה with ה.

The general sense of these clauses is well put by Aben Ezra. The success of everything depends upon the decree of Heaven. Without that decree human effort is vain. And by virtue of that decree (*so*)—not in proportion to human design, or pleasure, or effort—but by His own decree alone God giveth to the man that loveth Him (*His beloved*) sleep, the sweet reward of effort.

An excellent interpretation of the several clauses is given by the Targum:

* S. Mark i. 11.

"In vain do ye toil for yourselves, who are early in the morning in making for yourselves plunder, who delay and sit in harlotry, who eat the victuals of the poor, upon which they have toiled: suitably and rightly the Lord will give to His beloved sleep." Targum.

**3. Lo, children *are* an heritage of the Lord: *and* the fruit of the womb *is his* reward.**

A "goodly heritage" was accorded to David in the person of the child Solomon, the builder of "the house." Radak.

A curious turn is given by Rashi to this part of the Psalm. The "beloved" of God is the man who drives sleep from his eyes that he may Rashi. exercise himself in the Law of God. And the clause "So he giveth his beloved sleep," is explained to mean that God sustains him who thus repels sleep. The "children" of the present verse are the scholars and pupils whom such a man brings up, and who are to him as children. The last clause Rashi then takes without the pronoun "his" inserted in the italics of the Authorised Version: "A reward is the fruit of the belly;" that is, the fruit of the Law which is in the heart. He interprets it by the light of Prov. xxii. 18: "It is a pleasant thing if thou keep them in thy belly; they shall withal be fitted in thy lips." From Rashi's observations on this passage in Proverbs, I gather that he understands the "fruit" to be words. The reward of having the Law of God treasured in the heart is, that man is found with right words upon his lips.

The Latin writers have commented upon a somewhat different translation of the verse, which hardly Latin Writers. accords with the vowels of the Hebrew text. Still, the spirit of their interpretation is not inapplicable even to our translation. Their Version might stand thus in English:—*Lo, the inheritance of the Lord, even sons, is the reward of the fruit of the womb.* The fruit of the womb is Jesus of Nazareth, born of the womb of the Virgin; and the inheritance of the Lord are the members of His Church. So S. Augustine, S. Jerome, Cassiodorus, and Hugo of S. Caro.

One of the senses of "children of the youth" in the following verse—the Apostles—would suggest that the "inheritance" here spoken of is the *Clerus*, for which we pray: "And bless thine heritage"—the whole body of Apostolic ministers, whose function it is to carry forward the stream of Apostolic doctrine and use.

The Hebrew seems to imply that children are an heritage belonging to the Lord, and not an heritage given by the Lord, as most English readers appear to take it. The Targum likewise bears this out:

"Lo, a possession of the Lord are legitimate sons; a reward of good deeds are the children of the womb." *Targum.*

4. As arrows *are* in the hand of a mighty man; so *are* children of the youth.

Solomon, the builder of the house, was born to David towards the close of life, and from him therefore David had received no strength or help while he lived. Hence he reflects upon the support rendered to a man by children born to him while he is yet young—children who are as great an aid to him as are arrows to a mighty man. David had also, Radak observes, "children of youth," sons who were wise and power- *Radak.*

ful men, born to him in earlier life, of whom it is said (2 Sam. viii. 18), "And David's sons were princes," and who were all good to him, except Absalom and Adonijah.

S. Jerome discusses the Hebrew of this verse and the several translations that have been offered of it. He interprets the "children of youth," to be Christians, and quotes two examples in which God speaks of his own under the images of archery—(Zech. ix. 13, and Isa. xlix. 2). The discussion, which is quite worth consulting, will be found in the Letter to Marcella, beginning *Beatus Pamphilus Martyr.*

*S. Jerome.*

The curious phrase of the Vulgate "filii excussorum," as the equivalent of "children of the youth," almost defies reasonable interpretation. It might be rendered either "sons of those who shake off," or, passively, "sons of those shaken off." The passive participle in the Septuagint,* from which the Latin translation was made, seems to indicate that the latter sense was the one intended. S. Augustine, however, mentions that the former view had been taken by some; "those who shake off," being a

\* LXX. ἐκτετιναγμένων.

phrase for the Apostles, who were directed in a certain case to "shake off the dust from their feet;"* while their "sons" are the members of the Christian Church, which their preaching was the instrument of calling into existence.

Another interpretation makes the Apostles themselves the "sons of those who are shaken out," the descendants and inheritors, that is, of the Prophets, whose veiled meaning is explained, or "shaken out," by the Apostolic message.

It seems, however, possible to get an interpretation less far-fetched than either of these. Remember that the Greek of the Septuagint is not so much a "Version," as it is commonly called, in the strict sense of the term; but rather a Targum in Greek with a strong Christian intention. It is a thousand-fold easier to explain its many divergences from the traditional Hebrew by the hypothesis that it is a Christian paraphrase, and not a translation, of the original, differing therefore from that original with the same kind of freedom wherewith the Chaldee of Onkelos differs from it—far easier to explain the phænomena thus, than to adopt those fine-spun

* S. Matt. x. 14.

theories about the copyists incessantly mistaking one Hebrew letter for another, and thus by new combinations giving that new turn to the Hebrew text, which the Septuagint reproduces in Greek. I believe that the student of the Greek Scriptures, and consequently the student of the ancient Latin Scriptures too, which (it must be remembered) were derived from the Greek and not from the Hebrew— I believe that such a student will by this hypothesis reach a satisfactory explanation of many passages which without it would utterly baffle him.

Remembering, then, this character of the Greek and Latin Scriptures, we can take the "filii excussorum" quite literally, the *sons of those who have been shaken out*—shaken out, that is, either from their own land into captivity; or shaken out from the favour of God—Christians, that is to say, who are the true spiritual posterity of the chosen people. "Through their fall salvation is come unto the Gentiles." (Rom. xi. 11).

It should be noticed that the same figure in the same Greek and Latin words is adopted by Nehemiah with this kind of meaning: "Also I shook my lap and said, So God shake out every man from his house and from his labour that performeth not this promise, even thus be he shaken out and emptied." (Neh. v. 13).

Rashi, following up the line of interpretation which I have already indicated, takes the "children of youth," to be the pupils and scholars which the "beloved" made in his youth. Rashi.

The Targum follows the Hebrew :—

"As arrows in the hand of the mighty man, so are the sons of a young man." Targum.

5. Happy *is* the man that hath his quiver full of them: they shall not be ashamed, but they shall speak with the enemies in the gate.

As the children were spoken of under the figure of the arrows, so their home is called here the quiver. So both Aben Ezra and Radak.

*They.* The father and the sons.

*In the gate.* In public, before the eyes of all.

*The enemies* are, according to Rashi's line of interpretation, those who are opposed to them in disputation upon the Law. The Rashi.

children or disciples of the wise will not be put to shame in the debate. So too, according to the old Latin Gloss, He is not ashamed who speaks in Christ and seeks His honour, not his own: not ashamed, that is, when he shall speak with his enemies, that is, with heretics, in the gate, that is, in Christ.

<small>Gloss.</small>

The Latin writers have commented upon a version which substitutes "desire" for "quiver,"—*Blessed is the man who hath filled his desire from them*—from the preachers of Apostolic doctrine, that is. "Well, my brethren," asks S. Augustine, "who filleth his desire from them? Who loveth not the world."

The Targum here gives that line of thought which has been adopted by Rashi throughout the Psalm:—

"It is well with the man who filleth his school with them: they shall not be put to shame, when they shall contend with their enemies in the gate of the house of judgment."

<small>Targum.</small>

The phrase "house of judgment," so frequent in Targums and Hebrew writers, is a name for the Consistory Court at Jerusalem, composed of seventy-one members. It originated in the direction given to Moses: "Gather unto me seventy men of the elders of Israel, whom thou knowest to be the elders of the people, and officers over them; and bring them unto the tabernacle of the congregation, that they may stand there with thee." (Numb. xi. 16). In the Talmud* it is called *Great Sanhedrin*.

* Sanhedrin, cap. 1.

## CHAPTER XV.

### PSALM CXXVIII.

A Song of Degrees.

1. Blessed *is* every one that feareth the LORD; that walketh in his ways.

*Radak.* THE Psalm eulogizes the ways of him who retains the fear of the Lord through all the trials of the Captivity, and who accordingly will attain, either himself, or in the person of his children, to see the restoration of Jerusalem.

The walking in the ways of the Lord is not looked upon by the Hebrew commentators as a mere synonym of fearing the Lord. By both Aben Ezra and Radak that man is said to fear the Lord who from fear of Him observes the negative precepts of the Law ("Thou shalt not," etc.); while the man "that walketh in his ways" is he who is careful not to neglect the affirmative precepts. ("Thou shalt," etc.)

For the complete understanding of this comment, it should be known that amongst the Hebrew Doctors the Commandments of the Law of Moses are divided into affirmative and prohibitive precepts. Laws which say, "Do," and Laws which say, "Thou shalt not do." The following passage translated from the Talmud sums up their ideas upon the subject as concisely as possible: "Six hundred and thirteen precepts were spoken to Moses on Sinai—three hundred and sixty-five prohibitive, according to the number of days in the solar year; and two hundred and forty-eight affirmative, according to the number of parts in the body of man." (Makkoth cap. iii. fol. 23, 2.) The number of affirmative precepts is easily remembered, because it is the number made up in Hebrew notation by the letters of the word "Abraham"—the name which God substituted for "Abram," when He said to him (Gen. xvii. 1) "Be thou perfect"—perfect, Rashi explains, in observing the Covenant of Circumcision, which contained implicitly the later Law given to Moses.

According to Cassiodorus, Hugo of S. Caro, and the Gloss, the Psalm points to the ninth grade in Christian virtues, the fear of the *Latin Writers.*

Lord. This grade appropriately follows the preceding one—that spiritual joy in which man feels the sweetness of God, and accordingly fears lest he be severed from Him.

S. Augustine says distinctly there must be some hidden spiritual meaning in the Psalm, because there is a difficulty in the literal meaning of it. It seems to promise a numerous offspring to the man that feareth the Lord. The difficulty is that this blessing is not confined to the man that feareth the Lord. You know of a man who was ungodly, a heathen, sacrilegious, a worshipper of idols, whom numerous sons and grandsons have carried to the grave, an old man, bowed down with years, who had died in his bed. Clearly there must be some further meaning to meet the expressions of the Psalm. No one feareth the Lord except he be in the members of the Man, Christ Jesus; except he be amongst the members of His mystical Body, the Church. It is of the aggregate of such members—every such one—that the Psalm speaks. They are one with Him; what is true of Him is true of them: the "wife" is the Bride of Christ—to treat the second and third verses thus as

*S. Augustine.*

*1 Cor. xii. 27.*

an apostrophe to Christ helps us a little over the difficulty of the sudden change from third person to second, a peculiarity which is, of course, totally unexplained by those commentators who see in Psalms nothing but their literal sense. And the "children" are the members of the Church, "round about the table" of the Lord here, and privileged to eat and drink at His table, in the eternal Feast hereafter.

The Targum follows the Hebrew:—

"A Song which was said upon the steps of the abyss. Well is it with them who fear the Lord, who walk in His ways." <small>Targum.</small>

2. For thou shalt eat the labour of thine hands: happy *shalt* thou *be* and *it shall be* well with thee.

It is a blessing to a man to maintain himself by the sweat of his own brow, and not to be dependent upon what he can get from others. <small>Radak.</small>

*Happy shalt thou be.* The men of this world shall declare thee happy. *And it shall be well with thee.* God shall give thee a good <small>Radak.</small>

reward in the world to come. It shall be well with thee, then, both in this world and the next. So too the Midrash.

<small>Midrash Tehillim.</small>

This explanation of the twofold assertion of happiness is explicitly given by the Targum:—

"When thou eatest the labour of thine hands, it is well with thee in this world, and well (shall it) be for thee in the world to come."

<small>Targum.</small>

Both Cassiodorus and the Gloss take the verse as addressed to some one other than the person spoken of in the preceding verse—to Christ, that is, rather than to His members. The sudden change from "they" and "their" which the first verse would require, to pronouns of the second person in this verse, is at least too remarkable to be passed without some explanation. This is indeed one of the places where the mere naked Hebrew phrase itself seems to demand the Christian interpretation. It is not enough to say by way of comment, "Oh, the writer of the Psalm changes his grammar." Writers do not change their grammar without a reason. And what, I ask in such a case as this, can that reason be? If there were some hidden meaning lying beneath the letter of the holy Psalmist's words; if one moment he might legitimately eulogize the fearers of the Lord, and the next moment apostrophize Him in Whom all such fearers are gathered into One Body—if he might be allowed to do this, then his language becomes intelligible and natural enough. But if we are to cut ourselves off from this, and say that his words are nothing more than a plain matter-of-fact statement of the success that will commonly attend integrity—this, I submit, is to declare the interchanging of the pronouns totally unnecessary; and, in point of fact, it is tantamount to charging the writer of the Psalm with a looseness of language which no ordinary censor of phraseology would allow to pass, and which even a very modest estimate of the dignity of Scripture would most certainly exclude.

The Midrash associates this verse with the preceding one, and makes the two together a protest against mere sentimentality in religion. "Greater is he who gains by his labour than he who fears God." It means, of course, not that gain is better than godliness; but that he whose religion leads him to a zealous performance of duty

Midrash. Tehillim.

is superior to him whose religion is a mere fruitless sentiment. In the model religious man sentiment and duty are united. Hence, the mention of the "labour of the hands," in company with the "fear of the Lord."

3. Thy wife *shall be* as a fruitful vine by the sides of thine house: thy children like olive plants round about thy table.

The English Version seems to make a promise of this verse. According to the Hebrew, however, it might be, as Radak seems to take it, not only a promise but a direction. "It is a part of good morality that thou shouldest instruct thy wife to be as a fruitful vine by the sides of thine house." There is a singular beauty in the comparison of the wife to the vine. There is no other tree but the vine which men plant within the house. It, however, some men do plant within by the sides of the house; and when it is somewhat grown, they train it to the outside, so that its roots remain within the house, while its clusters hang outside. Just so, a modest wife will be concealed at home, "by the sides of the house," not in the doorway that she may court the gaze of all who come and go. Such a wife was Sarah. "And they said unto him, Where is Sarah thy wife? And he said, Behold, in the tent." (Gen. xviii. 9.) Her children on the contrary, like the grape-clusters when they have become strong and plentiful, go forth into the world for their several occupations and the needs of the household. The details of this picture are no doubt borrowed from the stricter usages of Oriental life with regard to feminine seclusion; but the *principle* that underlies the Hebrew's conception of family life is none the less essential to our Western civilization.

There is a twofold force in the comparison of such a wife's children with the olive plant. In the first place, says Radak, the olive admits no graft from any other tree; so the children of the modest wife are above the suspicion that they are the sons of any other father than their mother's husband. And further, the olive remains fresh and green through all the months of the year; so the sons of such a mother will continue at all times comely in their good deeds. *So, too, R. Joshua Ben Levi (one of the Doctors of the Gemoro) in the Midrash Tehillim.*

*Round about thy table;* because they will be

always at hand to serve thee as thou eatest; because they will never be driven forth from thy house, as degraded and debauched; and because they will never eat or drink themselves otherwise than at home.

 The verse appears to be taken by Aben Ezra as a promise, or at least a declaration, to the man who feareth the Lord. His wife is as the vine, because she bears him children in due season; and these children are themselves like olive plants in their strength and permanence.

<small>Aben Ezra.</small>

 The form אֶשְׁתְּךָ with ֶ under the א is remarked upon by Radak as an intentional variation from the more common form of the word אִשְׁתְּךָ.

<small>Radak.</small>

 The Midrash interprets as Radak does. The wife is as the fruitful vine, when she is modest and remains "in the sides of the house," just as Sarah was "in the tent," when inquiry was made of her whereabouts.

<small>Midrash Tehillim.</small>

 In the Targum, as in the Hebrew, the verb is omitted. It does not therefore determine whether the verse was taken as a promise or a direction :—

" Thy wife (shall be, *or* should be) as the vine that beareth fruit upon the side of thy house: thy children as the plants of olive round thy table." Targum.

S. Augustine says that the verse is said unto Christ, the wife being, of course, the Church; and then he draws out admirably the parallel of Eve suggested in the clause, *by the sides of thine house.* " Nor hath His wife been created from His side without a cause. When her spouse slept, Eve was created; when Christ died the Church was created; she was born of her husband's side, whence a rib had been withdrawn; and the Church was born of the side of her Spouse, when His side was transfixed with a lance and the Sacraments flowed forth." S. Aug. Enarr. ad loc.

Another line of thought is possible, which is adopted by Cassiodorus, Dionysius the Carthusian, and others. According to them the " wife " is Wisdom. Solomon used this very image in regard to Wisdom : " I loved her and sought her out from my youth, I desired to make her my spouse, and I was a lover of her beauty."[*] Elsewhere,

[*] Wisdom viii. 2.

too, this "spouse" is compared to the vine. "As the turpentine tree I stretched out my branches, and my branches are the branches of honour and grace. As the vine brought I forth pleasant savour, and my flowers are the fruit of honour and riches."* Remember too, in connection with this, that in the New Testament the Christ, Who is declared to be "the Wisdom of God,"† is careful to compare Himself with the vine. "I am the true Vine." (S. John xv. i.)

Nor is the application of the verse to the Christ confined to Christian exposition. The ancient Hebrew Midrash says that these expressions point to the Messiah, because of the same expressions in Genesis which have that application "Binding his foal unto the vine, and his ass's colt unto the choice vine." (Gen. xlix. 11.)

4. Behold, that thus shall the man be blessed that feareth the LORD.

The man that feareth the Lord will be blessed in his adoption of these principles and usages of life.

---

\* Ecclus. xxiv. 16, 17.     † 1 Cor. i. 24.

So Radak explains it—necessarily, from his having taken the former verse as a direction and not as a promise.

The Targum is just as the Hebrew:—

"Lo, for thus shall the man be blessed that feareth before the Lord." *Targum.*

Those who are willing to see nothing but a literal sense in Holy Scripture, should consider the difficulty in which such a verse as the present lands them. "Thus;" that is, in certain definite particulars, that have been laid down; in successful labour, in a domesticated wife, and in a numerous offspring—in the literal sense, it simply is contrary to experience that every one who fears the Lord is "thus" blessed. As Dionysius the Carthusian tersely puts it, Neither to Elijah nor to Jeremiah were these blessings granted; for each of them remained unmarried. The mere letter of such a passage as this—and there are many of them—forces us to a spiritual sense, if only that the expressions themselves may be not placed in antagonism with the facts.

5. The LORD shall bless thee out of Zion:

s

and thou shalt see the good of Jerusalem all the days of thy life.

*Out of Zion.* The allusion, says Aben Ezra, is to these blessings coming from God, Who in- habited the "house" that was fixed in Zion. He refers, of course, to the Temple. Yet, it must be remembered, the Temple was not, strictly speaking, upon Mount Zion, but upon Mount Moriah : and thus when we meet with this usage—so frequent in Hebrew writers, and adopted by them from the Scriptures themselves—of speaking of God's residence "upon Zion," we must explain it by a kind of synecdoche—pars pro toto—which treats any portion of the holy city as Zion.

<small>Aben Ezra. So also Radak.</small>

*See the good of Jerusalem,* sc. when Israel returns thither from her Captivity.

*All the days of thy life,* either in the Captivity, or on the return to Jerusalem.

The interpretation, thus adopted by the Hebrew writers, is the same in kind as that which the Christians have with a general unanimity employed.

*Sion* seems to be universally taken for the Church Militant; and some of them, Dionysius the Carthusian for example, take *Jerusalem* for the same—the Church, he says, at a distance from her Lord, Militant, to wit, warring, labouring, yet resting in the peace of Christ. Others, as Cassiodorus and Hugo of S. Caro, take *Jerusalem* for the Church Triumphant. This contrast between the two names, *Sion* and *Jerusalem*—as being respectively the Church Militant and the Church Triumphant—is valuable in ascertaining the force of many passages of Scripture, where there would seem to be a mere tautology but for this distinction.* So it is here. Jerusalem, says the former of the two writers named, is, being interpreted, the Vision of Peace, which shall then be seen, when Christ its Author shall be seen with the beatified mind, in whom all things that are good shall be seen; but that you may not believe this to refer to anything temporal, there is added, *All the days of thy life,* so that in the ineffable gift the full measure of eternity might be added.

\* The English reader may find this subject worked out in considerable detail by the late Dr. Neale, in an essay on the interpretation of Scripture, in the first volume of his Commentary on the Psalms. It is right, however, to say that the distinction remarked above is very far from being acknowledged by all the Latin expositors.

The Targum merely translates the Hebrew:—

<small>Targum.</small> "The Lord shall bless thee from Zion, and thou shalt see the good of Jerusalem all the days of thy life."

6. Yea, thou shalt see thy children's children, *and* peace upon Israel.

Thou shalt see peace upon Israel, in the redemption of the Captives, if the Redeemer come while thou art living; or if He come when thou art dead, in the resurrection, when the Creator shall raise thee with the righteous dead.

<small>Radak.</small>

Rashi, in his one solitary remark upon this Psalm, connects the promise of children's children with the certainty of inheritance. The reason for which a childless widow was to marry her husband's brother,* was that their offspring might succeed in the inheritance. In the case of the man "that feareth the Lord," his inheritance should be secure against all risks; he should "see his children's children."

<small>Rashi.</small>

<small>So, too, the Midrash.</small>

S. Augustine (and others have followed him) saw

* Deut. xxv. 6.

in "children" the good works of the Christian, and in "children's children" the reward of such works. Those, therefore, who shall see the eternal "peace upon Israel," are they "who stand around the Lord's table like olive-branches, so that the tree is not barren as was that fig-tree, where the Lord when hungry found no fruit."

The Targum is as the Hebrew:—

"And thou shalt see children of thy children: and peace upon Israel." *Targum.*

## CHAPTER XVI.

#### PSALM CXXIX.

A Song of Degrees.

**1. Many a time have they afflicted me from my youth, may Israel now say.**

THE Psalm turns, according to Radak, upon a comparison of the Captivity with human life—the beginning of it being likened to youth, and its prolongation to the time of age. The meaning of it, accordingly, is that from the very beginning of the Captivity the nation had been submitted to very grievous affliction. It is in reality a Psalm of praise to Almighty God, Who had not suffered them to be entirely swallowed up; the repetition of the phrase in the second verse serving to intensify the expression of praise, according to the usage of the sacred tongue.

S. Augustine remarks upon the shortness of the

Psalm contrasted with the weight of its contents: "As it is written, in the Gospel, of Zac- chæus that he was 'little of stature,' but mighty in works; as it is written of that widow who cast her two mites into the treasury, little was the money, but great was her charity; thus also this Psalm, if thou count the words, is short; if thou weigh the sentiments, is great." S. Aug. Enarr. ad loc.

In the "degrees" of Christian virtue the Psalm corresponds to the tenth step, which is patience in adversity.

*Many a time.* That is, says Cassiodorus, from the time of the first age, when Abel was killed by his wicked brother. At that time the persecution of the righteous began. From that time many others have been persecuted, as Lot, Job, and the rest of the Saints; and, as the climax of all, in the Passion of Christ Himself was the Church afflicted.

The Targum makes only a slight change at the beginning of the verse:—

"A Song which was sung upon the steps of the abyss. Many are they who afflicted me from my youth, may Israel now say." Targum.

2. Many a time have they afflicted me from my youth: yet they have not prevailed against me.

The form רַבַּת Aben Ezra explains as he did the same form in a previous passage of the Gradual Psalms (Ps. cxx. 6), that the ת is an exceptional, though not unprecedented, substitution for the more usual ה, without effecting any change of meaning. At the former passage he gives some analogous forms from other parts of the Scriptures.

*Aben Ezra.*

He adds that it is a kind of prophecy—it will be said by Israel time after time, Though they have afflicted me, yet they have not been able to destroy our name.

As in the preceding verse, the Targum takes the first word for the subject of the sentence:—

*Targum.*
"Many are they who afflicted me from my youth, but they were not able to harm me."

The Church, says Cassiodorus, properly adopts such language as this, because she groans under the persecutions of the wicked,

3. The plowers plowed upon my back: they made long their furrows.

A proverb, says Radak, for the greatness of the burdens and the cruelty they underwent in the Captivity. There is a special force in such a figure, for the plower as soon as he has made one furrow returns and makes another just like it, and gives his oxen no rest till the whole field is plowed up. When therefore the Psalmist says, *They made long their furrows,* he points to the conquerors giving their captives no rest from their servitude and their burdens.

Radak.

By Aben Ezra it is connected with the previous verse: "They have not prevailed against me, although the plowers plowed," etc. It is a proverb of contempt and degradation, like the phrase in Isa. li. 23: "Thou hast laid thy body as the ground."

Aben Ezra.

*Furrows.* לְמַעֲנִיתָם is not the usual word for *furrows*. It is thought worthy of special remark by Rashi, Aben Ezra, and Radak, in his "Book of Roots." All of them quote the other passage of Scripture where it occurs, 1 Sam. xiv. 14: "Within as it were half a furrow of an acre of land." Radak in his *Roots* explains it, according to its etymology, as the line or length between *turn* and *turn* (עֲנָה) of the plough.

<small>Book of Roots.</small>

Both the Ancient Latin Version and the Vulgate impart quite a different turn to the exposition of the Latin writers; putting, as those Versions do, "built" for "plowed," and "iniquity" for "furrows."

<small>Latin Writers.</small>

The word for "back" in the Targum has a wider range. It means "body," without reference to any particular part of it:—

"Upon my body plowers plowed: they prolonged their plowing (*or* their furrows)." Buxtorf gives both these meanings, with only this passage to determine it.*

<small>Targum.</small>

4. The LORD is righteous: he hath cut asunder the cords of the wicked.

*Hath cut asunder.* The past in place of the future. So both Radak and Aben Ezra take it. The Lord, because he is righteous

<small>Radak. Aben Ezra.</small>

* Buxtorf Lex. Chald. fol. 2213.

and just in his ways, will cut asunder the cord of the wicked. The cord is the cord whereby the yoke is bound: its severance therefore implies that they should no longer be able to plow upon the back of Israel.

*Cords.* It would almost seem that the English translators took עֲבוֹת for a feminine plural. It appears to be really a singular noun; the full form of the plural (עֲבוֹתוֹת) occurs in Hosea xi. 4: "With *bands* of love."

It will be noticed, however, that our translators are but following the Targum in treating the word as plural:—

"The righteous Lord hath severed the chains of the wicked." Targum.

The Latin writers here again do not help us in the exposition of our translation; because the Latin Version which they used had "necks" Writers. where we have "cords." The commentary, however, which has passed under the name of S. Jerome, admits, "Instead of *necks* it has in the Hebrew *cords* or *chains.*"

The idea of the *cord* belonging to a yoke is preserved in the Midrash. The abruptness of the clause, "He hath cut asunder" points to the swiftness of the deliverance which God shall give his people. Here the princes of the world subjugate them; but when the end comes, God will spend no time in remonstrance—"Thus, and thus have ye done to my children;" but He will come in suddenly and break the yoke, and cut asunder the yoke-bands, as it is said, "And I have broken the bands of your yoke." (Lev. xxvi. 13.)

<small>Midrash Tehillim.</small>

5. Let them all be confounded and turned back that hate Zion.

Or, more strictly, without the imprecation, as Radak puts it: When the Lord shall cut asunder the cord of the wicked, then all the haters of Zion shall be confounded, and turned back from their wicked plans against us.

<small>Radak.</small>

The nations of the world, bitterly exclaims Radak, cannot be said to hate Zion, because they engage in perpetual wars for the possession of it; but they hate the children of Zion, the people of Israel.

There is not necessarily any imprecation implied in the Targum:—

"They shall be put to shame, so that they turn backward—all the haters of Zion." *Targum.*

They who hate Sion, hate the Church, says S. Augustine. Sion is the Church. And they who hypocritically enter the Church, hate the Church. *S. Augustine.*

A new and subtle link of connection between the thought of the preceding verse and that of the present is hinted at by S. Jerome. In the last verse it was, "They plowed upon my back." Outrage was inflicted upon the Body of Christ. The Zion of the present verse is the Church, which is the mystical Body of Christ. *S. Jerome.*

6. Let them be as the grass *upon* the housetops, which withereth afore it groweth up.

*Grass upon the housetops* is grass that has no strength or vitality.

*It groweth up.* There is some difficulty about this word שַׁלַּף. The Prayer Book Version of the Psalm has, "Afore it be plucked up," which is more in accordance with the explanation of the word given by

Radak. He says it implies the extraction of a thing and the changing of its place. He quotes Ruth iv. 8, where the word occurs, "So he drew off (יִשְׁלֹף) his shoe;" remarking that there it is transitive, while here it is intransitive: "Afore it be plucked," rather than, "Afore one pluck it," as some have proposed to translate. Aben Ezra points out further that it applies to the drawing of a sword. It is found in Judges viii. 20 (A.V.): "But the youth *drew* not his sword." This last line of thought probably accounts for Buxtorf's rendering, which he got presumably from some or other of the Hebrew writers, "Afore one draw," sc., his blade to cut it.

<small>Buxtorf.
Lex. Hebr.
s. v.</small>

The Targum countenances the Authorised Version rather than the older one in the Prayer Book:—

<small>Targum.</small>

"They shall be as grass of the roofs, on which, before it bloom, there cometh an east wind (which), blows upon it and it withereth."

The word for "east" in this Targum, Walton's translator, renders "vehemens." I have been unable to discover why he does so.

Amongst the Latin writers, the grass upon the housetops points to the produce visible upon the heights of pride.

<small>Cassiod.
Hugo S. Car.</small>

7. Wherewith the mower filleth not his hand; nor he that bindeth sheaves his bosom.

From the grass upon the housetop there is no produce. The nations of the world, who follow a law of their own invention, are contrasted with Israel who had a law of God, and of whose obedience the language of an abundant harvest—in contrast with the infertility expressed by the present figure—has been already used in a Gradual Psalm. (Ps. cxxvi. 5.) "They that sow in tears shall reap in joy." See the commentary on that passage. <small>Aben Ezra. Radak.</small>

*His bosom*, that is, his arms. The word is so used in Isa. xlix. 22: "They shall bring thy sons in their arms (בְּחֹצֶן)." Rashi also quotes the use of the word in Nehem. v. 13, where it is rendered *lap*: "Also I shook my lap." So too Aben Ezra. <small>Rashi.</small>

The Targum is literal:—

"Whereof the mower filleth not his hand, nor the sheaf-collector his shoulder." <small>Targum.</small>

The figure of the mower and the sheaf-binder is

pointed by some to the circumstances of the Last Judgment, according to the saying of our Blessed Lord in S. Matt. xiii. 39: "The reapers are the angels."

<small>Dionysius Carthus. and others.</small>

The whole Psalm may be put into the mouth of our Lord Himself. He is in the truest sense Israel. From His youth up—from the time when Herod sought the life of the Holy Infant—men afflicted Him; yet they prevailed not against Him. Those who would have stoned Him, were baffled by His disappearance. (S. John viii. 59): those who would have seized Him, went backward and fell to the ground: even he who finally condemned Him, was told that he could have no power at all against Him except it were given him from above. (S. John xix. 11.) *The plowers plowed upon my back and made long furrows*, accurately describes the laceration produced by the scourges of the servants of Pilate. The *cord of the wicked*—the bands of death wherewith the wicked thought to bind Him—was severed in the resurrection. They that hated Zion, the newly-founded Church of the risen Lord, were confounded and turned back by the fact of its ever-increasing growth; it grows, but they, in S. Augustine's phrase, "have not the sap of bloom." It is the ultimate destiny of such that is described in the verse before us. In the Last Judgment they will not be of the wheat that is to be gathered into the Lord's barn. (S. Matt. xiii. 30.)

8. Neither do they which go by say, The blessing of the LORD *be* upon you : we bless you in the name of the LORD.

It was the usage of those who passed by to exchange a blessing with the reapers. Witness the conduct of Boaz in Ruth ii. 4. "And behold Boaz came from Bethlehem and said unto the reapers, The Lord be with you. And they answered him, The Lord bless thee." The Psalmist means, says Aben Ezra, that no one would praise the laws and morality of the nations of the world; accordingly he compared (in Ps. cxxvi.) Israel who kept the law of God to the sowers of good seed; while here he compares those who follow their own idolatrous vanities to the grass upon the housetops.

The responsory character of the two clauses be-

T

tween the reapers and the passers-by is well brought out by the Targum:—

<small>Targum.</small> "And those who pass by from thence say not, The blessing of the Lord be upon you: and they reply not to them, We bless you in the Name of the Lord."

In the view of the Christian writers, they who "go <small>Cassiodorus and others.</small> by" are the Saints of God, who pass by the world and hold it for nothing. S. Augustine, with greater particularity, assigns the term to Apostles and Prophets, who had no benediction for those who hate Zion. Dionysius the Carthusian likewise takes it for the Prophets. The Prophets, he says, spoke no good about the Jews, who put Christ to death, but much evil, as appears where it is thus said (according to the Vulgate and the Margin of the Authorised Version): "And they who shall deny Him shall be no more his people,"*—said with reference to the people who cried, 'We have no King but Cæsar.'

The opposite view to this is adopted in the Midrash. <small>Midrash Tehillim.</small> There, "they which go by," are the nations, the heathen, the enemies of the

* Dan. ix. 26.

people of God, who " go by," pass from this world. The last part of the verse, on the contrary, is put into the mouth of Israel. Although the transient heathen have no word of blessing for Israel, yet Israel says to them, " We bless you in the Name of the Lord."

## CHAPTER XVII.

**PSALM CXXX.**

A Song of Degrees.

1. Out of the depths have I cried unto Thee, O LORD.

IT is the Captivity that is here compared to depths of waters. So Radak; and Aben Ezra, who adds the particulars—from the depths of poverty, and contempt, and degradation, which distinguished the Captivity.

<small>Radak.</small>

This same line is adopted by the Christian interpreters, only that the Captivity is in their view one or other of those tyrannies under which the soul of humanity groans—wickedness, or sorrow, or other of the accidents of mortal life.

<small>Christian Expositors.</small>

The Targum is peculiar only in the usual heading :—

"A song which was sung upon the steps of the abyss. Out of the depths I have called Thee, O Lord." *Targum.*

The Psalm is the eleventh in the order of the Gradual Psalms, and treats of the eleventh step in the spiritual ascent, viz., penitential prayer. Its penitential character coincides with the fact of its being the eleventh of the Gradual Psalms; eleven being the number which contains the mystery of transgression in Scripture usage — the number which oversteps ten, which symbolizes the mystery of obedience—*e.g.*, ten commandments in the Law. A great mystery, says S. Augustine *S. Augustine.* in a Sermon,* was figured when it was commanded that the Tabernacle should be made. Many statements were made with numbers in the Law, by way of a great mystery. Amongst the rest the curtains of goats' hair were ordered to be made, not ten in number, but eleven (Exod. xxvi. 7); because by the covering of goats' hair the confession of sins is indicated. Some further illustration of this subject is given at the end of my commentary on this Psalm.

* De Verb. Dom. in Ev. sec. Matt. Sermon xv.

A strange application of the first clause is made <small>R. Jose in Midrash Tehillim.</small> by one of the Hebrew Doctors in the Midrash. He sees in it an anticipation of the rule given by our Blessed Lord that men should not stand in an elevated or conspicuous place to pray; because it is said, "*Out of the depths* have I cried unto Thee, O Lord."

2. LORD, hear my voice : let Thine ears be attentive to the voice of my supplications.

*Attentive.* To settle the vowel points of this word קַשֻּׁבוֹת, Radak observes that it is a <small>Radak.</small> word of the same form as שַׁכֻּלוֹת *bereaved* in Jerem. xviii. 21 : "Let their wives be bereaved of their children."

The Targum follows the Hebrew :—

<small>Targum.</small> "Lord, receive my prayer : let Thine ears be attentive to the voice of my prayers."

S. Augustine in a splendid passage * contrasts this prayer with the kind of language ordinarily adopted by men in the depths of wickedness and despair. "From henceforth I am lost, why do I not do what-

---

\* Enarr. in Pss. ad loc.

ever I have the power to do? What is the usual language of desperate robbers? The Judge will put me to the same death for ten murders as for five, as for one: why then do I not take advantage of every fresh opportunity? This is, *The wicked, when he hath reached the depth of evil deeds, despiseth.*\* But our Lord Jesus Christ, Who despised not even our deeps, Who hath deigned to descend to this life, promising remission of all sins; He raised man even from the deep, that he might cry from the deep beneath the weight of his sins, and that the sinner's voice might reach unto God; crying whence, save from the depth of evils?"

## 3. If Thou, LORD, shouldest mark iniquities, O LORD, who shall stand?

*Stand* appears to be taken by Radak in the sense of *continue, endure.* We shall be speedily consumed, if Thou, O Lord, markest our iniquities. On the other hand, Aben Ezra seems to give prominence to the idea of acquittal, justification, in *stand.* Make haste to save Radak. Aben Ezra.

\* Prov. xviii. 3. (Old Latin and Vulgate.)

me, and mention not to me my old sins, for I shall not be able to make answer.

The Targum word for "stand" would do either for endurance, or acquittal:—

<small>Targum.</small> "If Thou, Lord, shouldest keep iniquities, O Lord, who shall stand?"

4. But *there* is forgiveness with Thee, that Thou mayest be feared.

All the writers seem to be agreed, that the object of the verse is to ascribe the power of forgiveness to God exclusively. Whatever powers of various kinds He may have delegated to others, this, says the Psalmist, He has retained in His own hands.

Radak gives an interpretation, which he says he derived from his father of blessed memory—the famous Joseph Kimchi. <small>Joseph Kimchi.</small> Authority in the world was given by God to the Angels for them to execute His will; but the power of forgiveness was not lodged with them, but with God Himself, lest the reverence of the sons of men should be diverted from Him to them. The purpose of God's retention of this prerogative was that He might be feared.

Again, since God extends forgiveness, the sinner will feel that there is hope for him, and there is a chance that he may lay aside his sins and be converted to the fear of God. On the contrary, if God extended no forgiveness to the suppliant, the sinner, in sheer despair, would be tempted to continue in his own selfish ways. Thus, in a second way, the fact that there is forgiveness with God tends to His fear. So Aben Ezra explains it. *Aben Ezra.*

Rashi here exhibits his wonderful power of weaving Scripture with Scripture. The prerogative of forgiveness rests with God; it was not vested even in His emissary, the Angel, who preceded the host of Israel, of whom, notwithstanding all his imposing attributes, it is most expressly said (Exod. xxiii. 21), "He will not pardon your transgressions." *Rashi.*

The Targum seems to introduce a beautiful thought—that the true Being of God is seen in the attribute of forgiveness :—

"For there is forgiveness with Thee, that Thou mayest be seen." *Targum.*

The Commentary in the name of S. Jerome makes the verse an address to the Second Person of the Trinity :—

S. Jerome.
"For Thou wilt reconcile us to the Father by the Cross."

5. I wait for the LORD, my soul doth wait, and in His word do I hope.

*I wait. My soul doth wait.* The double expectation that God will in this world rescue him from bondage, and in death will gather his soul to Himself. So Radak.

Radak.

Rashi paraphrases it: Lo, I am amongst those who look for redemption.

Rashi.

*His word.* His promise, says Radak, that He will bring me out of the Captivity. So, too, Aben Ezra.

The way in which the Targum handles "word" is worth notice. We have seen before,* that the Targum habitually introduces "word" where neither it, nor any suggestion of it, occurs in the Hebrew text, making "the word of the Lord" the ordinary

\* See on Ps. cxxi. 7, and on Ps. cxxiv. 8.

equivalent of "the Lord." In the present verse, however, where we might have expected a similar phrase, the Targum seems to go out of its way to avoid it. Is it that the Targumists felt the notion of personality attaching to the phrase "the word of the Lord," that they shrank from using it, except where they saw in the original some personal action indicated? Their paraphrase stands thus :—

"I waited for the Lord; my soul waited; and for His glory I have delayed." Targum.

"Glory," however, no less than "Word," is a name of the Christ, Who is the "brightness of the Father's glory." (Heb. i.) And in this sense the last clause of the verse is taken by many of the Christian writers.

6. My soul *waiteth* for the LORD more than they that watch for the morning : *I say more than* they that watch for the morning.

The Prayer Book Version puts it—"Before the morning watch." If we take *before* as meaning *more than, rather than*, it will accord with the explanation of the preposition (מ) which is given by Aben Ezra.

*Aben Ezra.* Just as the night watch look for the morning, strengthening and comforting their hearts with the prospect of sleep on its arrival, so intently and confidently the soul of the Psalmist is directed to the Lord.

The watching for the morning is interpreted by *Radak.* Radak of those who rise in the early watches of the morning for prayer. The repetition of the phrase "they that watch for the morning," expresses the fact that this watching for prayer takes place morning after morning. According *Rashi.* to Rashi, also, the repetition expresses the continued expectation of the soul.

The sentiment, adds Radak, is that of every devout individual in the Captivity.

The purpose of the "watching" is distinctly assigned by the Targum:—

"My soul delayeth for the Lord more than those *Targum.* who keep the watch of the morning, who keep it for the offering of the morning oblation."

*Cassiodorus.* Some have seen in the mention of the morning watch an allusion to the Resurrection of the Lord, and the fruitless watch that was kept by the soldiers at the Sepulchre. It should be noted, that the Hebrew preposition would be rendered by "from," even more ordinarily and naturally, than by "before," or "more than." And thus even the strictly literal translation of the Hebrew furnishes a splendid sense for Christians, which is not possible for those who reject the facts of Christianity. My soul waiteth for the Lord from the morning watch—from the resurrection morning, that is. From that time the hope of the Church is stayed upon the Lord even to the night, that is, the end of the world. This, indeed, is one of those clauses (of which, in my belief, there are many) where the facts of the Gospel enable us easily and literally to translate a piece of Hebrew, which, without those facts, must always occasion more or less perplexity to the translator. It will thus be seen by the learned, that the Old Latin Psalter, which has maintained its place in the Vulgate, though in no sense a translation of the Hebrew, is nevertheless like its prototype the Septuagint, strictly accurate in its character of a Targum, giving the Christian sense of the verse before us. "Usque ad noctem," it will be observed, has absolutely no equivalent at all in the Hebrew text of the verse.

7. Let Israel hope in the LORD: for with the LORD *there is* mercy, and with Him *is* plenteous redemption.

<small>Radak, it appears, would translate it, *Hope, O Israel, in the Lord;* for he explains that the verb here is in the imperative mood of the Pihel modification. Aben Ezra, too, eminently the grammatical commentator, specially remarks that the verb is in the imperative mood. Leeser, I observe, though generally following the Hebrew authorities, translates *Let Israel wait for the Lord.* But it is difficult to see any reason why, in any revised English translation that may be achieved, the lead of Radak and Aben Ezra should not be followed. Israel is to hope, because the Lord will assuredly deliver the nation from its bondage, for He always shows mercy to the sons of men.</small>

<small>Radak. Aben Ezra.</small>

<small>*Plenteous redemption.* Redemption that has been multiplied, beginning with the deliverance from Egypt, and is still unexhausted. The Christian writers, too,</small>

have insisted on the epithet *plenteous*. Our Redeemer, S. Gregory the Great points out, is a fountain so copious, that no "depths" of sin are deep enough to warrant despair. In the same strain, S. Augustine sees that it answers a possible objection on the part of the penitent. The Head might rise again, because It was not weighed down with sins, there was no sin in Him; what shall we do? Shall we hope for such a resurrection as went before in the Lord, whilst we are weighed down by our sins?

<small>S. Greg. Mag.</small>

<small>S. Aug. Enarr. ad loc.</small>

The first verb is taken by the Targum as simply indicative:—

"Israel hopes for the Lord: for with the Lord is mercy, and abundant redemption with Him." <small>Targum.</small>

## 8. And He shall redeem Israel from all his iniquities.

*He.* The pronoun is emphatic. If thou sayest, How shall He rescue me, seeing I am full of iniquities? He it is that shall redeem thee from them. First, He shall forgive Israel

<small>Radak.</small>

his past sins, and then put it into his heart to return to God, after which his Captivity shall be turned.

What can be the meaning of this strange emphasising of the pronoun? any reader might ask. It must surely indicate some fact out of the common. The Christian interpreter has, of course, no difficulty in giving an amply sufficient explanation of the seemingly superfluous pronoun. Out of the common itself, it does call attention to a fact out of the common about the redemption that is contemplated. God, it is true, was to redeem. But if that were all, there were no need to signalize the pronoun here, more than elsewhere when God is named. But the Psalmist seems to point out that there is something exceptional about this redemption. It was to be effected, as we know, in the Person of Him who took the Manhood upon Himself. It must have been this pronoun, I suspect, that made S. Jerome, the Hebrew scholar, remark: "The Son Himself, when the fulness of the Gentiles is come in, shall save the residue of Israel by the remission of their sins."

*S. Jerome.*

The clause, says Aben Ezra, is contrasted with the thought of a previous verse : "If Thou, Lord, shouldest mark iniquities." Aben Ezra.

The Targum is quite literal :—

"And He"—emphasised, as in the Hebrew—
"shall redeem Israel from all his iniquities." Targum.

This is an appropriate place for reverting to the fact, that this one of the Gradual Psalms is also the sixth of the Penitential Psalms of the Christian Church. It will at least form a *memoria technica* for remembering its place in the series of Gradual Psalms, to record S. Augustine's observation that a Penitential Psalm is the eleventh *S. Augustine.* of the Gradual Psalms, the number eleven conveying the mystery of transgression, as that lying next beyond the number ten, which conveys the mystery of obedience (Ten Commandments). Notice the *eleven* curtains of goat's hair that were to be made (Exod. xxvi. 7) for the tabernacle; and S. Augustine's disquisition upon it in his treatise *De Civitate Dei*, lib. xv. cap. 20. Contrast the eleven descendants of Adam through sinful Cain, enumerated in Gen. iv. 16-22, with the ten descendants of Adam to Noah through the God-fearing line of Seth, in Gen. v. 3-29.

## CHAPTER XVIII.

### PSALM CXXXI.

*A Song of Degrees of David.*

1. LORD, my heart is not haughty, nor mine eyes lofty: neither do I exercise myself in great matters, or in things too high for me.

HUMILITY is the precursor of mercy. The Psalm is spoken by David about himself; but it is placed here amongst the Gradual Psalms as applicable to the exiles in Babylon. As David bore himself humbly, so also must Israel in their Captivity, and this will be the most certain guarantee of their ultimate deliverance, according to Isa. lvii. 15: "For thus saith the high and lofty One that inhabiteth eternity, Whose Name is Holy; I dwell in the high and holy place, with him also that is of a contrite and humble spirit, to revive the spirit of the humble and to revive the heart of the contrite ones." Rashi illustrates the humility of David by the modest character of the appointments of his residence and Court, all of which were in remarkable contrast with the sumptuous expenditure of his son Solomon. The latter says of himself: "I made me great works; I builded me houses ; I planted me vineyards : I made me gardens and orchards, and I planted trees in them of all kinds of fruits; I made me pools of water, to water therewith the wood that bringeth forth trees. I got me servants and maidens, and had servants born in my house ; also I had great possessions of great and small cattle above all that were in Jerusalem before me : I gathered me also silver and gold, and the peculiar treasure of kings, and of the provinces : I gat me men singers and women singers, and the delights of the sons of men, as musical instruments, and that of all sorts." (Eccles. ii. 4-8.)

<small>Rashi.</small>

The two clauses, *my heart is not haughty*, and, *nor mine eyes lofty*, express two distinct things, says Aben Ezra. The former repudiates pride as it exists secretly in the heart; the latter, as it shows itself in outward bearing. Radak also concurs in this exposition. Several of the Christian writers have it too.

Both Aben Ezra and Radak think it necessary to observe that the word for "exercise myself" (הִלַּכְתִּי) is intransitive, though it belongs to the Pihel modification which usually carries a transitive sense. Aben Ezra quotes two passages (Ps. xxxviii. 7; Job xxx. 28)—I may add that there are several others—where the same form has the intransitive force; though he subjoins that if it be taken as a transitive verb, then "my heart" must be understood—*I have not trained my heart*.

*The great matters* Radak understands to be the mysteries of the Godhead. In handling these the Psalmist had conducted intellect modestly and reverentially.

<small>Radak.</small>

The Targum adds nothing but the enlargement of the title:—

"A song which was sung upon the steps of the abyss. Lord, my heart is not exalted, nor mine eyes lifted up, and I have not walked in great matters and in wonders beyond me."

<small>Targum.</small>

The place of the Psalm, as pointing to the twelfth of the degrees of Christian virtue, cannot be better illustrated than by the words of the commentary that carries the name of S. Jerome. It is a Psalm, "which in the person of the Prophet exhibits to us the humility which Christ in the flesh was about to carry." <small>S. Jerome.</small>

The extension which S. Augustine gives it is admirable: "For we have often warned you, beloved, that it ought not to be received as <small>S. Aug. En. ad loc.</small> the voice of one man singing, but of all who are in Christ's Body."

An objection is anticipated by Dionysius the Carthusian. Humility is the basis and foundation of spiritual progress. True: <small>Dion. Carth.</small> yet humility, as it is described in the Psalms, properly occupies a late place in the rank of virtues. For it is the matured, developed, practised humility of the advanced saint, who for the glory of God and the building of Christ does not shrink from describing even his own attainments: as S. Paul, "I have laboured more abundantly than they all;" (1 Cor. xv. 10;) and Job, "My heart shall not reproach me so long as I live." (Job xxvii. 6.)

The case of Pilate is adduced by Cassiodorus as an example of one who exercised himself in great matters, when he said to our Blessed Lord, "Knowest thou not that I have power to crucify

Thee, and have power to release Thee?" (S. John xix. 10.)

Simon Magus too he adduces, as an instance of one handling things "too high" for him. Simon was fascinated by the power, not by the holiness of the Apostles, and wished to do such things as they did, without himself being such. S. Augustine also gives this illustration.

Against those who would use the verse to prohibit the study of the deeper mysteries of the Scripture, Dionysius the Carthusian quotes not only the example of the holiest men who have striven to explain the most difficult texts, but also the direct precept of Scripture itself—"Increasing in the knowledge of God." (Col. i. 10.)

*Dion. Carth.*

2. Surely I have behaved and quieted myself, as a child that is weaned of his mother; my soul *is* even as a weaned child.

*Surely.* The words (אִם לֹא "if not") are a common formula in the Holy Tongue for introducing an oath. Thus here, "If I have not behaved and quieted myself, let so

*Radak.*

and so happen to me ;" *i.e.*, surely I have behaved, etc.

*Child that is weaned.* This seems to be the real meaning of the word—*Weanling*, rather than *suckling* as Leeser renders it. It must be admitted, however, that he has the very high authority of Rashi for doing so. But see the word in Isa. xi. 8, "And the weaned child (גָּמוּל) shall put his hand on the cockatrice' den." It is necessary to insist on this in order to interpret the similitude as Radak does. Further, the word that in our version is "of" (עָלָי) he seems to take in its proper meaning, "upon"—*I have behaved and quieted myself, as a weanling is (dependent) upon his mother.* Just as the young child in its first attempts to walk depends, not upon its own strength, but upon its mother; so in handling the mysteries of Divine truth, I have not depended upon my own strength of intellect.

Nothing, I venture to say, can be more complete than such an exposition dependent simply upon accuracy of translation. Radak suggests a reason for the particular figure employed by the Psalmist. The Kabbalah—the body of traditional exposition—is to him as a mother. Catholic theology, a Christian might observe, adopts the sentiment, and says the same thing about the witness of the Church.

Aben Ezra apparently would express the figure in precisely the same way: and he sees in it a tacit reference to the phrase of the preceding verse, *Neither do I exercise* myself; lit., *I have not walked.*

<small>Aben Ezra.</small>

The English Version has shirked the difficulty presented by the word עָלַי in the last clause, by omitting it altogether. Aben Ezra grapples with it. He explains it as equivalent to בעיני "in my own eyes, in my own estimation." *As the weanling in my own estimation is my soul.* A revised translation might well rectify the defect. Leeser puts it, *Like a suckling is in me my soul.* In reality he follows the lead of Rashi, who would paraphrase the verse thus:

<small>Rashi.</small>

I have laid upon thee, (sc. upon God) my soul and quieted it, as the sucking child is laid upon its mother's breast; in thy sight my soul in me is like the suckling. It thus expresses the entire dependence of the humble soul upon God; but the exposition seems less satisfactory than what I have given above.

A different turn to the figure is given by some of the

Latin writers. The weaned child is deprived of that which it most desires. So if the heart is haughty and the eyes lofty, the soul will be deprived of its eternal reward. By pride the soul is cut off from Christ, its true Food; and as the mother, when she sees her child unfit for taking meat, giveth him meat, but meat that hath passed through her own flesh; so the soul finds its Food upon the bosom of the Church. S. Augustine's remarks seem to imply this way of taking the figure. *Hugo Card. Gloss.*

The Targum employs a word which points decidedly to the weaning, the completion (the word implies *completion*) of the period of suckling the child, rather than to the suckling period itself:—

"Surely I have laid hand upon mouth and have silenced my soul, till it heard the matters of the Law; as the weanling upon the breast of its mother, I have grown strong in the Law, as the weanling upon me is my soul." *Targum.*

3. Let Israel hope in the LORD from henceforth and for ever.

*Hope.* The verb, says Aben Ezra, is imperative.

In a revised translation it might perhaps more accurately stand, as Radak clearly takes it, "Hope, O Israel, in the Lord." See the same amendment required at Ps. cxxx. 7. Radak too seems to take the phrase as elliptical: "Hope, O Israel, in the Lord, and He shall give thee thy hope from henceforth and for ever."

Nothing is added by the Targum:—

Targum. "Israel shall hope in the Lord from the present time and for ever."

S. Augustine comments upon a strictly literal rendering of the Hebrew in the closing words "from this time forth and even unto eternity." "Until we arrive at eternity," he explains it, "let us trust in the Lord God; because when we have reached eternity, there will be no longer hope, but the thing itself will be ours (jam spes non erit, sed ipsa res erit.)"

The Midrash Tehillim gives nothing on this Psalm.

## CHAPTER XIX.

### PSALM CXXXII.

### A Song of Degrees.

**1.** LORD, remember David, *and* all his afflictions;

DAVID said this Psalm when he built the altar in the threshing-floor of Araunah the Jebusite by the direction of Gad the prophet, and "offered burnt offerings and peace offerings, and called upon the Lord: and He answered him from heaven by fire." (1 Chron. xxi. 26.) And David "said, This is the house of the Lord God, and this is the altar of the burnt offering for Israel;" but until that day the site for the temple was not known. Yet Nathan the prophet had previously told* him that he should not build the temple, but that his son Solomon should do so. And inasmuch as David had devoted himself to prepare for the erection of the

<small>Radak.</small>

---
* 2 Sam. vii.

temple, he asks, "Lord, remember David, and all his afflictions; and though I am not worthy to build, yet accept the intention for the deed; and remember all the trouble I have taken for its sake; for I have driven sleep from mine eyes in the multitude of my thoughts about it. I vowed and sware that I would not rest until I entered it; and I found no refreshment of spirit in my house, after that the house of the Lord was not to be built."

In support of this interpretation it should be observed that the Hebrew word for "afflictions" is akin to the word for "trouble" in 1 Chron. xxii. 14: "Now, behold, in my *trouble* I have prepared for the house of the Lord an hundred thousand talents of gold..."

Rashi concurs in referring these expressions to the trouble that David gave himself to ascertain the place where the temple should be built.

Rashi.

By Aben Ezra, likewise, the Psalm is referred to the same period, when David and the elders of Israel were clothed in sackcloth on account of the plague that was among the people.*
This writer, however, appears to consider that the

Aben Ezra.

* 1 Chron. xxi. 16.

"afflictions" of David arose in some degree from the difficulty of knowing where he should offer a sacrifice for the removal of the scourge; for "the tabernacle of the Lord, which Moses made in the wilderness, and the altar of the burnt-offering, were at that season in the high-place at Gibeon,"* and were therefore not immediately accessible to David.

The somewhat ambiguous form in the word for "afflictions" is, according to Aben Ezra, עֻנּוֹת to be taken for a noun derived from the Pual formation of the root.

Except in the title, the Targum adds nothing to the Hebrew:—

"A song which was sung upon the steps of the abyss. Lord, remember to David all his affliction." Targum.

The Psalm corresponds to the thirteenth step in the "degrees" of spiritual progress; and, as such, it speaks prophetically of the Advent of the Son of God. So the Latin Commentary that carries the name of S. Jerome takes it. Dionysius the Carthusian, however, represents it somewhat differently. According to him, it has a right to be the thirteenth

* 1 Chron. xxi. 29.

step, because it treats of the spiritual building of the house within—the holy soul; and when this is adorned with virtues, then the house of Christ is built.

The Latin writers have a turn of meaning different to that given above, owing to the particular word upon which they had to comment. In place of "afflictions" they had "meekness," *mansuetudo*. As applied to the literal David, S. Augustine sees in the word a reference to his self-restraint, upon those occasions when his enemy Saul was completely in his power. If by David we understand Christ, the word is an anticipation of that very character, which our Blessed Lord was careful to claim for himself, "I am meek and lowly of heart." It should be observed that the Christ is in the Old Testament not unfrequently called simply *David*, without apology, simile, figure, or explanation of any kind—nay, He is so called even in passages where the primary or historic sense of the name is absolutely inadmissible. When, for example, Ezekiel says, "And I will set up one shepherd over them, and he shall feed them, even My servant David"— whom could he mean by *David?* Not, of course, the

S. Augustine.

successor of Saul: for he had been dead some four hundred years when Ezekiel wrote.

It might make modern Christians less reluctant to recognize the Christ when David is spoken of, if they remembered how many incidents in the life of David, too trivial for mention but for some ulterior significance in them, have counterparts in the life of our Lord, and are perhaps set down in Holy Scripture precisely because they were a rehearsal of parts in the great drama that was to follow in the Person of David's Son. Take by itself any one of those incidents in which it is possible to detect a foreshadowing of the Christ; and, though you might be surprised at the exactness of the parallel,—though you might even be willing to pay a compliment to the ingenuity of the adaptation,—yet you might shrink from calling it anything but a coincidence, in what you are content to believe is plain prosaic narrative. But take a string of such analogies, and mark its cumulative effect upon your own mind. Observe how, at his very first introduction upon the divine page, David is represented as the keeper of his father's sheep:[*] how this fact is again and again insisted on,

[*] 1 Sam. xvi. 11.

often when it does not seem to help the matter in hand: how Saul sent messengers with a summons cast in this particular form, "Send me David thy son, *which is with the sheep:*"\* how David himself reverts to it upon an occasion when its mention seems almost inconsistent with the characteristic modesty of a brave man, "Thy servant *kept his father's sheep,* and there came a lion and a bear:"† observe how the same apparently trivial fact has got imbedded in one of the most majestic of all the Psalms, "He chose David also his servant, and took him away from the sheep-folds:"‡—grasp the prominence given to this shepherd character of David, and then transfer your thought to Him who claimed to be the Good Shepherd *par excellence,* and came here to seek and to save that which was lost and strayed from the fold of the Father. Observe, again, how David, at the very onset of his career, exhibited himself as the Deliverer of the people of God from their enemies; how he was sent, and sent too by his father, to sustain his brethren in their conflict, and to sustain them with bread, moreover; and then mark

\* 1 Sam. xvi. 19.   † 1 Sam. xvii. 34.
‡ Ps. lxxviii. 71.

how Jesus declared that He was sent by His Father to feed His brethren—even all the sons of men—with the true bread from heaven, which was His Own Self. Think, again, of David having been anointed much earlier in the secresy of his father's house, yet not coming forward as king till he was thirty years old; and then think of that pointed statement of the evangelist about Jesus, Who also had been from all eternity the Anointed Son in the mansions of His Father—that "Jesus Himself began to be about thirty years of age"\* when He came forward to claim His kingdom over the hearts and consciences of men. Think of David in the Cave of Adullam, represented as the rallying point of the debtor, the distressed, and those who had any bitterness of soul; and then think of Jesus, the Man of Sorrows, Who is the centre of thought in the prayer that God would "forgive us our debts," and who constituted Himself a resting-place for all who travail and are heavy laden. Think of David sustaining his companions in their difficulties with the hallowed bread taken from under the hand of the priest; and then remember that in the days of their faintness Christ has also chosen to

\* S. Luke iii. 23.

sustain His followers by a Sacrament of Holy Bread. Think of David pronounced mad amongst the Philistines; and then think of the blasphemy of the Jews against the Lord,—" He hath a devil, and is mad;" and then as you advance into the Passion of the Christ, think of the persecution of David on the part of Absalom; remember how David's lamentation for his rebellious son took this particular shape,— "Would God I had died for thee,"—exactly the description of what Jesus did for His persecutors. Remember how, when Absalom took arms, though many ways of flight were open to him, yet David took the way of the Mount of Olives—exactly the direction taken by Jesus after the Last Supper. Remember how both of David and of Jesus it is remarked that he passed "over the brook Kedron,"— Kedron, a stream of so little importance, as altogether to disappear at certain seasons of the year; how David is recorded to have wept at Mount Olivet, and then how it was from one of the summits of the same Olivet that Jesus came in sight of the Holy City and wept; how Absalom, the persecutor of David, at the last met his death by hanging by the head from a tree, and then how Judas, the arch-persecutor of Jesus, is said to have gone and hanged himself,—make an effort of thought, and gather up all this together, and then you will feel, I venture to say, that these coincidences (as we began by calling them) are too systematic to be unintentional; that the history of David has for Christians an interest and a significance far deeper than any that could ever attach to the history of Alexander or of Napoleon; and that it could only have been written as it is written, to teach the world to see behind the figure of David in the drama nothing less than the Person of the Christ.

2. How he sware unto the LORD, and vowed a vow unto the mighty God of Jacob.

A repetition of the same fact in different words.

The phrase "mighty God of Jacob" indicates him whom Jacob called his mighty one; as in Jacob's blessing upon Joseph: "The arms of his hands were made strong by the hands of the Mighty God of Jacob"—(Gen. xlix. 24.) —an expression used by Jacob, because God was his

Radak.

deliverer, his strength and support in all his distresses.

The reason why he mentions Jacob here is because in his dream Jacob saw the site of the Temple, the steps of which were the ladder that he saw.* It was with an allusion to the Temple, and not to Bethel where he lay, that he said, "How dreadful is this place! this is none other but the house of God, and this is the gate of Heaven."† Jacob however, though in his dream he saw the future Temple, yet on awaking did not reveal its site, that being a privilege reserved by God for David. There is a propriety in David's mention of Jacob in connection with the Temple, because it was to Jacob that the revelation of the chosen spot was first made; for although Abraham was commanded to offer his son Isaac as a burnt-offering on the same spot, yet there is nothing in Scripture to show that he was acquainted with its selection as the site of the future Temple.

This association of the passage about Jacob's dream with the destined site of the Temple is too curious to be unnoticed; yet it is difficult to see how in its literal sense such application can be reconciled

* Gen. xxviii. 12. † Ibid. 17.

with S. Jerome's statement that Bethel was about twelve miles from Jerusalem.*

A similar method (not however embarrassed by such particularity of detail) of accounting for the mention of the "God of Jacob" is adopted by Aben Ezra. Jacob "vowed a vow," when he declared "this.... shall be God's house."† David accordingly preserves a reminiscence of the fact, when he vowed a vow in connection with a similar subject. <small>Aben Ezra.</small>

Instead of "how he swore," Aben Ezra appears to take the first word as a particle of time. Rather "when he swore."

The Targum substantially follows the Hebrew:—

"Who swore before the Lord (and) vowed to the Mighty One of Jacob." <small>Targum.</small>

Treating the Psalm as a Psalm of the Advent of the Christ, the "vow" is, according to Cassiodorus, the vow of the Son of God to reconcile the world to the Father by His Own Incarnation.

---

\* S. Jer. *De locis Hebraicis.* s.v. *Agai.*

† Gen. xxviii. 20, et seq. "And Jacob vowed a vow, saying, If God will be with me, and will keep me in this way that I go.... then shall the LORD be my God, and this stone, which I have set for a pillar, shall be God's house."

3. Surely I will not come into the tabernacle of my house, nor go up into my bed.

<small>Radak.</small> An hyperbole, meaning that he derived no pleasure from his own house and bed until he had found a place for the *Lord*. The same spirit was exhibited in David's words to Nathan the prophet: "See now, I dwell in an house of cedar, but the ark of God dwelleth within curtains." (2 Sam. vii. 2.)

"My bed" is in Hebrew "the couch of my bed," sc. the couch upon which a bed worthy of a king is spread.

<small>Aben Ezra.</small> Our translation of the verse is justified by Aben Ezra, who remarks that אם is here to be translated not in its usual sense of "if,"—"if I shall come"—but as introducing a vow, "I will not come." This idiom, it may be observed, is more or less missed by our existing translation of Heb. iv. 5: "And in this place again, If they shall enter into my rest"—a translation which is the more curious from the fact that the idiom in the present Psalm is hit off exactly in the preceding chapter, Heb. iii. 11:

"So I sware in My wrath, They shall not enter into My rest."

The Targum gives a new turn to the former part of the verse:—

"Surely I will not go in unto my wife, I will not mount into the couch of my bed." *Targum.*

If we refer the Psalm to the Christ, the "tabernacle of my house" is, according to both S. Jerome and Cassiodorus, the dwelling-place of God in heaven; and in this and the two following verses we have allusion to our Lord's return thither, after His resurrection, with the flesh that He had assumed—that flesh which was an "habitation for the Mighty God of Jacob."

**4. I will not give sleep to mine eyes, *or* slumber to mine eyelids,**

"Sleep," *i.e.*, regular sleep.

Upon the form of the word for "sleep" (שְׁנָת) Radak remarks in his *Book of Roots* that it is not the construct form of the noun; the ת being in place of the more usual ה. The peculiarity of the form is discussed at considerable length by Aben

Ezra upon Ps. cxviii. 14, where the word וְזִמְרָת

<small>Aben Ezra.</small> presents an analogous difficulty. He comes to the conclusion that in the present instance שְׁנָת is in construction with the following word לְעֵינָי the ל being redundant. As an example of a similar redundancy we may quote the form in Ezek. x. 3, עֹמְדִים מִימִין לַבַּיִת, where, he observes,[*] מִימִין is clearly derived from the construct form of the noun, and the ל with the following word is therefore redundant.

<small>Radak.</small> "Slumber to mine eyelids," merely a change of expression for the same thing.

It is remarked, however, by Aben Ezra that the <small>Aben Ezra.</small> Psalmist, in commencing this verse with the same particle (אִם) as the preceding verse, intended to throw all possible emphasis into his vow. The two clauses of this verse need not be taken as a mere repetition of the same thing, since one of them may have reference to the midday sleep in which

---

[*] The form actually quoted by Aben Ezra is לִימִין לבית. But after careful search I fail to find any such phrase in Scripture, and can only conclude, that he had in mind the expression of Ezekiel's, which I have inserted above. The alteration does not affect his argument.

Easterns are said to indulge. The two co-ordinate expressions of the preceding verse—"the tabernacle of my house" and "my bed,"—perhaps lend some colour of probability to this interpretation.

5. Until I find out a place for the LORD, an habitation for the mighty God of Jacob.

Until it is known where the sanctuary of God should be. *A place for the Lord*: the whole earth, observes Aben Ezra, is the Lord's; yet some places are chosen rather than others: so that Jacob could say of one spot, "This is the gate of heaven." Rashi. Aben Ezra.

The word for "habitation" is in the plural, indicating that there should be three temples. Radak.

It is to be presumed that David Kimchi here refers to the Temple of Solomon, the Temple of Zerubbabel, built after the Babylonian Captivity (Ezra v. 2), and the Temple of Herod, which appears in the New Testament.

The Targum reproduces the peculiarity of the Hebrew in putting "habitation" in the plural:—

"Until I find a place for building the Sanctuary of the Lord, the habitations of the Mighty One of Jacob." *Targum.*

In the term "habitation"—tabernacle, or tent, in the Latin—S. Augustine sees an allusion to the Church militant. "A tabernacle applies rather to soldiers in the field; tabernacles are used for soldiers ready for action," he says. The Hebrew word, however, does not contain any special reference to "tent," as the Latin rendering of it here does. *S. Augustine.*

The Targum is word for word as the Hebrew:—

"Surely I will not give sleep to mine eyes, to mine eyelids slumber." *Targum.*

The "bed," the "sleep," and the "slumber" point, according to S. Jerome, to the eternal rest of the Christ. He promises not to return to that rest, unless by His resurrection He first constructed in man, that is to say, in humanity, a worthy "place" for God the Father; and that "place" is, the congregation of the Church. *S. Jerome.*

6. Lo, we heard of it at Ephratah: we found it in the fields of the wood.

Ephrath was the birthplace of David. Cf. 1 Sam. xvii. 12: "Now David was the son of that Ephrathite of Beth-lehem-judah, whose name was Jesse." Radak.

David says, then, that up to this day we knew not for certain the site of the Temple; only at Ephrath, where he grew up, we heard from the ancients that not Shiloh, nor Nob, nor Gibeon, was chosen, but that the place selected should be revealed; and now we have found it in the field, in the floor of Araunah the Jebusite. So Aben Ezra.

"The wood" refers to the trees that were there.

By Aben Ezra, likewise, Ephratah is taken to mean Bethlehem, the import of the whole clause being that men had heard in past days, by the mouth of the Prophets, that the chosen place was to be near Bethlehem—as the site of the Temple actually was—but exactly in which direction from Bethlehem was not known.

Maimonides takes the mention of Ephratah, as pointing to the birthplace of David. We heard of it—presumably the site of the Temple—by the instrumentality of David, who was of Ephratah. So quoted by Aben Ezra.

Rashi's exegesis is somewhat obscure from its extreme brevity. "We heard of it—the glad tidings." That may mean the announcement that the site for the Temple had been discovered; or it might mean, I conceive, the announcement consequent upon that discovery, and contained in the following verse: "We will go into His tabernacles: we will worship at His footstool."

*Rashi.*

The Targum appears to take it in this last way:—
"On all sides we heard the glad cry, Let us go . . . ." But the difficulty of fixing what "it" refers to, probably constituted one of the reasons which led Castellio to say of the passage, "Hujus loci sententiam non intelligo." S. Augustine interprets "it" in yet another way:—*Heard of it.* Heard of what? A place for the Lord.

*Targum.*

*S. Augustine.*

In Hebrew the pronoun "it" is feminine. The reason of this suggests to Aben Ezra quite another interpretation, which has much to recommend it. According to him the pronoun contains an allusion to the Shechinah,* or visible presence of

---

\* It should be noticed that the word *Shechinah* to express the indwelling Presence of God does not occur in the text of Holy

God, which was vouchsafed to the Temple. It is this Presence, found in the fields of Araunah, that is indicated by the "fire," sent from God as an answer to David's sacrifice and prayer. "And He answered him from heaven *by fire* upon the altar of burnt-offering." (1 Chron. xxi. 26.)

It should be noted that the word Shechinah is closely connected with the word for "tabernacle," in verse 7; and "habitation" מִשְׁכָּנוֹת in verse 5.

Aben Ezra.

For the explanation of the phrase "at Ephratah," Rashi suggests two methods which are peculiar to himself. Let us take the historic method first. *Ephratah* he connects (as he does elsewhere) with *Ephraim*, and "at Ephratah,"—or, more properly, "in Ephratah"—is equivalent to "in the Ephraimite;" that is, in the Book of Joshua, who belonged to the tribe of Ephraim, and whose lineage is traced back to Ephraim in

Rashi.

Scripture, though it is common in the Targum of Onkelos; to which, indeed, our use of the term is probably due. According to ancient tradition it was one of the five things which were absent from the second Temple; a want, which according to the Talmud is, in a mystery, indicated by the omission of ה (5) at the end of וְאֶכָּבֵד "And I will be glorified," in Haggai i. 8.

1 Chron. vii. 22-27. The question then arises, How did they "hear of it;" hear, that is, of the future distinction of Jerusalem as the locality of the Divine Presence *—how did they hear of this in the Book of Joshua? The answer lies in the fact that Jerusalem is brought into notice *as* Jerusalem first in the Book of Joshua. (Josh. xv. 8.) So that Israel would say with literal exactness, "We heard of it in the Ephraimite."

This very remarkable interpretation—for as such I must regard it—of a difficult clause, furnishes a good example of that amazing textual knowledge which systematically enables the Hebrew doctors to weave together passages of Scripture the most remote from each other. Unexpected as such an interpretation is to most Christians, it must be admitted to be remarkably in accordance with the facts of Holy

---

\* The commentary of Rashi is very difficult to understand, and needs to be itself—as some of his commentaries actually are—accompanied by a commentary. But after much deliberation about it, I imagine the meaning is as I have given it above. That exegesis of this very troublesome phrase of the Psalms is, in my judgment, worthy of especial remark, as it is perfectly in accordance with the facts of Holy Scripture, and is one of a class of interpretations which commonly escape the notice of Christian expositors.

Scripture. It *is* the case that the character of Joshua, *as* an Ephraimite, is pointedly traced out in the aforesaid chapter of the first Book of Chronicles; the genealogy, it will be noticed, stops with him. It *is* the case that in the Book of Joshua, the Ephraimite, "we hear of" Jerusalem for the first time; and it *is* the case, moreover, that in the passage under notice in the Book of the Ephraimite, the mention of Jerusalem seems gratuitous and (so to speak) unnecessary—"And the border went up by the Valley of the Son of Hinnom unto the south side of the Jebusites; the same is Jerusalem"—a mention therefore which we are not surprised the Psalmist should fix upon as significant.

The only link in the chain of this exegesis that remains to be made good, is the question whether "in Ephratah"* can be properly connected with *Ephraim*: whether, in fact, the "th" of *Ephrath* could in any way arise out of a derivative of *Ephraim*. Rashi has himself anticipated the objection, by quoting the analogous form in 1 Sam. i. 1 :—

"Now there was a certain man of Ramathaim-zophim, of Mount Ephraim, and his name was

* בְּאֶפְרָתָה.

Elkanah, the son of Jeroham, the son of Elihu, the son of Tohu, the son of Zuph, an Ephrathite,"— where *Ephrathite* means, according to Rashi, *Ephraimite*. To this I would add, that in 1 Kings xi. 26: "And Jeroboam the son of of Nebat, an Ephrathite of Zereda," the same word (אֶפְרָתִי) is used to describe the condition of Jeroboam as an Ephraimite.

<small>So also Targum.</small>

The mystic interpretation (Aggadah) of *in Ephratah*, makes it equivalent to *in a distinguished and eminent place*. So likewise Rashi interprets the kindred word discussed above in 1 Sam. i. 1, "a man of noble birth." And in Ruth i. 2, the phrase "Ephrathites of Bethlehem-judah" has, besides its literal meaning, the mystic sense of "distinguished men of Bethlehem-judah." It must be admitted, however, that the etymology upon which this interpretation rests is difficult to trace, and is precarious when found.

<small>Mystic Sense.</small>

If, however, following Radak and Maimonides, we take Ephratah to indicate the birthplace of David, the door is at once opened for the interpretation adopted by S. Cyril of Jerusalem, who applies the verse to the Birth of the Christ in His Human

Nature, of which Nature the Ark in the Temple—so prominent a thought in this Psalm—is mystically the representative.\*

The remark of S. Jerome is to the same effect. *We heard of it at Ephratah,* that is, in Bethlehem; where first the Church was heard of, and in which the Lord Christ took flesh; in which also Rachel, the beloved of Israel, who is a type of the Church, rests. *The fields of the wood* are, with him and others, the nations of the world, formerly unfruitful and covered (as S. Augustine puts it) with the thorns of idolatry, but now brought in to the obedience of Christ. S. Jerome.

The enlargements of the Targum are curious here, and open out new lines of thought:—

"Lo, we heard of it" (the pronoun is feminine here, as in the Hebrew) "in Ephrath, we found it in the field of the wood (thicket) of Libanus, the place where the fathers of old prayed." Targum.

**7. We will go into His tabernacles: we will worship at His footstool.**

\* S. Cyr. Jer. Catech. xii. 9. (Oxf. Ed. s. 20.)

Since we have found the chosen spot, from this day forward let us go into it, because it is His tabernacle.

*Radak.*

His footstool is in Truth; which is established before the throne of the Most High.

*His tabernacles*—the place where David built an altar, and where he was answered "from heaven by fire upon the altar of burnt offering." (1 Chron. xxi. 26.) And of which he said, "This is the house of the Lord God." (Ib. xxii. 1.)

*Aben Ezra.*

It is shown by Joseph Mede that "footstool" in this and kindred passages must mean either (1) the Holy of Holies; or (2) the Ark of the Covenant, which stood therein. In an admirable sermon upon this text he justifies the Christian practice of turning towards the altar during prayer. (See Sermon No. 7, Book II.)

*Mede.*

The Targum follows the Hebrew:—

"We will go into His tabernacle; we will prostrate ourselves at His footstool."

*Targum.*

8. Arise, O Lord, into Thy rest; Thou, and the Ark of Thy strength.

These three verses were recited (in substance and, approximately, in terms) by Solomon at the dedication of the Temple. (Cf. 2 Chron. vi. 41, 42.) Radak.

"Thy rest," or, This place where Thy Presence is finally settled.

"Thou" points to the manifestation of the Divine glory at the dedication of the Temple, after they had introduced the Ark into the most holy place. Cf. 2 Chron. v. 14: "The glory of the Lord had filled the house of God."

The Targum makes a slight change:—

"Arise, O Lord, dwell in the house of His abode with Thy rest, Thou and the Ark, in which is Thy Law." Targum.

*Arise.* Ye know already, says S. Augustine, who slept and who rose again. . . . The Body of Christ, that was born of Mary, hath been understood by some to be the Ark of Sanctification; so that the words, *Arise, O Lord, into Thy resting-place, Thou and the Ark of Thy sanctification*—so the verse runs in the Latin translation—mean, Arise with Thy Body, that they who believe not may handle. S. Augustine.

So, too, S. Jerome: "Now Thou hast fulfilled Thine oath; Thou hast paid Thy vow; now Thou hast found out a place for the Lord; now from Thy Side Thou hast produced the Church; arise now from the dead; return into the Tabernacle and depart to the rest, of which Thou hast spoken above."

<small>S. Jerome.</small>

**9. Let thy priests be clothed with righteousness, and let thy saints shout for joy.**

"Thy priests," *i.e.*, in their ministration. Let them be clothed with the garments of the priesthood which are garments of righteousness.

<small>Radak.</small>

"Let thy saints shout," refers to the singing and playing of the Levites before the Lord. Cf. 2 Chron. v. 12, 13: "Also the Levites which were the singers, all of them of Asaph, of Heman, of Jeduthun, with their sons and their brethren, being arrayed in white linen, having cymbals and psalteries and harps, stood at the east end of the altar, and with them an hundred and twenty priests sounding with the trumpets.

"It came even to pass, as the trumpeters and singers were as one, to make one sound to be heard in praising and thanking the Lord; and when they lifted up their voice with the trumpets and cymbals and instruments of music, and praised the Lord, saying, For He is good; for His mercy endureth for ever: that then the house was filled with a cloud, even the house of the Lord."

In agreement with this is the interpretation adopted by Aben Ezra, that while the "priests" are the sons of Aaron, the "saints" are the Levites, specially spoken of as "the singers" in the passage quoted above; the "shouting for joy" being, of course, their official shout in the execution of their function.

<small>Aben Ezra.</small>

The priests are said to be "clothed in righteousness" —the righteousness, that is, inculcated in the Law— because they were the teachers of the Law and judges of Israel. On this judicial function of the Aaronic priesthood see Deut. xvii. 9; xix. 17; and especially the explicit declaration of Deut. xxi. 5: "And the priests, the sons of Levi, shall come near. . . . and by their word shall every controversy and every stroke be tried."

The Targum distinctly interprets the Saints of this verse as Levites :—

<blockquote>Targum.

"Thy priests shall be clothed with the garments of righteousness : and thy holy Levites shall utter praises over the offerings."</blockquote>

Over and above the obvious interpretation of Christians, the royal "priesthood," putting on righteousness, Cassiodorus gives the further hint that Christ is the "righteousness" spoken of. "This is His Name whereby He shall be called, The Lord our Righteousness." (Jer. xxiii. 6.) The prayer of the verse therefore is, that Christians may be clothed with Christ Himself. "As many of you as have been baptized into Christ, have put on Christ." (Gal. iii. 27.)

10. For thy servant David's sake turn not away the face of thine anointed.

<blockquote>Radak.

For David's sake, because to him the glory of God was revealed in the fire at the floor of Araunah.* For his sake God, he trusts, should accept whatever prayer David himself offers</blockquote>

* 1 Chron. xxi. 26.

in this chosen place, and should "turn not away the face" of Solomon his son in the prayer that he might offer subsequently.

This part of the Psalm bears a strong likeness to the concluding verses of Solomon's prayer,* with which it should be compared.

The first clause, "For thy servant David's sake," Aben Ezra thinks should be connected with the preceding verses: Arise, O Lord, for thy servant David's sake. This enables us to take "thine anointed," as meaning David himself—for David's sake arise and turn not away thine anointed. Aben Ezra.

Rashi agrees with Radak in referring "thine anointed" to Solomon. He connects it with a curious Hebrew tradition which he gives at length in his comment upon the closing words of Ps. xxiv. When Solomon came up to bring the Ark of the Covenant of the Lord into the Holy of Holies, the gates kept themselves firmly closed, and Solomon said four and twenty Psalms; but he was not heard till he recited the words mentioning David at the end of his prayer in 2 Chron. vi. 42: "O Lord God, turn not away the face of Rashi.

\* 2 Chron. vi. 41, 42.

thine anointed: remember the mercies of David thy servant."

The Targum refers this verse to the introduction of the Ark into the Temple:—

<small>Targum.</small> "On account of the innocency of David thy servant, when the Ark enters into the midst of the gates Thou shalt not turn away the face of Solomon thine anointed."

These words are addressed to God the Father, says <small>S. Augustine.</small> S. Augustine. They are a prayer to God on behalf of the remnant of Israel, that in turning His Presence towards the Gentiles, a remnant of the Jews might be saved. The prayer was fulfilled, the same writer adds, in the Twelve Apostles, in the more than five hundred brethren, to whom the Lord showed Himself after His resurrection, and in the many thousands baptized, who laid the price of their possessions at the Apostles' feet.

11. The LORD hath sworn *in* truth unto David: he will not turn from it; Of the fruit of thy body will I set upon thy throne.

The word of the Lord is the oath of the Lord.

The "truth that He sware unto David" is the promise conveyed to him by Nathan the Prophet, "I will set up thy seed after thee, which shall proceed out of thy bowels, and I will establish his kingdom." (2 Sam. vii. 12.)

*Radak.*

"*In* truth : He will not shrink from it," points to the permanence of the promise made through Nathan— "Thine house and thy kingdom shall be established for ever before thee." (2 Sam. vii. 16.) "It," that is to say, refers to "truth."

Nothing is added by the Targum :—

"The Lord sware to David in truth; He will not turn from it (sc. from truth); Of the fruit of thy bowels I will set a king upon thy throne."

*Targum.*

It is urged by S. Cyril of Jerusalem (Catech. xii. 10), and somewhere, I think, by S. Augustine, that the Scriptural promises of a succession to the throne of David assert too much for them to find their fulfilment in the accession of Solomon. When for instance it is said, *His seed shall endure for ever, and his throne as the sun before me* (Ps. lxxxix. 36), "Solomon's throne," observes S. Cyril, "endured not as the sun." In all such places it is, in fact, Christ and

not Solomon that is spoken of. The Father, says S.
Jerome, swears the truth to God Incarnate,
that He will give Him a Spiritual seed, begotten of the Body that He took.

*S. Jerome.*

12. If thy children will keep my covenant and my testimony that I shall teach them, their children shall also sit upon thy throne for evermore.

The Hebrew form (עֵדוֹת) for "Covenant" is peculiar. It is to be taken as a singular noun (with the pronominal suffix in the usual form), and as equivalent to the more ordinary form עֵדוּת, with ו.* Aben Ezra concurs in this view.

*Radak.*

He suggests, however, as an alternative, that it may be an anomalous word compounded from the ideas in singular and plural—that is, I presume, that the anomalous form of the word is designed to affirm at once the multiplicity and the unity of the testimonies

---

\* Radak confirms this view in the *Book of Roots* (ספר השרשים) —his famous Hebrew Lexicon, written in Hebrew, to which subsequent Hebrew Lexicography has been so much indebted.

of God. As an analogous Hebrew form he quotes מַכֹּתְךָ in Deut. xxviii. 59.

"That I shall teach them." The form (זוֹ) of the pronoun, again, is peculiar. It is equivalent to the feminine (זֹאת) of the demonstrative pronoun. In the *Book of Roots* \* Radak quotes the last clause of Hos. vii. 16 as containing a similar form.†

The covenant and the testimony had been already given; nor would there ever be another to supersede the law of Moses. It was the true interpretation of the Law that God was promising to teach them; and this He would do by the mouth of the prophets.

With regard to the grammatical structure of the clause, "that I shall teach them," some Christian writers think that the demonstrative pronoun in Hebrew (זוֹ) does duty for the relative, much as "that" is often used for "which" in English. Rashi, on the contrary, is of opinion that there is an ellipsis of the relative, the pronoun here being a *bonâ fide* demonstrative. He gives the full form thus : זוֹ אֲשֶׁר אלמדם.

---

\* s. v. זה.

† זוֹ לַעֲגָם בְּאֶרֶץ מִצְרָיִם This *shall be* their derision in the land of Egypt.

The pronoun is taken in this latter way by the Targum:—

> "If thy sons keep My covenant and those My testimonies which I teach them, their sons also shall for ever sit upon thy seat."

*Targum.*

Christian commentators offer two distinct interpretations of the clause, "sit upon thy seat." By the one class it is thought to be the "sitting in heavenly places"—the reward of faithful obedience—that is pointed to; by the other class it is applied to apostles, pastors and doctors, who may be said to "sit in the seat" of Christ. Dionysius the Carthusian gives the latter view: S. Jerome gives the former. The latter writer also interprets "their children" of the good works produced by the faithful, and which shall abide with them in the heavenly places. "Their works do follow them." (Rev. xiv. 13.)

On the word "if" which introduces the condition annexed to the promises made to David, the Hebrew Midrash observes that in the Bible three things were given upon conditions, and two things without any condition subjoined. The three which depended on conditions are the Land of Israel, the Sanctuary, and the Kingdom of the house of David.

*Midrash Tehillim.*

The Land of Israel, because it is said before their admission to the promised land: "Take heed to yourselves that your heart be not deceived, and ye turn aside and serve other gods and worship them. . . . lest ye perish quickly from off the good land which the Lord giveth you." (Deut. xi. 16, 17).

The Sanctuary, because it is said of it, concerning this house which thou art in building, if thou wilt walk in My statutes. . . then will I perform My word with thee, which I spake unto David thy father. (1 Kings vi. 12.)

The Kingdom of the house of David, because in the present verse it is said, If thy children will keep my covenant . . . their children also shall sit upon thy throne for evermore.

On the other hand, the Book of the Law and the Covenant of Aaron were given without any attendant condition. "Moses commanded us a law, even the inheritance of the congregation of Jacob." (Deut. xxxiii. 4.)

And of the Covenant of Aaron God said unconditionally, "It is a Covenant of salt for ever before the Lord unto thee and to thy seed with thee." (Numb. xviii. 19.)

13. For the LORD hath chosen Zion; He hath desired *it* for his habitation.

In 2 Sam. v. 7, we are told: "David took (sc. from the Jebusites) the strong hold of Zion; the same *is* the city of David." In this verse of the Psalm David says in effect: "And I am sure that God hath chosen in* Zion what I took." For in the city of Zion the glory of the Shechinah was revealed,† and God longed for it for a dwelling-place for Himself.

<small>Radak.</small>

There is a difficulty in the mention of Zion. For, strictly speaking, the Temple was not situated upon Zion, but upon the adjoining Mount Moriah. It is this apparent difficulty which, I suppose, Aben Ezra has in view when he says that mention is made here of Zion, because Zion was called the city of David. (See 2 Sam. v. 7, 9; 1 Kings viii. 1.) It should be observed, that in David's time the Ark of the Covenant of the Lord

<small>Aben Ezra.</small>

---

\* This appears, according to Radak, to be the explanation of the ב prefixed to ציון. The prefix thus does something more than merely introduce the object of the verb.

† See above on v. 6.

was lodged literally in Zion, and the leading feature in the ceremonial at the dedication of the Temple by Solomon was the transportation of the Ark from Zion to its new abode in Moriah. "Solomon assembled the elders of Israel, and all the heads of the tribes . . . that they might bring up the Ark of the Covenant of the Lord out of the city of David, which is Zion." (1 Kings viii. 1.) The solution of the difficulty appears to lie in the altered meaning of the term *Zion*. Zion meant, at first, a particular mount; then it became synonymous (as, I suppose, Aben Ezra means to indicate) with the *City of David*, whatever the boundaries of that city might be. So that when Moriah became included in the City of David, Moriah got spoken of as Zion; very much as in our own language we do not hesitate to speak of (say) Westminster as London, though London, properly so called, constitutes but a small portion of our modern metropolis. Mr. Lewin, I remember (though I have not his work at hand for quotation), in his work upon Jerusalem, makes a remark to the effect that Zion became a poetic name, rather than a designation of any defined geographical limit.

The Targum follows the Hebrew:—

<small>Targum.</small> "For the Lord delighted in Zion: He desired her for an habitation for Himself."

Zion, says S. Augustine, is the Church herself.

The Hebrew doctors of the Midrash remark upon <small>Midrash Tehillim.</small> the exclusive effect which the "choice" of God has. Before God chose Jerusalem, all the land of Israel was a permitted place of sacrifice. So before Aaron was chosen, all Israel were admissible to priesthood; and before David, all Israel were fit recipients of the royal authority.

**14. This *is* my rest for ever: here will I dwell: for I have desired it.**

The Ark, which was symbolically the throne of the Divine Presence, hitherto had moved about from place to place: now accompanying the chosen people in their journeys (Josh. iii. 3) and their warfare (Josh. vi. 6); now captured by the Philistines (1 Sam. iv. 11). <small>Radak.</small> For the future the Divine Presence should continue in the Temple, to which David looked forward.

The Targum expressly mentions the Shechinah:—

"This is the rest of my Presence (Shechinah): here will I dwell, for I desired her." Targum.

The words, says Cassiodorus, are those of God the Father. They are not to be confined literally to the earthly Jerusalem, which has been often overthrown, but are to be understood of the Church, which is to endure for ever. Tropologically, they are applied by S. Jerome to the faithful soul which is cleansed from sin, and so made the rest and abode of God. Cassiodorus.

S. Jerome.

### 15. I will abundantly bless her provisions: I will satisfy her poor with bread.

It was on Mount Moriah that the Temple was built. There is an affinity between the name "Moriah" and the word for "the former rain" (Joel ii. 23) מוֹרֶה which was one of the causes of the abundant produce that should be consequent upon the presence of God in His Temple. So abundant should the blessing be, that not even the poor in the City of God should be in want. Radak.

The Targum is literal:—

"Her provision I will abundantly bless: and her
<small>Targum.</small> poor shall be satisfied with bread."

The Latin writers comment upon a version which has "widow" in place of "provision." They apply the word either to the Church or to the faithful soul, alike desolate in the world and bereft of all help but that of God. S. Jerome remarks that the Latin rendering is due to the change of a single letter in the Greek version from which it was made—χήραν for θήραν.

*Satisfy her poor with bread.* God Himself, says S. Augustine, is their bread. The bread came down upon the earth. "I am the living Bread that came down from heaven." (S. John vi. 51.)

16. I will also clothe her priests with salvation: and her saints shall shout aloud with joy.

Because the priests are clothed in priestly apparel
<small>Radak.</small> for my service, I will clothe them\* with garments of salvation, so that they shall be saved by Me.

\* This, I imagine, must be Radak's meaning: though in my copy the reading is אלבישה, "I will clothe her."

*Her Saints.* The priests were the subject of the first clause of the verse; and the Levites are the subject of the second, under the title of Saints. Thus it is explained by both Aben Ezra and Radak.

The Levites, Radak explains, are spoken of as *Saints*, or holy ones, with an allusion to the blessing pronounced upon the tribe by Moses, Deut. xxxiii. 8: Radak.

"And of Levi he said, Let thy Thummim and thy Urim be with thy Holy One, Whom thou didst prove at Massah. . . ." The word for *holy one* is the same as that here used for *saints*. חֲסִידֶיהָ

It appears from 2 Chron. v. 12, "Also the Levites which were the singers. . . . being arrayed in white linen, having cymbals and psalteries and harps. . . ." that some of their duties were musical. The promise of God therefore is that because they had shouted and played for the glory of His Name, He would so multiply good upon them that they should shout for their own gladness of heart.

In a previous verse, the Targum interpreted "Saints" as Levites: here it does not do so, except by implication :—

"And her priests I will clothe with garments of redemption: and her saints shall give much praise." *Targum.*

The first of the two clauses in the verse S. Augustine interprets and illustrates by the saying of the Apostle: "As many of you as have been baptized into Christ, have put on Christ." (Gal. iii. 27.)

*Her priests,* says Hugo of S. Caro, are all the faithful of the Church, who present their bodies a living sacrifice, holy, acceptable, to God. So too *her saints* are those who are put into the state of saints by Baptism. This reference gives rise to the mention of the Baptist in the following verse, according to S. Augustine.

A third way of interpreting the two classes of "priests and saints" is that adopted by the Latin Gloss. The first class is there taken for prelates in the Church, and the second for clergy subordinate to them. This, it will be observed, is not altogether unlike the line of the Hebrew commentators, which takes the two classes to be Priests and Levites respectively.

17. There will I make the horn of David

to bud: I have ordained a lamp for mine Anointed.

*The horn*, the symbol of strength and sovereignty. The verse is to be referred altogether to the Messiah, as is the kindred prophecy of Jer. xxiii. 5: "Behold, the days come, saith the Lord, that I will raise unto David a righteous Branch." Radak.

The same Messianic drift apparently is seen in this verse by Aben Ezra. For he says that it is a prophecy of the perpetual continuance of the kingdom of David—a continuance, I may add, which can be discovered nowhere else than in the kingdom of the Christ. Aben Ezra.

*Ordained a lamp for mine Anointed*, that is, I will set up a King who shall illuminate the people as a lamp. This idea is found also in Christian expositors. With S. Augustine the "lantern" which God had ordained for the Christ was His Human Nature.\* That lantern, says S. Augustine, He lighted as He hung upon the Cross, and therewith He sought the lost

---

\* See S. Aug. Enarr. in Ps. ciii. Sermo IV.

piece of money. But even more beautiful is the application of the "lantern" to S. John the Baptist, of whom the Lord Himself said (S. John v. 35): "He was a burning and a shining light." See S. Augustine's discussion of this last passage, where he says, "All prophecy was one great lantern" (Omnis prophetia una magna lucerna.) S. Aug. Tract. in Joan. Evang. xxiii. Cf. 2 Pet. i. 19.

S. Jerome, and indeed most of the subsequent writers, agree in taking S. John the Baptist to be the "lantern."

In connection with S. John the Baptist, too, S. Augustine has an interpretation of the "horn," which is quite his own. The horn is the symbol of exaltation. The true exaltation consists in self-abasement. "What is spiritual loftiness, save to trust in Christ? not to say, It is my work, I baptize; but, *He it is which baptizeth.*" (S. John i. 33.) There was, we may add, the same deep spiritual exaltation in the Baptist's contrast betwixt himself and the Christ: *He must increase, but I must decrease.*" (S. John iii. 30.)

The Targum paraphrases the first clause:—

"There will I cause to spring up a glorious king for the house of David: I ordained a lamp for my Christ." Targum.

18. His enemies will I clothe with shame: but upon himself shall his crown flourish.

Radak observes that some of the Hebrew interpreters have seen here an allusion to the holy garments for Aaron in Exod. xxviii. 36: Radak.
"And thou shalt make a plate of pure gold, and grave upon it, like the engravings of a signet, HOLINESS TO THE LORD." The word for "plate" in this passage is akin to the verb, "shall flourish," in the Psalm.* The effect of this would be to make the verse a reference to the priestly character of the Christ—"His crown shall be the mitre-plate."

It is well observed by Aben Ezra that the two clauses of the verse correspond respectively with the two preceding verses. The priests Aben Ezra.
of Zion should be clothed with salvation; and here, by way of contrast, the enemies should be clothed with shame. It should be noted that the structure

* The words are respectively ציץ and יציץ.

of the two parallel clauses corresponds exactly in Hebrew, word answering to word. In the second part of this verse, the parallelism is sustained no longer by way of contrast, but of resumption. Before, the horn of David should be made to bud: here, his crown should flourish upon himself.

Rashi explains the difficult word יָצִיץ (flourish) by יָאִיר (be brilliant) and illustrates its meaning by the kindred word (נֹצְצִים) in Ezek. i. 7, which Christian lexicographers, following, I suppose, the Lexicon of Radak,* commonly put under a different root, and which the English translators have rendered "sparkled."

The Targum is quite literal:—

Targum.     "His enemies will I clothe with garments of shame: but upon him shall his crown flourish."

The clothing of the enemies of "David" with shame is referred both by S. Jerome and by Cassiodorus to His Second Advent, when they shall see Him in His Majesty.

* Ezekiel's word Radak himself puts under the root נוץ. He remarks that Rabbi Judah has referred it to a form נצץ, but endeavours to show that he was ill advised in doing so.

Amongst Christian writers, S. Jerome seems to adopt the same explanation of the "crown," as that given by Radak amongst the Hebrew authorities. It is the "crown" of the eternal priesthood of the Christ, who is consecrated, says the Apostle, for evermore. (Heb. vii. 28.)

Behold — Dionysius the Carthusian ends his exposition—we have heard a glorious and mysterious Psalm, in which the Incarnation of the Christ and the institution of the Church are figured with much beauty. Tropologically, also, the Psalm admonishes us to swear and vow a vow that we will not come into the tabernacle of our house, until within ourselves we find a place for the Lord, purifying our hearts from superfluous care, from inordinate affection, and from all sloth.

It was, no doubt, some one, or perhaps all, of these last meanings that caused this one of the Gradual Psalms to be selected *Eucharistic Use.* for recitation by those about to celebrate the Holy Communion of the Lord's Supper. It is appointed to be said by Priest and Deacons as a preparation for the service in the Divine Liturgy, according to the rite and ceremonies of the Orthodox Armenian Church of S. Gregory the Illuminator.*

* Translated from the Armenian, with an Introduction and Notes, by the Rev. S. C. Malan, M.A., Vicar of Broadwindsor, and Prebendary of Sarum. London; Nutt. 1870.

## CHAPTER XX.

**PSALM CXXXIII.**

A Song of Degrees of David.

1. Behold, how good and how pleasant *it* is for brethren to dwell|| together in unity! 　　|| Heb. *even together.*

THE Psalm must be taken in connection with "the two Anointed Ones" of Zechariah, the prophet of the Return from Captivity.* These two are, in Radak's view, the Messiah who was to come as a king, and the high-priest at the time of His coming. 　Radak. And these two are "brethren" in their eminence and their lordship over Israel. The Christ should sit (dwell—the same word in Hebrew) upon the throne of judgment and sovereignty, governing Israel: and the high-priest should instruct them in the Law; and one should not be jealous of the other. Each

* Zech. iv. 14.

should "dwell" upon the throne of eminence; and how good and how pleasant should such "dwellings" be! The Psalm then in this exegesis is an anticipation of the kingdom of the Christ.

The meaning of the difficult particle "even," omitted in the Authorised Version, is explained by some of the Hebrew commentators as being significant. The phrase גַּם יָחַד (even together) is intended to strengthen the idea of their unity. As they should be one in eminence, so they should be brethren likewise in vesture,* and together, moreover, in unity of purpose. Compare Zechariah's declaration: "The counsel of peace shall be between them both." (Zech. vi. 13.) It should be observed, however, that in the verse of Zechariah the English translation appears to make the subject of all the verbs the same, though in Hebrew it is not necessarily so.

Under the head of grammatical explanation, Aben Ezra draws attention to the fact that דָּבָר (thing) is omitted; the words expressed טוֹב and נָעִים being *bonâ fide* adjectives.

Aben Ezra.

In his view the Psalm connects itself with the

---

* So my copy of Radak has it (בלבושם), but I question if the reading is correct.

preceding. There the promise from God had been, "There will I make the horn of David to bud," (Ps. cxxxii. 17.) that is, the house of David should be set up. Here the Psalmist affirms that in the days of Solomon the house of David should be undivided. Under this interpretation the גַּם (*also* or *even*) in its strange position points to the priests, who are likewise to be comprehended in the national unity. It might be observed that it was through a strange priesthood and their ministrations that this unity was broken in the time of Jeroboam.

As an alternative interpretation, Aben Ezra would refer the Psalm to the community of the priests, dwelling as brethren together; the גַּם in this instance signalizing the high-priest as being embraced in the unity.

But this strange word גַּם seems to come out with most force in the exegesis of Rashi, who explains the drift of the Psalm differently, though still with reference to the building of the Temple by Solomon. When God should dwell in His sanctuary with Israel, who are called brethren and friends, then should God *also* (גַּם) be united (יַחַד) with them.

Rashi.

The Targum makes a slight enlargement besides that in the title:—

*Targum.* "A song which was sung upon the steps of the abyss. Behold, how good and how sweet it is to dwell in Zion and Jerusalem as two brothers indeed as one."

In the Christian exegesis, the Psalm corresponds to the fourteenth of the steps of Christian virtue, and accordingly speaks of charity.

The association of the two qualities *good* and *pleasant* in this charity is much insisted on by S. Jerome. There are many things which are good but which are not at the same time pleasant. Martyrdom is one such thing. In charity, however, both these merits are united. The "brethren" spoken of are spiritual brethren, rather than brethren after the flesh. The dwelling together of these latter is often a source of discord rather than of unity. The example of Esau and Jacob is a case in point. The "brethren" of the Psalm are such as our Lord intended when He said to the holy women after His resurrection, "Go tell My brethren." (S. Matt. xxviii. 10.)

The Psalm is specially interpreted as a praise of

the monastic life. This is found in most of the Latin writers. We have it as early as S. Augustine, and we have it also in Dionysius the Carthusian in the middle age. The Psalm is true in a sense of all Christians, says S. Jerome; but it is especially true of the monastic fraternities. Even in the Churches the "unity" is very far from perfect; one is in a hurry to go home, another to go to the play, and a third is thinking of his gain. But in the monastery how different! There all have the same mind and aim.

2. *It is* like the precious ointment upon the head, that ran down upon the beard, *even* Aaron's beard; that went down to the skirts of his garments;

The vowel-point of כ in כַּשֶּׁמֶן indicating the presence of the definite Article shows that the Psalmist has in view some particular ointment, viz., the Ointment of the Holy Unction. To the same degree, he says, shall the dwelling of the "brethren" be good and pleasant as the anointing of the priest is good

<small>Radak. So Rashi; and Aben Ezra likewise on the presence of the Hebr. Article.</small>

and pleasant on the day when he is elected high-priest.

Two reasons may be assigned why mention is made of the Unction of the Priest and not of the Unction of King David. First, because Unction was originated in the case of Aaron, who was anointed when God tabernacled in Israel and the tabernacle was set up; and so likewise would it be that when the Sanctuary was built, the Christ should stand upon the earth as King, and God should tabernacle there. (Compare the Christian Doctrine of the Incarnation.) And, secondly, because the Unction of Aaron took place in the sight of all Israel, while the Unction of David was effected in the privacy of his home in the presence only of Jesse, his brethren, and the elders of Bethlehem: and so likewise, in the future, the exhibition of the Christ—the one of the two "brethren"—should take place before the eyes of all Israel and of the Gentiles; distinguished, that is, by the publicity that attended the Unction of Aaron and not by the secrecy that was observed in that of David.

*Ran down upon the beard.* Sc. upon the occasion

[side notes: Radak. So also Aben Ezra.]

of Aaron's consecration by Moses. The ceremony is described in Lev. viii. 1-13. The "garments" spoken of in the Psalm are the official garments of priesthood, with which Moses invested him before the Unction.  *Radak.*

The word translated "skirts"—more properly, perhaps, *edge*—is explained by Radak to mean the collar of the holy robe. Rashi gives the same interpretation, adding that upon the collar the beard rested.  *Rashi.*

The details of the Anointing are explained at length by Radak. He says that Moses first poured the oil—the Hebrew word for "ointment" in the Psalm is the same as that (שֶׁמֶן) for "oil" in the chapter from Leviticus— upon Aaron's head, from whence it ran down upon the beard and the holy raiment; and that afterwards with the oil he made the sign of the Greek letter Gamma (γ or Γ) — Quære: can this be connected with the sign of the Cross?—between his eyebrows.  *Radak.*

The word for "garments" here (מִדּוֹתָיו) is used of the "linen garment" of the priest in Lev. vi. 3. (vi. 10. A.V.)

2 A

The word for "skirts" is in the Targum also rendered simply "border:"—

Targum.
" (It is) as the precious ointment which was poured upon the head, descending upon the beard, the beard of Aaron, descending upon the border of his garments."

A Hebrew treatise* commenting upon the present verse explains that the reference is to "the High-Priest above, at the right hand of the King, a Priest for ever"—that is, to the Christ.

This exactly accords with the description given by

S. Jerome.
S. Jerome. The beard is the index of a man. The Anointing of the Eternal Spirit descended from the Divine Word upon the beard—that is, upon the perfect man.

With S. Augustine, the "beard" stands for the

S. Augustine.
Apostles and first Saints who contended for the faith of Christ our "Head," and the Sacerdotal "garment" is the Church. The Unction of the Spirit descended from the "Head," the Christ, and being conducted through Apostles

---

* The *Sohar Chadash*, fol. 41-3, quoted by Mr. McCaul in his work on the Epistle to the Hebrews. I have no access to the treatise in the original.

as its channels, descended upon the "garment" of the Church.

3. As the dew of Hermon, *and as the dew* that descended upon the mountains of Zion: for there the LORD commanded the blessing, *even* life for evermore.

The apparent difficulty that lies in the Hebrew, nakedly translated, of the first clause is obliterated by the translation above. That difficulty, however, is fully exhibited in the older translation of the Prayer Book:—

"Like as the dew of Hermon: which fell upon the hill of Sion."

That translation presents exactly the succession of the Hebrew words. The difficulty arises from the fact that Sion lay far to the south of Hermon, and therefore could not literally receive the dew of Hermon. One or two methods have been suggested by modern commentators to overcome the difficulty. It has been said (1) that it was only by a figure that the dew of Hermon in the north was supposed to fall upon Zion in the south. By others it has been thought (2) that "dew of Hermon" was used as a generic term for "dew" simply; very much, I would suggest, as *India-rubber* amongst ourselves would be used for any preparation of caoutchouc, though not necessarily coming from India. But the easiest and most natural interpretation (3) seems to be

*Radak.*

that adopted by the English translators, and adopted probably from Radak. Indeed, we have here probably an example of their admirable familiarity with the traditional interpretation treasured up from antiquity in the writings of the Hebrew doctors—a familiarity, I am bound to say, which is very far in advance of what is discernible in the bulk of more recent writers, and which has taught me, without saying that they are exempt from error, to be very cautious in amending any seeming eccentricities in their version.

Aben Ezra gives, on his own part, a decided preference to the same view as Radak; though he mentions that Maimonides has debated the

*Maimonides.*

question, and interprets it, "As the dew of Hermon, of whose descent the hills of Zion are worthy."

It should be observed, that the Hebrew participle

might, perhaps, with more propriety be translated as a present than as a past—"that descends," rather than "that descended," as the A. V. The Hebrew commentators seem to be unanimous in viewing it under this aspect.

The apparently arbitrary insertion of the words in italics, *and as the dew*, in order to overcome the geographical difficulty of the Hebrew, has, I repeat, good Hebrew authority. Take "as the dew" twice, says Radak: it is just as if it had said, "As the dew of Hermon, as the dew which descends upon the mountains of Zion." Radak.

*Hermon* is specified as furnishing an example of the magnitude of the mountains in the land of Israel: and *mountains of Zion*, because there should be the seat and origin of the Messiah's kingdom. "And of Sion it shall be reported that He was born in her." (Ps. lxxxvii. 5, P. B. V.).

The words *Hermon* and *Sion* occur together again in another passage: "Even unto mount Sion, which is Hermon." (Deut. iv. 48.)

The joint mention of the anointing oil and the dew points to the two "brethren" who, according to Radak, form the subject of the Radak.

Psalm—the Kingly Christ and the High-priest; the oil of course indicating the High-priest, as has been shown above; and the "dew" indicating the king, according to the similitude in Prov. xix. 12: "The king's wrath is as the roaring of a lion; but his favour is as dew upon the grass." In the mention of "dew," too, there is a further allusion to the redemption from Captivity—and (a Christian writer may add) from that sorer Captivity under evil, of which Babylon was a figure—in harmony with the promise in Micah v. 7: "And the remnant of Jacob shall be in the midst of many people as a dew from the Lord." And yet once again, the dew is said to fall *upon the mountains*, as being the spots that stand most in need of it.

Rashi gives an explanation of his own, as well as one from the Talmud. In his own view, the formula in this and the preceding verse, "It is *like* (כְּ) the precious ointment . . . *As* (כְּ) the dew of Hermon . . ." ought to be taken thus, "*As* (כְּ) the precious ointment. . . . *So* (כְּ) the dew of Hermon. . . ." In this way, it follows the analogous formula in Hosea iv. 9. Like people, like priest (כְּעָם כַּכֹּהֵן). He ignores altogether the geographical difficulty dis-

<small>Rashi.</small>

cussed above. "As the precious oil, so pleasant is the dew of Hermon, which is higher than the mountains of Zion. The dew, moreover, descending from Hermon upon the mountains of Zion is as the anointing oil, which imported greatness and distinction. So the dew of Zion imports honour and glory for Israel." Rashi, however, adds that the ancient Hebrew doctors have applied the "dwelling of brothers" to Moses and Aaron, and that in one of the sections of the Mishna\* the whole Psalm is expounded of transgression with the Oil of Unction; though to what transgression in particular he refers I have been unable to discover. Possibly it means the absence of transgression—that Moses and Aaron were at one in not transgressing in the matter.

A curious soliloquy on the part of each of the two brothers, Moses and Aaron, is given in the Hebrew Midrash. Each would be intensely *Midrash Tehillim.* anxious lest any mistake should have been made in the details of Aaron's Anointing, as commanded by God. Moses said to himself, Perchance, though God forbid that it be so, I have erred with the Oil of

\* הוריות.

Unction. The Divine Voice answers him and says, It is as the dew of Hermon (N.B. The Midrash has the same translation as Rashi, which I have given above: *As* the ointment, *So* the dew). What is dew? There is no error in it. Assuredly then there is no error in the ointment. But then Aaron would say within himself in his anxiety, Though Moses has not erred, yet perchance I have done so. And him the Divine Voice answers, Behold how good and how pleasant is the dwelling of brothers, *yea, together:* Moses has not erred, and so neither hast thou erred.

The interpretation of the verse is made by S. Jerome to turn upon the meaning of the name Hermon, which, he rightly says, is *anathema, rejected, reprobate.* The Divine Scripture was first committed to the Jew, who has become reprobate in his unbelief, and it has now descended upon Zion, to wit, the Christian Church.

S. Jerome.

The Psalmist would have it understood, says S. Augustine, that it is of God's grace (figured by the dew) that brethren dwell together in unity.

S. Augustine.

For *there*, that is, upon the mountain of Zion. "Oh, that the salvation were given unto Israel out of Sion."

(Ps. liii. 7; P. B. V.)   Sion is the figure of the Church. *There* in the Church the Lord hath promised the blessing of life for evermore.

*Blessing* is, in Aben Ezra's view, the produce of the earth upon which the life (in the next clause) of man depends. Aben Ezra.

*For evermore*, that is, in the world to come. Radak.

The Targum gives no help in solving the difficulties discussed above:—

"As the dew of Hermon, descending upon the mountains of Zion: for there the Lord enjoined the blessing, life for evermore." Targum.

Our life, says S. Jerome, is Christ. He who confesses Christ shall receive life for evermore. S. Jerome.

## CHAPTER XXI.

### PSALM CXXXIV.

A Song of Degrees.

Behold, bless ye the LORD, all ye servants of the LORD, which by night stand in the house of the LORD.

THIS Psalm is in a measure connected with the pre-
<small>Aben Ezra.</small> ceding by both Aben Ezra and Radak.
<small>Radak.</small> *Behold*, calls attention to the fact with which that Psalm concludes, viz., that the Lord had commanded a blessing for them. The summons, therefore, now is that blessing should be reciprocated for blessing.

There seems to be a difference of opinion as to the persons indicated by *Servants*, and consequently
<small>Aben Ezra.</small> as to the subsequent action of the Psalm.
Aben Ezra (and he has apparently other Hebrew authorities with him) takes *Servant* to mean

the priest; drawing from this intention of the Psalm an interpretation of *by night*. So great was the privilege conferred by God upon the ranks of the priesthood, that *their* service of praise for the blessings, by which they were distinguished, should not cease even by night.

Radak, on the contrary, expressly disowns this line of exegesis. The *Servants* of the Lord are, in his judgment, the wise and holy, who by night rise from their beds and enter into the house of God for prayer and praise. According to the Midrash they are the wise, who spend the night in the study of the law of God. Radak.<br>Midrash Tehillim.

The Targum emphasises that character in the Psalm which has led the Christian Church to make this a Compline Psalm:—

"A song which was sung upon the steps of the abyss. Behold, bless the Lord, all ye servants of the Lord, who stand upon the watch-house of the sanctuary of the Lord, and who praise Him by night." Targum.

It corresponds to the fifteenth and last of the steps of Christian virtue, and speaks accordingly of love to God, thus supplementing the Dion. Carth.

preceding Psalm, which was a Psalm of love to our neighbour.

*By night.* That is to say, in the course of this world, which is in Scripture spoken of under the figure of night. "The night is far spent, the day is at hand." (Rom. xiii. 12.) So it is taken by S. Jerome and several of the Christian writers.

<small>Christian Writers.</small>

Yet the literal sense of the word can never be lost sight of by us since the Church has adopted this as one of the Night Psalms in the Compline Office. With this sense the Psalm applies to the work of those holy persons who pray while others sleep. It has a parallel in the thought of Bishop Ken, in lines which form part of his Evening Hymn, though they are omitted from the abbreviated forms of the hymn in common use:—

> "You, my blest Guardian, whilst I sleep,
> Close to my bed your Vigils keep,
> Divine love into me instil,
> Stop all the avenues of ill.
>
> Thought to thought with my soul converse,
> Celestial joys to me rehearse,
> And in my stead all the night long,
> Sing to my God a grateful song."

It used to be a favourite proverb with the late good

Bishop Hamilton of Sarum—I heard him say it many times, but I have not been able to find whose the saying is—"Stat mundus precibus sanctorum"—The world stands by the prayers of the saints.

2. Lift up your hands‖ *in* the Sanctuary, and bless the LORD.  ‖ Or, *in holiness*.

*In the Sanctuary.* So the Hebrew word is explained by Radak. The Midrash, however, takes it as in the margin, *in holiness*, that is to say, washed, technically clean. Indeed this verse is made the basis of one of the rules of the Talmud about what are called the "three connections" —acts, that is, that are to be connected, and to follow one immediately upon the other. One of those "connections" is that the benediction is to follow immediately upon the washing of the hands. This gives a decided preponderance of Hebrew authority in favour of the translation in the A.V. margin, rather than that of the text. <small>Radak. Midrash Tehillim.</small>

*Lift up your hands*, sc., in prayer, if *Servants* in the former verse be taken for the faithful people. But *lift up your hands* in the act <small>Aben Ezra.</small>

of benediction, if the Psalm be addressed to the Priests. It is identically the phrase used of Aaron in Levit. ix. 22: "And Aaron lifted up his hand towards the people and blessed them."

*Bless ye the Lord*, are the words of the Cantor according to Radak. On the other hand, Aben Ezra remarks, that the formula is to the present day the benediction of priests.

The Targum employs a technical word, which leaves us free to interpret the lifting up of the hands either of prayer or of benediction :—

Targum. "Lift up your hands of (*or* with) holiness, ye priests, upon the holy rostrum, and bless the Lord."

The "holy rostrum" here introduced is the raised platform in the Temple or in the Synagogue, from which prayers were said, psalms were sung, and the recitation of the public offices took place. So far the Targum might be thought to favour the interpretation of "lifting the hands" as referring to prayer. It is not so in reality, however. For the priests were specially required to ascend the rostrum to give the benediction to the people. The directions for the priestly benediction are given in Numb. vi. 23 :

"Speak unto Aaron and unto his sons, saying, On this wise ye shall bless the children of Israel." Buxtorf quotes* the Targum of Jonathan on the passage, as explaining that the Sons of Aaron should do so and so, "when they stretch out their hands *upon the rostrum.*" Further, the Targum name for the rostrum (*Ducan*) at length came to be used to signify the blessing itself. It is discussed in this sense by Wagenseil upon the Treatise Sotah in the Talmud. Surenhusius' Mishna, vol. iii., p. 265, col. i.: ed. 1520. Amsterdam. I conclude therefore that the Targum rather supports, than otherwise, the interpretation which would refer the "lifting up the hands" to the act of benediction rather than that of prayer, and which has, in my judgment, the most to recommend it.

S. Jerome and several of the Latin writers offer yet another meaning for the phrase "lift up your hands;" lift them in good deeds: lift them, as Moses lifted his in the conflict with Amalek, and as Jesus lifted His upon the Cross. S. Jerome and others.

* Lex. Chald. s.v. דּוּכָן.

3. The LORD that made Heaven and earth bless thee out of Zion.

In the opinion of the commentators, says Radak, these are words which the priests address to Israel in giving them benediction. But in my opinion, he adds, they are the words of the Cantor, who said *Bless ye the Lord* at the end of the former verse; the meaning being, If ye will bless the Lord, then the Lord will bless you.

*Radak.*

*That made heaven*, which pours blessings upon the world: *and earth*, which yields its produce for a blessing at the command of God.

*Out of Zion*, because Zion was the seat of the Divine glory, and from thence the blessing should proceed to all Israel.

Rashi has no comment on this Psalm.

The Targum is quite literal:—

*Targum.*

"The Lord shall bless thee out of Zion, Who made Heaven and earth."

S. Jerome gives a similar intention to the verse to that which Radak (above) says was given by the ancient Hebrew interpreters. He makes it, that is to say, a response to what went

*S. Jerome.*

before, and uttered by a different speaker. The verse, he says, is spoken by the Holy Spirit, or at least by the Prophet speaking in the Spirit. And thus it forms a kind of close to the whole group of Gradual Psalms: Thou who hast thus mounted up the successive steps of Christian perfection; who hast done so and so; who hast trust in God, and humility, and the other grades of virtue; who blessest God; who liftest up thy hands in the Sanctuary—receive also thy reward. The Lord that made Heaven and earth bless thee out of Zion. The Lord who made thee—earth, if thou art a sinner, and Heaven, if thou art a saint—bless thee out of the Heavenly Jerusalem, where is bliss and where are the archangels, and the rest of the Powers, and Apostles, and Prophets, and holy Martyrs, and the throngs of Angels and Saints, who follow the Lamb whithersoever He goeth.

"And after these things I heard a great voice of much people in Heaven, saying, Alleluia." (Rev. xix. 1.) The next word in the Hebrew Psalter that immediately follows the Gradual Psalms, which have pictured the Christian's ascent to Heaven—the very next word is *Hallelujah:* Praise ye the Lord.

## CHAPTER XXII.

### THE PREVALENCE OF THE ODD NUMBER.

THE preference of the Church for the odd number in the recitation of the Psalms has been already noticed incidentally in this work. But as the subject is one that has escaped the attention of many, I subjoin here a few facts that I have been able to observe in connection with it.

It may be thought perhaps that such a detail is beneath the notice of the Christian Church; and that if the result of any observations can be recorded *{The prevalence not accidental.}* which do seem to indicate a preference for the odd number, yet the seeming preference arises from accident more probably than from design. A presumption to the contrary, however, is at once raised by the emphatic manner in which the odd number is made imperative by the ancient regulation as to the number of Collects which should day by day be said in the Offices of the Church.

In the ancient Eucharistic Rite of Sarum the rubric as to number in the Collects stands thus:—

It should be noted that on all Sundays and Feasts, when the choir is ruled throughout the year this principle is generally observed, that at Mass there are said just so many Collects as were said at Matins save on Christmas Day: with this condition, however, that at Mass *the odd number of the said Collects be always maintained*, except in the Octave of Christmas only.

\* \* \* \* \* \*

It is to be observed that according to the use of Sarum there are never said more than seven Collects at Mass, because God only appointed seven petitions in the Lord's prayer.\* \* \* \* \*

---

\* Notandum quod in omnibus Dominicis et in festis cum regimine chori per totum annum, hoc generaliter observatur, ut ad missam tot dicantur Collectæ quot dicebantur ad Matutinas, nisi in die Nativitatis Domini: ita tamen quod ad missam impar numerus ipsarum Collectarum semper custodiatur: nisi in hebdomada Nativitatis Domini tantum.

\* \* \* \* \* \* \* \*

Notandum est quod secundum usum Sarum nunquam dicuntur ultra septem Orationes ad Missam quia Deus in Oratione Dominicali tantum constituit septem petitiones. Missale ad usum Insignis et præclaræ Ecclesiæ Sarum. Burntisland, 1861, pp. 4, 6.

It probably has escaped the notice of many, that the principle laid down in this ancient rubric is not altogether unrecognized in our existing Book of Common Prayer. At the end of the Order for Holy Communion there is a group of six Collects, which are "to be said after the Offertory, when there is no Communion, every such day one or more; and the same may be said also, as often as occasion shall serve, after the Collects either of Morning or Evening Prayer, Communion or Litany, by the discretion of the Minister." The "occasion," referred to here, arises probably when the assigned Collects of the day would, if unsupplemented by one or more of these occasional Collects, violate the ancient requirements of the odd and even numbers. Thus in our own Reformed Prayer Book there would be just one day in the year when the tale of Collects would necessarily reach the lawful maximum of seven. That day is Good Friday. There are the three Collects appointed for the day; these to be followed by the Collect for Ash Wednesday, making four; the two invariable Collects (for Peace and Grace) at Matins, six; and one of those occasional Collects added to make the odd number, seven.

*The English Prayer Book.*

I am not acquainted with any explicit declaration that the same rule of odd numbers was to be maintained in the Psalms. But, as a fact, the same rule was commonly maintained nevertheless. There are many examples in which its influence may fairly be presumed; while there are also many in which the same influence can be clearly and unquestionably traced.

The Greek Psalter furnishes an example of the latter class. The Psalms, it is well known, are there divided into twenty sections, which are called Kathismata, and of which the group of Gradual Psalms forms the eighteenth. If we number the Psalms as they are numbered in the Hebrew Psalter, the division is as follows:—

Kathisma i. comprises Psalms i. to viii.
,, ii. ,, ,, ix. to xvii.
,, iii. ,, ,, xviii. to xxiv.
,, iv. ,, ,, xxv. to xxxii.
,, v. ,, ,, xxxiii. to xxxvii.
,, vi. ,, ,, xxxviii. to xlvi.
,, vii. ,, ,, xlvii. to lv.
,, viii. ,, ,, lvi. to lxiv.

Kathisma ix. comprises Psalms lxv. to lxx.
,, x. ,, ,, lxxi. to lxxvii.
,, xi. ,, ,, lxxviii. to lxxxv.
,, xii. ,, ,, lxxxvi. to xci.
,, xiii. ,, ,, xcii. to ci.
,, xiv. ,, ,, cii. to cv.
,, xv. ,, ,, cvi. to cix.
,, xvi. ,, ,, cx. to cxviii.
,, xvii. ,, ,, cxix.
,, xviii. ,, ,, cxx. to cxxxiv.
,, xix. ,, ,, cxxxv. to cxliii.
,, xx. ,, ,, cxliv. to cl.

Now it will be observed that some of these sections contain an even and some an odd number of Psalms. But what is to my present purpose is this: that in the cases where such number is even, the odd number is artificially produced, by grouping two or more Psalms together, and saying them as one, with the "Gloria" only after the last of them. Every Kathisma is, in fact, subdivided into three sections, each of which is called a Stasis; even the solitary Psalm of the seventeenth Kathisma is so divided; and only at the end of each Stasis is the formula which corresponds to our "Gloria" recited. We have, then, here in the Greek Psalter a highly artificial arrangement for securing the odd number. The fact that the particular odd number is uniformly three, may suggest to us the reason which led early Christianity to its preference for the odd number. It was probably because such number best furnished a memorial of the Trinity.

Let us pass now to a Latin Psalter, and we shall find the same principle at work. In the Sarum Rite, if the number of Psalms for an Office happened to be odd, well: but if it happened to be even, then the odd number was often artificially produced by omitting a "Gloria," and saying two or more Psalms as one. Thus, in the Office for Compline the Psalms were invariable throughout the year, and they were four in number (Psalms iv., xxxi. (to end of verse 6), xci., and cxxxiv.). But then the "Gloria" is omitted after the third, the two last being said as one, and the odd number produced. In some modern translations, I observe, this little point is missed, a "Gloria" being prescribed after each of the four Psalms.

*Use of Sarum.*

Once again. At the four Central Offices of the

day,—Prime, Terce, Sext, and None,—Psalm cxix. is said throughout, a portion being assigned to each. But here again the same principle is enforced. At Sext, for instance, six portions (Octaves) of the Psalm are appointed. But the "Gloria" is to be said only at the end of every sixteen verses, and not at the end of every eight as with ourselves, the odd number being thus secured.

Another good illustration of the principle under discussion is furnished by the Psalms at Matins on Sundays. Those Psalms are divided into three groups, each of which, I need hardly say, is called a Nocturn. Now the second and third of these Nocturns consist each of them of three Psalms, every one of which has its own "Gloria Patri." Here the odd number might be thought to be undesigned. The first Nocturn, however, seems to be little short of fatal to such a supposition. For though it contains twelve Psalms, and seems at first glance to negative altogether the principle in question, yet we find that these twelve Psalms are practically made into three, by grouping some of them together as one, and reciting them under a common "Gloria Patri." And thus the first Nocturn of the Sunday Matins, instead of being evidence against the alleged principle of a regard for the odd numbers, furnishes, when more closely examined, the strongest possible confirmation of it.

These are but specimens of a usage which might be further illustrated by almost any number of examples that are to be found in the ancient Services. It does not, indeed, appear that the rule of the odd number was observed without exceptions. Such a rule, however unmistakeably it might have influenced the Service Book, would nevertheless have been compelled, from time to time, to yield to one or other of those many exigencies which control the details of daily devotion. We may admit, then, that the preference for the odd number was by no means absolute and paramount: still, in admitting exceptions, we are bound to add that cases which look like exceptions in one book do not unfrequently, by a different arrangement, in another book—for there is some diversity in little points amongst the books—present themselves as most convincing, because artificial, illustrations of the rule.

It will no doubt surprise some readers to learn that the ancient preference for the odd number in regulating the Psalms of a Service is traceable even in our own Book of Common Prayer. In that book we have two groups of Psalms, one for Morning and one for Evening Prayer, assigned to each of the thirty days of the month. There are, therefore, sixty groups in all. Of these, thirty-nine contain an odd number, and twenty-one have an even number of Psalms. The difference is considerable, approximating, as it does, to the proportion of two to one. Still it is not so considerable, it may be felt, as to eliminate the possibility of its being the result of accident rather than design. But let us examine the arrangement a little more closely, and we shall find that the probability of its being designed is very much increased. In the first three days of the month, that is to say the first six groups, every group is odd. It begins to look as though the compilers *started*, at all events, with the preference for excluding even numbers in their mechanical distribution of the hundred and fifty Psalms over the thirty days of the month. Further, split the month into two halves, and we have the astonishing fact that of the thirty-nine odd groups no less than twenty-four occur in the first fifteen days, the odd and even groups being

<small>Psalms in the Prayer Book.</small>

exactly balanced in the last fifteen days of the cycle. Such a fact, I submit, raises a strong presumption that the compilers began with the ancient preference for the odd number; that they worked it out as far as convenient in so mechanical a disposition; and that, as their scheme approached its close, they found their preference, as might have been expected, less and less practicable, owing possibly to the length of individual Psalms, or the quantity of the Psalter still left to their disposal.

There are still remaining some considerations which point to the conclusion that the an- *Proper Psalms.* cient principle has not been without its influence in the modern Services of the Church of England. There are six days in the year for which we have Proper Psalms appointed, giving us twelve groups in all. Of these, no less than nine contain the odd number of Psalms, only three being exceptions to the rule. A glance at the Psalms which form these exceptions will suffice to furnish a probable explanation of them. They all contain Psalms of unusual length. It was probably the length of the individual Psalms which the compilers felt it desirable to employ for the three occasions in question which led them to sacrifice the claims,—considerable, yet not paramount, claims of the ancient precedent under notice.

Under this head of the subject, it remains only to be noticed that in every single one of the Occasional Forms which contain Psalms— those, namely for Matrimony, the Visitation of the Sick, the Burial of the Dead, the Churching of Women, and the Commination—in every one of these, with a possible exception in the Burial Service, the rule of the odd number is maintained.

*Occasional Services.*

I conclude with noticing an ancient usage in the recitation of the Psalms in Cathedral churches— a usage which will furnish some little confirmation of what has been said, but which has further an interest of its own, because its existence is not so generally known. In this Cathedral of Sarum a certain number of Psalms were assigned to each one of the Prebendaries for daily recitation by him. The same custom is recorded by the late Dean Milman as having prevailed in S. Paul's Cathedral. The same custom prevails too at Lincoln, where, I have been informed, the initial words of each man's Psalms are written up over his stall,

*Cathedral Recitation.*

and where, I know, the present Bishop (Mackenzie) of Nottingham has taken occasion to write and publish a series of Meditations upon his portion of Psalms. Probably the same custom prevailed everywhere. In Æthiopian and Abyssinian monasteries, which contained a great number of monks, the entire Psalter was said immediately before dinner, by being divided among the monks.* I have before me the list as it was prescribed to the clergy of this Cathedral of Sarum; and, because specimens of such lists are not easily accessible, I transcribe it here. The places named in the first column are the names of the several prebends:—

| | |
|---|---|
| 1. Prima pars Altaris. | Ps. i., Beatus vir. |
| | Ps. ii., Quare fremuerunt. |
| | Ps. iii., Domine quid. |
| | Ps. iv., Cum invocarem. |
| | Ps. v., Verba mea auribus. |
| 2. Potterne. | Ps. vi., Domine, ne in furore. |
| | Ps. vii., Domine, Deus meus. |
| | Ps. viii., Domine, Dominus noster. |

* So says the famous writer on Ritual, Zaccarias. Bibliotheca Ritualis, vol. i. p. 95, fin. ed. Romæ, 1776.

| | |
|---|---|
| 3. Brickles-worth. | Ps. ix., Confitebor tibi. (N.B. This included Ps. x., which in the Latin Psalter formed part of it.) |
| 4. Ramsbury. | Ps. xi., In Domino confido. |
| | Ps. xii., Salvum me fac. |
| | Ps. xiii., Usque quo, Domine. |
| | Ps. xiv., Dixit insipiens. |
| 5. Charminster. | Ps. xv., Domine, quis habitabit. |
| | Ps. xvi., Conserva me. |
| | Ps. xvii., Exaudi. |
| 6. Calne. | Ps. xviii., Diligam te. |
| 7. Heytesbury. | Ps. xix., Cœli enarrant. |
| | Ps. xx., Exaudiat. |
| | Ps. xxi., Domine, in virtute tuâ. |
| 8. Graham (Grantham). | Ps. xxii., Deus, Deus meus respice. |
| | Ps. xxiii., Dominus regit me. |
| | Ps. xxiv., Domini est terra. |
| 9. Graham. | Ps. xxv., Ad te, Domine, levavi. |
| | Ps. xxvi., Judica me, Domine. |
| | Ps. xxvii., Dominus illuminatio mea. |
| | Ps. xxviii., Ad te Domine clamavi. |

10. Bedewynde.   Ps. xxix., Afferte Domino.
                 Ps. xxx., Exaltabo.
                 Ps. xxxi., In te Domine speravi.
11. Urda.        Ps. xxxii., Beati, quorum.
    (? Woodford.) Ps. xxxiii., Exultate, justi.
                 Ps. xxxiv., Benedicam.
12. Blewberry.   Ps. xxxv., Judica, Domine, nocentes.
                 Ps. xxxvi., Injustus.
13. Schipton.    Ps. xxxvii., Noli æmulari.
                 Ps. xxxviii., Domine, ne in furore.
                 Ps. xxxix., Dixi, custodiam.
14. Becton.      Ps. xl., Expectans.
                 Ps. xli., Beatus qui.
                 Ps. xlii., Quemadmodum.
                 Ps. xliii., Judica.
15. Shireborne.  Ps. xliv., Deus, auribus.
                 Ps. xlv., Eructavit.
                 Ps. xlvi., Dominus noster refugium.
                 Ps. xlvii., Omnes gentes.
                 Ps. xlviii., Magnus Deus.

16. Stratton.        Ps. xlix., Audite hæc.
                     Ps. l., Deus Deorum.
                     Ps. li., Miserere.
17. Hortune.         Ps. lii., Quid gloriaris.
                     Ps. liii., Dixit insipiens.
                     Ps. liv., Domine in nomine tuo.
                     Ps. lv., Exaudi Deus orationem meum ne.
18. Chesyngbury.     Ps. lvi, Miserere mei.
                     Ps. lvii., Miserere mei.
                     Ps. lviii., Si vero utique.
                     Ps. lix., Eripe me.
19. Begminster       Ps. lx., Deus, repulisti.
    prima.           Ps. lxi., Exaudi, Deus.
                     Ps. lxii., Nonne Deo.
                     Ps. lxiii., Deus, Deus meus.
20. Begminster       Ps. lxiv., Exaudi, Deus orationem meam.
    Secunda.
                     Ps. lxv., Te decet.
                     Ps. lxvi., Jubilate Deo.
21. Bishopston.      Ps. lxvii., Deus misereatur.
                     Ps. lxviii., Exurgat Deus.
22. Husseburn.       Ps. lxix., Salvum me fac.

23. Netheraven.     Ps. lxx., Deus in adjutorium.
                    Ps. lxxi., In te, Domine, spe-
                        ravi.
                    Ps. lxxii., Deus, judicium.
24. Netherbury      Ps. lxxiii., Quam bonus.
   in Ecclesia.     Ps. lxxiv., Ut quid, Deus.
25. Slepe.          Ps. lxxv., Confitebimur.
                    Ps. lxxvi., Notus in Judæa.
                    Ps. lxxvii., Voce meâ.
26. Netherbury      Ps. lxxviii., Attendite.
   in terrâ.
27. Awelton.        Ps. lxxix., Deus, venerunt.
                    Ps. lxxx., Qui regis Israel.
                    Ps. lxxxi., Exultate Deo.
                    Ps. lxxxii., Deus stetit.
28. Awelton Pan-    Ps. lxxxiii., Deus, quis similis.
   cras.            Ps. lxxxiv., Quam dilecta.
                    Ps. lxxxv., Benedixisti, Do-
                        mine.
29. Etemynster      Ps. lxxxvi., Inclina, Domine.
   Mag.             Ps. lxxxvii., Fundamenta.
                    Ps. lxxxviii., Domine Deus.
30. Grymston.       Ps. lxxxix., Misericordias Do-
                        mini.

| | |
|---|---|
| 31. Durneford. | Ps. xc., Domine, refugium. |
| | Ps. xci., Qui habitat. |
| | Ps. xcii., Bonum est confiteri. |
| | Ps. xciii., Dominus regnavit. |
| 32. Writtelston. | Ps. xciv., Deus ultionum. |
| (? Writhlington.) | Ps. xcv., Venite. |
| | Ps. xcvi., Cantate. |
| | Ps. xcvii., Dominus regnavit. |
| 33. Wynelsford. | Ps. xcviii., Cantate. |
| (Wilsford.) | Ps. xcix., Dominus regnavit. |
| | Ps. c., Jubilate. |
| | Ps. ci., Misericordiam. |
| | Ps. cii., Domine, exaudi. |
| 34. Rotesfen. | Ps. ciii., Benedic (1.) |
| | Ps. civ., Benedic (2.) |
| 35. Combe. | Ps. cv., Confitemini (1.) |
| 36. Rotecamp. | Ps. cvi., Confitemini (2.) |
| (? Roscombe.) | |
| 37. Yatminster. | Ps. cvii., Confitemini (3.) |
| 38. Yatesbury. | Ps. cviii., Paratum cor. |
| | Ps. cix., Deus laudum. |

| | |
|---|---|
| 39. Axeford. | Ps. cx., Dixit Dominus. |
| | Ps. cxi., Confitebor. |
| | Ps. cxii., Beatus vir. |
| | Ps. cxiii., Laudate pueri. |
| | Ps. cxiv., In exitu. |
| 40. Warminster. | Ps. cxvi., Dilexi. |
| | Ps. cxvii., Laudate. |
| | Ps. cxviii., Confitemini. |
| 41. Stratford. | Ps. cxix., Beati immaculati, 1-48. |
| 42. Preston. | Ps. cxix., (Memor esto) 49-128. |
| 43. Bemynstre. | Ps. cxix., (Mirabilia) 129-176. |
| | Ps. cxx., Ad Dominum. |
| | Ps. cxxi., Levavi oculos. |
| 44. Teynton. | Ps. cxxii., Lætatus. |
| | Ps. cxxiii., Ad te levavi. |
| | Ps. cxxiv., Nisi quia Dominus. |
| | Ps. cxxv., Qui confidunt. |
| | Ps. cxxvi., In convertendo. |
| | Ps. cxxvii., Nisi Dominus ædificavit. |
| | Ps. cxxviii., Beati omnes. |
| | Ps. cxxix., Sæpe expugnaverunt. |
| | Ps. cxxx., De profundis. |
| | Ps. cxxxi., Domini, non est. |

| | |
|---|---|
| 45. Toryntona. | Ps. cxxxii., Memento, Domine. |
| | Ps. cxxxiii., Ecce, quam bonum. |
| | Ps. cxxxiv., Ecce nunc. |
| | Ps. cxxxv., Laudate Nomen Domini. |
| | Ps. cxxxvi., Confitemini. |
| | Ps. cxxxvii., Super flumina. |
| 46. Media pars principalis Altaris. | Ps. cxxxviii., Confitebor. |
| | Ps. cxxxix., Domine, probasti. |
| | Ps. cxl., Eripe me. |
| | Ps. cxli., Domine, clamavi. |
| | Ps. cxlii., Voce mea ad Dominum. |
| 47. Ferendona. | Ps. cxliii., Domine, exaudi. |
| | Ps. cxliv., Benedictus Dominus. |
| | Ps. cxlv., Exaltabo te. |
| | Ps. cxlvi, Lauda, anima mea. |
| 48. Cerdestock. | Ps. cxlvii., (1-11) Laudate Dominum. |
| | Ps. cxlvii., (12-end) Laudate Jerusalem. |
| | Ps. cxlviii., Laudate Dominum. |
| | Ps. cxlix., Cantate Domino. |

| | |
|---|---|
| 49. Lym. | Ps. cl., Laudate Dominum. cum Letania. |
| 50. Uphaven. | Confitebor. (Isaiah xii.) |
| | Ego Dixi. (Isaiah xxxviii. 10.) |
| | Exultavit Cor. (1 Sam. ii. 1.) |
| 51. Lodre. | Cantemus Domino. (Exod. xv. i.) |
| (? Podre.) | Domine audivi. (Habakkuk iii.) |
| 52. Okeburne. | Audite cœli. (Deut. xxxii.) |

The distribution of the Psalms amongst the Clergy seems to have varied in different Churches. The explanation, however, which Marten gives[*] with respect to the Church of Amiens, probably applies to all Cathedral Churches. He says that anciently the entire Psalter was recited at Amiens daily throughout the year, "in conventu," that is, with all the Canons present; but that on account of the burden of such a service, a portion of the Psalter was subsequently assigned for recitation to each Canon, so as to ensure the daily recitation of the whole Psalter within the ecclesiastical body. In connection with this, it will be interesting to remark, in passing, that the reception

[*] De Antiquis Ecclesiæ Ritibus, Lib. iv., cap. xviii, 19: Tom. 3, p. 62. Ed. 1764. Antwerp.

of the book of the Psalter from the hands of the Precentor formed a part of the ceremonial at the admission of a new Canon, certainly in the Church of Paris, and probably elsewhere too.*

It has been suggested to me that the distribution of the Psalms amongst the Clergy of Sarum probably formed the basis of that distribution of them over the days of the month which is prescribed to the modern English Clergy in the Book of Common Prayer. There are indeed sixty sections, two for each day in the latter, while there are but fifty-two in the former list. Yet on comparing the two, it will be found that the divisions in the two lists correspond in a much larger number of cases than might have been expected.

The immediate reason, however, why I quote the scheme here is, because it shows a preponderance of odd numbers in the Psalms apportioned to each clergyman. Taking the first forty-nine of these groups, which dispose of the Psalms properly so called, and counting the Psalms according to the numbering and arrangement in the Latin Psalter, we have thirty

* De Antiquis Ecclesiæ Ritibus, Lib. i., cap. v., Ordo i.: Tom. 2, p. 182.

groups which contain an odd number of Psalms against nineteen which contain an even number—a ratio of very nearly five to three.

Look, in short, where we will, and we find traces, more or less distinct, of the fact that ancient Christianity was careful even of such a detail as the number of Psalms that should be assigned to an Office; that it recognized, and, of course, transmuted with its own higher purpose and intention, the old Pagan principle that "God delights in the odd number;"[*] that—to state the matter dispassionately —the rule of the odd number in Divine Service was preferred, but, as certainly, was not absolute.

[*] "Numero Deus impare gaudet."—Virgil Ecl. 8, 75.

## CHAPTER XXIII.

### THE INFLUENCE OF HEBREW WRITERS UPON THE ENGLISH BIBLE.

THE numerous commentaries which have been written in Hebrew and kindred languages, constitute a region of Scriptural exegesis traversed by so few readers amongst ourselves, that I have thought it worth while to collect a few examples, which might convey some idea of the manner in which our English Bible has been influenced by them. There is, indeed, ample evidence on the face of the English Bible itself, that the translators of it were acquainted with the Hebrew writers that are best accredited. In many a passage where the translation of the Original is open to debate, the decision seems to have been taken in the direction of traditional acceptation, which was learned from one or other of the leading Hebrew authorities. It is, perhaps, almost superfluous for me to say, that we cannot accept everything that is said by a Hebrew writer about the Holy Scriptures for the single reason that a Hebrew says it, any more than we can accept everything that is said by Englishmen about Shakespeare. Still, upon the whole, Englishmen are by far the best authorities about Shakespeare. And so, when we have made every deduction from the value of the Hebrew commentators for much that to our generation appears fanciful, far-fetched, uncritical, sometimes even childish, and often, when measured by our beliefs, heretical and false; still we have in them a body of exposition, descending even to the treatment of minute anomalies in grammar, and preserving much of what has been said and believed about the Scriptures in the most remote past— a storehouse of native and traditionary acceptation, which no modern translators can with impunity ignore. It was a sound position that was taken up by one of the profoundest Semitic scholars the English clergy ever had—one of that famous band of the seventeenth century, whose intellect and acquirements served to make the English clergy, according to the flattering proverb, the amazement of the world: "The Jews I look on, as especially in this case, to be had regard to, not because the language is now to them as a mother-tongue vulgarly spoken, as anciently, when the Scriptures of the Old Testament were written, it was; but because divers of them looking on it as their ancient inheritance, strive to recover the possession of it by a constant practice and study in it from their infancy, and by that means many of them have become more expert, than usually others, in it."*

The influence of Hebrew and Chaldee authorities in the English Bible will be most pointedly exhibited, if I adduce some passages wherein it has been allowed to override the claims of an interpretation which had been hitherto current amongst Christians. This, then, seems to have been the case with the eight-times-reiterated formula in the first two chapters of Amos. Allowance being made for the change of name in each instance, it stands thus:—

"Thus saith the Lord; For three transgressions of Damascus and for four, I will not turn away *the punishment* thereof." (Amos i. 3.)

Now "the punishment," it will be observed, is an insertion of the translators, and has no equivalent in

* Pocock, Preface to "Commentary on the Prophecy of Hosea."

the Original. The Hebrew phrase here might be simply rendered "I will not turn it." The same word actually is so rendered—"I will restore it"—in Judges xvii. 3, and elsewhere. Our translators even felt that the plain, ordinary sense of the phrase would not be altogether inapposite here—a feeling which they indicated by giving in the Margin the alternative rendering "I will not convert it." Further, this last rendering had acquired amongst Christians a kind of traditional right to acceptance from its very antiquity. For it had secured a place in the ancient Latin Version of the Vulgate ("non convertam eum"), and so was practically the only rendering of the passage known in the Christian world of the West; and, going back even to pre-Christian times, it was the rendering adopted in the still older Greek translation of the Septuagint. Why, then, was a rendering with so many considerations in its favour ousted from the English text? I can see no reason, except the fact that some of the great authorities of the Hebrew nation took the clause as we have it now. The Chaldee Targum may be taken as the representative of such authorities, and it here employs a verb, which Buxtorf, in his great Chaldee Lexicon, explains as "remit," and which therefore points to the punishment, and not to the nation, as that which God asserts He would not "turn."

A similar influence is discernible in the translation of a familiar passage, Isa. v. 1, "My well-beloved hath a vineyard in a very fruitful hill." The alternative in the Margin shows that there was a doubt or a difficulty in the translation of it. The end of the verse stands in the Margin thus: "in the horn of the Son of oil." The "Son of oil" is an ordinary Hebrew idiom, and need not detain us; but what is the warrant for translating the common Hebrew word for "horn" by "hill?" For it is by no means imperative to do so. Render it "horn," and we can get a very good sense. S. Jerome does not scruple to render it "horn" (cornu) in his translation, and expounds it in his comment; the Vulgate renders it so; the Septuagint renders it so; it was so understood by Greek as well as Latin Fathers; our own translators felt it was quite open to translate it so. Why, then, in the face of this unison of authority, why translate it "hill?" The simple answer is, that there is authority of Hebrew doctors for translating it so. Rashi, it is true, renders it "corner;" but Radak renders it "hill," and he quotes the Targum as the warrant for doing so. The Hebrew usage, which allows the same word to represent the two ideas of "horn" and "hill," may be compared with the corresponding idiom in modern German, seen in such a word as "Matterhorn," the name of the famous Swiss mountain.

Another good example of the deference which was paid by our translators to the authority of the Hebrew writers, is furnished by a later verse in the same chapter :—

"Therefore is the anger of the Lord kindled against His people, and He hath stretched forth His hand against them, and hath smitten them : and the hills did tremble, and their carcases were torn in the midst of the streets. For all this His anger is not turned away, but His hand is stretched out still." (Isa. v. 25.)

Now, in place of "torn" in this passage the Margin gives the words "as dung." But why, we may ask, are we offered two translations so widely sundered as these ? Surely a translator may be fairly expected to make up his mind about a word within somewhat narrower limits than these? The answer, no doubt, is that the Hebrew doctors themselves are at issue upon the question. When these latter had given no decisive ruling upon a point, then our translators felt themselves incompetent to settle it: and therefore while they put "torn" in the text on the authority of Aben Ezra and Radak, yet they offered as an alternative in the Margin the rendering "as dung," which rests upon the no less venerable authority of Rashi and the Targum.

Again: a verse in the Minor Prophets shows incidentally how the English translators allied themselves with the best Hebrew authorities. In Zech. ii. 6 (ii. 10 Hebr.) we have this:—

"Ho, ho, *come forth*, and flee from the land of the north, saith the Lord: for I have spread you abroad as the four winds of the heaven, saith the Lord."

The words "come forth" are an insertion on the part of the translators, having no equivalent in the Original. Whence then did they get them? Not from the ancient versions which Christians had been in the habit of using: for neither the Greek of the Septuagint, nor the Latin of the Vulgate, have anything corresponding to them; and both alike are consequently forced to omit the next word "and" (existing in the Hebrew), which makes an insertion of some kind or other necessary. No; the inserted words are the product, it can hardly be doubted, of the translators' acquaintance with the Hebrew Commentary of Radak, who says that "the 'and' indicates the ellipsis of a word, as if it were 'come forth and flee.'" It is he who supplies the identical words which our translators have selected for the stoppage of the gap.

There is yet one other passage of Zechariah, which I cite in evidence because of an incidental interest that it possesses for Christians:—

"And the Lord showed me four carpenters." (Zech. i. 20.)

Why "carpenters?" There is nothing here to show that they wrought in wood. The word is one of very frequent occurrence in the Hebrew Scriptures; and in a considerable majority of instances it appears to mean "smiths," or "artificers" generally. In some passages it is accompanied by other words, which restrict it to artificers *in wood;* and there, of course, it is represented by "carpenters." But there are only four passages (Isa. xli. 7 ; Ezra iii. 7 ; Jer. xxiv. 1 ; xxix. 2) without this qualification, where it is rendered " carpenters ;" and even in one of these, the passage in Ezra, the English translators have offered the wider alternative of " workmen" in the Margin. On what authority then, it may be asked, have they in the passage before us restricted the word specifically to "workmen" in wood, and given us " carpenters" as the equivalent? Conceivably the old Greek of the Septuagint, which here gives the very word afterwards applied to designate the trade of our Blessed Lord, may have influenced them. Yet they were not in the habit of following the translation of the Septuagint, where it stands alone, in a doubtful phrase. And here the authority of Radak was no doubt that which finally determined the complexion which the English Bible should give to the clause before us. He it is who explains that the word " artificer" is here to be understood just as it is in the fuller phrase—" artificer in wood," or " carpenter" in Isaiah xliv. 13; and thus unconsciously justifies the old Greek translators in having chosen precisely that word, which was destined at a later epoch in the New Testament to describe the employment of our Blessed Lord in the home at Nazareth: "Is not this the carpenter?"

A familiar passage in the Pentateuch would, by the introduction of a single word, create a strong presumption that the English translators allowed the Hebrew writers to have an influence with them, which often carried the day over all other considerations. The narrative of Korah is introduced thus:—

"Now Korah, the son of Izhar, the son of Kohath, the son of Levi, and Dathan and Abiram, the sons of Eliab, and On, the son of Peleth, sons of Reuben, took *men*." (Numb. xvi. 1.)

It will be observed that the word "men" is really the comment of the translators. The Hebrew is elliptical, and says simply "took." But took what? Why "men?" Whence did the translators get this method of supplying the hiatus? There are many other ways of supplying it in vogue. It never was supplied in this particular way in any of the versions of the Scriptures that had hitherto been in circulation amongst Christians. The ancient Greek of the Septuagint did not do it so. Nor the Latin of the Vulgate, that every one had used for centuries in the

Western Church. Luther in his German does not take it so. The modern English translation of Dr. Leeser does not take it so.* Whence then did our translators get their rendering? From their knowledge of the Hebrew writers, there cannot be a question. From Aben Ezra, and from Rashi; the former of whom explicitly directs that "men" is to be supplied in the hiatus, and the latter suggests it as an alternative of two methods, which he gives.

There is an important passage in the Pentateuch in which it has become the fashion to suspect and discredit a word adopted by our translators. It is the word "meek," as descriptive of the character of Moses in Numbers xii. 3:—

* It may be convenient to subjoin in a note some of the various proposals that have been made for filling the gap in the Hebrew of this verse:—

The Septuagint gives "spoke," probably "took *words.*" Καὶ ἐλάλησε Κορὲ.

The Vulgate omits the verb altogether, "Ecce autem Core."

The ancient Chaldee of Onkelos gives "separated himself;" that is, probably, as Rashi explains, "took *himself*" to one side.

Luther turns the verse, "Und Korah, der Sohn Jezehars, des Sohnes Kahaths, des Sohnes Levi, sammt Dathan und Abiram, u. s. w.," omitting the verb altogether.

And, finally, Dr. Leeser represents it by "was presumptuous."

"Now the man Moses was very meek, above all the men which were upon the face of the earth."

I call the passage important, because the history of Moses was in many respects a rehearsal of the history of the Christ Who was to come; and in this character of meekness we have that most novel and most winning of all the attributes that Jesus appropriated to Himself—a character, it will be believed, which was far too prominent in Jesus for it to have been altogether unmentioned in some one or other of His Types in the Old Testament; but which would be actually ascribed to no one of them, if it cannot be sustained in reference to Moses in the passage under consideration. It is worthy of notice that the Greek word adopted by the ancient translators of the Septuagint is substantially the same Greek word as that which the Evangelist employs in our Blessed Lord's saying of Himself: "I am *meek* and lowly in heart." (S. Matt. xi. 29.) Of late years, however, the word "meek" has fallen under suspicion as inadequately representing the Hebrew word applied to Moses in the Pentateuch. The distinguished author of the article upon Moses in the Dictionary of the Bible gives expression to the feeling. "The word 'meek,'" says Dean Stanley, "is hardly an adequate reading of the Hebrew term עָנָו which should rather be 'much enduring;' and, in fact, his onslaught on the Egyptian, and his sudden dashing the tables on the ground, indicate rather the reverse of what we should call 'meekness.' "[*] The same feeling was long ago expressed by Luther, who translates that Moses was, not meek, but, "geplagt," smitten, afflicted. In deciding the question, then, whether we should cling to some such translation as our own, or adopt in its place some such reading as that which Luther's German suggests, we ought to remember that our translators, at all events, chose that which had the leading Hebrew authorities on its side. Consciously and intelligently chose it, we might venture to say; for they could not have been ignorant that the fundamental idea of so common a Hebrew word as this was that of *affliction*, and not that of *meekness*. Yet even Gesenius, who is not wont to be particularly tender towards received translations, when comparative philology does not run upon exactly

[*] Smith's Dictionary of the Bible. Art. Moses.

the same lines with them—but even he admits\* that *meek* is the import of the word in the passage before us. And so our translators, it may be believed, deliberately rejected the sense of 'much enduring,' which is the more common, but by no means universal significance of the word, and chose the reading 'meek' with all the train of ideas that the word entails, because it had the preponderance, and even, so far as I know, the monopoly of Hebrew authority in its favour. Rashi comments upon the adjective in two words, and says it means here, "lowly and patient." Aben Ezra expands the same idea at somewhat greater length. The meaning of it is, he says, that Moses sought not eminence above his brethren. The Chaldee Targum represents it by a word which indeed comes from the same root as the Hebrew word, but which Buxtorf in his great Lexicon translates, "humble, meek, mild," and which is, moreover, identically the same word as that with which the Chaldee paraphrases the term in Zech. ix. 9: "Rejoice greatly, O daughter of Zion; shout, O daughter of Jerusalem : behold, thy king cometh

---

\* Sola *mansuetudinis* significatione legitur Num. xii. 3. Ges. Thesaurus Ling : Heb. et Chald., p. 1049.

unto thee: he is just and having salvation: *lowly*, and riding upon an ass, and upon a colt, the foal of an ass." The Hebrew word, in short, which the sacred writer applies to Moses, does no doubt mean primarily, "stricken, afflicted, having much to bear:" but gathering together such authorities as these, we may say that it also describes the disposition of one who has borne that much well and nobly; that it designates that chastened, unresentful temper, not always unallied with a self-forgetful courage that may be disastrous or even fatal to an aggressor, when it is stirred to the vindication of another's wrong—that temper, which is in the highest sense "much enduring," because it is the product of a long experience in the art of doing so; which is neither weak, nor languid, nor unintelligent, nor cowardly; and which deservedly goes far to entitle him who has acquired it to be signalised as "meek."

# SUPPLEMENT

## TO CHAPTER I.

SINCE the early sheets of this work were in type, a friend, who has been good enough to read my proofs, has more than once drawn my attention to a passage of Scripture which I have left unnoticed in the argument of my first Chapter. I cannot do better than give his remarks in his own words. He says:—

"I still think that 2 Chron. ix. 11, bears very strongly on the subject you have in hand. 'And the king made of the algum-trees terraces to the House of the Lord, and to the king's palace, and *harps and psalteries for singers*: and there were none such seen before in the land of Judah.' My Bagster has this note to terraces: 'or stays; *Hebrew*, highways.' The Septuagint has 'καὶ ἐποίησεν ὁ βασιλεὺς τὰ ξύλα τὰ πεύκινα ἀναβάσεις τῷ οἴκῳ τοῦ κυρίου.' Vulgate, 'gradus in domo Domini.' Here you have the word for 'goings up,' and also a word of which 'gradual' is the derivative. Hence it would be scarcely too much to argue, that this verse gives an account of the first makings of those 'steps;' of their connection with vocal and instrumental sacred music; and of their being devised originally by Solomon."

It may be remarked, that the Hebrew word here translated "stairs" in the Margin, is not the identical word employed in the Titles of the Gradual Psalms. This fact might, at first sight, appear to invalidate the argument sketched above. In reality, however, it does not do so. For no less an authority than Rashi explains that the Hebrew word in the Chronicles means "steps." It is a derivative of the same root that, according to Radak, gives us the term "Selah,"—a word which is generally admitted to be a musical term of some kind or other, and therefore, perhaps, to be expected in a series of Orchestral Psalms, but which nevertheless, it was long ago observed by S. Gregory of Nyssa,[*] does not occur in the Gradual Psalms.

[*] S. Greg. Nyss. in Pss. cap. x. p. 320, ed. Paris, 1638.

# INDEX.

Aaron's Anointing, details of, 353.
Abraham's servants, 86.
—— name of, change of, 88, 247.
Absalom, 234, 306.
Abyss, steps of the, 10.
Abyssinian Monasteries, the Psalms in, 381.
Accent, effect of, in fixing meaning of a word in Hebrew, 195.
Adam, generations between, and Noah, 289.
Adonijah, 234.
Adullam, Cave of, typical of Christ, 305.
Advent, the Second, 344.
Æthiopian Monasteries, the Psalms in, 381.
Aggadah, how far analogous to Christian exposition, 76.
Aijeleth Shahar, 131.
Alamoth, 131.
Allegoria, 43.
Amen, as Name of Christ, 89.
Amiens, the Psalter at, 389.
Anagogia, 43.
Angelic Orders, 150.
Anomaly of grammar, 56.
Anticipation of New Testament phrases in the Psalms, 134, 141, 147, 149, 173, 177, 179, 180, 193, 214, 220, 224, 232, 236, 255, 302.
Antiphon, intercalary, 126.

Apostles, 241.
Aquinas on Interpretation, 51.
Ark, type of Christ, 321.
Armenian Psalter, 106.
—— Liturgy, 346.
Ascension of Christ, 311.
Ascent, 3, 7, 131.

Bellarmine, on clerical ignorance of the Psalter, xix.
Benedictine Psalter, Gradual Psalms in, 101.
Benedictions, how begun, 93.
—— in Hebrew Service, 125.
—— Hebrew Ceremonial of, 366.
Bethlehem, burial-place of Rachel, 321.
Book of Roots, Radak's, 189, 311, 330, 344.
Brethren, what, 350.
Breviary. See Sarum Portfory.

Cain, descendants of Adam through, 289.
Canon, a division of Armenian Psalter, 106.
Captivity, going up from the, 12.
—— particular character of the distress in the, 131, 134, 208, 211.
—— fourfold, 82.

Carpenters, four, 399.
Cathedrals, recitation of Psalms in, 380.
Chaldee tenses, 213, 215.
Children, how applied, 251, 332.
Christ our Peace, in the Psalms, 147.
Christian exposition continuous with more ancient Hebrew, 67.
—— interpretation of Old Testament, argument for, 303.
Christianity, debt of, to Hebrew nation, xviii.
Church militant, 314.
Churching of women, 103.
Circumcision, covenant of, its scope, 247.
Collects, rule of, 371.
Compline Psalm, 54, 94, 364.
—— Hebrew precedent for, 122.
Confirmation Office, 103.
Consecration of Bishop, 104.
Coronation, 104.
Council of Laodicæa, 106.
—— Sixth General, 106.
Cross, sign of the, 353.

David, name of, in Gradual Psalms, 163.
——, name of, its presence how to be explained, 164, 166.
—— a Name of Christ, 178, 232.
—— how a type of Christ, 303.
Day of Judgment, 149, 153, 177, 272.
Defective Hebrew phrases, how sometimes explained, 146.
Degrees, 4, 8.
Delitzsch on the tenses in Hebrew, 219, note.
Deliverance, Songs of, 21.

De Rossi on Titles of Gradual Psalms, 30.
Despair, 278.
Dionysius the Carthusian on Interpretation, 47.
Dream of Jacob, 308.

Elevation of voice, 8.
Eleven, significance of, 277, 289.
English Version, apparent variation of, from Hebrew Original, 151, 167, 168, 174, 201, 203, 239, 267, 296, 310, 348,
—— its general trustworthiness, viii.
Ephratah discussed, 315.
Epistles, subscriptions to, 33.
Eschatology, Hebrew, 218.
Eucharist foreshadowed, 87.
Eucharistic preparation, 345.
Ewald on the tenses in Hebrew, 215, note.

Feasts, going up to, 7, 173.
Feminine life in Scriptures, 253.
Fifteen, import of, 89.
Forgiveness, 280.

Gate, 243.
Gemoro, 17.
Gloria Patri, how said, 92.
Goat's hair, the eleven curtains of, 289.
Good, as a designation of the Law, 209.
Grace before meat, 123.
Gradual Psalms, Term explained, 3.
—— which, 1,
—— eminence of, 91.
Gradual, in Eucharist, 2.

Gradual Psalms, versicles in, 92.
—— furnish last Psalm of the day, 94.
—— Office of, 95, 108.
—— at Burial, 97.
—— in Benedictine Psalter, 101.
—— at Vespers, 94.
—— a Kathisma, 106, 107.
—— in Lent, 108.
—— in winter, 120.
Greek Psalter, 373.
Gregory, S., the Illuminator, 346.

Hamilton, favourite saying of Bishop, 365.
Harvest, 223.
Hebrew interpretation the parent of Christian, 66.
—— the four heads of, 73.
—— Messianic character of, 77, 230.
Hebrew ritual, 120.
—— literature, neglect of, ix.
—— the attempt to learn. Statement of attainable re-results, xvi.
Hermon, 355.
Hills, interpreted by Latin writers, 151.
Hillel on interpretation, 68.
Horn, 396.
House of judgment, 244.
Humility, 290.

Incarnation in the Psalms, 159, 214.
Inspiration, alleged by Hebrew writers, 229.
Interpretation, branches of, 42, 47.
—— mystic, 45.

Interpretation, scheme of, 63.
—— spiritual, demanded by grammar of the sacred tongue, 222, 250.
—— specimen of Hebrew, in several branches, 230.
—— spiritual, demanded by the facts, 248, 257, 329.

Jacob, in the Psalms, 222.
Jah, name of, attached to the tribes, 175.
Jarchi, the name a mistake, xi.
Jerusalem, interpretations of, 51.
—— English form of the word, traceable to what, 168, note.
—— figure of the Church; 179, 206, 214.
—— first mention of, 318.
Jew and Christian, real seat of the controversy between, 78.
Jonath-Elem-Rechokim, 131.
Joseph, in the Gradual Psalms, 227.
Joshua, distinguished as an Ephraimite, 318.
Juniper, story of, in the Midrash, 138.

Kabbalah, 295.
Kathismata, 106, 107, 373.
Kedar, 141, 142.
Ken, Bishop, 364.
Kennicott on Titles of Gradual Psalms, 30.
Kitto, Cyclopædia of Biblical Literature, xiii.

Lantern, 341.
Law, classification of precepts in the, 247.

Leeser, his version of the Old Testament, 170.
Levites, function of, 324.
—— designated as Saints, 339.
Liddon, on Hebrew writers, vii.
Lincoln, the Psalter at, 380.

Mahalath, 131.
Maimonides on interpretation, 76.
—— how designated, xii.
Manna, interpretation of, 50.
Marriage Service, 102.
Marten, on division of Psalms, 389.
Massorah, 189.
Mede, on posture in prayer, 322.
Meek, an epithet of Moses, justified, 402.
Mesech, explanations of, 139.
Messianic character of Hebrew exposition, 77, 147, 256.
Mezuzah, on doors of Hebrew dwellings, 157.
Midrash Tehillim, xiii., 13.
—— antiquity of contents of, 75.
Missal, Sarum, 371.
Mistress, a name of Christ, 185.
Monastery, life in, 351.
Moral interpretation, in the Midrash, 233.
Moriah, 334, 337.
Moses, the Good, 209.

Nameless Psalm, 131.
Nathan, in the Gradual Psalms, 230.
New Moon, 122.
Night, 122, 124.
Nocturn, 376.

None, Psalms at Office of, 376.
Number of Psalms in an Office, rule for fixing, 92.
Numerals, explained by Hebrew writers, 83.

Obedience, indicated by ten, 289.
Odd number, trace of in Prayer Book, 372.
—— artificial production of, 375.
"Of" in the phrase "A Psalm of David," 228.
Office of the Eucharist, 102.
—— Compline, 54, 94.
—— the Dead, 97.
—— the Gradual Psalms, 108.
—— the Blessed Virgin, 99.
—— the Sick, 118.
Old Latin Psalter, 285.
Orchestra of Temple, 18, 19.

Passage of the Red Sea, 195.
Past, for future in Scripture, 132, 266.
Paul's, the Psalter at S., 380.
Peace, what, 147, 179.
Pearson on the Creed, source of quotations in, xiv.
Penitential Psalm, Coincidence of, with a Gradual Psalm, 289.
Persecution, 263.
Pharaoh's daughter, Solomon's marriage with, 229.
Philology, argument from, 20.
Pocock on value of Hebrew writers, 394.
Portfory. See Sarum Portfory.
Prayer Book, arrangement of Psalms in the, 378.

Priests, judicial function of Aaronic, 325.
Prime, Psalms at, 376.
Printed Bibles, 29.
Progress in virtue, 132.
Promises, three, with conditions annexed, 332.
Prophecy, a lantern, 342.
Proskyria, 105.
Psalms, several, under one Gloria Patri, 374, 375.
—— the backbone of Hebrew Services, 128.
Psalter, Greek, 373.
Purim, Feast of, 123.

Quantity of Psalms in Services, 128.
Queen's Coronation, Gradual Psalms at, 104.

Radak, the name explained, xi.
Rain, excessive, Gradual Psalms in, 120.
Rashi, the name explained, xi.
Redeemer in Ruth, 81.
Redemption, exceptional character of, 288.
Repetition, force of, in Scripture, 262.
Resurrection, 214, 233, 285, 323.
Right hand, import of, in Scripture, 158.
Rostrum, 366.
Russian Church, 105.
Ruth, gifts of Boaz to, 80.

Salaam, a salutation, 144.
Salisbury Cathedral, the Psalter at, 381.

Salutation, mode of, 273.
S. Ambrose, on Joseph as type of Christ, 227.
Sanhedrin, Great, 245.
Sarum Portfory, 97, 116, 118.
—— its title, 129.
—— Missal, 371.
S. Augustine on penitence, 142.
—— on possessions, 186.
S. Bernard on interpretation, 47.
Scourging of Christ, 269.
Scrivener on Subscriptions to Epistles, 33.
Sentiment, the function of, in religion, 252.
Septuagint, character of, 241.
—— variations of, from Hebrew, how to be explained, 242.
—— a Greek Targum, 285.
Seth, descendants of Adam through, 289.
Sext, Psalms at, 376.
Shechinah in Targum, 176.
—— absence of, in second Temple, 317.
Shew-bread, Christ seen in David's action with, 305.
Shiloh, joined with Jerusalem, 171.
Sick, Office for recovery of, 118.
Sion. See "Zion."
S. Jerome on Interpretation, 43, 45.
Slander, a leading feature of Israel's suffering in the Captivity, 131, 134, 208, 211.
Solomon, 228.
—— a name of Christ in Scripture, 232.
—— lavish expenditure of, 291.

Song of Songs, modern neglect of, 101.
Song of Moses and of the Lamb, 220.
South, Scriptural use of, 221.
Stanley, Dean, remarks on "meek," 403.
Stasis, in Greek Psalter, 374.
Steps, 4, 15.
—— shape of the, 17.
Subscriptions to Epistles in New Testament, 32.
—— rise of, 33.
—— external evidence against, 40, 41.
Success, the secret of, 167.

Tabernacle, coverings of, 277.
Tabernacles, Feast of, 20, 121.
Talmud, age of, 74.
—— on classification of commands in the Law of Moses, 247.
Targum, 9.
—— curious title to Gradual Psalms in, 10, 132 al.
—— date of, 152.
—— Christian doctrine of the Word in, 160, 192, 198, 201, 283.
—— in Greek, 241.
Temple, David's longing to build, 165, 230.
—— of the Lord's Body rebuilt, 232.
Temples, three, 313.
Tenses, difficulty in use of Hebrew, 57, 58, 64, 215.
—— character of, 215.
Terce, Psalms at, 376.
Titles to Psalms.
—— Length of, 23.
—— Inseparable, 24.

Titles to Psalms.
—— Why suspected, 27.
—— External evidence for, 30.
—— Not like Subscriptions to Epistles, 31, 40.
—— Internal evidence subsidiary, 36.
—— Ancient writers on, 38.
—— Tenacity of, in Hebrew rite, 127.
Trinity, memorial of, 375.
Tropologia, 43, 231.

Unity, in Jerusalem, how explained, 169.
Unusual Hebrew forms, 143, 148, 155, 183, 186, 188, 194, 196, 210, 254, 264, 311, 330, 331.

Valley of the Doves, a name of Jerusalem, 190.
Versicles in Gradual Psalms, 92, 199.
Vespers, Gradual Psalms at, 94.

Watch at the Tomb, 285.
Water, Gradual Psalms associated with, 10, 11, 120.
Water-drawing, Hebrew Feast of the, 121.
Winter, Gradual Psalms in, 120.
Word, Christian Doctrine of the, in Targum, 160, 192, 198, 201.
Words compared to arrows in the Midrash, 137.

Zaccarias, on distribution of Psalms, 381.

Zechariah, the Vision of, 347.
Zion, figure of the Church, 213.
—— how described as the site of the Temple, 258.
Zion, relation of, to Jerusalem in Scriptural language, 259.
—— topographical limit of the term, 335.

---

Swift and Co., Regent Press, King Street, Regent Street, W.

# BY THE SAME AUTHOR.

*8vo. cloth, 4s.*

## THE LEGEND OF CHRISTIAN ART.

"Unlocks the beauties of sculpture and painted windows."—*Guardian.*

"A proof that Christian iconography is beginning to be better understood among us."—*Saturday Review.*

"A series of well-told, simple, pointed biographies."—*Standard.*

"A useful guide to a very large province in the domains of sculpture and painting."—*Spectator.*

---

*8vo. sewed. Sixpence.*

## AT THE CRATER OF VESUVIUS IN ERUPTION. A WORD-PICTURE.

---

*8vo. sewed.*

## THE CATHEDRAL GLORY. A Chapter upon Rights and Responsibilities; being the substance of a Sermon preached in the Nave of Salisbury Cathedral, on the Festival of the Dedication of the Cathedral.

---

SALISBURY: BROWN & CO.
LONDON: SIMPKIN, MARSHALL & CO.

*October*, 1873.

# WORKS

PUBLISHED BY

## J. T. HAYES, LYALL PLACE, EATON SQUARE;

AND

## 4, HENRIETTA STREET, COVENT GARDEN.

## BY REV. W. J. E. BENNETT.

A DEFENCE OF THE CATHOLIC FAITH; Being a Reply to the late Charge of the Bishop of Bath and Wells. By W. J. E. BENNETT, Vicar of Froome-Selwood. 2s 6d.; by post, 2s. 8d.

THE "MISSION" SERMONS AT S. PAUL'S, KNIGHTSBRIDGE, in 1869. By Rev. W. J. E. BENNETT, Froome-Selwood. 7s. 6d.; by post, 8s.

A PLEA FOR TOLERATION IN THE CHURCH OF ENGLAND. By W. J. E. BENNETT. Fourth and Cheap Edition. 1s.; by post, 1s. 1d.

OBEDIENCE TO THE LESSER, (The State); DISOBEDIENCE TO THE GREATER, (The Church). By W. J. E. BENNETT. 6d.; by post, 7d.

AGAINST STATE INTERFERENCE IN MATTERS SPIRITUAL: A Reprint from a work entitled "*Remains of Richard Hurrell Froude.*" Preface by W. J. E. BENNETT. 2s.; by post, 2s. 2d.

THE CHURCH'S BROKEN UNITY. Edited by W. J. E. BENNETT, Froome-Selwood. Vol. I., PRESBYTERIANISM AND IRVINGISM. Vol. II., ANABAPTISM, INDEPENDENCY, AND QUAKERS. Vol. III., ON METHODISM, AND THE SWEDENBORGIANS. Each of the first Three Volumes 3s. 6d.; by post, 3s. 10d. Vols. IV. and V., ON ROMANISM. Each, 4s. 6d.; by post, 4s. 10d.

B

## BY E. S. FFOULKES, B.D.

**THE ATHANASIAN CREED RECONSIDERED**; Being an Appendix to "The Athanasian Creed; by Whom Written," &c. 2s. 6d.; by post, 2s. 9d.

**THE ATHANASIAN CREED**: By Whom Written, and by Whom Published; together with some further Inquiries as to Creeds in general. Followed by the APPENDIX: "The Athanasian Creed Reconsidered." 9s.; by post, 9s. 7d.

**DIFFICULTIES OF THE DAY, AND HOW TO MEET THEM.** Eight Sermons at S. Augustine's, Queen's Gate. Second Thousand. 3s. 6d.; by post, 3s. 10d.

**THE CHURCH'S CREED; THE ROMAN INDEX.** In one vol. Cloth. 4s.; by post, 4s. 3d.

Or, separately, as under:—

**THE CHURCH'S CREED OR THE CROWN'S CREED?** Sixteenth Thousand. 1s. 6d.; by post, 1s. 7d.

**THE ROMAN INDEX AND ITS LATE PROCEEDINGS.** Sixth Thousand. 1s. 6d.; by post, 1s. 8d.

**IS THE WESTERN CHURCH UNDER ANATHEMA?** Third Thousand. 1s.; by post, 1s. 1d.

**UNION AT HOME FIRST.** The A.P.U.C. Sermon at All Saints', Lambeth. 1s; by post, 1s. 1d.

---

## BY REV. DR. LEE.

**THE VALIDITY OF THE HOLY ORDERS OF THE CHURCH OF ENGLAND**, Maintained and Vindicated both Theologically and Historically; with Foot-Notes, Tables of Consecrations and Appendices. By the Rev. FREDERICK GEORGE LEE, D.C.L., All Saints', Lambeth. Dedicated to the Archbishop of Canterbury. 8vo., 572 pages. 16s.; by post, 17s.

**SANCTA CLARA ON THE THIRTY-NINE ARTICLES.** Reprinted from the Edition in Latin of 1646, with a Translation, together with Expositions and Comments in English from the Theological Problems and Propositions of the same writer, and with additional Notes and References. Edited by the Rev. FREDERICK GEORGE LEE, D.C.L. 5s.; by post, 5s. 5d.

## LITURGICAL, &c.

**THE ARMENIAN CHURCH**; Its History, Liturgy, Doctrine, and Ceremonies. By E. F. K. FORTESCUE. With an Appendix by Rev. S. C. MALAN, Vicar of Broadwindsor, etc. 7s. 6d.; by post, 8s. Illustrated.

**THE NIGHT HOURS OF THE CHURCH**: being the Matin Office. Vol. I. From Advent to Trinity. Vol. II. Trinity-tide. Partly arranged by the late Rev. Dr. NEALE, and completed by the Members of S. Margaret's, East Grinsted. 7s. 6d.; by post, 8s. (*Vol. III. is in the Press.*)

**THE LITURGICAL "REASON WHY:"** Being a Series of Papers on the Principles of the Book of Common Prayer. By Rev. A. WILLIAMS, Culmington, Salop; Author of "Home Sermons," &c. 4s.; by post, 4s. 4d.

**THE RITUAL "REASON WHY:"** Being 450 Ritual Explanations. By C. WALKER, Author of "Liturgy of the Church of Sarum," &c. 4s.; by post, 4s. 4d.

**PLAIN WORDS ON THE PSALMS**: As translated in the Book of Common Prayer. By MARY E. SIMPSON, Author of "Ploughing and Sowing," &c. With Commendation by the Rev. WALSHAM HOW, M.A., Whittington, Salop. 6s.; by post, 6s. 6d.

**THE SERVICES OF THE CHURCH**: According to the Use of the Illustrious Church of Sarum. Edited by CHARLES WALKER, Author of "The Liturgy of Church of Sarum," "The Ritual Reason Why," &c. 4s.; by post, 4s. 3d. In Morocco, 7s. 6d. to 12s. 6d.

**NOTITIA LITURGICA**; Containing Plain Directions for a Low and a High Celebration; Matins and Evensong; Holy Baptism, Confirmation, Holy Matrimony, and Churching of Women; Visitation of the Sick, and Burial of the Dead; Processions; Prayers before and after Service; Brief Rules for Sacristans. With an Office for the Admission of a Chorister. 8d.; by post, 9d.

**THE LITURGY OF THE CHURCH OF SARUM**. Translated from the Latin, and with an Introduction and Explanatory Notes. By CHARLES WALKER, Author of "The Ritual Reason Why," "The Services of the Church according to the Use of Sarum," &c. With Introduction by Rev. T. T. CARTER, M.A., of Clewer 5s.; by post, 5s. 5d.

**THE KISS OF PEACE**: or, ENGLAND AND ROME AT ONE ON THE HOLY EUCHARIST. By GERARD F. COBB. 7s. 6d.; by post, 8s.

**SEQUEL TO THE KISS OF PEACE.** 5s. 6d.; by post, 5s. 10d. (This sequel may be had separately.)

**RITUAL EXPLANATIONS.** By Rev. C. J. ELIOT, sometime Fellow of Corpus Christi College. 4d.; post, 5d.
The subjects dealt with are:—The Separation of the Sexes during Public Worship—The Rising of the Congregation at the Entrance and Departure of the Priests—Reverent Inclination of the Body at sundry portions of the Service—Choral Celebrations and Eucharistic Ritual and the Worship of non-Communicants—The mixing of a little Water with the Wine—The Sequence of Colours—Processions with Cross and Banners on solemn occasions.

## BY C. E. WILLING.

**THE BOOK OF COMMON PRAISE: HYMNS WITH TUNES FOR THE SERVICE OF THE CHURCH OF ENGLAND.** Arranged and principally composed by C. E. WILLING, Organist of the Foundling, and late of All Saints', Margaret-street. To which are added Chants for the Magnificat and Nunc Dimittis, and Responses for Advent and Lent, as sung at All Saints; with fourteen new Double Chants, &c.

a. HYMNS & TUNES. Bound in cloth, 3s. 6d.; postage, 4d.
b. THE SAME. Limp cloth flush, 2s. 6d.; postage, 3½d.
c. TUNES ONLY. Suitable for Hymns Ancient and Modern, the People's Hymnal, and all the modern Hymn Books. Bound in cloth, 1s. 6d.; postage, 2d.
d. THE SAME. Limp cloth flush, 1s.; postage, 2d.
e. WORDS OF HYMNS ONLY. Bound in cloth, 8d.; postage, 1½d.
f. THE SAME. Limp cloth, 6d.; postage, 1d.

**THE PSALTER, CANTICLES, AND THE PROPER PSALMS FOR CERTAIN DAYS.** Pointed for Chanting by C. E. WILLING. 2s.; by post, 2s. 2½d.

**THE PSALTER, CANTICLES, &c.** Pointed for Chanting. By C. E. WILLING. 1s.; by post, 1s. 2d.

**THE CANTICLES, EASTER ANTHEMS, AND ATHANASIAN CREED.** Pointed for Chanting by C. E. WILLING. 3d.; postage, ½d.; per dozen, nett, 2s. 6d.

**SAFE HOME!** Funeral Hymn. By the late Rev. Dr. NEALE; Music by C. E. WILLING. 4d.; postage, ½d.

# HISTORICAL, THEOLOGICAL, DOCTRINAL,
### ETC.

**HELPS TO HOLINESS; or, RULES OF FASTING,** Almsgiving, and Prayer. By Rev. C.W. FURSE, Principal, Theological Training College, Cuddesdon. 3s.; by post, 3s. 3d.

**LIFE OF S. ELIZABETH OF HUNGARY.** Vol. I. of "Church Biographies." Edited by C. A. JONES, Author of "A History of the Church," &c. 5s.; by post, 5s. 4d.

**LIFE OF ST. VINCENT DE PAUL.** Vol. II. of "Church Biographies." Edited by C. A. JONES. 5s.; by post, 5s. 4d. (Vol. III. will be "Life of St. Jane Frances de Chantal.")

**SERMONS ON THE PARABLE OF THE PRODIGAL SON.** By Rev. T. HANCOCK, Assistant Priest of St. Stephen's, Lewisham. 2s. 6d.; by post, 2s. 8d.

**CHURCH AND NO CHURCH:** Plain Essays on Leading Church Subjects of the Day. 4s. 6d.; by post, 4s. 9d.

**THE VIRGIN MARY AND THE TRADITIONS OF PAINTERS.** By Rev. J. G. CLAY, British Chaplain at Messina. 6s.; by post, 6s. 4d.

**A COMMENTARY ON THE AUTHORIZED VERSION OF THE GOSPEL OF ST. JOHN.** Compared with the Sinaitic, Vatican, and Alexandrian MSS.; also with Dean ALFORD's Revised Translation. By Rev. F. H. DUNWELL, Hensall (late Hastings Exhibitioner, Queen's College, Oxford). 15s.; postage, 9d.

**A HISTORY OF THE CHURCH.** From the Day of Pentecost to the great Schism between East and West. By C. A. JONES, Author of "Church Stories for Sundays." Preface by Dr. LITTLEDALE. 6s.; by post, 6s. 4½d.

**BIBLE HISTORY (OLD TESTAMENT); From the** Foundation of the World to the Return of the Jews from Captivity. By C. A. JONES, Author of "A History of the Church," &c. 6s.; postage, 5d.

**BIBLE HISTORY (NEW TESTAMENT); From the** Birth of Our Lord to the Establishment of Christianity. By C. A. JONES, Author of "A History of the Church," &c. 6s.; Postage, 5d.

**THE BABEL OF THE SECTS AND THE UNITY OF PENTECOST.** By Rev. H. T. EDWARDS, Carnarvon. 2s. 6d.; by post, 2s. 8d.

**SERMONS ON THE RE-UNION OF CHRISTENDOM.** BY MEMBERS OF THE ENGLISH, ROMAN, AND GREEK CHURCHES. First and Second Series. Each Volume 5s.; by post, 5s. 4d.

**ESSAYS ON THE RE-UNION OF CHRISTENDOM.** BY MEMBERS OF THE ENGLISH, ROMAN, AND GREEK CHURCHES. Introductory Essay by Rev. Dr. PUSEY. 6s.; by post, 6s. 4d.

**SERMONS, ON DOCTRINE AND PRACTICE.** By Rev. Dr. OLDKNOW, Bordesley. 4s.; by post 4s. 3d.

**STORIES ABOUT THE GREAT KING:** for the Little Ones of the Church. By Rev. W. H. B. PROBY, Author of "Lessons on the Kingdom." 3s. 6d.; postage, 3d.

**LESSONS ON THE KINGDOM:** for the Little Ones. (Second Edition.) By Author of "Stories about the Great King." 2s.; by post 2s. 2d.

**THE FATHERS OF THE CHURCH:** being the Lives of St. Clement of Rome—St. Ignatius—St. Polycarp—St. Justin—St. Irenæus—Tertullian—St. Clement of Alexandria—Origen. By Author of "Tales of Kirkbeck." 5s.; by post, 5s. 5d.

**THE UNION REVIEW:** A Magazine of Catholic Literature and Art. By Contributors of the Anglican, Greek, and Roman Churches. In Bi-monthly Nos., 2s. each; by post, 2s. 2d. Annual Subscription, 12s.

**A.P.U.C.—CORPORATE RE-UNION, NOT INDIVIDUAL SECESSION:** Two Sermons. By Rev. W. H. P. WARD and DR. LITTLEDALE. 6d.; by post, 7d.

**SOUR GRAPES OF DIS-UNION.** A Sermon by Rev. Dr. LEE. 6d.; by post, 7d.

**A COMPARISON OF THE FUNDAMENTAL DOCTRINES** of the Anglican and Greek Churches. By Rev. J. O. BAGDON. 1s.; by post, 1s. 1d.

**THE HOLY EASTERN CHURCH.** Preface by Rev. Dr. LITTLEDALE. 3s. 6d.; by post, 3s. 10d.

**PERE GRATRY ON PAPAL INFALLIBILITY.** 3s. 6d., cloth; by post, 3s. 10d.

**REDEMPTION: SOME ASPECTS OF THE WORK OF CHRIST CONSIDERED.** By Rev. R. M. BENSON, Evangelist Father, Cowley. 5s.; by post, 5s. 6d.

**PROTESTANT OR CATHOLIC?** A Lecture at Cambridge. By Rev. S. BARING-GOULD, Author of "Curiosities of Olden Time," &c. 6d.; by post, 7d.

**PHARISAIC PROSELYTISM: A FORGOTTEN CHAPTER IN EARLY CHURCH HISTORY.** By Rev. Dr. LITTLEDALE. 1s.; by post, 1s. 1d.

**THE LITTLE ONES IN SUNDAY SCHOOLS; or, A NEW AND INTERESTING WAY OF TEACHING HOLY SCRIPTURE TO YOUNG CHILDREN.** Part I. Edited by Rev. W. W. LA BARTE. 5s.; by post, 5s. 4d.

**THE CHURCH'S COMPREHENSIVENESS.—THE IDEA AND DUTY.** An Address at Leeds Congress, 1872. By Rev. Dr. IRONS. 6d. by post 6½d.

**THE SACRED LIFE OF OUR LORD JESUS CHRIST.** (A Reading Book for Children.) By the Rev. Dr. IRONS. 1s.; by post, 1s. 1d.

**THE SACRED WORDS OF OUR LORD JESUS CHRIST.** By the Rev. Dr. IRONS. 2s; by post, 2s. 2d.

**ATHANASIUS CONTRA MUNDUM.** By Rev. Dr. IRONS, Prebendary of S. Paul's, and Rector of St. Mary's, Woolnoth. 3s. 6d.; by post, 3s. 9d.

**THE BIBLE AND ITS INTERPRETERS: ITS MIRACLES AND PROPHECIES.** By Dr. IRONS, Second Edition. 6s.; by post, 6s. 6d.

**EUCHARISTIC SERMONS BY GREAT PREACHERS** (From the Latin). By Rev. J. M. ASHLEY, Fewston, Ottley, Yorkshire. 5s.; by post, 5s. 4d.

**A YEAR WITH GREAT PREACHERS; or, SERMONS UPON THE GOSPELS FOR EVERY SUNDAY IN THE YEAR.** Edited from the Latin: By J. M. ASHLEY, B.C.L., Fewston, Ottley, Yorkshire. In Two Vols.—I. Advent to Whitsun Day; II. Trinity-tide. Each (separate) 5s.; postage 4½d.

**A FESTIVAL YEAR WITH GREAT PREACHERS;** Or, Sermons for every Festival in the Year. Edited, from the Latin, by J. M. ASHLEY. 6s.; by post, 6s. 6d.

**THE HOMILIES OF S. THOMAS AQUINAS UPON THE EPISTLES AND GOSPELS FOR EVERY SUNDAY AND FESTIVAL.** Translated by Rev. J. M. ASHLEY, Author of "A Year with Great Preachers," &c. 4s. 6d.; by post, 4s. 10d.

**A DIGEST OF THE DOCTRINE OF S. THOMAS AQUINAS ON THE MYSTERY OF THE INCARNATION.** By the Author of "A Digest of the Doctrine of S. Thomas on the Sacraments." 6s.; by post, 6s. 4d.

**MEMORANDA OF ANGELICAL DOCTRINE FROM LADY DAY TO THE ASCENSION.** By the same Author. 1s. 6d.; by post, 1s. 7d.

**A DIGEST OF THE DOCTRINE OF S. THOMAS AQUINAS ON THE SACRAMENTS.** By the same Author. 7s.; by post, 7s. 5d.

## BY THE LATE REV. DR. NEALE.

**OCCASIONAL SERMONS.** By the late Rev. Dr. NEALE. 3s. 6d.; by post, 3s. 9d.

**SERMONS FOR CHILDREN.** Third Edition. By the late Rev. Dr. NEALE. 3s. 6d.; by post, 3s. 9d.

**CATECHETICAL NOTES AND CLASS QUESTIONS**: Literal and Mystical. Second Edition. By the late Rev. Dr. NEALE. 5s.; by post, 5s. 5d.

**NEALE AND BENNETT ON "CHURCH DIFFICULTIES."** 6s.; by Post. 6s. 6d.

**SERMONS ON THE APOCALYPSE—On the NAME OF JESUS**; and on the last Chapter of PROVERBS. By the late Rev. Dr NEALE. 5s.; by post, 5s. 4d.

**SERMONS ON PASSAGES OF "THE PSALMS."** By the late Rev. Dr. NEALE. 5s.; by post, 5s. 4d.

**"THE SONG OF SONGS."** A Volume of beautiful Sermons thereon. By the late Rev. J. M. NEALE. Edited by the Rev. J. HASKOLL. *Many are added which have never hitherto been published.* Second Edition, considerably Enlarged, 6s.; by post, 6s. 4d.

**ORIGINAL SEQUENCES, HYMNS, AND OTHER ECCLESIASTICAL VERSES.** By the late Rev. Dr. NEALE. Second Edition. 2s. 6d.; by post, 2s. 9d.

**STABAT MATER SPECIOSA: FULL OF BEAUTY STOOD THE MOTHER.** By the late Rev. J. M. NEALE. Now first translated. 1s.; by post, 1s. 2d.

**HYMNS SUITABLE FOR INVALIDS, ORIGINAL** or Translated, by the late Rev. J. M. NEALE. With a Preface by the Rev. Dr. LITTLEDALE. In paper cover, 6d.; by Post, 7d.; in cloth, 1s.; by Post 1s. 1d. A fine Edition on Toned Paper, cloth, 2s.; by post, 2s. 2d.

**THE RHYTHM OF BERNARD OF MORLAIX**, on the CELESTIAL COUNTRY. Edited and Translated by the late Rev. J. M. NEALE. New Edition, beautifully printed on Toned Paper. 2s. in cloth; by Post, 2s. 2d.; in French morocco, 4s. 6d.; by Post, 4s. 9d.; in morocco, 7s. 6d.; by post, 7s. 9d. Cheap edition 9d.; by post, 10d.

**HYMNS, CHIEFLY MEDIÆVAL, ON THE JOYS** and GLORIES of PARADISE. By the late Rev. J. M. NEALE. Companion Volume to "The Rhythm of Bernard of Morlaix." 1s. 6d.; by post, 1s. 7d.

**THE REVISION OF THE LECTIONARY.** A Letter to the late Bp. of Salisbury. 1s.; by post 1s. 1d.

**SERMONS ON BLESSED SACRAMENT.** By the Rev. J. M. NEALE. Third Edition. 2s. 6d.; by Post, 2s. 9d.

**NOTES, ECCLESIOLOGICAL & PICTURESQUE,** on DALMATIA, CROATIA, &c.; with a visit to MONTENEGRO. By the late Rev. J. M. NEALE. 6s.; by post, 6s. 4d.

**THE PRIMITIVE LITURGIES** (in Greek) OF S. MARK, S. CLEMENT, S. JAMES, S. CHRYSOSTOM, AND S. BASIL. Edited by the late Dr. NEALE. Preface by Dr. LITTLEDALE. Second Edition. 6s.; by post, 6s. 4d. Calf, 10s. 6d. (for Presents); by post, 11s.

**THE LITURGY OF S. MARK.** And, THE LITURGY OF S. JAMES. In Greek. By the late Rev. J. M. NEALE. 1s. each; by post, 1s. 1d.

**THE TRANSLATIONS OF THE PRIMITIVE LITURGIES** OF SS. MARK, JAMES, CLEMENT, CHRYSOSTOM and BASIL, and THE CHURCH OF MALABAR. With Introduction and Appendices, by the late Rev. J. M. NEALE, D.D., and the Rev. R. F. LITTLEDALE, LL.D. Second Edition, enlarged. 4s.; by post, 4s. 4d.

**THE HYMNS OF THE EASTERN CHURCH:** Translated by late Rev. J. M. NEALE, D.D. New and larger type Edition. 2s. 6d.; by post, 2s. 9d.

**"THE CHRISTIAN NURSE;" AND HER MISSION IN THE SICK ROOM.** Translated from the French of Father Gautrelet, by one of the Sisters of S. Margaret's, East Grinstead; and Edited by the late Rev. J. M. NEALE. 2s.; by post, 2s. 1d.

**AN INVALUABLE SERMON HELP—THE MORAL CONCORDANCES OF S. ANTONY OF PADUA.** Translated, Verified, and Adapted to Modern Use, by Rev. J. M. NEALE; with Additions from the "*Promptuarium Morale Sacræ*" of THOMAS HIBERNICUS, an Irish Franciscan of the 14th Century. With Preface by Dr. LITTLEDALE. Third Edition. 3s. 6d.; by post, 3s. 9d.

**TEXT EMBLEMS:** Twelve beautiful Designs, engraved by Dalziel, illustrating the Mystical Interpretation of as many Verses from the Old Testament. By the late Rev. J. M. NEALE. Second Edition. 2s.; by post, 2s. 2d.

## ON MEDITATION, DEVOTION, &c.

**ON PAROCHIAL MISSIONS.** By the Evangelist Fathers, Cowley. 2s. 6d.; postage, 2d.

**THE EVANGELIST LIBRARY CATECHISM.** PART I. By the Evangelist Fathers, Cowley. 3s.; by post, 3s. 3d.

**THE MANUAL OF INTERCESSORY PRAYER.** Edited by Rev. R. M. BENSON. Limp cloth, 9d.; cloth boards, 1s. 3d.; Postage, 1d.

**TRACTS BY THE EVANGELIST FATHERS.** A packet of all Published. 1s. 8d; by post, 1s. 10d.

**CONFERENCES WITH GOD;** being Meditations for Every Day of the Year. By C. C. STURM. Translated from the German by a Layman. Second Edition, 640 pages. 6s.; by post, 6s. 6d. In 12 Parts, 6d. each.

**SHORT DEVOTIONS,** primarily for the Young; with the Collects and Psalms of David. 1s. 6d.; by post, 1s. 8d. An Edition without the Psalms of David, 6d.; by post, 7d.

**THE LITURGY OF THE CHURCH OF ENGLAND:** An Altar Manual for Hearers or Communicants. Limp Cloth, 1s. 1d.; Stiff Cloth, 1s. 3d. Postage, 1d.

**MANUAL OF DEVOTIONS FOR THE BLESSED SACRAMENT, ATTENDANCE, COMMUNION, PREPARATION, and THANKSGIVING.** With Preface by the Rev. FREDERICK G. LEE, D.C.L. 32mo. Editions: limp cloth, 6d.; boards, 1s.; postage, 1d. In calf, 3s. 6d.; by post, 3s. 7d. 12mo. Edition, 1s. 6d.; by post, 1s. 7d.

**THE HOLY OBLATION;** A Manual of Doctrine, Instructions, and Devotions relative to the Blessed Eucharist. By an ANGLO-CATHOLIC PRIEST. In roan, 2s.; in morocco, 4s.; postage 2d.

**BISHOP WILSON** (Sodor and Man) **ON THE LORD'S SUPPER.** Rubricated Edition. With Notes. In cloth 1s.; by post 1s. 1d., or, With Appendix and copious Notes; in cloth, 2s.; in morocco, 5s. to 8s.; postage, 3d.

**BISHOP WILSON'S SACRA PRIVATA.** In cloth, 2s.; in morocco, 5s. to 8s.; postage, 3d.

**THE VENERABLE SACRAMENT OF THE ALTAR.** By ST. THOMAS AQUINAS. Preface by the Rev. W. J. E. BENNETT. 3s.; by Post, 3s. 3d.

**THE SORROW OF JESUS.** A Companion for Holy Week; intended for the use of Religious Societies. Third Edition. 1s.; by post, 1s. 1d.

**BUND'S AIDS TO A HOLY LIFE;** in Forms of Self-Examination. New Edition, 1s.; by post, 1s. 1d.

**PRAYERS AND NOTES:** extracted from the MSS. of the late Sir Robert and Lady Wilmot, of Chaddesden: with Preface by the Rev. T. T. CARTER, Clewer. 7s. 6d.; by post, 8s.

**SHORT PRAYERS FOR BUSY MEN AND WOMEN.** From a Bodleian MS. 2d.; by post, 3d.

**PRAYERS FOR CHILDREN;** with **DEVOTIONS** for the HOLY SACRIFICE, HYMNS, &c. By Rev. F. G. LEE, D.C.L. With Frontispiece. 1s.; by post, 1s. 1d.

**DEVOTIONS FOR SISTERS OF MERCY.** Edited by the Rev. T. CARTER, Clewer. Part I.—For Daily Use, 1s. 6d.; by post, 1s. 7d. II.—Different Necessities, 1s.; by post, 1s. 1d. III.—Forgiveness of Sins, 1s.; by post, 1s. 1d. IV.—Holy Communion, 2s.; by post, 2s. 2d. V.—To the Holy Ghost, 1s.; by post, 1s. 1d. VI.—To our Lord, 1s.; by post, 1s. 1d. VII.—On The Passion, 1s.; by post, 1s. 1d. VIII.—On Sickness, 1s. 6d.; by post, 1s. 7d. Two vols., cloth, 10s.; postage, 8d.

**THE LITTLE HOURS FOR BUSY PERSONS.** By an ASSOCIATE of the CLEWER SISTERHOOD. 4d.; by post, 4½d.

**SIX STEPS TO PERFECTION.** Cut from the Works of M. Olier. By same Author. 4d.; by post, 4½d.

**HINTS ON RELIGIOUS EDUCATION.** By same Author. 6d.; by post, 6½d.

**A PRAYER BOOK FOR THE YOUNG;** or a Complete Guide to Public and Private Devotion. Edited by CHARLES WALKER. Second Edition, carefully Revised and Re-arranged. 700 pages. 4s.; by post, 4s. 3d. In various morocco bindings, 7s. 6d. to 12s. 6d.; postage, 6d. Cheap Edition, 3s.; by post. 3s. 2d.

**THE LAST HOURS OF JESUS:** being Colloquies on The Passion. From the German. 6d.; by post, 7d.

**SUGGESTIONS FOR THE DUE AND REVERENT CELEBRATION OF THE HOLY EUCHARIST.** 6d.; by Post, 7d.

**SHORT DAILY READINGS AT FAMILY OR PRIVATE PRAYER**, mainly drawn from Ancient Sources; following the Church's Course of Teaching for the Year. By Rev. J. B. WILKINSON. Vol. I., from Advent to Lent; II., Lent to Ascension; III., From Ascension to Sixteenth Sunday after Trinity. IV., completing Trinity-tide, with Readings for all the Saints' Days. In four Volumes. Separated, each 5s. 6d.; by post, 6s.

**REPENTANCE AND HOLY LIVING**: being Meditations on the Lord's Prayer and the Seven Penitential Psalms. By the Rev. J. B. WILKINSON, Author of "The Parables," &c. 2s. 6d.; by post, 2s. 8d.

**THE PARABLES OF OUR LORD: THIRTY-SIX INSTRUCTIONS THEREON; BEING PLAIN SERMONS ON THESE SUBJECTS** By Rev. J. B. WILKINSON. 6s.; by post, 6s. 4d.

**MEDITATIONS ON THE PENITENTIAL PSALMS.** By the Rev. J. B. WILKINSON. 1s.; by post, 1s. 1d.

**MEDITATIONS ON THE LORD'S PRAYER.** By Rev. J. B. WILKINSON. 1s. 6d., by post, 1s. 7d.

**AIDS TO MENTAL PRAYER, &c.** By Rev. J. B. WILKINSON, Author of "Daily Readings," "On the Parables," &c. 1s. 6d.; by post, 1s. 7d.

**HOUSEHOLD PRAYERS.** Preface by Dr. WILBERFORCE, Bishop of Winchester. 1s. 6d.; by post, 1s. 7d.

**THE REFORMED MONASTERY; or, THE LOVE OF JESUS**: A Sure and Short, Pleasant and Easy Way to Heaven; in Meditations, Directions, and Resolutions to Love and Obey Jesus unto Death. Preface by the Rev. F. G. LEE, D.C.L. (Being a Reprint of the said Work by Dr. BOILEAU, Chaplain to Dr. Fell, Bishop of Oxford, 1675.) 3s.; by post, 3s. 4d.

**FENELON'S COUNSELS TO THOSE WHO ARE LIVING IN THE WORLD.** Edited by W. J. E. BENNETT, Froome-Selwood. Large paper Edition, calf, 4s. 6d., by post, 4s. 8d. Cheaper Edition, 1s.; stiff cloth, red edges, 1s. 6d.; postage, 1d.

**FENELON ON FREQUENT COMMUNION.** Edited by W. J. E. BENNETT, Froome-Selwood. 6d.; post, 6½d.

**LITANIES, TRANSLATED BY THE LATE REV.
DR. NEALE:**—On the Resurrection—On the Holy Name
—Of the Holy Ghost—For the Saints—Of the Blessed Sacrament—Of Reparation to the Blessed Sacrament—Of the
Passion—For the Faithful Departed; together with "The
Way of the Cross," and "The Hours of the Passion."
cloth limp, 1s. 6d.; cloth turned in, 2s.; postage, 1d.

**ADVICE TO THE YOUNG ON TEMPTATION IN
SIN.** By Monsignor DE SEGUR. 1s. 6d; by post, 1s. 8d.

**PONDER AND PRAY: THE PENITENT'S
PATHWAY.** Translated by Rev. F. HUMPHREY.
2s.; by post, 2s. 2d.

**THE DUTIES OF FATHERS AND MOTHERS.**
By ARVISENET. Edited by the Rev. G. C. WHITE,
S. Barnabas', Pimlico. 1s. 6d.; by post, 1s. 7d.

**AVRILLON'S DEVOTIONS AT THE BLESSED
SACRAMENT.** (Translated). 1s.; by post, 1s. 1d.

**THE LITTLE WAY OF PARADISE.** Translated
from the Italian. 2s.; by post, 2s. 2d.

**DEVOTIONS ON THE COMMUNION OF SAINTS.**
Compiled from the "Paradise for the Christian Soul,"
and other sources. For the use of English Churchmen.
Part I.—Communion with the Faithful Departed.
Part II.—Communion with the Saints and Angels. By
CHARLES WALKER, Author of "The Liturgy of the
Church of Sarum." "The Ritual Reason Why." &c.
With Preface by RICHARD F. LITTLEDALE, LL.D.,
D.C.L. 2s. 6d.; by post, 2s. 8d.

**ON CHRISTIAN CARE OF THE DYING AND
THE DEAD.** Illustrated. 3s. 6d.; by post, 3s. 9d.

**THE OFFICE OF TENEBRÆ.** Second Edition.
(Published for the Guild of S. Alban.) 1s. 6d.; by post,
1s. 8d. The Words only, 2d.; by post, 2½d.

**FASTING VERSUS EVENING COMMUNION.**
By F. H. D. 6d.; by post, 7d.

**IMPRESSIONS OF THE AMMERGAU PASSION-
PLAY.** (1870.) By an Oxonian. 6d.; by post, 7d.

## TALES, &c.

**A LITTLE LIFE IN A GREAT CITY.** By the Author of "Church Stories for the Sundays and Holy-days," &c. 2s.; by post, 2s. 2d.

**THE CITY OF THE PLAIN, AND OTHER TALES.** With Preface by Rev. E. H. BLYTH, Hammersmith. 2s., by post, 2s. 2d.

**LOVE AND HATE.** By Author of "An Object in Life," "Our Christian Calling," "Letters to Young Servants," &c. 2s.; by post, 2s. 2d.

**THE ROYAL CRADLE**; and other Carols. By S. D. N., Author of "Chronicles of St. Mary's." 2s. 6d.; by post, 2s. 8d.

**THE SAINTS OF OLD**; being Sketches of the Holy Days in the Kalendar of the English Church. By Author of "Church Stories for Sundays, &c.," "Our Childhood's Pattern," &c. 3s.; by post, 3s. 4d.

**CHURCH STORIES FOR THE SUNDAYS, HOLY-DAYS, AND FAST-DAYS OF THE CHRISTIAN YEAR.** In Fifteen Parts. Each, 1s.; by post, 1s. 1½d. Or, in Four Vols. Cloth, each 5s.; by post, 5s. 4½d. And in Eight thinner Vols. Cloth, each 2s. 6d.; postage, 2½d.

**OUR CHILDHOOD'S PATTERN: BEING NINE TALES BASED ON INCIDENTS IN THE LIFE OF THE HOLY CHILD JESUS.** By Author of "Church Stories for Sundays," &c.; and "Saints of Old," &c, 2s. 6d.; by post, 2s. 9d.

**OSWALD, THE YOUNG ARTIST.** A Tale for Boys. (Inculcating the necessity of a reverential attention when assisting in the Public Worship.) By C. WALKER, Author of "The Ritual Reason Why." 1s. 6d.; by post, 1s. 8d.

**NORWEGIAN TALES; EVENINGS AT OAKWOOD.** Translated by ELLEN WHITE. Preface by Rev. S. BARING-GOULD, Author of "Curious Myths," &c. 3s. 6d. by post, 3s. 9d.

**COUSIN EUSTACE; or CONVERSATIONS WITH A DISSENTER ON THE PRAYER BOOK.** By the Author of "Tales of Kirkbeck," "Aunt Atta," "Lives of the Fathers," &c. 5s. 6d.; by post, 6s.

**RHINELAND AND ITS LEGENDS**; with Other Tales. Translated from the German. By the Translator of "God still works Miracles," &c. With Preface by W. J. E. BENNETT. 3s. 6d.; by post, 3s. 9d.

**CURIOSITIES OF OLDEN TIMES.** A new work by the Rev. S. BARING-GOULD. 6s.; by post, 6s. 4d.

**CHURCH BALLADS** (First Series.) In a Packet of Twelve. 2s.; by post, 2s. 2d.

**CHURCH BALLADS** (Second Series) FOR THE FESTIVALS THROUGHOUT THE YEAR. 3s. 6d.; by post, 3s. 9d.

**WAYLAND WELL**: A Tale for Adults. By the Author of "Crystal Finlaison's Narrative," &c. 5s.; by post, 5s. 5d.

**ONLY A GHOST.** By IRENÆUS THE DEACON. 1s.; by post, 1s. 1d.

**SIR HENRY APPLETON**: A Tale of the Great Rebellion. By the Rev. W. E. HEYGATE, Rector of Brighstone, Isle of Wight. 470 pp. 5s.; by post, 5s. 6d.

**TALES OF KIRKBECK.** First, Second, and Third Series. By Author of "Cousin Eustace," &c. Preface by W. J. E. BENNETT. Each Vol. 3s. 6d.; by post, 3s. 10d.

**A COMMON-PLACE STORY**: by Author of "Cousin Eustace," "Tales of Kirkbeck," &c. Edited by W. J. E. BENNETT. 2s. 6d.; by post, 2s. 8d.

**AUNT ATTA.** A Tale for little Nephews and Nieces. By Author of "Tales of Kirkbeck," &c. Edited by W. J. E. BENNETT. 3s. 6d.; by post, 3s. 9d. Cheap Edition 2s. 6d.; by post, 2s. 8d.

**AUNT ATTA AGAIN**; or, THE LONG VACATION. Edited by W. J. E. BENNETT. 3s. 6d.; by post 3s. 9d. Cheap Edition 2s. 6d.; by post, 2s. 8d.

**THE FARM OF APTONGA**: A Story of the Times of S. Cyprian. By the late Dr. NEALE. 2s.; by post, 2s. 2d.

**DAYS AT LEIGHSCOMBE.** A New Tale for Children. 2s.; by post, 2s. 2d.

**THREE STORIES**: ("USE OF A FLOWER," "A LONG DAY," and "WHILE THE RAIN LASTED.") By the Author of "Days at Leighscombe." 2s. 6d.; by post, 2s. 9d.

**USE OF A FLOWER.** By the Author of "Days at Leighscombe." 9d. by post, 9½d.

**A LONG DAY.** By the Author of "Days at Leighscombe." 6d.; by post, 6½d.

**WHILE THE RAIN LASTED.** By the Author of 'Days at Leighscombe." 9d. by post 9½d.

LIFE AND TIMES OF S. EDWARD THE CONFESSOR. By CECILIA MAC GREGOR. 2s. 6d.; by post, 2s. 9d.
CHRISTINE; OR, THE KING'S DAUGHTER. 2s.; by post, 2s. 2d.
THE CHILDREN'S GUILD. By Author of The Abbey Farm." 2s. 6d.; by post, 2s. 9d.
FROM DARKNESS TO LIGHT. A Confirmation Tale. 2s. 6d.; by post, 2s. 9d.
HAROLD AUSTIN: A Tale. By the Author of "From Darkness to Light." 2s.; by post, 2s. 2d.
THE VICTORIES OF THE SAINTS: Stories for Children, from Church History. New Edition. By Rev. Dr. NEALE. 2s.; by post, 2s. 2d.
THE PILGRIM; AND OTHER ALLEGORIES. 1s. 6d.; by post, 1s. 8d.
HENRY OF EICHENFELS, AND CHRISTMAS EVE. By Rev. W. B. FLOWER. 1s.; by post, 1s. 1d.
REGINALD GRÆME; By the Rev. CLAUDE MAGNAY. 2s. 6d.; by post, 2s. 8d.
BLANCHE MORTIMER. By E. M. S. 3s.; by post, 3s. 2d.
THE LIFE OF S. PAUL. By Rev. Dr. BIBER. 2s. 6d.; by post, 2s. 9d.

HISTORICAL LECTURES ON THE EARLY BRITISH, ANGLO-SAXON, AND NORMAN PERIOD. Intended for the Use of Teachers of English History. By Mrs. FRANCES A. TREVELYAN. Partly Edited by the late Rev. CHARLES MARRIOTT, Oriel College, Oxford. (I. Roman Invasion to the Norman Conquest. II. William I. to Henry II. III. Henry II. to Henry III.) Each Volume 7s. 6d.; by post, 8s.
SPANISH TOWNS AND SPANISH PICTURES. By Mrs. W. A. TOLLEMACHE. With Photographs, &c. Second Edition, 7s. 6d.; by post, 8s.
RESURGAM, AND OTHER VERSES. By the late G. F. JACKSON. Edited with a short Biography by his Brother, the Rev. H. MARSHALL JACKSON. 3s.; by post, 3s. 3d.

J. T. HAYES, LYALL PLACE, EATON SQUARE;
AND
4, HENRIETTA STREET, COVENT GARDEN.